STONER McTAVISH

by
Sarah Dreher

New Victoria Publishers, Inc.

a feminist literary and cultural organization
located at 7 Bank Street,
Lebanon, New Hampshire 03766

For Lis—
    who brings me memories for tomorrow

CHAPTER I

"I know what you need," Marylou said.

"What?" It was muggy in the travel agency. Stoner's hand stuck to the page as she angrily scratched out one tentative schedule and filled in another. The paper was limp as worn cotton.

"Love."

"I don't need love, Marylou. I need air conditioning."

"Romance," Marylou said, placidly spreading Boursin on a rye thin. "Passion, excitement, anguish."

Stoner grunted. "These people are crazy. Can you imagine what Disney World is like in this weather?"

"You haven't been in love since What's-her-face?"

"Agatha." Stoner rummaged in her desk drawer. "Did you take the United schedule?"

"No. How long has it been?"

"I had it this morning."

"Since you were in love."

"Not long enough," Stoner said. "Are you sure you didn't take it?"

"Two years? Three years. Much too long." Marylou brushed at a crumb that had nested in her frilled blouse. "It isn't healthy for you to go that long without being in love."

Stoner shot her a glance of annoyance. "For heaven's sake, Marylou, I have work to do."

"It's made you dull."

"Thank you."

Marylou sighed. "Moonlit walks along the Charles. Skinny-dipping at Crane's beach..."

"It's too hot to be in love, if I knew anyone I wanted to be in love with, which I don't, so if you don't mind I have to..."

"Dull, dull, dull," said Marylou. "Have a cracker."

Stoner threw her pencil down. "I don't want a cracker. I don't want to be in love. All I want is the United Airlines schedule."

"Maybe my mother knows some nice available woman in Wellfleet."

"Marylou..." She wasn't in the mood for this. Murderous impulses stirred.

Her friend and partner looked at her sheepisly. "It might be cooler in Wellfleet than in Boston."

"It might," Stoner said evenly, "be cooler in Hell. The United schedule, please?"

"I don't have it. Honest. You'll have to call them." She poured a plastic cup of wine for Stoner and one for herself. "They'll put you on 'hold', you know."

"What else can I do? United Airlines isn't tuned into my thoughts."

"And only marginally to our telephone," said Marylou.

She dialled the reservation desk and was put on 'hold'. Leaning back in her chair, she tapped the receiver against the palm of her hand and rocked furiously.

"You really should relax," Marylou said seriously. "This isn't good for you."

"We have to make a living. This isn't a non-profit organization."

"It is in summer. You worry too much. We're making ends meet."

"Barely," Stoner said. She took a swallow of wine and rubbed at her forehead with the heel of her hand. "Just once I'd like to have enough money to do something special for Aunt Hermione. Do you know, in the twelve years I've lived with her, I've never been able to do more than pay my own way."

"Oh, Stoner, she doesn't care about that."

"I do." She finished off her wine. "Look at me. Thirty-one years old and all I can do is 'make ends meet'."

Marylou refilled her glass. "My mother says this kind of thinking is normal at our age."

"Somehow that doesn't comfort me." Stoner listened to the phone for a second. "Damn it, if they're going to put me on 'hold', they could spare me the Muzak. I feel like I'm at the dentist."

Marylou plucked at her skirt. "I think I've gained another pound."

"I'm not surprised. You've eaten three bagels with cream cheese — whole bagels, not halves — and half a box of crackers since nine o'clock this morning."

"Women cannot live on air alone, rich with pollutants though it may be."

"*And* we went out for lunch."

"Lunch was lunch," said Marylou.

"Then don't complain about your weight."

"I can't help my weight, it's hereditary."

Stoner shook her head helplessly. "Marylou, both your parents look like victims of chronic anorexia."

"Nature abhors repetition," said Marylou.

"One of these days," Stoner said, "they're going to carry me out of here, kicking and screaming, in a strait-jacket."

Marylou considered her well-supplied bosom and frowned. "Do you think I'm repulsive?"

"Oh, Marylou, of course I don't."

The phone clicked and a breathy voice crooned, "Good afternoon. United Airlines. May I help you?"

Stoner covered the mouthpiece with her hand. "It's her," she whispered. Marylou dove for the extension on her desk.

"One moment, please," Stoner said in a secretarial voice, and waited. Then she cleared her throat. "Hi. This is Stoner McTavish, of Kesselbaum and McTavish."

"Oh." The voice turned icy. "What can I do for you?"

Marylou convulsed silently and hung up. "I love it, I love it."

2

Tilting back her chair, Stoner propped her foot against the edge of her desk and spent the next ten minutes untangling airline tickets. As she was finished, Marylou shouted, "Call back next week. We're having sex-change operations."

Stoner laughed. "Really, Marylou."

Marylou dismissed United Airlines with a flick of her wrist. "So she hates women. I'll bet she falls all over Crimson Travel."

"What makes my day," Stoner said, grinning, "is knowing I've ruined hers."

"I have an idea. Call back and ask her out."

"Never!"

"Why not?"

"She might accept." Bracing herself, Stoner attacked the mail. As usual, it was all brochures. Three new resort hotels in the Virgin Islands, an All-American Las Vegas fly-drive vacation special (with free breakfast, casino tokens, and complimentary in-room cocktail), notices of Christmas cruises to Rio. "This is cute," Stoner said, holding up a mimeographed sheet.

"What?"

"A dog-sled tour of the Arctic Circle."

Marylou glanced up. "Maybe you should try it."

"It's in January." She got up to file the folders in their appropriate niches.

"I was in love with you once," said Marylou.

Stoner looked at her. "You?"

"During my polymorphous-perverse adolescence."

"Marylou, I didn't know."

Marylou sighed. "It happened the first time I saw you. Remember the night my mother brought you home to dinner?"

Stoner remembered. It had struck her then as peculiar behavior for one's psychotherapist. In the intervening years she had learned that nothing was peculiar for Dr. Kesselbaum.

"God, you were adorable," Marylou said. "The way you hung back in the doorway in those faded jeans and workshirt, staring at your moth-eaten sneakers."

"Moths don't eat sneakers," Stoner said, feeling herself blush.

"And when you finally looked up at me, with those green eyes, I thought Halley's Comet had just struck the Boston Common."

Stoner brushed her hair back in a nervous gesture.

"And you kept doing that. All evening. I remember every word you said that night. 'This is very good' — I believe over the Big Macs. 'No, thank you,' to seconds on fries. And 'I'm sorry' about twenty-three times." Marylou tapped the desk with her pencil. "You know, I've always suspected Edith was trying to fix us up."

"I thought you were straight," Stoner said.

"I am now, but back then it was anything goes. She didn't care what direction my impulses went in, as long as they went somewhere and stayed."

3

"You never said anything."

Marylou shrugged. "Anyone with two ounces of brains could tell a relationship with you would have to be serious. I wasn't about to sign up for that."

Stoner stood like a piece of abandoned luggage in the middle of the room and wondered what to do with her hands. "Do you — uh — I mean, are you still —"

"Of course not, silly. Do you think I'd have sat here for seven years, day after day, eating my heart out? I'd have trapped you in the coat closet and ripped your clothes off long ago." She opened a bill with a silver letter opener. "Shit, the electicity's gone up again. Anyway, I prefer men in bed, God knows why. Are you going to stand there all day?"

Earlobes flaming, Stoner lurched back to her desk and dropped into her chair. "I hope..." she said hesitantly "... I haven't treated you badly."

"No, love, you haven't treated me badly. I can't help my sexual orientation any more than you can." She looked at Stoner for a minute. "You know, you haven't changed a bit."

Stoner threw a pencil at her. It missed. "I have, too."

"How?"

"I'm older."

"Not discernibly. Beneath that womanly — and, I might say, still terribly attractive — exterior, there beats the heart of a spring lamb."

That did it. Stoner got up. "I'm leaving."

"You can't. I'm coming home for dinner with you. Aunt Hermione said it was an emergency. I wonder what kind of wine goes with emergencies."

Stoner's stomach gave a lurch. "My parents are here."

"Oh, Stoner, you know she would have warned you."

"I suppose so."

"Still and all," Marylou mused, "it *is* strange. Your aunt hasn't declared an emergency since 1970, when the cat ate the Blue Runners."

"Huh?"

"Don't you remember? It was the night she taught me — and I use the term loosely — to play Mah Jongg."

Stoner grinned. "She won ten dollars from you."

"Your aunt," announced Marylou, "is a sweet old lady. She is also a crook."

Marylou turned back to her work. Stoner watched her. So Marylou had been in love with her, all those years ago. She wondered what she would have done if she'd known. Stoner sighed. She knew exactly what she would have done. Run like hell. Back in those days her lesbianism had terrified her even in its latent, embryonic stage. Brought to the surface, it would have sent her leaping from the top of the Bunker Hill Monument. Sex of any kind had frightened her then. Well, to be perfectly honest, it still made her uneasy. And then there were her parents, her mother alternately screaming at her and collapsing into hysterics, her father looking at her as if she were something dragged up from the ocean floor to leave evil-smelling stains on the living room rug... And no matter how much Aunt

Hermione snorted her disgust at them and informed them they were lucky, their only child could have come home dragging an unwanted and illegitimate baby, and how would they keep *that* from the neighbors whose opinion they obviously valued above the happiness of their own daughter... But they reminded Aunt Hermione that Stoner was their daughter, not hers, and only seventeen to boot, and if they wanted to make her unhappy it was their right — not to say duty — and Hermione could keep her Beacon Hill nose out of their Rhode Island business, and what did she know anyway, having no children of her own, and never married, and that looked pretty strange, too, by the way, and if she knew what was good for her she'd stick to her palm reading and Blue Runner Beans, there were Places people like her could End Up and they weren't exactly Country Clubs, either, so she'd better watch her P's and Q's... Which sent Aunt Hermione off into peals of laughter.

Sometimes it even made Stoner laugh, except after they'd slammed down the phone and Aunt Hermione was cut off, it wasn't funny any more.

One night Stoner knew she had had enough. After all, when your mother repeatedly tells you you make her sick, you either give in, get out, or learn to ignore it. And Stoner had never been able to ignore anything, particularly if it was unpleasant — which Dr. Kesselbaum pointed out to her, not as a criticism, Stoner dear, but so that she would be careful to surround herself with benign environments and loving persons. But that night the air had sparked and crackled with violence and useless tears, and Stoner, not daring to let herself think about what she was doing, had done the only thing she knew. She had run to Aunt Hermione.

She packed what she could into an old knapsack, and waited until the house was quiet. Terrified, she crept down the stairs, stole fifty dollars from her mother's pocketbook, and caught a bus to Boston.

At Park Square Terminal, her courage disintegrated. Aunt Hermione would hate her for this. It was cowardly, irresponsible, and unfair. She would send her away — or worse, send her back. She couldn't face Aunt Hermione.

For two days she hung around the city, sleeping in the bus station, staring across the fall-stripped Public Gardens at her aunt's brownstone fortress, haunted by the look of hurt in her little dog's eyes as she pushed him gently back inside and closed the door. But finally, hungry, exhausted, her nerves ragged, she dragged herself up the steps and rang the bell.

"Well," said Aunt Hermione, "it's about time."

Stoner looked up at her aunt's soft, round face ringed with frizzed gray hair, and broke down. "Please don't make me go back," she mumbled.

Aunt Hermione pulled her forward in a lavendar-scented embrace. "Don't be an ass," she said, and wiped the tears from Stoner's face with the sleeve of her house dress. "Come into the kitchen. I'll make us a pot of tea."

Stoner huddled cross-legged on the sagging love-seat that graced one corner of her aunt's kitchen. Morning sunlight poured through lace curtains, spilling leafy shadows on the polished wood floor. Prisms in each window shattered the light into rainbows against eggshell walls. Wicker birdcages filled with trailing plants hung by the doors and over the sink and table.

"My sister was always a bitch." Aunt Hermione puttered about slamming cupboard doors. She found some Danish pastries and shoved them into the oven. "Probably stale, but they'll do. When did you eat last?"

"Huh? Oh, I ... I'm not sure."

"Something horrifying in a restaurant, no doubt. I tell you, Stoner, civilization has departed downtown Boston. I remember when you could get a gracious meal any time of the day or night. Served with *style*, mind you. Now look. Pewter Pots. *McDonald's*, for the love of Heaven. Not even a decent Walgreen's counter. The Parker House is an abortion. No wonder people act like cattle. I haven't had a decent omelette in years."

"Did you talk to them?" Stoner asked timidly.

"I assure you I complained long and loud, for all the good it does these days."

"What?"

"I've called the mayor's office, the planning board, the attorney general, even the governor. I might as well talk in my sleep." She glanced at Stoner. "Oh, your parents. I told them you weren't here. You weren't, were you?"

"What did they say?"

Aunt Hermione planted her hands on her hips. "My dear, at my age I shouldn't be subjected to what *they* said to *me*. Don't, I beg you, ask me to repeat it in *your* tender ears."

In spite of herself, Stoner smiled. The nutmeg odor of pastries reached her.

"Whoops!" Aunt Hermione flew to the oven and swept out the rolls. "Here you go."

She handed Stoner the plate and a little tray with butter and a knife. "Tea in a minute. Those are good. Given to me by a client, a marvelous cook, pays me in calories."

"How is business, Aunt Hermione?" Stoner asked politely, trying not to wolf her food and act like cattle.

"Booming. It's the occult fad, of course. Suddenly having your palm read is fashionable. Personally, I prefer working with *serious* students of the Mysteries, not these fly-by-nights. Next year they'll be opening savings accounts and voting Republican. Still, as my father used to say, make hay while the sun shines."

The copper kettle sang. Aunt Hermione tossed several kinds of loose tea into a pot she had been warming, and poured in the water. "Strawberry, mint, and chamomile. You need bracing up."

Stoner blushed. "I haven't had a bath in three days."

"Never be ashamed of dirt honestly come by," said Aunt Hermione. She looked Stoner up and down. "A little sleep wouldn't hurt, either." She propped her elbows on the table, chin in hands. Her blue eyes were alert as a sparrow's behind rhinestone-studded, plastic-framed glasses.

"So you finally did it. Stoner, I'm proud of you."

"You are?"

"Though it took you long enough. Even a dog would have the sense to leave that house of horrors. I never could understand Helen, and not because she's ten years younger than me. Of course, she'd have you think I'm a hundred years older and she was an accident of menopause. Always had to have her own way, wanted everyone around her to re-arrange themselves to suit her."

"That's about the size of it," Stoner said bitterly.

"Meaner than cat pee. I don't mind telling you, it frightened me when you turned out to be a girl. She set out to make you a carbon copy of herself." Aunt Hermione frowned. "I used to tell her, 'Helen, if you love yourself so much, fill the house with mirrors. But leave that child alone!'"

She poured tea and handed a cup to Stoner. "And that father of yours. Pardon my French, but he wouldn't say 'shit' if he had a mouthful. Old Angus' mind must have been elsewhere when he fathered *him*."

Stoner curled up in the corner of the loveseat and felt — tentatively — safe. Aunt Hermione delivered another Danish. "Did I ever tell you," she asked, "about the time I won you from her in a card game?"

Stoner shook her head.

"You were a week old. I'd talked her into a game of gin. She loves to play, but hates to lose. So I cheated, and took her to the cleaners. Now, your mother would squeeze a nickel 'til it screams. I let her run up a tidy little tab and offered her a choice — pay up or give you to me."

"Was she shocked?" Stoner asked, a little shocked herself.

"It fried her undies. After the smoke cleared she tried to weasel out of it. 'A gambling debt's a gambling debt,' I said. But I settled for naming you. Maybe I should have held out."

"I never knew," Stoner said.

"Well, I'm not surprised. Yes, named you after Lucy B. Stone. I was a great admirer of hers. Helen was livid. She always hated feminists."

"How much did it cost you?"

"Five hundred bucks."

Stoner whistled.

"It was cheap for the pleasure it gave me to know every time she called you she'd be reminded of Lucy B." Aunt Hermione assumed an innocent air. "If I'd known then what I know now, I'd have insisted on Gertrude Stein."

Stoner looked down at her hands and blushed.

"Oh, don't be like that," Aunt Hermione said. "It warms my heart on long winter nights, knowing that Helen produced a Sapphic." She stirred her tea. "We have to plan our strategy, Stoner. We're not going to get off this easily."

"I don't want to make trouble for you, Aunt Hermione."

"Trouble! I *love* trouble." She glanced at her lapel watch. "But now I must go and meditate. I have a client in twenty minutes."

I'll get a job," Stoner said eagerly.

Aunt Hermione looked at her sharply. "You will not. Tomorrow we go down to B.U. and enroll you for the spring semester. No niece of mine is going to be a hippie drop-out.''

Stoner felt tears spring to her eyes.

"Now," her aunt said firmly, "you finish those pastries, have a bath, and rest. I use the front parlor for readings. Otherwise, the house is yours.''

"Thank you," Stoner muttered. "I think I'll sit here for a while.''

"Good enough. Don't answer the phone." She got up to leave, then turned. "Stoner, nobody's going to make you go back there, ever.''

She sighed heavily. Four weeks from Labor Day, and counting. They went on vacation the last two weeks in August, and invariably capped it off with dinner in Boston with their renegade daughter. Perhaps a holiday just wasn't a holiday without unpleasantness.

"I should just tell them not to come," she said aloud.

"That might work," said Marylou. "Tell who not to come?''

"My parents.''

Marylou glanced up. "Is it that time already? I haven't ordered the Christmas cards.''

"You don't send Christmas cards.''

"*We* do, remember? Business?" She leaned back in her chair. "Look, love, why don't you let me book them on a tour? I can arrange it so they'll never been seen again in this life.''

"It wouldn't work.''

"After eight years of misplacing luggage, we should be able to lose your family.''

"I can't," Stoner said. "I'd feel too guilty.''

"You don't have to lift a finger. Say the word, I'll take care of it all, and we'll never mention it again. I have connections.''

"Mafia?''

"The skycaps at Logan are on the take." Marylou went back to work.

This is ridiculous. Normal thirty-one-year old women do not spend their time worrying about getting along with or away from their parents. Normal thirty-one-year old women worry about husbands (lack thereof), careers, calories, split-ends, toilet bowls, diaper absorbency, ring-around-the-collar, feminine hygiene, perspiration, and unwanted pregnancy.

"What are you brooding about?" Marylou asked.

"Ring-around-the-collar.''

"Do you have it?''

"I don't think so.''

"Do I?''

"No.''

Marylou sighed. "Well, would you mind worrying about that bus tour to Tanglewood? We promised them Previn, and they're going to get Linda Ronstadt.''

"Maybe they won't notice.''

"Out of 35 music-lovers, someone's bound to notice.''

Wearily, Stoner reached for the Tanglewood schedule. "You know

8

what this means, don't you? Thirty-five phone calls."

"Thirty-six. You'd better check with Lenox first."

She compared the schedule with her calendar. "It *is* Previn. Look."

Marylou peered over her shoulder. "That's last year's schedule, love."

"For God's sake," Stoner said, throwing it down, "do we have to keep everything that comes across the desk?"

"Not me, pal. You're the one who's saving it all for the archives."

"Well, you never know."

Maybe Marylou's right. Maybe I do need to be in love. God knows, I need *something*. I'm restless, bored, indecisive, and a coward. Well, I've always been a coward. And sometimes I've been indecisive. But not like this. Or have I? Jesus, I can't even make up my mind about *that*.

Two years. That isn't very long, is it? It doesn't hurt any more. But if it doesn't hurt any more, why don't I want to get involved with anyone? Because I haven't met anyone I want to be involved with, that's why. You don't just decide you want to be involved and go out and pick someone up, like a head of lettuce. You don't just put "love" on the shopping list and whip on down to Filene's basement, for God's sake. I'm not interested, that's all. This isn't a movie, this is life. There are more things in Life than Love.

Name three. Okay, there's work. Even Freud admitted that. Love and Work. And there's... there's... the Red Sox. The *Red Sox*? I don't even like baseball. The Imminent Nuclear Holocaust? Now, there's something I could *really* get into. Makes you glad to be alive just thinking about it.

What I'd *really* better get into is Linda Ronstadt at Lenox. Thirty-six phone calls? It can't be that bad. Nothing could be that bad. Could it?

***

"All right," Marylou said briskly. "We're closing the store."

Stoner looked up. "What time is it?"

"Three fifteen." Marylou folded down the top of the waxed paper wrapping on her box of Triscuits with an air of finality.

"We can't do that."

"We work for ourselves."

"Why?" Stoner crossed to Marylou's desk and slipped a paper clip over the folded wrapper.

"Because we can't get along with anyone else." Marylou stared at the crackers. "Honest to God, you're so compulsive."

"Why are we leaving?"

"You're brooding. It's bad for business. We're supposed to radiate the fun and romance of travel."

"You should talk," Stoner said. "I don't even remember the last time you were out of Boston."

"I went to the Cape in 1973."

"Under duress."

"No, by bus."

"You don't even visit your mother, and it's only two hours to Wellfleet."

9

"Travel," said Marylou, "is tawdry. If you enjoy being chewed by sand fleas, *you* visit my mother."

"You don't see your father from April to October."

Marylou swept the crumbs from her desk. Some of them managed to hit the waste basket. "Max is perfectly happy with his seaweed and organic fertilizers."

"Seaweed *is* organic fertilizer." Stoner glared down at the crumbs. "Are you going to leave those there? We could get rats."

"Good!" Marylou shrilled. "Rats would be better company than you." She touched Stoner's hand. "Dear old friend," she said gently, "you know I love you. But your moods are abominable."

Stoner hung her head. "I'm sorry."

"What's wrong with you?" She waited for a moment. "Out with it, Stoner."

"I'm ... frightened."

"Of what?"

"What if they're here?"

"Your parents?"

Stoner nodded.

"Love, they can't do anything to you. You're over twenty-one."

"And a freak."

"You're not a freak," Marylou said firmly. "Kesselbaums do not associate with freaks."

Stoner had to laugh. "You Kesselbaums *are* freaks."

"That's why we don't associate with freaks," Marylou said, locking her desk drawer. "It would be redundant." She dropped the keys in her pocketbook. "Are you coming, or should I leave you here to delight the janitor?"

***

They reached the town house overlooking the Public Gardens. The air hovered over the city like stagnant water. Even the traffic was subdued. Leaves of maples and beeches drooped listlessly from exhausted branches. The pigeons barely moved, muttering to themselves as they scratched half-heartedly at the cracks in the sidewalk. At the foot of the steps, Stoner froze.

"They're here. I know it."

"Aunt Hermione wouldn't do that to you," Marylou said.

"Maybe she didn't have any choice."

"If that's the case, we'd better get in there, because they probably have her bound and gagged in the hall closet."

Frightened, miserable, and feeling ridiculous, Stoner sat on the step. "I hate myself."

"Why?"

"At my age, to be afraid of my parents."

Marylou straightened her skirt, which had managed to circumnavigate her waist. "Well, they get pretty nasty. Personally, I don't know why you let them talk you into going out to dinner every time they get in the mood to visit the big city."

10

Stoner ran her hand through her hair. "They'd make such a *mess* if I refused."

"Judging from your description of those dinners, it's already untidy."

"You must think I'm an awful coward," she said, not daring to look up.

"Stoner, I have a mother who is rumored to be a psychoanalyst of some repute. She drives a white Lincoln Continental convertible, pumps her own gas to save money, and litters the house with plastic cartons from fast food restaurants. My father is so gentle he goes into a depression when he has to thin the beets. And my sister's one aim in life is to go on living peacefully in her bungalow in Hawaii with four children who don't know what it is to wear clothes, and keep me supplied with kona coffee and macadamia nuts." She shrugged. "What do I know about being afraid of families?"

Stoner was silent.

"When you went to dinner with them last April, you came home and drank yourself into oblivion. For the next three days you went around apologizing for being alive. From that, I can only conclude they are not charming people."

"They tried to have Aunt Hermione arrested for taking me in."

"I know."

"They almost had me put in a mental hospital. If your mother hadn't..."

Marylou took her by the shoulders and shook her. "Stoner, listen to me. That was a long time ago. It didn't work then, and it wouldn't work now. They can make you feel awful, but they can't interfere with your life."

Stoner looked up at her and sighed. "I'm sorry."

"Come on," Marylou said, pulling her to her feet. She shoved Stoner ahead of her up the steps. "Oh, shit," she muttered. "I forgot the wine."

Stoner made coffee while Marylou browsed through the breadbox. "I'm afraid there isn't much around," Stoner said. "Mrs. Bakhoven's on vacation."

"How inconsiderate," Marylou said, tackling the refrigerator.

"Aunt Hermione told her she was going to take a trip, so she did."

"Anything would be better than what I have at home. Mother came down last weekend and unloaded all the summer squash on me." She found a left-over piece of cherry pie and carried it to the table in triumph. "Know what I love about your aunt? She's dependable."

Stoner poured coffee and sat down. "If the emergency isn't my parents, what is it?"

"She didn't say."

"Didn't you ask?" She was beginning to feel cold on the inside of her face, a sure sign of impending panic.

"Well, it obviously wasn't too serious to wait until dinner."

"After dinner. We never discuss anything serious while we eat. She says it throws the electrolytes off balance."

"Probably does," Marylou said.

Aunt Hermione burst through the swinging door, rope beads clattering. "Quick," she exclaimed. "Coffee."

11

She flung herself onto the love seat as Stoner got up to get a cup. "Did you make more fresh, Stoner?"

"Yes."

"The thermos pitcher is full."

"Oh," Stoner said sheepishly. "I didn't think."

Marylou waved her fork. "You shouldn't use those things, Aunt Hermione. They're barbaric. They put them in motel rooms."

"How would you know?" Stoner asked.

"I know," said Aunt Hermione, "but this one came in the mail. I hadn't ordered it, of course. I'd never order such an ugly thing, especially not from a mail-order house. But there it was. I thought it might be a sign."

Stoner couldn't stand it any longer. "My parents are here, aren't they?"

"Oh, my God," Aunt Hermione said. "I thought we'd seen the last of them for at least six months, and it's only..." she counted backward to April..."four."

"I thought that was the emergency," Stoner said. "I thought they were here."

Aunt Hermione stared at her. "Here? In *this* house? Really, Stoner."

"She's having a bad day," Marylou said.

"Probably premenstrual tension. Thank God for menopause."

"I think," said Marylou, "she needs to be in love."

"Marylou..." Stoner warned.

"Why, Marylou, what a perfectly lovely idea. Who do you have in mind?"

Stoner rubbed her hands over her face. "I don't need to be in love. I was only afraid my parents were here. I was afraid you'd asked them to dinner."

Aunt Hermione exchanged a look with Marylou. "You know, Marylou, sometimes I think Stoner's a little ... slow. Did your mother ever mention possible brain damage?"

"Aunt Hermione," Stoner said between clenched teeth. "What is the emergency?"

"You'll have to wait." Her aunt waggled a finger at her. "It has to do with a client of mine, Eleanor Burton. I think she should explain it herself."

"Oh." Stoner felt herself go limp. "Is that who you were with just now?"

Aunt Hermione gave a weary sigh. "No, that was a new one. A young man. Very intense, very sincere, and very, very mystical. But the dullest palm I ever saw. That boy is going to have a life that would bore an accountant. My imagination is strained to the quick."

"Have some cherry pie," Marylou said sympathetically.

"Thank you, dear, no. It's Table Talk."

Marylou dropped her fork and clutched her throat. "I'm poisoned!"

Stoner laughed. "It's all right. I had it for breakfast."

"Ugh," Marylou said. "You are revolting."

CHAPTER 2

Stoner tried to divide her attention between the meal, the conversation, and the globed brass wall sconces in which beeswax candles glowed bravely. The light was gold, the shadows sepia, the air touched with a gentle sweetness. From time to time she stole a surreptitious glance at Mrs. Burton, and wondered what was troubling her. The elderly woman was delicate, almost frail. The lines around her eyes were deepened with worry. The hollows in her cheeks were stark, not with age, Stoner thought, but with sleeplessness. Her fingers scurried over the silverware and around the hem of her napkin. Stoner fought down a desire to throw decorum to the winds and demand to know what was wrong.

She tried to involve herself in the proceedings. "My father thinks," Marylou was saying, "weeds are the coming thing. They retain moisture, shade tender seedlings, and can act as trap crops for insects."

"But so untidy," Aunt Hermione said. "What do you think, Eleanor?"

Mrs. Burton looked up from her plate. "I beg your pardon?"

"What do you think of weeds?"

"Lovely," Mrs. Burton murmured, and picked politely at the veal marsala.

"Have some more wine, Eleanor." Aunt Hermione filled her glass. "My personal preference..." She turned back to Marylou "... is the French intensive method. Very practical for city gardens."

"Yes," said Marylou, "but we have only begun to understand weeds. The possibilities are limitless. Consider amaranth."

Stoner smiled to herself. Consider amaranth, indeed. Marylou was as likely to eat amaranth as an Egg McMuffin.

"Well," Aunt Hermione said, "I'm all in favor of progress, but you can't convince me pigweed is good for anything."

"Except pigs," Stoner offered.

Marylou and Aunt Hermione stared at her as if she had lost her mind. "You can't keep pigs in Boston," Marylou said. "There are ordinances."

"I only meant..."

"I didn't know you liked pigs," Aunt Hermione said.

"They're all right."

Aunt Hermione turned to the others. "Sometimes I wish we didn't live in the city. I know Stoner would love a dog, but it would have to be a very small dog, and small dogs are so unsatisfying. Especially if you're the rough-and-tumble sort like Stoner."

"I am not," Stoner protested.

"Only with dogs, dear. But pigs! I don't imagine you'd be allowed to keep even a very small, very clean pig."

"I don't want to keep pigs," Stoner said.

"But if you'd like to see pigs, we could run out to Drumlin Farm. I'm sure they must have pigs there, don't you agree, Eleanor?"

"Lovely," said Mrs. Burton, and poured herself another glass of wine. "Perhaps they'll let you touch one, though I personally find the idea chilling. But you know what you're doing, Stoner. You always do."

Well, Aunt Hermione was off and running. If there were time, and any hope of success, she might try to clarify the situation. But Aunt Hermione was devoted to her tangents, on occasion even fanatic about them, and there was nothing to be done but let her run down.

Not that Stoner had anything against pigs. They seemed like affable creatures, though some people claimed they could be vicious. But what could they do except ram you with their snouts? And that could be easily sidestepped. She had heard that they liked to swim in the ocean, which inspired peculiar images of great herds — flocks? — coveys? — of them stampeding the beaches and racing off to France to dig truffles. She wondered how they managed to swim with those tiny hooves. Perhaps the whole thing was a rumor, a bit of misinformation planted by the government to divert the public's attention from the fact that the economy was going to hell in a peach basket.

Meanwhile, there was the current emergency on the home front. Not that anyone was behaving with any urgency, except perhaps Mrs. Burton, who was going to be completely snockered by dessert. Aunt Hermione, of course, believed in Fate, which relieved her of the necessity for immediate action in any situation — a position which Stoner sometimes coveted, and which sometimes made her want to go screaming off into the night. Marylou, on the other hand, was so passionately embedded in whatever was going on at the moment that everything else — past, future, or nuclear arms build-up — faded into misty obscurity.

Stoner envied them, although the thought of living like that terrified her. As Aunt Hermione was fond of saying, "Stoner always has to know where the exits are."

She glanced at Mrs. Burton, who was beginning to tremble slowly or sway rapidly. It was difficult to tell which. What, she wondered again, would bring a sweet little old lady to such desperate straits. Sweet little old lady? Eleanor was little — that much was evident — but was she sweet? Was she a lady? Was she even, when you came right down to it, old? Older than Aunt Hermione, at least in spirit, but not by much. But old people had been known to do amazing things. Even *sweet* old people. Even sweet old *ladies*. Look at those two in "Arsenic and Old Lace" — bodies stacked like cordwood in the basement. Were there bodies stacked in Mrs. Burton's basement? If so, how many? No more than one, of that she was firmly certain. Mrs. Burton clearly lacked the disposition for multiple murder.

One body, then. Circumstances? A trusted boarder turned unexpectedly violent. The elderly woman strikes back in fear and self-defense. The fireplace poker. A discreet burial under the coal-pile. The anxiety and remorse become unbearable. In the safety and semi-darkness of the palmist's parlor she unburdens herself of her guilty secret. What to do next? Aunt Hermione suggests that Stoner and Marylou, being more worldly, would have some ideas.

"Don't worry," Stoner blurted out. "I'm sure we can convince them it was an accident."

"Oh, I tried," Mrs. Burton said. "Not an accident, but a mistake. She wouldn't listen."

"Ignore Stoner," Marylou said. "She talks to herself."

"So does *she*," Mrs. Burton whimpered. Her chin trembled.

"I suggest we go into the parlor." Aunt Hermione stood and folded her napkin. "We can have our Linzer torte there."

"None for me, thank you," Mrs. Burton said. "I'll just have some more of this lovely wine."

Marylou rolled her eyes. "Linzer torte! Aunt Hermione, you old fox, why didn't you tell me? I've stuffed myself on dinner."

"You can take yours with you, Marylou. I got an extra one, just for you."

"You should be canonized."

"Impossible," Aunt Hermione said. "I'm agnostic."

"I'd pray to you nightly," said Marylou.

"Well, you're free to do that, dear. Stoner, would you give Eleanor a hand? She seems to have misplaced her sense of balance."

The heavy drapes in the parlor were closed, but the room was cool. Overhead, a Tiffany ceiling lamp cast a soft, multi-colored glow. Stoner slouched in an overstuffed Lawson chair, while Aunt Hermione perched on the edge of a Shaker ladder-back and unrolled her knitting. "I hope you don't mind, Eleanor," she said. "Busy fingers clear the brain."

Mrs. Burton plucked at her sleeve. "Of course," she muttered in a preoccupied way. Marylou refilled their wine glasses, though Stoner had barely touched hers.

"Well!" Marylou plopped herself down on the sofa beside Mrs. Burton. The older woman bounced. "Now for the mystery."

"Marylou..." Stoner warned.

Mrs. Burton clutched her pocketbook. "You'll probably think I'm a silly old fool, imagining things."

This didn't sound like skeleton-in-the-coalpile stuff. "Not at all," Stoner said.

"My granddaughter does," Mrs. Burton said sadly. She sighed. "Sometimes I doubt my own senses." She took a healthy swallow of wine and sat upright. "But I know what I know, and I suspect what I suspect. And I *know* something terrible is going to happen."

This was sounding less and less like accidental murder.

Mrs. Burton glanced around a little wildly. "She was never very popular, you know. Shy, and insecure. She thought nobody liked her. So when *he* came along she was swept off her feet. But I'm sure he knows about the money, and she's changed the will, and..."

Stoner held up her hand. "Mrs. Burton," she said, leaning forward, "please try to tell us the whole story, from the beginning. Take all the time you need."

"Thank you, dear." Mrs. Burton drew a deep breath. She rummaged in her purse and pulled out a photograph. "This is my granddaughter, Gwen." She passed the picture to Aunt Hermione. "She was married last week to a Bryan Oxnard. Gwen, my daughter's daughter, was orphaned in her teens. Her parents were killed in an airplane accident. It was a charter flight. To Venice."

"We lost one like that once," Marylou said.

"This wouldn't have been your fault," said Mrs. Burton. "They were from Atlanta."

Aunt Hermione clucked sympathetically.

"Her brother was in Australia, so Gwyneth came to live with me. It had been so long since there were children in the house. Perhaps I was remiss. I thought I was giving her all the love she needed, but ..." Mrs. Burton pulled a crumpled lace handkerchief from her sleeve and dabbed at her eyes.

"Please go on," Stoner said.

"Her parents left her comfortably well off. The money was in a trust fund until she was 25. After that she could do as she wished with it. She decided to leave it to accumulate."

"Sensible," said Aunt Hermione, a little disapprovingly.

"How old is she now?" Stoner asked.

"Thirty. About two months ago he started showing up at the house." She emptied her wine glass. Marylou refilled it.

"He?" Stoner asked.

"Bryan Oxnard, of course," said Marylou. "Pay attention, Stoner."

Stoner glanced at her. "I'm trying. So Gwyneth ... Gwen ..."

"They're the same person," Mrs. Burton said. "Gwen is short for Gwyneth."

"Celtic," Aunt Hermione said.

"... married Bryan," Stoner pressed on, "after only knowing him a short time, and changed her will, leaving — I assume — her money to him."

"That's it!" Mrs. Burton exclaimed. "Clever girl."

"Woman," Stoner said.

Aunt Hermione nodded proudly. "Now, you just leave everything to Stoner."

Marylou laughed.

"Please," said Stoner, "tell me more."

"Daphne and Richard, Gwen's parents, were married in 1945. April. It was an exciting time. The war was drawing to a close, the boys were returning. Gwen's father had been wounded in action. I believe he dropped a case of ammunition on his foot, in Brighton. Daphne met him in an Army hospital. She was doing volunteer work, you see."

"Yes," Stoner said. "I meant, tell me more about Bryan..."

Mrs. Burton ignored her. "That was in January. Three months later, they were married." A look of horror crossed her face. "Oh, dear. You don't suppose precipitous marriages run in the family, do you?"

"I don't think it's hereditary," said Marylou. "On the other hand, given an environment in which such a thing is an acceptable form of behavior..." She gestured, palms up. "...anything might happen."

"Marylou's mother is a well-known psychoanalyst," Aunt Hermione explained.

"How very sweet," said Mrs. Burton.

Stoner sighed. "You were saying about Gwen..."

"Donald, the older child, was born just nine months after the wedding.

16

A honeymoon child."

"Aquarius or Pisces?" Aunt Hermione asked.

"Aquarius. Gwyneth is the Pisces. Cancer rising."

"Dear, dear," said Aunt Hermione. Her ball of yarn rolled off her lap and under the sofa. Stoner retrieved it. "Very emotional."

Stoner was nearing hysterics. "Please, what about Bryan?"

Mrs. Burton thought for a moment. "I believe he's a ... Leo. Yes, that's right. Leo."

Stoner rubbed her face in desperation. "What else do you know about him?" she asked as calmly as she could.

"Very little," said Mrs. Burton. "He *said* he was new in town, working in the trust department at the bank."

Uh-oh. "And was he?"

"What?"

"Working in the trust department?"

"Oh, yes. That much was true." Mrs. Burton leaned forward and tapped Stoner's hand. "You must understand, Gwen considers herself an ordinary-looking girl."

"Woman," Stoner said.

Marylou, on her way to refill her glass, took the picture from Aunt Hermione. She whistled.

"She was a darling baby," Mrs. Burton said. "Could I have just a touch more of that lovely wine, dear? Thank you. A good baby. Never cried, slept through the night almost from the first. She's been that way ever since, sweet and agreeable, never complaining, always eager to please..." Her voice broke. "There was never a cross word between us until *he* came along."

Marylou passed Stoner the picture. She looked at it, and gulped. Gwen was no beauty in the conventional sense, but even though the photograph was taken from a distance and slightly blurred — Instamatic, Stoner thought — the woman projected a warmth and vulnerability... For some reason, Stoner found herself blushing. "She's ... lovely," she said.

"How about more wine?" Marylou asked. "I'll get another bottle." On her way out of the room, she gave Stoner a look.

"Stop that," Stoner said under her breath. She turned to Mrs. Burton. "I take it," she said, hoping her voice wasn't shaking, "you and — uh — Gwen disagreed about Bryan."

"It was horrible," Mrs. Burton began to cry again.

"There, there," Aunt Hermione murmured, and attached a new ball of yarn to her knitting.

Mrs. Burton pulled herself together. "I suppose it was really my daughter's fault."

"It was?" Stoner looked at her blankly.

"That Gwyneth was so ... easy. Daphne was vivacious. The center of attention wherever she went. Gwen was always in the shadows. Even her friends were charmed. The minute Daphne entered the room, they forgot all about her."

"That's unfair," Stoner muttered.

"I suggested to Daphne that she stay out of the way when Gwen was entertaining, but of course she wouldn't hear of it. Daphne was an irresistible child. By the time I realized how self-centered she was, the damage was done."

"It wasn't your fault," Stoner said sympathetically. She had known baby *femmes fatales* herself. They were born that way, and barring disfiguring plastic surgery, there was nothing to be done but trip them into mud puddles.

"Gwen never had many beaux. I tried to warn her about Bryan, but she refused to listen. They were married last week." She resumed sobbing.

"Would you like a glass of water?" Stoner asked.

Aunt Hermione refilled her wine glass.

"Thank you. They're on their honeymoon, in Grand Teton National Park. Jackson Hole. That's in Wyoming."

"Yes," said Stoner. "I know."

"South of Yellowstone."

Stoner pushed her hair to the side. "What makes you suspect Bryan Oxnard of ... evil motives?"

"I don't trust him. And, as Harry pointed out, it's very suspicious about the will."

"Harry?"

"Harriman Smythe, our family lawyer."

"I see," said Stoner, not seeing.

"We had tea together only yesterday, at the Copley. You should try it, Hermione. It's very gracious."

"I shall," said Aunt Hermione.

"Har ... Mr. Smythe told me quite by accident ... Mr. Smythe would never betray a confidence ... he told me that Gwen had changed her will. She left everything..."

"To Bryan Oxnard," Stoner finished.

"Exactly." Mrs. Burton's eyes turned watery.

Playing a hunch, she turned to her aunt. "Could you keep Marylou in the kitchen for a while? I'd like to speak with Mrs. Burton alone."

"Of course," Aunt Hermione said, and gathered up her yarn. "I'll see if she's hungry."

She studied the older woman, who was now sitting quite calmly, her hands in her lap. In repose, she was lovely, the kind of soft, cream-skinned woman grandmothers are supposed to be. The kind who have seen hurts come and go, and know they don't last forever. The kind who stay up nights worrying if you're late, but never tell you about it in the morning. The kind who give you books for your birthday when your mother insists on slips and bras, and wrap them themselves. And try never to make you feel guilty, embarrassed, or ashamed. Who say things like, "Leave the girl alone, Helen. She's only a child."

She cleared her throat. "I thought it might be easier to talk if it were just us."

Mrs. Burton smiled tentatively. "I appreciate that, Stoner. I've had entirely too much to drink on top of a wrenching two weeks." She glanced

18

toward the empty doorway. "And frankly, though I find your friend delightful, she is somewhat ... overstimulating.

"I'm afraid I've gone all to pieces about this business. Gwyneth and I have never had a serious disagreement before, you see. But I feel so *sure* I'm right about him, and she's just as positive she's right, and ... well, it's quite a helpless feeling."

"I understand."

"Once I realized what I was doing, I knew I had to ... what do you young people call it? ... 'play it cool'."

Stoner laughed. "I'm not *that* young."

"I'm afraid I may have damaged our relationship beyond repair."

"I'm sure you're wrong," Stoner said. "Not after all these years."

"Love should never be taken for granted. I did hurt her, Stoner, I can't forgive myself for that." She paused to take a sip of wine, changed her mind, and put the glass down. "Chattering like a magpie," she mused. "At my age, one has to be so careful to keep up appearances."

Stoner rested her arms on her knees. "Could you tell me, please, what you've done about the situation up to now?"

"Something terrible," the woman said. "Unthinkable."

"Unthinkable?"

Mrs. Burton fumbled with her cuffs. "I went to the police."

"Well, that seems appropriate."

"It was humiliating." Her eyes flashed. "They were barely polite. Obviously, they were convinced I'm a nattering old fool."

And there was the difference between Mrs. Burton and Aunt Hermione, who would have marched directly to the mayor's office to rail against the idiocy of entrusting the safety and well-being of an entire city to a bunch of insensitive, incompetent babies.

"If you ever have reason to call on the authorities," Mrs. Burton said, "do it before you reach fifty. After that, they won't give you the time of day."

"Did they advise you in any way?"

"They said I had to have Hard Evidence. A bloody corpse, no doubt."

"No doubt," Stoner agreed. "Have you looked into Bryan's background?"

"It occurred to me to make discrete inquiries at the bank, some weeks ago. But it seems like poor form."

"You might do that now."

"Not in person. It could get back to Gwen, don't you see?"

Stoner nooded. "I might be able to help you there."

"That would be lovely, of course. But it would take time, and I'm afraid time is what we don't have."

"Really?"

"Gwen called me last night from Wyoming ... I had gotten her to agree to that, at least ... and I had the most exact premonition that I'd ... that I'd never see her again." She seemed about to break down again, and took herself in hand. "What frightens me is that I *never* have premonitions. After I left the police, I came directly to Hermione. She wasn't very encouraging."

"What did she say?" Stoner asked, beginning to be alarmed.

"That there is danger. Definite danager. She *connected* with Bryan in some way. I'm not sure how these things work."

"Neither am I. But they work."

"You don't suppose she was only being tactful, do you?"

"I doubt it. Tact isn't her long suit." Stoner contemplated the pattern on the rug. "What do you want me to do?"

"Go out there and, well, keep an eye on things."

"*Spy* on them?"

"Such a harsh word. But, yes, spy."

"Mrs. Burton," she said, "I wouldn't know how to go about it."

The older woman dismissed Stoner's objection with a wave of her hand. "Of course you would. Hermione says you're clever."

"Not *that* clever." Hide behind bushes? Lurk in doorways? Peep through windows? She hadn't done those things since she was ten.

"You could run into them in a casual sort of way. Ingratiate yourself..."

"Ingratiate myself?"

"Befriend them. I'm sure you'd like my granddaughter."

"I'm sure I would, but ..."

"And I know she'd like you. Perhaps you could uncover the truth." She fixed Stoner with an even gaze. "She needs a friend very much, Stoner."

"But what if you're wrong about him?"

Mrs. Burton smiled. "I'm fully prepared to eat a great deal of crow. And to adjust to a grandson-in-law I don't like very much."

Stoner glanced at Gwen's picture, and fought down a tiny flurry of excitement. Rational. We have to be rational here. "May I take some time to think about it?"

"Speed is of the essence. Even now it may be too ... oh, dear."

"Overnight," Stoner said quickly. "I can't ... couldn't do anything until tomorrow, anyway. Meanwhile, if you ... uh ... hear from her, will you call me?"

"Immediately." She stood up. "I have to be off. If there's dreadful news, I don't want to hear it from my answering machine." They started toward the door. "When I was your age, we delivered bad news in person. Even a phone call would have been unthinkable. Anything goes nowadays, doesn't it?"

"Would you like Marylou to accompany you home?" Stoner asked, pulling the woman's coat from the hall closet.

"Why, that's an excellent idea. She'd reduce a mugger's mind to pudding, wouldn't she?" She pulled on her gloves. "Thank you so much for your help. Hermione promised you wouldn't let me down."

Stoner felt the walls closing in. "I'll consider it. That's all I can say right now."

"I'd go out there myself, you know, but that wouldn't do at all."

"Not at all. It has to be someone they don't know."

"And what good would I be around mountains?"

"To tell you the truth, Mrs. Burton, I believe you could handle yourself in any situation."

"You're very sweet," the woman said, and patted Stoner's cheek.

"May I keep the picture for tonight?" Self-conscious, she grinned awkwardly. "It might help me to decide."

"Of course. And you'll need it, won't you, to identify her?"

"If I ..."

Mrs. Burton sighed. "Oh, I hope I'm wrong. I do want her to be happy."

"I'm sure you do."

"I've behaved so badly up to now. Do you think she'll ever forgive me?"

"I'm sure she will."

"Love makes us do strange things." She checked her purse for her house key.

"It certainly does."

"But what else is there?" She touched Stoner's arm. "I think I'm ready for Marylou now."

When they had left, Stoner turned to her aunt. "Do you think it's as bad as she says?"

"As bad, if not worse."

Stoner rammed her hands into her back pockets. "For Heaven's sake, Aunt Hermione, what have you gotten me into?"

Alone in her room, Stoner leaned against the open window and gazed down into the night-darkened pocket garden. The tall buildings, standing shoulder to shoulder around the tiny open space, obliterated street noises. Listening carefully, she thought she could hear the whisper and creak of squash vines growing secretly in the blackness. She sighed deeply, and permitted herself a single unworthy thought.

Much as she loved Marylou and Aunt Hermione — and she loved them with all her heart — she sometimes, in the midst of their clatter and ease of living, felt lonely. Sometimes she longed to spend an hour with someone who was fearful of strangers, who couldn't let a telephone ring unanswered, was silenced by sunsets, grouchy when tired, timid in department stores, awkward when touched — someone, in short, who was merely normally neurotic. She sighed again. It really was an unworthy thought.

Stoner clicked on the bedside lamp and studied the blurred snapshot. There was something about the woman's eyes... Guarded, aware that her picture was being taken, and not altogether comfortable with it. *That*, she thought, was an emotion she could understand.

Her fingertips tingled oddly. Stoner wiped her hands on her pajamas. What, in the name of Heaven, was she going to do about this situation? It was ridiculous, something out of a soap opera or a late-night movie. People didn't go around marrying for money and murdering their wives. Not in Real Life. Well, not in real life as *she* knew it. And there didn't even seem to be much money involved here. Now, if they were talking about millions ... since she didn't really believe there *were* people with millions, after all Newport was obviously a movie set ... if they were talking about millions, it was possible. If you could believe in one impossibility, you could believe in the other.

But even granting the impossibilities, how could she take this job? She wasn't clever, she knew nothing about this kind of thing, and she didn't even own a trench coat. Better to leave it in the hands of a professional. A private detective. That's what she'd advise Mrs. Burton to do. Stoner was better off — they were all better off — if she stayed home doing what she did best. Filling out travel vouchers.

She glanced once more, wistfully, at the photograph, and climbed into bed. Convinced she had made the right decision, she turned out the light. Someday, she hoped, she would meet Gwen Oxnard.

***

"Well," said Aunt Hermione over breakfast.

"Well?"

"Are you going to do it?"

Stoner looked up. "I thought meals were sacrosanct."

Aunt Hermione put her coffee cup down with an impatient gesture. "Honestly, Stoner, sometimes you think like a dog."

"Huh?"

"I tell you to stay off the couch, and you're afraid to get on *any* of the furniture."

Stoner rubbed her eyes sleepily. "Only because you keep changing the rules."

"All right, Stoner." Aunt Hermione poured her a second cup of coffee. "I know that McTavish set of jaw. You've reached a decision, and I want to know what it is."

"I thought my father was weak-willed."

"I'm referring to *Angus* McTavish," Aunt Hermione said. "When are you leaving?"

Stoner stirred her coffee. "I'm not. I think she should hire a private detective."

"I already suggested that. She won't do it."

"Why not?"

"She doesn't want her family business known to outsiders, and she doesn't trust strangers."

"I'm a stranger." She took a sip of coffee.

"But she's known me for years."

Stoner cocked her head on one side and looked hard at her aunt. "Do I really *have* a choice?"

"Of course not," said Aunt Hermione, buttering a croissant.

***

Stoner let the door to the travel agency slam behind her and dropped her shoulder bag onto her desk. "Well," she said grimly, "I'm going to do it."

"Wonderful," said Marylou. She picked up a packet of papers. "Now, you'll take the 1:10 from Logan. United, I'm afraid. You have a through flight, with a 45 minute layout at O'Hare, arriving in Denver at 6:03 local time."

"Marylou..."

"You don't have to pack much. You can get your disguise when you get there."

22

"My *disguise*."

Marylou gave her an exasperated look. "You'll stand out like a sore thumb in those eastern clothes. You want to look like a tourist, blend in with the scenery, which I understand is magnificent. Take your knapsack, hiking boots, and other essentials." She tossed a pile of Jackson Hole brochures on the desk. "Study these."

"Wait a minute..."

"At Denver you change to Frontier Airlines, whatever that is, which takes you into Jackson. I've rented you a car. You have reservations at Timberline Lodge, where Gwen and Bryan are staying."

"How did you find that out?"

"I talked to Mrs. Burton this morning. She's offered to pay your expenses, plus a little extra for your trouble. She has a terrible hangover."

Stoner sagged against the desk. "You set me up."

Marylou stopped shuffling papers. "Set you up?"

"You and Aunt Hermione," she said angrily. "I'm tempted not to do it."

"I didn't mean..."

"Oh, forget it, Marylou. You never mean." She sat down and began rummaging through a desk drawer. "Damn it, where did I put the Jessamys' Amtrak tickets?"

Marylou came over to her. "Stoner, I'm sorry. Really I am."

Stoner folder her arms and stared straight ahead. Her mouth was tight. "It *could* be dangerous, you know."

"I didn't think."

Stoner hummed to herself.

"You kept the picture, didn't you?" Marylou asked meekly.

"Yes, I kept the picture."

"Well..." Marylou shrugged, and drew apologetic circles on the desk top with her fingertip.

Stoner melted. "All right." She flipped through the airline tickets and sat bolt upright. "Marylou, these are one-way tickets."

"I didn't know when you'd be coming back."

Stoner laughed. "For a minute I thought you didn't expect me to."

Marylou looked at her. "You're scared."

"You bet I'm scared."

"What can happen to you?"

Exasperated, Stoner brushed her hair to the side. "Theoretically, I'm going out there to stop a murder. What do *you* think can happen?"

"Aunt Hermione must know it's going to be all right."

"Aunt Hermione doesn't do readings for family or close friends."

"Oh," said Marylou. She brightened. "Take a gun."

"I don't know how to use a gun."

"It's easy. You just poke that little doo-hickey that hangs down... Don't you?"

"Marylou, I am *not* going to walk around Wyoming with a gun."

"Why not? Everyone else does."

Stoner groaned. "That's only in the movies."

"Well, what the heck? Mrs. Burton's probably imagining the whole thing."

23

"I hope so."

"Will you write?"

"Every day."

Marylou hugged her. "Hey, the change will do you good. And think of the aesthetics..."

"I know," Stoner said. "I've always wanted to see the Tetons."

"I wasn't referring to the mountains," said Marylou.

CHAPTER 3

Her first view of the Midwest from 30,000 feet convinced Stoner of the virtues of air travel. Far below stretched mile after mile of perfect, tawny squares, their symmetry reinforced by ruler-straight roads. Occasionally a single farmhouse appeared, surrounded by trees, sturdy, solitary, like a lost migratory bird storm-driven into an empty sea. A tractor crept beetle-like across a field. It would take at least two days to drive across that.

On the other hand, a car would provide her with something she had longed for periodically since the plane left Boston — the opportunity to turn back. Only discipline, self-restraint, and a double Manhattan had kept her from stowing away on the next flight back east from Chicago. Stoner leaned her head against the back of the seat and gazed at the top of the airliner's wing. The sky was darkening a little, washing out toward the western horizon. A wisp of cloud drifted by the window.

The cities east of the Mississippi fell below the earth's curve. She felt a stirring of excitement. Those were the Great Plains below, the home of the now-vanished buffalo herds, wagon trains, Arapahoe, Pony Express, the land rush, the Dust Bowl. Pioneers had set out to cross them not knowing what lay on the other side — or if there would *be* another side. Men were driven to violence, and women to insanity, by the isolation, the uncertainty, and the wind. The life was unimaginable, even now. It must be tens of miles between the farm houses. Housewives would go days, even weeks, without seeing another woman's face. They cleaned, cooked, grew vegetables, and watched television. Day after day, an entire lifetime. What did you do if you were lonely? What did you do if your husband abused you? What, in God's name, did you do if you were a lesbian? Well, you probably did the same thing in any event — got out if you could. And if you can't, grit your teeth, try not to feel, and hope like hell there was a life after death — or after Nebraska, whichever came first.

The flight attendant leaned over her, breaking her reverie. ''Landing in ten minutes, Miss McTavish.''

''Ms.'', Stoner said automatically.

Ahead now she could see the front range of the Rockies, a thin, mauve-gray line of ragged bumps. Then the plane tipped forward, its engines slowing. The mountains grew larger; sharp peaks fringed the lavender sky. The tiny diamond lights of Denver twinkled in the haze. Stoner felt a lump in her throat. She was in the West.

***

The little two-engined Frontier Airlines plane bumped and dipped over wind-currents like potholes in the sky. Stoner glanced around at the other passengers and felt conspicuous in her eastern clothes. The Denver flight had carried mostly business suits and light dresses, but the locals clearly preferred jeans and plaid western shirts.

25

They paused briefly in Laramie to deliver a few summer college students, then took off northwest. The sky was still light, but fading rapidly. A planet sparkled on the horizon. Night came on in a rush.

Her seatmate gestured out the window. "Medicine Bows," he said. Below lay snow-capped mountains. "Glaciers."

He was a middle-aged man in polyester jeans and pointed cowboy boots. An unremarkable looking person. This was the first time in an hour he had spoken.

"I notice there's no sunset," Stoner said. "Is that usual?"

He nodded. "Dry."

"Do you live in Jackson?"

"Moose. Fish and Wildlife. Wapiti."

"Moose, fish, wildlife, and wapiti?"

"Government service," he grunted. "Live in Moose."

"Wapiti?" Stoner asked tentatively.

"Research the wapiti. Elk. 'Cept they aren't elk, they're wapiti."

"Oh," Stoner said. She vaguely remembered reading something about the National Elk Refuge in a brochure.

"Look like elk," the man said. "But they aren't elk."

"Wapiti," Stoner said.

He grunted again, in a pleased sort of way. "Wapiti.' He appraised her clothes. "Tourist."

Stoner shooked her head. "I'm here ... on business."

"Good. Too damn many tourists. Government?"

"No, I'm with a ... " she hesitated, "... travel agency. In Boston?" she finished hopefully.

"Damned tourist."

"No," Stoner said urgently. "I'm not a tourist."

"Make your living off of them."

"But I don't like them."

"Oughta make your living off something you like."

"Well, I do like some of them. But not the kind that think the world is their personal playground."

"Lotta them around," said Fish and Wildlife.

"And there are plenty of places for them."

"For instance?"

"Las Vegas, most of Florida, and Atlantic City."

She thought he smiled a little, but it could have been a hallucination.

"Somebody's always after something in this valley," the man growled. "What are you after?"

"I only want to look around," Stoner said. "To get a feel for the place, so I don't recommend it to the wrong people."

Fish and Wildlife stared at her. "You want to look the place over so you can keep people away?"

Stoner nodded eagerly.

"Some kind of a kook," he said. "Want a drink?"

Stoner looked toward the tail of the plane. If there was any sort of a galley, it was bound to contain nothing more than third-class mail. "Do they serve drinks on this flight?"

26

"Nope." He pulled a flask from his battered brief case, wiped the opening on his sleeve, and passed it to her.

Feeling as if she were being initiated into some ancient tribal rite, Stoner offered up a quick prayer to whoever might be listening, and took a healthy swallow. It was straight, warm gin. "Thank you," she gasped.

"Good stuff." He put the flask away without drinking.

"Yes, indeed." It was, she noticed with some amazement, possible to shudder invisibly. It all had to do with pressure on the back teeth. "You're not drinking?"

"Rots my insides." He sighed and settled back comfortably. "Been out here five years, probably stay another five. If it's still here. Trappers, tuskers, now tourists."

"Tuskers?" Stoner asked, alarmed.

"Came out here looking for wapiti's eye teeth, 'tusks' they called them. Killed the animals, pulled out the teeth, and left the rest."

"Whatever for?"

"You ever heard of the B.P.O.E.?"

Stoner nodded. "The Elks."

"Biggest Pigs On Earth. Used the teeth on their watch fobs."

"But they aren't elk," Stoner protested. "They're wapiti."

"Killed hundreds of thousands. Damn near wiped out the herd."

"Oh, God," Stoner said.

"Well, they got the herd protected. Now it's tourists.

"Campgrounds, ski trails, snowmobiles, trail bikes. Damn recreational vehicles. Whole towns cut out of the forest. Condominiums. You go take a look at that damn Teton Village. Swiss Chalets, French Restaurants. People want to come out to Wyoming and pretend they're in Europe. Why don't they just go to Europe?" He glared at her. "You tell me that."

"I don't know," Stoner mumbled.

"Well, if you ever find out, let me know. I certainly would be interested in that information." he sighed. "Jackson Hole used to be sacred land to the Indians. No one knows why, but they wouldn't even camp here. Some say it was because so many tribes passed through the valley going from here to there, they agreed among themselves nobody'd stake a claim so there wouldn't be any jealousy. But they weren't much for laying claim on land anyway. I figure they believed the Great Spirit lived in the mountains. You see if they don't strike you that way. But you'll never get any damn tourist to swallow that."

Stoner was becoming more and more depressed.

"Profit," her companion said morosely. "Land developers hit the Mother Lode in Jackson Hole. Buy up a few acres with a view, put out some slick advertising, sit back and rake in the profits."

"Why would anyone sell to them?" Stoner asked.

"Main way to make a living out here, if you don't make pots or sell trinkets, is ranching. Hard work, heartbreak, hardship, and bankruptcy — ranchers' life cycle."

To break the cloud of gloom that was settling over her, Stoner looked out the window. The mountains had fallen behind. They were over flat land again. Sand and sagebrush glowed oddly in the near darkness. The view was unbroken by towns, buildings, or even lights.

"Water," the government agent said abruptly. "That's what you easterners never understand. You get more rain in two months than we see in a year. Gotta be without water to appreciate it."

That was true enough. In New England, water was always coming down, running off, freezing, melting, hanging in the air, leaking into the cellar, or evaporating off the hillsides. It made your hair stringy, your clothes smell, your bread mold, and your garden rot. It flooded your carburator, stained your walls, and caused you to dress funny.

"You got too much foliage," he went on. "Spend half your life pulling weeds and cutting underbrush. Out here the trick is to get anything to grow. We got trees and plants on the higher elevations, up where you can't get to them. But down on the plains it takes a sagebrush 50 years to mature. And then it ain't worth much."

"I'm sorry," Stoner said, irrelevantly.

"So we don't take kindly to folks coming in, not looking where they step, carving on trees, breaking and killing. And calling it fun." He glanced over at her. "Talk to the Forest Service, they'll tell you the same. We try to protect an acre here, a tree there. But we're losing. We can slow it down, but sooner or later they'll have it all."

"There must be *some* hope," Stoner said desperately.

"Well, they got Jackson Hole made into a National Park. That's something. At least until those jackasses in Washington change their minds and sell the whole damn thing to land developers. There they are."

Stoner whirled around, half expecting to see platoons of land developers and legislators trooping down the aisle. "Who?"

"Tetons."

Through the darkness she could just make out the landing field, and behind it massive black shadows of mountains. To the north a river glowed silver in reflected moonlight. Jackson lay at the south end of the dark basin of Jackson Hole. "What are those?" she asked, indicating an isolated cluster of lights.

"One of the lodges," the man said. He glanced around, orienting himself. "Signal Mountain, probably. On Jackson Lake."

Stoner looked more closely, and saw a sprawling body of water like spilled mercury. Farther to the north, another cluster of lights cut into the darkness.

"Jackson Lake Lodge," her companion said.

"Is everything out here named Jackson?"

"Just about. Jackson was an early trapper. Set his traps along the Snake."

"Can you see Timberline Lodge from here?"

He shook his head. "It's in the forest at the base of Teewinot. That where you're staying?"

"Yes."

"Ted and Stell Perkins' place. Nice folks. Probably won't see much of Ted, though. He's restless. Stell runs one of the best kitchens in the park."

"French?" Stoner asked.

28

Fish and Wildlife laughed, an act of which Stoner had thought him incapable. "Stell wouldn't serve anything she couldn't pronounce."

The two lodges floated like ocean liners in a gray sea of darkness and moonlight. Stoner could feel her heart begin to pound. She sat up, clutching the back of the seat ahead, trying to see everything at once. The pilot banked the plane and began his decent. She leaned back, hands trembling.

"Tell me," she said as calmly as she could, "what's the quickest way to get your bearings around here?"

"Tourists," the man sighed. "Always in a hurry."

"Please."

"Well, *Bonney's Guide* is pretty good. Hasn't been updated since 1972, but it's still the best around. The Natural History Association would have that, and some others. Or you could pick it up at the entrance station in Moose. Plan to ride any?"

"Horseback?" Stoner shook her head. "I'm terrified of horses. But I might hike."

"Get a topographic map, and don't go anywhere without it. Stay away from the back country. Dangerous territory out there, and the altitude can do strange things to you."

The plane bounced and sputtered to a stop. "Son of a bitch got the thing landed," the man said. "Swear to God, some day he's going to set it down in Granite Canyon." He pulled a topcoat from the overhead rack. "Better get out a coat. Freeze your ass off dressed like that. Have a nice trip." He stalked off down the aisle. "Tourists," Stoner heard him mutter.

She stood alone on the deserted runway, feeling as much as seeing the hulking Tentons before her. Under a half-moon the mountains were barely visible, but their presence was unmistakable. Smears of florescence marked the glaciers on the high peaks, and she could make out, as her eyes became accustomed to darkness, the jagged, tooth-like spires. But mostly she felt their heavy, placid impersonality. There was something ominous about it. Stoner felt her body tense.

She picked up her car and a map of the Park. At least it wasn't going to be easy to get lost. Only two major roads ran through the area, Rockefeller Highway to the east, and Teton Park Road, with a one-way cutoff near Jenny Lake, to the west. Between them stretched Baseline and Antelope Flats, and the twisting Snake River. Timberline Lodge lay at the edge of Lupine Meadows, nestled against the mountains along Cottonwood Creek.

Her anxiety lifted as she drove north though the deserted night. The car's headlights picked up clumps of sagebrush along the road. Now and then tiny pairs of eyes flashed at her and disappeared. Buckrail fences, X's of rough saplings supporting horizontal poles, lined the highway. That was all. No trees, no other cars, only the glow of her dashboard lights and the silence, and the brooding mountains. The night air was crisp; it made her feel a little drunk to breathe it. Fish and Wildlife was right. She *did* want to see everything at once. The moonlight teased her with shadows.

She turned in at the dirt road marked with the small, discreet sign. Timberline Lodge. The rough bridge and cattle guard rattled as she crossed them and pulled into the parking lot. Closing the screen door quietly behind her, Stoner was surprised to see that the lobby was nearly deserted. The walls were made of varnished logs, rough-chiseled and crossed at the corners. The main lodge was in the shape of a squat L. Directly opposite the front door stood the entrance to what must be the dining room, identified by the Highlands Room sign over the arch. To its right was an exit, and next to that the Stampede Room, probably the bar. A soft glow filtered from the doorway, along with the incongruous murmur of a television set. It sounded like a late movie. Stoner glanced at her watch. Eleven-fifteen. Back home it would be after one.

A fireplace filled the north wall, blazing logs sending up fingers of flame and sharp popping sounds. Two young men sat reading by the fire, their feet propped on the raised stone hearth. The room dwarfed them. Everything was so quiet. Feeling awkward and a little self-conscious, she tapped the bell.

A tall, thin woman appeared from the dining room, wiping her hands on an apron. Her hair was brown and streaked with gray, her eyes a dark hazel. "You must be Stoner McTavish," she said, holding out her hand. "We've been waiting for you."

Stoner shook her hand, startled by the roughness of her skin, the firmness of her grip. "I'm sorry," she said. "I didn't mean to sneak in like a thief in the night."

"Sneak in? They can hear that cattle guard all the way over to the Jenny Lake campgrounds. I've been after Ted to fix that loose rail for six years. I'm Stell Perkins. Call me Stell. Want a cup of coffee?"

"That would be nice," Stoner said.

"Park your suitcase behind the desk. How was the flight?"

"A little confusing. I mean, I've never seen scenery like this before. What I've seen of it, I mean." For some reason she felt about fifteen years old. "Is there always so much — space?"

Stell laughed and threw an arm around her shoulders, leading her into the dining room. "Sometimes there's more. You don't mind sitting in the kitchen, do you?"

A single lamp burning in the Highlands Room lit up huge windows, black against the night. "Those look out on the Cathedral Group," Stell explained. "Middle, Grand, Owen, and Teewinot. It's impressive in daylight."

Stoner glanced around the room. Another fireplace, its fire burned down to coals, stood against the south wall. The tables were made of varnished wood, the chairs of wood and rawhide. A gigantic wagon wheel studded with lamps hung in the center of the room.

"It's like something out of a movie," Stoner said, dazzled.

"I suppose it is. Everything out here's in pretty much the same style. Except the new places like Teton Village. Sorry about the sauna."

"I beg your pardon?"

"Your partner — Kesselbaum? — when she called to make the reservation. Asked about a sauna."

Stoner felt her face redden. "I hate saunas. They make me feel like something growing in a lab." She glanced at Stell. "Marylou's a little crazy."

30

Stell shrugged. "Who isn't? Let me give you the official rundown on the place, then you can relax. We have about sixty guests here at any one time. Thirty in the cabins and thirty in the lodge rooms upstairs. Fortunately, Little Bear was available."

"Little Bear?"

"Our overflow cabin. Comfortable for two, but since most of our guests are families, it's sometimes empty. Or a large party will take Big Bear and put some of the children in Little."

"I see," Stoner said.

"It's on the end, so you'll have plenty of privacy. Come on." She held open the door to the kitchen, and Stoner stepped inside. It was love at first sight. Backed onto the dining room fireplace was still another, complete with built-in brick warming ovens. Over the andirons, a huge black kettle hung from an iron bar. An old Border Collie blinked up at her from its mat by the fire. "That's Chipper," Stell said. "Not good for much but loving any more. She's a little deaf, and kind of slow, but she was a great mouser in her time. Weren't you, girl?"

Stell bent and scratched Chipper behind the ears. The dog panted with ecstasy.

"Hope you don't mind a little informality," the older woman said, pulling two heavy white mugs from the cupboards over the sink. She filled them from a tin pot that sat on the back burner of a monstrous black gas stove. "Sugar?"

"No, thanks."

A device resembling a bucket was clamped to the large butcher-block table that ran the length of the kitchen. Stell turned a crank in the top of it. "Mind if I finish up here while we talk? Sourdough bread's one of our drawing cards."

"I shouldn't think you'd need an attraction," Stoner said. "This is a beautiful place."

"Thanks. It was my husband's family's ranch, long before there was a National Park here. Then they ran a dude ranch for a while, and finally turned it into what we have here. It's one of the few private holdings left inside the Park."

Stoner took a swallow of coffee. The sharp bitterness of it made her eyes pop open. "Good heavens!" she said.

Stell laughed. "Cowboy coffee. Water and grounds boiled up together, with a few eggshells tossed in to settle it."

"It doesn't taste very settled," Stoner said. "I mean..."

"You'll get used to the flavor. It isn't as hard on the nerves as it tastes. There." Stell turned the dough out onto the floured tabletop and began to shape the loaves.

"How many of those do you make a day?" Stoner asked.

Stell brushed the hair from her forehead, leaving behind a streak of white. "We have our regular guests for breakfast, plus about ten extras — local artists and Forest Service personnel. Lunch, usually about fifteen, and twenty or so box lunches. At dinner we expect around forty. I probably make up thirty loaves a day."

Stoner whistled. "That's a lot of work."

31

"No more than making three," Stell said. "By the way, if you're not going to be here for dinner, we'd appreciate it if you'd let Pat know. She's the headwaitress. You can tell her at breakfast. And if you want a box lunch, order that at breakfast, too. You can pick it up after nine."

"Should I tell you if I don't want breakfast?"

"You will. These mountains play havoc with your diet."

Stoner leaned her arms on the table and sipped her coffee. "I notice it's awfully quiet here," she said. "Is that because there are so many families?"

"The altitude. Knocks you out if you're not used to it. You saw our little bar?"

Stoner nodded.

"Tony, the bartender, is willing to stay open all night, but it usually clears out by twelve." Stell slipped loaves of dough into the line of waiting pans. "Now that I think about it, I've never seen Tony sleep."

"Maybe he's a vampire," Stoner said.

Stell grinned. "Maybe." She wiped her hands on a towel. "Now, what else can I tell you about Timberline?" She gestured toward the dining room. "You've seen the Highlands Room. Just outside the door under the stairs, next to the bar, is a campfire circle. The local rangers give talks on Thursday nights. Or a guest might want to talk about hobbies or travels. Once in a while we have a church service on Sunday morning, if there's a minister staying here. But we don't encourage it."

"Why not?"

"Well, it tends to make the guests nervous, like it's something they ought to do. Kind of ruins a vacation." She rinsed out a dishcloth and scrubbed briefly at the sink. "From the campfire there are two paths, one to Jenny Lake and one to Taggart. They're marked. There's a telephone in your room. Our nearest doctor is in Jackson, but there's a nurse at Jackson Lake Lodge for emergencies. We have our own stables. If you want to go riding or hiking, it's a good idea to register. That way, if anything happens, sooner or later someone will come looking for you. Of course, that isn't necessary on the popular trails. Our wrangler's name is Jake. Kind of taciturn, but don't let that put you off. Our waitresses and cabin girls are college students. Sheets are changed every three days. Have I forgotten anything?"

"I doubt it," Stoner said. She was beginning to feel sleepy.

"Don't hesitate to ask." Stell tossed her apron over the edge of the sink. "Your partner said not to let you do anything damnfool. You planning to do anything damnfool?"

Stoner laughed. "That's just Marylou. She's..."

"... a little crazy. All the same, it pays to be careful. This is tricky territory out here."

"It can't be any worse than Boston."

"Yes, it can. Out here, if anything happens to you, you're on your own." She squeezed Stoner's shoulder affectionately. "Let me show you how to find your cabin."

Stoner finished her coffee and followed Stell into the lobby.

"Here," Stell said, pointing to a rough chart. "Go back out the way you

32

came in, into the parking lot. Rockchuck, Wapiti, Bobcat, Elk, and Bronco are to your left as you face the road. Coyote, Mustang, Big Bear, and Little Bear are on the right. Little Bear is up the mountain a few yards. The nights are pretty cold now, so I lit your fire. Throw a couple of logs on before you go on to bed, and it should hold until morning.''

Stifling a yawn, Stoner picked up her key and suitcase. "Thanks, Stell. Oh, by the way, I was supposed to look someone up while I was here. Could you tell me where the Oxnards are staying?''

An odd look flickered over Stell's face. "Friends of yours?''

"Friends of a friend. I've never met them.''

"The Nez Perce suite, upstairs.''

Stoner hesitated. "Is something wrong?''

"No,'' Stell said, and shrugged. "The wife seems nice enough. I just can't warm up to the husband. Some people affect you that way, I guess. Put you off right away, you finally convince yourself it was all in your mind...''

"And six months later you find out you were right,'' Stoner finished. "What puts you off about Bryan Oxnard?''

Stell frowned thoughtfully. "I can't say for sure. A little too self-confident for my taste. It takes a touch of insecurity to add salt to the stew. Know what I mean?''

"I certainly do.''

"Suppose I shouldn't gossip, but seeing as how we're in the same line of work, so to speak...''

"I won't say anything,'' Stoner said.

"That reminds me. Your partner said to make sure you don't come home with fifty pounds of brochures the way you usually do. Said you couldn't afford the extra freight.''

Stoner laughed. "She's trying to save enough money in petty cash to buy us a food processor.''

"Why do you need a food processor in a travel agency?''

"You'd have to know Marylou to understand,'' Stoner said.

"Well, you'd best trot on up the path. Mornings start early around here.''

"I don't know.'' She yawned openly. "Maybe I'll sleep in.''

"Not when the birds start up,'' Stell said.

Stoner stepped out into the cold mountain air and glanced up. Even with the moon half full and nesting overhead, she thought she could see every star in the universe. Above her stretched the Milky Way, a diamond ribbon tossed carelessly down. Other stars and galaxies lay like scattered grain across the royal blue velvet sky. A Perseid meteor cut the night. My God, she thought, the beauty is going to kill me.

She crossed the parking lot and trudged up a dirt trail, past the darkened cabins toward Little Bear. Lodgepole pines spread their branches silently overhead. Stars twinkled through their needles. The still air smelled faintly of pine and an odd, acrid scent from wildflowers that bloomed in open spaces. The silence was almost tangible, a breath drawn and held, broken only by the inconsequential sound of her footsteps.

33

Little Bear stood apart from the others, a tiny cabin built of logs, diminutive and complete as a child's playhouse. Colored light seeped from the windows through bright curtains. A roofed porch held rocking chairs. Clumps of fireweed surrounded the foundation. Stoner lifted the latch and stepped inside. The fire hissed and sizzled on the flagstone hearth, flanked by deep, comfortable-looking chairs with rope springs. Against one wall was a writing table. The opposite wall held the door to the bath. Bright Indian rugs warmed the floor. Beside the front door were two twin beds separated by a nightstand, and facing them the dresser and closet. Everywhere she looked her eyes met the friendly glow of polished wood. It was too much. Stoner dropped her suitcase, sat on the edge of the bed, and wept.

***

She was awake almost before dawn, rested and eager to confront the mountains. Scrambling into her clothes, she stepped out on the porch. To her left the Tetons thrust their granite peaks into an ice-blue sky. Snow fields lay deep in the crevices and dusted the tips of the summits. Forests of pine and aspen spilled down the lower slopes, and meadows of wild flowers shouted with color. To her right she could make out the dry, low hills of the Gros Ventre Range. The valley between was a powdery gray-green. And over it all that incredible, endless sky. She thought it would tear the heart from her.

She looked as long as she could bear. Glutted with scenery, she hurried down the path to the lodge.

The doors to the dining room were closed, but groups of hikers and backpackers were already in the lobby, bustling about with an air of un-washed self-importance. Somewhere along the line, she thought, she was lacking an essential chromosome — the one that thrilled at the risk of life and limb, not to say exposure, for the dubious pleasure of dangling from rocks at the end of a rope. Of freezing, sweating, consumed by mos-quitoes, drenched by rain, baked by the sun — all to down a can of Budweiser on top of a mountain while jumping up and down in slow mo-tion and flashing the "We're Number One" sign. In this crowd, most of the steel-toed boots, doughnut socks, *lederhosen*, ropes, and picks decorated *male* bodies. Which undoubtedly explained something. Didn't it?

The dining room doors swung open. Backpackers sprinted for tables, jostling, shoving, poking with elbows, and shouting obscenities with boyish good humor. Stoner waited until they were seated, and peeked tentatively around the edge of the door. There, behind floor-to-ceiling windows, were the mountains, framed by aspens and gazing placidly down on an alpine meadow. She closed her eyes and clenched her fists. "I can't bear it," she said aloud.

"You must be new here," said a masculine voice at her elbow.

Stoner whirled around to see a tall, rugged-looking man in Forest Ser-vice green. His eyes were deep-set and blue as the sky, his hair reddish

34

brown but salted with gray. He wore wire-rimmed glasses. A black plastic name tag over his left breast pocket read, "Flanagan."

"I ... uh ... got in last night."

"First time I saw them," the man said, gesturing in the general direction of the dining room, "I locked myself in my room and had a couple of good, stiff drinks."

"The mountains?" Stoner asked. "Or the hikers?"

"Both."

Stoner held out her hand. "Stoner McTavish."

"Flanagan," he said, giving her hand a hearty shake. "John."

One of the Lodge employees passed. "Yo, Smokey," he called.

The ranger's face fell. "Yo, Tim."

"Smokey?" Stoner asked.

"It's the hat," he groused. "The Smokey Bear hat."

"Oh." She had a sudden picture of herself, standing on a bit of high ground, yelling, "Smokey!", and watching the entire Forest Service converge from every corner of the Park. "It must be very confusing," she said, "if they call all of you Smokey."

Flanagan sighed. "They don't. Just me."

"Why?"

"I have special problems. Would you do me the pleasure of joining me for breakfast?"

"I'd be delighted."

As they crossed the threshold, she felt a sudden faint prickling at the base of her spine. Today, in fact any minute, she would meet the real Gwen Owens. I'm not ready, she thought. Slip quietly away before it's too late.

Smokey was leading her to a table for two, offering her the seat that faced the window. Stoner declined. If she could watch the door, perhaps she would see Gwen before Gwen saw her. It would give her the advantage...

A waitress brought them coffee and menus. "Watch out for that stuff," Smokey said, indicating the coffee.

"I know. I had some last night." She noticed she was stirring sugar into her cup. She put her spoon down. "I don't take sugar," she explained.

He looked at her, raised one eyebrow, and returned to the menu.

Nerves, nerves. Now what is the point of this, she asked herself sternly. You meet people every day. Yes, she replied, but you don't meet *her* every day.

She tried to focus on her table companion. "You mentioned special problems."

Smokey glanced around, then leaned across the table. "Movie people," he said under his breath.

"Movie people."

Stoner shook her head. "I've missed something." An elderly couple entered the dining room. Not them.

"They make movies out here, for ... obvious reasons." He nodded discreetly toward the mountains.

"Please," Stoner said. "Not until I've eaten."

The waitress came to take their orders. Thinking she'd better stick to familiar routines, Stoner chose sweet rolls.

"Have something more," Smokey said. "This altitude makes you wicked hungry."

"I'll take my chances." Considering the way her stomach was tightening, keeping *anything* down was going to be a miracle. If Marylou were here, she'd take Stoner outside and make her scream.

"What's a short stack?" she asked, to make conversation.

"Flapjacks, two. A tall stack is four." He took a swallow of coffee.

The lobby was mercifully empty. Maybe they wouldn't come. "Tell me about the movie people."

"Well," Smokey said, leaning back in his chair, "most of these buckos are city types. Raised on cement and supermarkets, if you know what I mean. But we have a very fragile ecology out here."

"I know," Stoner said. "I heard about it from Fish and Wildlife."

"Fish and Wildlife! What do *they* know? Sit around on their fat duffs in air conditioned offices. Write reports no one ever reads, if they have any sense, and couldn't understand if they did. They should be out *here*..." He stabbed the table with his finger. "... where things are happening."

"Movie people?" Stoner suggested timidly.

"Yes. Well, when they make a movie here, the government — God rest its soul — assigns the Forest Service to the set. To make sure they don't destroy anything."

Someone was standing in the door! No, it was only a small child looking for its mother. "No rain," Stoner muttered.

"These Hollywood characters," Smokey said. "You'd think they'd understand about rain, not being overly endowed in that commodity themselves." He snorted. "Money, that's all they understand. Break something, buy a new one. But you can't buy rain, and plants need rain, and wildlife need plants, and who are you looking for, darlin'?"

"What? No ... nobody. I'm sorry. You were saying about rain?"

Smokey grinned at her discomfort. "I'm the one that gets to ride herd on that bunch."

"I see." Confused, she brushed her hair to the side. She was going to run. Any minute now, she was going to leap up, create a disturbance, and bolt. Concentrate, she told herself sharply. "I thought this had something to do with... I can't remember."

"The nickname, McTavish."

"Of course. The nickname." She was beginning to feel dizzy. "I think I'd better have breakfast after all."

Smokey signalled the waitress. "*They* started this 'Smokey' business," he said when she had ordered. "They think it's cute."

"Can you get a different assignment?"

"The Forest Service is like the Army," he grumbled. "And the worst of it is, they *like* me. Word gets around. So any time a company comes out here it's the same thing, 'Where's Smokey Flanagan?' Well," he spread his hands in a gesture of helplessness, "gotta keep the taxpayers happy."

Stoner had to smile. "I think you like it."

"Like it! McTavish, you're pulling my leg."

Stoner shrugged. He glared at her. "Well," he said, "I guess it could be worse. Bunk mate of mine has to do nature walks up in the Colter Bay area. That's *real* hard time. What's a girl like you doing out here alone?"

"Please," Stoner said, wincing, "don't call me girl."

"I meant no offense," he apologized.

"That's all right. I just prefer it." She took a swallow of coffee and glanced uneasily toward the door. It was beginning to look as if they weren't coming. "I'm here on sort of a business trip. I run a travel agency..."

"Humph," said Smokey.

Stoner rubbed her forehead. "Oh, please, I went through it all with Fish and Wildlife."

"Through what?"

"Tourists, tuskers, ecology, and wapiti."

Smokey laughed. "That must have been Harry. That gentleman was born with a tick up his..." He broke off and cleared his throat. "Excuse me."

"I like that," Stoner said. "May I quote you?"

"All I meant to imply, McTavish," he said gruffly, "is that the travel business is a lousy business to be in."

"It has its compensations. We get discounts."

The waitress brought their orders. "Stell giving you a discount?" Smokey asked.

"I don't know."

"If she does, it won't be because she's looking for business. She doesn't need any more business. But she might do it if she likes you. Stell's a funny gal." He looked at her. "Is that all right? To say 'gal'?"

"Sure. I'm sorry, Smokey. I don't mean to be a pain."

He shrugged it off. "Some things sit right with you, some don't. I wouldn't take kindly to anyone calling me a Mick."

It was getting late. If they were going to come at all, it would have to be soon. The climbers had left in a noisy crowd — off to terrorize the wildlife, no doubt. The waitresses were sponging off the tables in a leisurely fashion. The few diners left were taking their time. Stoner chewed thoughtfully on her pancakes and syrup and watched the door. The prickling at the base of her spine had nearly subsided.

"Who *are* you looking for?" Smokey asked.

"The granddaughter of a friend of my aunt," Stoner said, blushing unreasonably. "We've never met."

"What's the name?"

"Gwen Owens. She's on her honeymoon."

He looked at her quizzically. "Alone?"

"With her husband. Bryan Oxnard. Have you run into them, by any chance?"

"Not likely, if they're honeymooners. Newlyweds tend to sleep late. Where are they from?"

"Boston."

"Boston!" His eyes lit up. "You're from Boston, McTavish? Is it true they serve green beer on St. Patrick's Day?"

"Some places. You've never been to Boston?"

He shook his head sadly, looking somewhat like a wet Basset. "I've never been east of Omaha."

"Where were you born?"

"Nevada."

"I didn't know there were Irish in Nevada."

"There aren't," Smokey said, "since I left."

Stoner laughed. "Nevada. Another stereotype shot to hell. And there are so few good ones left."

"Well," Smokey said, mopping up pancake syrup with a forkful of pork chop, "I'm afraid I'm not one of them."

"Oh, Smokey," Stoner said. "Did I insult you?"

"Nah. It's what I'd expect from a Scot." He winked at her.

"Speaking of stereotypes," Stoner said, "there seem to be an inordinate number of fireplaces out here."

"Most of the folks don't stay through the winter. A fireplace gives off enough heat to cut the chill through October."

"Do you have to stay all year?"

"Sure do," he said.

"What do you do for meals?"

"Take turns and suffer. We have one fellow, cooks so badly we suspect he's a Park Service plant."

Out of the corner of her eye, Stoner noticed a couple entering the dining room. Her stomach gave a lurch. "Smokey, that's them!"

Gwen's picture had excited her. The real thing — the honest-to-God, live, technicolor, 3-D, stereophonic panavision woman stunned her. About average height. (Stoner realized on the spot that she disliked tall women.) On the thin side but firm-bodied. (And skinny women.) Her hair was a light, doe-skin brown. (Her absolutely all-time favorite hair color.) Her features clear but soft. (No sharp noses and high cheekbones for her, not in a million years.) From this distance, she couldn't see her eyes. (Big eyes ate you alive. Stoner didn't know what she had ever seen in them.) And she was wearing a soft plaid western shirt, khaki pants, and desert boots. (As did anyone with good taste.)

"I think you'd better breathe, darlin'," Smokey said.

Humiliated, she let out all her breath at once, and cleared her throat. "Uh, handsome couple," she muttered.

"He's not bad, either," said Smokey.

She watched them cross the room and take a table. Bryan hovered over his wife with a slightly condescending air. No, he wasn't bad-looking, if you liked tall, broad-shouldered men with wavy black hair and piercing eyes.

"He looks as if he stepped out a deodorant commercial," Stoner said.

"Maybe he did."

"No, he's a banker."

Smokey gave a disgusted grunt.

"Don't you like bankers?"

"They're all right," Smokey said, "for a race of people that were found living in caves at the end of World War II."

Stoner laughed. "Have you had unpleasant experiences with bankers?"

"Have you had pleasant ones?"

"Well," Stoner said, "Bryan isn't really a banker. I mean, he works in a bank, but I don't think he's a banker."

"What is he, then?"

Stoner ran her hand through her hair. "I'm not sure."

Gwen was looking at the menu. Bryan seemed to be advising her, making suggestions. For God's sake, this wasn't the Ritz Carlton. He was wearing a bolo tie and suede jacket, new jeans and white shirt. Probably sat around in the evening in a bulky sweater with leather patches on the sleeves. When he had ordered (Mrs. Burton had apparently neglected to mention that Gwen was mute, and therefore incapable of ordering for herself), he reached across the table and stroked Gwen's arm with a forefinger. When he lifted her hand to his lips, Stoner shoved back her chair. "Excuse me," she mumbled, and stood up.

"Something wrong?"

"I hate sex over orange juice."

By the time she had reached their table, Stoner had taken herself in hand. "Hi," she said casually.

Gwen looked up and Stoner felt the floor lurch beneath her feet. My God, mahogany eyes. She rammed her hands into her pockets. "Are you..." Her mouth was dry. "Are you by any chance Gwen Owens?"

Bryan had risen halfway from his chair. "Oxnard," he said brusquely. "Gwen Oxnard."

"Yes, of course, and you must be Byron."

"Bryan. And you?"

"Oh, uh, my name's McTavish. Sto ... Stoner McTavish. You don't know me."

Gwen smiled. "No, I don't think I do." She had a voice like velvet. Stoner wanted to scream.

"My grandmother and your aunt ... I mean, my aunt and your grandmother are friends. She had dinner with us the other night — your grandmother. I said I'd look you up."

"Well, I'm very happy to meet you," Gwen said, and held out her hand. Stoner took it. "Will you join us?"

"No, really, I..." She stared at Gwen.

"Nonsense," said Bryan. Stoner jumped. She had forgotten about him. "At least a cup of coffee."

Stoner dropped unceremoniously into the chair he held for her.

"Excuse me," Gwen said, and gently withdrew her hand.

"Oh, sorry."

Stoner took a deep breath. She had to get on top of this. Mercifully, the waitress arrived. "Coffee, please,"she said. "Black."

"They always serve it black out here unless you ask," Gwen said. "A bit of regional culture we've picked up."

"That's nice."

"So you know my grandmother?"

Stoner nodded. "She's my aunt's client. Hermione Moore."

"The clairvoyant," Gwen said. "Grandmother's spoken of her often. She never mentioned a niece."

"Aunt Hermione doesn't involve me in her business much," Stoner said. "She says I'm too excitable."

"Are you?" Bryan asked.

"Am I what?"

"Excitable."

"I don't ... think so." Only at the moment.

"Gwen's grandmother is excitable," Bryan said. "Highly excitable." Gwen looked down at the table. "Please, Bryan."

"I'm sorry, honey," Bryan said. "Every time I think of what she did to you..."

Gwen glanced at Stoner. "My grandmother didn't want us to marry when we did," she said, almost apologetically. "I'm afraid it's created some ... unpleasant feelings."

"Well," Stoner said, "that happens."

"Are you married?" Bryan asked. For some reason, the question sounded rude, as if he were asking her if she wore underwear.

"No, I'm not."

"It's very painful," he said, "when one's family disapproves of the person one loves."

Tell me about it, Stoner thought. I wrote the book.

"Did she say anything about it to you?" Gwen asked.

Oh, shit. What do I do now?

"Gwen," Bryan said firmly, "I'm sure Stoner ... it is Stoner, isn't it? Odd name. I'm sure she isn't interested in our little problems."

She nearly laughed in his face.

"Besides," he went on silkily, "you have to live your own life now. You were under her domination long enough."

"It didn't feel like domination," Gwen said.

Bryan smiled. "Gentle tyranny is an elusive thing."

Prick. Stoner peered into the depths of her coffee cup. She took a long swallow, knowing it was too hot.

"She chooses to believe I married Gwen for her money," Bryan explained. "It's my theory she expected Gwen to be companionship and security for her old age."

"Can't we drop it?" Gwen asked testily.

He covered Gwen's hand with his own. Consumed it, Stoner thought. "I'm sorry, darling." He turned to Stoner. "You see? Even two thousand miles away she manages to come between us. Is this your first trip here?"

Stoner nodded, and wondered how fast she could drink the coffee without risking permanent tissue damage.

"Staying long?"

"I'm not sure. It depends on how soon I get the information I need."

40

"Information?" Gwen asked.

"I work for a travel agency. I have to see what facilities they have here. Motels, museums, entertainment, that sort of thing."

"Listen." Gwen touched Stoner's hand. She felt it in her toes. "We've been here nearly a week. We could show you some of the high spots."

Stoner could hardly believe her ears. "I don't want to impose."

"It wouldn't be imposing. Would it, Bryan?"

He smiled tightly. "Of course not."

"I don't have any plans for today," Gwen said. "Bryan has a business meeting with some people he met."

Business? On a honeymoon?

Gwen looked at her husband. "You wouldn't miss me for a few hours, would you?"

"I thought you were dying to read that mystery."

"I didn't want you to feel guilty about leaving me." Bryan was silent. "And I haven't talked to another woman in a week."

"What difference does that make?"

Gwen looked puzzled. "I thought you understood these things."

Bryan gave a condescending half-smile. "Of course I do. You know I try to be sensitive to women's issues."

Choke on it, Oxnard. "Well, I really have to go into Jackson," Stoner said. "The only appropriate things I brought are a knapsack and a pair of old hiking boots."

"I'd expect a travel agent to be better prepared," Bryan said sweetly.

"You have us confused with boy scouts." She gave him her most winning smile. "As a matter of fact, one of our clients had to cancel his trip here at the last minute. I took his reservations."

"Look," Gwen said, "why don't we drive into town this morning? You can get your clothes, and I'll talk to the outfitters about our camping trip."

"Camping trip?"

"Next Thursday. A week from tomorrow. It's Bryan's birthday."

Something in Stoner's head gave a little "click." Interesting.

"Sounds like fun," she said. "Where are you going?"

"Secret," Bryan said.

"He won't tell me," Gwen said. "Somewhere he used to go with his father."

"Oh," said Stoner. "Then you're from around here?"

Bryan glanced toward her table. "I think your friend's leaving."

"I'll meet you at the campfire circle," Gwen said. "In an hour?"

Stoner got up. "In an hour. Thanks for the coffee."

She hurried back to her table. "I'm sorry, Smokey. I didn't mean to run out on you."

He eyed her shrewdly. "You look as though it was successful."

"Yes, well..." she said, "...that's done. Now I can enjoy my vacation."

"Good," Smokey said heartily. "Nothing worse than being on vacation and having to run errands."

"Smokey," she said as he pushed back his chair. "Do you try to be sensitive to women's issues?"

"Huh?"

Stoner laughed. "Have a good day. Don't take any wooden movie stars."

He looked down at her. "Know what, McTavish? You're up to something." He swept his check from the table and left.

Transparent, Stoner thought, nervously brushing her hair back from her forehead. Marylou had often accused her of that. "You're not an open book, you're a public library." This situation called for caution, circumspection. Plan every move. Don't be caught off guard. Glancing down, she noticed she was drumming her fingers on the tabletop, and nearly laughed aloud. Who was she kidding? It was a beautiful day, Wyoming waited for her, and she was going to Jackson with Gwen.

CHAPTER 4

Stoner arrived at the campfire circle fifteen minutes early. She sat on one of the rough log benches that ringed the little amphitheatre, propped her feet on the bench below, folded her arms, and glared at the Tetons. They were truly remarkable, great chiselled blocks of blue-gray granite, ice age glaciers still clinging to their peaks. Time, cold, and wind had carved deep canyons and filed the summits to knife-like points. Stoner looked at her map. Grand Teton, directly in front of her, was the tallest, 13,766 feet above sea level. Teton Glacier was visible even at this distance. To the south of Grand, Middle and South Tetons perched like younger twins, and to the north Mt. Owen and Teewinot. The mountains sparkled in the morning air.

She breathed deeply, feeling a little light-headed. At her feet a golden-mantled ground squirrel darted among the logs. A shrill squawk caught her attention, and she turned to see a Canada jay fly off with its bread-crust prize. In the meadow beyond, scarlet and purple flowers competed for attention. Stretching her arms above her head, Stoner wished she could absorb the view into every cell and crevice in her body. "Oh, glorious," she said aloud.

"Isn't it?"

She turned and looked directly into Gwen's brown eyes. Her stomach gave a tiny leap.

"The three central ones are the Cathedrals," Gwen said, and dropped down beside her. "I tried to read out here one afternoon. All I could do was stare."

"Do you suppose, living out here, you'd get used to them?"

"It would be too bad, wouldn't it?"

"Gwen," Stoner said, "I hope this isn't causing any trouble between you and Bryan."

Gwen laughed. Christ, even her *laugh* was velvet. "It's good for him to trip over his politics now and then. It keeps him humble." She smiled to herself. "He means well. Ready to go?"

At the parking lot exit, Stoner hesitated. "This is ridiculous, but I'm completely disoriented."

"I went through the same thing," Gwen said. "Look, the Tetons are always in the west. If they're on your right, you're going toward Jackson. On your left, toward Yellowstone."

"What if they're behind me?" Stoner asked, turning right.

"Then you're not going anywhere."

Stoner laughed.

"Seriously. East of the Big Horns is the Great State of Suspended Animation. Bryan and I bought a car in Detroit and drove out from there. There's a section of Interstate 90 that stretches from Moorcroft — where all the socks go that get lost in the dryer — to Buffalo. There's nothing on it. I mean *nothing*. Desert, sage, dust, and sun. And snakes, lots of snakes. you can drive for almost 100 miles without seeing any sign of human life, and not much of any other kind. I was getting nervous, and Bryan was grim, and there were evangelists on every radio station. Then, all of a sudden, there's this huge green sign, with an arrow pointing down a dirt track. And it says 'Crazy Woman Creek'."

"Good heavens," said Stoner.

"I screamed, and Bryan would have wrecked the car if there had been anything to run into. After that we tried to keep the conversation a little snappier. Really, Stoner, how did they do it?"

"Who? What?"

"The pioneers. I teach history, but the books never tell you *how* they did it. Or why."

"Maybe they were crazy to start with," Stoner said.

"Every now and then, while we were driving that road, I'd remember that it follows one of the old wagon trails. And I'd think, 'We're driving over the bones of thousands of people who didn't make it'."

"Good grief," Stoner said, glancing at her. "Do you torture yourself with thoughts like that often?"

"Not unless I absolutely have to."

The car hummed through the soft morning air, past sage-dotted flatlands, over sparkling creeks banked by ivory river stones. Groves of cottonwoods lined the creekbeds, and tossed their silky filaments on the breeze. Dusty buttes rose from the valley floor. The dessicated Gros Ventre Mountains enclosed the basin to the east. Over it all stretched the blue, blue sky. It made Stoner want to sing.

***

Snow King Mountain closed off the southern end of the valley. The town of Jackson hugged the flatland at its base. Some of the shops were just opening. Stoner ambled beside Gwen along the wooden sidewalk that surrounded the town park. A stage coach stood by the square, horses jangling their bridles. The crowd of big-eyed children stared in awe as the driver took endless pains with the harness. Art galleries proliferated behind weathered wood store fronts. Everyone, it seemed, had paintings for sale. Most of them were of the Tetons.

"We should ship a few dozen of those back home," Stoner said, "and exchange them for Motif #1's."

"Cynic," Gwen said.

They passed the Dry Goods Store. "I think that's what you're looking for. Let's meet in the park in an hour. Or do you want me to help?"

"No," Stoner said quickly. "Trying on clothes is personal."

Her new jeans and plaid shirt were a little stiff and uncomfortable, and Stoner felt conspicuously tourist-like as she settled down on the park bench to wait. She had another pair of jeans, several cotton and flannel shirts, and a Levi jacket in one paper bag. Her eastern clothes were stuffed in the other. Folding her hands behind her neck, she leaned her head against the back of the bench and listened to the country and western music from a bar down the street. The west was truly amazing. Well, there weren't many cowboys around that she could see, and somehow savings banks and laundromats had never figured prominently in her fantasies, but she wasn't disappointed. I'm in Wyoming, she thought. I'm really in Wyoming. Even the license plates excited her.

She heard a low whistle and turned. "You look gorgeous," Gwen said.

Stoner blushed down to the tips of her toes. "Thanks," she murmured, sitting up.

"Ah, the promised appropriately scuffed boots."

"From my old Cambridge Women's Center days."

Gwen laughed. "I remember those days. I'm surprised we never ran into each other. Maybe we did."

Stoner shook her head. "I'd have remembered."

"Actually, I was only there for a CR group and a couple of self-defense workshops. What did you do there?"

"Uh, hung around." She hesitated. Oh, what the hell, better now than later. "And taught a course. Alternative Lifestyles."

Gwen's eyes lit up. "No kidding? I wanted to take that course, but I didn't qualify."

"Yeah." Stoner made a careful study of the sidewalk between her feet. "We were ... " she cleared her throat "...pretty selective in those days."

"Funny I didn't recognize your name, though."

"We didn't publicize the names. FBI scare." Stoner realized she was talking through her teeth. All right, all right, now you know. What do you think?

Gwen put her hand on Stoner's arm. "Relax," she said quietly. She looked around the square. "What do you want to do now? It's too early for lunch, altitude or no altitude."

"Anything you like," Stoner said, not daring to look at her. For some strange reason, she felt like crying.

"Well," Gwen said, still touching her arm, "we could do tacky trinkets and souvenirs. Unaffordable works of art. The latest in exploitation of Native Americans."

Stoner smiled a little. "Now who's a cynic?"

Gwen sighed. "I know. Life was so simple before Social Awareness. My entire childhood is an embarrassment." She gave Stoner a light slap on the leg. "Come on. Let's go over to the Wort Hotel and have a drink."

"I thought you said it was too early for lunch." She ventured a glance at Gwen.

"I wasn't suggesting lunch." She got up, grabbed one of Stoner's bundles, and started off.

"Don't leave me," Stoner shouted. "I'm lost!"

Gwen turned back, laughing. "Well catch up, dummy."

They crossed at the light and started down the side street. "If you ever feel the walls closing in," Gwen said, indicating the Teton Book Store, "go in there. They have a women's section."

"Really?"

"Rudimentary, and in the basement, but it's better than nothing."

"Gwen," Stoner said, "are you really taking me someplace called the Wart Hotel."

"The *Wort* Hotel. You'll like it, I promise."

The bar was quiet, cool, and dark, permeated with the ever-present aroma of varnished wood. Stoner slouched a little in her chair, gripping her beer like an axe-handle. Gwen ran her finger lightly around the rim of her glass.

"Tell me about your Aunt Hermione," she said. "Does she believe in palmistry, or is she...?" She hesitated.

"A charlatan? No, she believes it."

"Do you?"

"I don't know. She's done amazing things. And life's so odd I want to keep an open mind. Every time I don't believe in something, it happens."

"That must simplify things," Gwen said.

"What?"

"If you want something to happen, all you have to do is not believe in it. Want another beer?"

Stoner nodded. I really should say something, she thought. We can't just drop it like that. She took a deep breath. "Listen, Gwen, I really appreciate you understanding about..."

"Don't," Gwen said.

"But..."

"I said *don't*. It isn't a big thing."

"It is to me."

"All right, but don't *appreciate*, for God's sake."

"But, I *do* appre..."

"Well, *don't!*" Gwen shouted. The bartender and three customers looked up.

"Now see what you've done?" Stoner said.

"*I've* done?"

Stoner started to giggle.

"You're crocked," Gwen said.

The waitress brought their beers.

"Look, Stoner, I haven't spent my entire life locked in an apartment in Watertown..."

"Is that where you live? Watertown?"

Gwen sighed. "Do you want to discuss this, or don't you?"

"Whatever you want."

"I'm not the one who brought it up."

"Then let's not discuss it."

"Stoner..."

She raked her hair with her hand. "I'm sorry. It makes me... nervous."

"I'm the one it's supposed to make nervous," Gwen said.

"Does it?"

"What?"

"Make you nervous?"

Gwen covered Stoner's hand with her own and squeezed it. "You are not the first lesbian I've met. You are not the first lesbian I've talked to.

46

You are not the first lesbian I've touched. You may, however, be the first lesbian into whose face I have hurled a glass of beer."

"At these prices?" Stoner said.

Gwen laughed. My God, if you could package that laugh, it'd be a sell-out in every Wimmin's book and record store in the country. We'd dance to it, take baths to it, make love to it... She took a deep breath and tried to think of a way to change the subject.

"How did your parents take it?" Gwen asked.

"Take what?"

"You being a lesbian."

"Not very well." She took a swallow of beer. "I had to run away from home, and then they tried to have me committed to a mental hospital."

"I didn't know that was possible."

"It was back then."

Gwen looked at her. "I think that's terrible."

"Well." She shrugged. "They're not very nice people."

"Do you ever see them now?"

"Once in a while. Sometimes I think I'm still looking for a mother." Did I really say that?

"What about Ms. Moore?"

"Aunt Hermione's ... half friend, half grandmother, I guess. There's a difference, but I'm not sure what it is." She glanced up. "You probably think that's silly, a woman my age."

"Not at all."

"Maybe what I really want is approval."

"Well," Gwen said, "Ms. Moore must approve of you."

"Oh, she does. She relishes it."

"'It' being your sexual preference."

"Yeah." She shifted uncomfortably. "And I'm grateful for that, I really am. But it's not the same."

"Not the same as some nice, solid, middle-aged woman who goes to P.T.A. meetings and shops at the local supermarket."

"I suppose that's what I mean," Stoner said, feeling foolish and a little ashamed.

"Well, I can understand that."

"You can?"

"Of course."

"The crazy thing," Stoner said, "is that I really don't like that normal world very much."

"Still and all, I can see where you might want to belong, once in a while. There are so many of them."

Stoner laughed. "Millions."

"Billions," Gwen said. She traced a series of wavy lines on the tabletop with her finger. "I feel different, too."

"From what?"

"People who don't worry about being loved." She laughed a little uneasily. "That's my particular obsession."

"That's a hard one," Stoner said gently.

"It makes me timid."

"You don't strike me as timid."

"Well, this is a little out of character for me. Maybe it's you."

"Me?" Stoner squeaked.

"You're very .. comfortable."

If there's anything I'm not, Gwen Owens Oxnard, it's comfortable. My hands are shaking, my stomach is experiencing free-fall, and I'm oozing self-disclosure at every pore. I may be a little drunk but I am *not* comfortable. "Thank you."

"Well, you're lucky," Gwen said. "You want a mother, so your judgment is suspect only with women more than twenty years older than you. I can be taken advantage of by women, men, children, peers, elders, youngers, dogs, cats, and tropical fish."

And Bryan Oxnards.

"And guinea pigs," Gwen went on. "I once made an absolute fool of myself over a guinea pig."

"I hope it was a nice guinea pig."

"It was a wonderful guinea pig. I called it Miss MacIntosh, My Darling."

"After your favorite teacher?" Stoner asked hopefully.

"After a book. Every summer of my life, since I was sixteen, I've set out to read *Miss MacIntosh, My Darling.* I've never finished it. Come to think of it, I've never met anyone who did."

"Well, you see, you're normal." "She had red hair."

"Who?"

"Miss MacIntosh, my darling."

"The guinea pig."

"Miss MacIntosh. The guinea pig had grey hair."

"Then why did you name it Miss MacIntosh?"

Gwen looked at her. "I haven't the slightest idea. It was a very large book. And a very small guinea pig."

"Gwen, are you drunk?"

"Never," Gwen said firmly, and finished off her beer.

"I think we'd better have lunch."

"Am I making a fool of myself?"

"Not yet."

"Don't let me make a fool of myself."

I hereby devote my life to not letting you make a fool of yourself. It will require 24-hour surveillance.

"Have you ever made a fool of yourself?" Gwen asked.

"Frequently."

"I made a fool of myself over Bryan."

Stoner looked at her.

"Really, I did. I married a man I'd only known for a few months. That makes me a fool in anybody's eyes, doesn't it?"

There must be some polite, non-committal response to a question like that. "Uh ... " Stoner said ungraciously, "why did you?"

"I was afraid this was the summer I might finish *Miss MacIntosh, My Darling.*"

"Seriously."

"He makes me feel exciting."

"You *are* exciting."

They stared at each other in a moment of mutual recognition of the embarrassing fact that someone had just overstepped the bounds of propriety. Jesus.

"So are you," Gwen said softly.

Stoner cleared her throat and tried to shift into reverse. "Do you want to be loved 'just for yourself', as they say?"

"Well, I'm willing to put some effort into it. A great deal of effort at times, I'm afraid. Do you think they really serve food in this place, or is it only a rumor?"

"I'll find a waitress," Stoner said, and jumped up.

"Waitperson."

Stoner looked down at her, a strange, subterranean twitching in her hands. Nothing wrong with a friendly little touch, if you make it casual. Casual is the operative word. Very casual.

She patted Gwen's shoulder clumsily. "Wait here, person."

***

"Has your aunt read your palm?" Gwen asked.

Stoner took a healthy bite of hamburger. "She says reading for friends and family members is unprofessional. I think she's spent too much time around Dr. Kesselbaum."

"Dr. Kesselbaum?"

"Marylou's mother. She's a psychoanalyst."

"Marylou?"

"Her mother. Marylou runs the agency with me."

"Is she your lover?"

Stoner laughed. "She may be into kinky, but it's in mixed company. Do you think there's salmnella in that cole slaw?"

"I doubt it," Gwen said.

"She hates to travel."

"Hates to travel."

"But she likes slides. She goes to our clients' homes to look at their vacation pictures. Once she threw a party at the agency for everyone to show their slides, but no one came. She forgot to send the invitations."

"I see. Well, you'll have some to show her when you get home."

"Oh, my God," Stoner said, "I forgot my camera."

Gwen choked on a French fry. "If you make me disgrace myself, I'll never forgive you." She took a drink of beer. "I mean it, Stoner. I'll carry resentment to my grave."

"Don't say that," she snapped.

"What?"

"Don't talk about dying."

"I'm sorry."

She took a moment to get control of herself. "It makes me uneasy," she said apologetically. "I don't like to think of people dying."

There was a long, awkward silence.

"Personal reasons?" Gwen asked

Oh, God, I've given her the impression... "Nothing like that." She forced a smile. "Superstitious, I guess. I don't know why. Aunt Hermione says I'm going to live to seventy-two."

"That must be comforting."

"Is that her only work?"

"Well, she cheats at cards. And sells McTavish Blue Runners."

"Sells what?"

"The McTavish Blue Runner Stringless Hybrid Snap Bean. Have you heard of it?"

Gwen stared at her. "I hope not. Is it legal?"

"My grandfather developed it," Stoner explained. "On my father's side. Aunt Hermione's my mother's sister, but when he — un— died, he left it to her. Aunt Hermione. He said she was full of piss and vinegar, while *his* side of the family was full of pee and wind." She felt herself turning scarlet. "It ... it was a little joke of his," she went on helplessly.

"You have green eyes." Gwen said. "But I guess you know that."

"'The McTavish Blue Runner,'" she raced on, trying to out-distance herself, "as our flyer explains, 'is a highly prolific dwarf green bean suitable for container growing."

"My, my," Gwen said.

"It's a mutant. The only one of its kind. Aunt Hermione was invited to join the New England Horticultural Society, and had a mild flirtation with James Whitehead. Esquire. During intermission at the Boston Symphony. They never consummated it. It was Mendelssohn night."

"How appropriate."

"She and Mrs. Whitehead go to all the Hort. meetings together."

"*Hort* meetings?"

"Horticultural Society," Stoner explained.

"Hort," Gwen said thoughtfully. "It sounds like something earthworms do. 'How's your garden?' 'Not so good. The worms didn't hort this year.' Want another beer?"

"I'd better not." A fresh convey of giggles formed near the top of her rib-cage.

"You must lead a fascinating life," Gwen said. "All that horting and all." The giggles took flight. Stoner put her head in her hands and gave in.

"If Jackson has ordinances against public drunkenness," Gwen said, "we're about to be ordinanced."

Stoner glanced up, and gave the approaching bartender a reassuring smile. He retreated to the safety of his cash register. "I don't know what's wrong with me."

Gwen leaned forward. "It's the altitude," she whispered. "It carbonates the blood."

"Why are you whispering?"

"I don't want to offend the natives. One never knows."

"Carbonated blood," Stoner mused. "I wonder what they'd think of *that* on Beacon Hill."

"Is that where you live?"

50

"In one of the old Brownstones. With Aunt Hermione."

"And the McTavish Blue Runners."

"We had a cat once," Stoner said, "but it died."

"I'm sorry."

"We didn't get along."

Gwen shot her an amused look. "I thought you didn't want to talk about dying? Or is it only *me* who's not supposed to talk about it?"

"I'm not myself," Stoner said. "I'm not sure who I am, but it's definitely not me."

"A distant cousin, no doubt."

"Maybe."

"Stoner," Gwen said, suddenly serious, "is my grandmother very angry with me?"

Angry with you? Who could be angry with you? "I don't think so."

"I said things I wish I hadn't." She rubbed the back of her neck. "I'm afraid I took a position, and then wouldn't budge."

"Well," Stoner said, "I imagine it works both ways."

"I'd been grinding along for years, teaching, dating now and then, but nothing special. And then Bryan came along."

On his white charger.

"He proposed to me every night for a month. I kept putting him off. I didn't want him to wake up some morning, and look over at me, and be ... disappointed."

Jesus. Stoner pushed the food around on her plate. "What made you decide to..." Cave in.

"He was offered a job in Chicago. He said it was driving him crazy, being with me..." She gave an embarrassed smile. "... but knowing I wouldn't... have him."

You should have given him a quick tiptoe through the tulips and packed him on the night flight to O'Hare.

"He said if I didn't marry him, he'd take the Chicago job."

Aw, *shit*. *That* one was so old, *rigor mortis* had come and gone. She stared down at the table. Put on the brakes, pal. You have absolutely, positively no reason to take this attitude toward Bryan Oxnard. For all you know, he loves dogs and small children, and helps old ladies cross the street. A veritable prince of a fellow. "Well," she said.

"Maybe I did the wrong thing," Gwen went on. "Maybe I should have waited. I just don't know any more."

Stoner glanced up. "Second thoughts?"

"Not really. We've been together twenty-four hours a day for a week, and he's been ... wonderful. I mean, if we can survive Interstate 90, the rest should be a breeze. Shouldn't it?"

"Sure."

"But I wish he understood Grandmother. I wish I did."

"She's worried about you, that's all. People worry about the people they love." Sometimes with very good reason.

"I guess so," Gwen said. "I just feel rotten about it."

Oh, God, don't look so sad. I can't bear it. "Gwen," she said firmly, "your grandmother's going through a hard time, but it'll be all right."

51

Lighten it up. "She wasn't opening any veins when we had dinner with her the other night. At this very moment, she's probably getting sloshed on sherry with Aunt Hermione, and learning how to cheat at solitaire."

Gwen laughed. "You're probably right. I worry too much."

"So do I. I'm the world's champion worrier." She indicated Gwen's plate. "Finished?"

"Yes. What would you like to do now?"

That, my fawn-haired, brown-eyed, velvet-voice friend, is a dangerous question. "You're the tour guide on this one."

"We could stop by the Elk Refuge on the way back."

"Wapiti," Stoner said. "Look like elk, but they aren't elk. Wapiti."

Gwen pushed her chair back and stood up. "Do you really think they're drinking sherry back in Boston?"

"If I know Aunt Hermione."

"It's only eleven o'clock in the morning there. Grandmother's too old to drink at that hour."

"That," said Stoner, "is an ageist remark. You'd be drummed out of the Cambridge Women's Center in disgrace."

"Serve them right," Gwen said, "for keeping me out of Alternative Lifestyles." She reached for the check.

Stoner grabbed it. "I'll take that."

"Why, Stoner, are you being butch?"

She hooked her thumbs through her belt loops. "Yeah, doll, I'm being butch."

***

The day was fading fast, too fast. The afternoon wind blew hot and dry through the open car windows. The mountains were softer now, dusty air blurring the harsh outlines. They stopped at the Moose Visitors' Center, where Stoner pretended a fascination she didn't feel, over maps, photographs, and bits of history. Trying to drag out the afternoon. Trying to keep it from ending. But it was ending. Next stop, Timberline Lodge.

"You know what?" Gwen asked as the sagebrush hurtled by the window.

"What?"

"It's going to be awfully nice, having you for a friend."

Hey, this friendship has a future. She wrenched the car back into the right lane.

"Bryan's going to like you, too."

Terrific. She stared at the road, an old song running through her head. ("Keep your mind on your driving, keep your hands on the wheel, keep your stupid eyes on the road ahead...")

Gwen touched her shoulder. "Stoner, have I done something wrong?"

She pulled herself out of a morass of emotions. "Not at all," she said, avoiding Gwen's eyes. "I'm sorry. My head isn't too clear. Must be the altitude."

"It's been a nice day."

"Yes, it has." ("We're havin' fun, sittin' in the back seat...")

"Let's do it again."

"Any time." ("Kissin' and huggin' with Fred.")

"I have," Gwen said. "I've done something wrong."

Stoner looked at her. "No, you haven't." Except be the most amazing woman I've ever met in my life. "We're awfully late. Do you think Bryan will be angry?"

"I hope not."

"If he is, tell him it was my fault."

"I will not," Gwen said. "Why should I?"

"Because it was my pleasure."

"Oh, Stoner what a lovely thing to say."

She took the Lodge turnoff too fast, and plowed to a dusty halt in the parking lot.

"Well," Gwen said.

"Well..."

"Maybe we'll see you tonight. We usually have a drink in the Stampede Room before dinner."

"I'll look for you."

Gwen hesitated. "What are you going to do with the rest of the day?"

"I thought I'd hike up to Taggart Lake."

"It's a beautiful walk," Gwen said. "But what isn't, out here?" She rested her hand on Stoner's shoulder. "Don't let the altitude get you."

Stoner touched her hand. "Thanks for everything."

"Next time," Gwen said, "I'll be butch." She slipped from the car and disappeared into the Lodge.

The dust curled and settled.

***

"McTavish and Kesselbaum. Good afternoon."

Stoner clamped the phone between her cheek and shoulder, and untied her shoelaces. "Hi, Marylou."

"Stoner! What's wrong ?"

"Nothing's wrong."

"You sound funny."

"I'm trying to get my boots off. Are you busy?"

Marylou laughed. "Don't I wish. Business has been so slow I'm thinking of giving up caviar."

Pulling off her boots, Stoner grunted.

"Oh, my God," Marylou said. "Is there a moose in your room?"

"No, that was me."

"Well, it didn't take you long to pick up some strange habits."

"I met them," Stoner said.

She could imagine Marylou leaning forward over her desk, ready to gossip. "What are they like?"

"Marylou, she's fabulous. We went in to Jackson and got high at the Wort Hotel..."

"Stoner!" Marylou shrieked. "Come home immediately. Take the next plane. Take a bus."

"What?"

"You don't know what you might pick up in a place like that."

53

Smiling, Stoner stretched out on the bed. "I didn't even pick up a brochure. We had lunch."

"Where, the Herpes Bar and Grill?"

"You're going to love her. She's warm, and gentle, and has a wonderful sense of humor. Her eyes... Marylou, what are you humming?"

"Me? Nothing."

Stoner sat up. "Yes, you are. It's 'Tammy's in love'."

"Oh."

"Marylou, I am *not* in love."

"Of course not."

"I'm not."

"I didn't say a word."

Stoner took a deep breath. "Marylou."

"What?"

"How are things there?"

"Fine," Marylou said. "I'm just holding the fort here in the heat and humidity while you go lusting all over the state of Wyoming."

"*I...am...not...lusting.*"

"Dear Stoner, I — who am an authority on lust — know lust when I hear it."

"She's a married woman, Marylou."

"I didn't say you had good judgement. I only said you were lusting."

"I'm going to hang up," Stoner said.

"Okay."

"Marylou?"

"Yes? Who's this?"

Stoner shoved her hair back from her face. "Stop that."

"Stoner? I thought you'd hung up."

"This is costing us money."

Marylou sighed. "I'd better pencil in a new target date for the food processor."

"Seriously, I need to talk to you."

She could almost see Marylou's shrug. "It's your dime."

"I have a problem about Bryan. I don't like him."

"Good," said Marylou. "Gwen won't have to worry about you taking him away from her."

Stoner steeled herself. When Marylou was in this kind of a mood there was nothing to do but push on. "He could be as innocent as a babe, and I wouldn't believe it. I *want* him to be a villain. I mean, I don't want him to hurt her. She loves him. A lot. And she's happy. I don't want to spoil that. But ... hell, I'm all mixed up."

"You don't have to like him, Stoner."

"But I think I should be more ... objective."

"Well, that would be completely out of character for you, wouldn't it?"

Stoner gripped the phone. "Marylou, *help* me."

"Here's how it looks to me, love." She could hear paper crackling in the background. "The way it looks to me is this..."

"Don't stall. I know you're eating."

"Right. Now, in cases like this, the dispassionate approach may not be the best way to go. After all, emotion is a powerful motivator. And, under the circumstances, loving the alleged victim and hating the alleged suspect is undoubtedly the ideal combination — inspiring thoroughness, dedication, zeal, and perseverence."

"Marylou," Stoner said, "will you put it in English for me?"

"In a word, love go out there and nab the bastard."

***

Stoner checked her trail guide and decided she had plenty of time to get to Taggart Lake and back before sundown. Even though it was a popular trail, she had no desire to be caught by the darkness, street lights being at a premium. From the trail parking lot, she crossed a section of flatland dotted with sage and wild grasses, and then she was in the forest. She forded quick, bright Taggart Creek and began climbing upward. Tall stands of fir gave way to lupine-dotted meadow, and back again to forest. Now she could really feel the altitude. Her legs ached, her knees trembled. She had to stop often to catch her breath. She jumped the creek again, circled a meadow, and found herself on the shore of the lake. Serene and self-contained, it sparkled in the sunlight, reflecting the mountains. Huge boulders edged the shore where she stood. Finding a flat rock, she stretched out on her stomach and gazed into the shallow waters. She dipped a hand in the lake and was shocked by the coldness. Of course, glacial runoff. This was nothing like the warm, muddy ponds back home, that hid creepy things in their murky depths. Stoner rolled over on her back and gave herself up to the stillness and the searing rays of the sun.

***

It was crowded, but there were seats at the bar. Stoner ordered a Manhattan. Six young and very dirty men had apparently returned recently from a climb. They grumbled good-naturedly, and were consuming beer like water. "Christ," she heard one say, "I thought I'd bought it out there. That's it for me."

One less foot trampling wildflowers. Stoner smiled to herself. The jukebox in the corner played country western music. Well, it beat disco. Tony, the bartender, was in his glory, serving drinks with the speed and dexterity that would be the envy of any Space Invaders jockey. Stoner twisted a leg around the barstool and swirled the ice in her glass.

The honeymooners weren't there. Probably in their room, doing whatever honeymooners did at six o'clock in the evening. She preferred not to think too closely about that. Time for some serious figuring. She grabbed Tony as he passed, hoped she hadn't thrown his timing off for the night, and borrowed a pencil. Make a list. Stoner was a great believer in lists. She made several a day, and promptly lost them. But the important thing was to make them. It fixed things in the mind. Or something. Taking a drink, she spread out her napkin.

55

First, how to find out more about Bryan? Well, Marylou was checking his credentials at the bank. That would tell them something, though probably only what he wanted known. Resumes could be faked. Most of them apparently were, judging by what she read in the papers — when she had the stomach to read the papers. He claimed to be from Wyoming, so there should be a birth record. She'd have to go to Cheyenne for that. It could be time consuming. And what would that tell her, except that Bryan Oxnard indeed existed, which fact was already fairly well established. Police record. How in the world would she find out about that? Let Marylou worry about it. What could she do from here? All right, whose idea was the will? That might come out in conversation, if she could steer it right. Does Bryan have any plans involving large sums of money? The camping trip, what did that entail? And what is his *real* attitude toward Gwen? And why the rush to get married? She didn't believe the Chicago story for a minute, but if he really loved her, couldn't bear to wake up in the morning and face the day without her —

The trouble was — Stoner finished her drink and ordered another — Gwen. Gwen believed Bryan loved her. Okay, so that happens. But if Stoner was right, and Bryan was a rat, Gwen was going to end up dead or disillusioned. Stoner had never been dead, but she had been disillusioned, and it wasn't a nice feeling. And what if *she* were wrong? What if Bryan were as innocent as a babe, a victim of malicious gossip or Mrs. Burton's overactive imagination? What if Stoner were suffering from some kind of psychic astigmatism which rendered her blind to Bryan's obvious virtues? Well, no harm done, then. Unless Gwen found out why she was really here — which would send one budding friendship down the toilet. Or if she didn't find out. Then they could be friends, and Stoner would have the dubious pleasure of sitting around watching that fugitive from a deodorant commercial nibbling on Gwen's fingertips.

Stoner McTavish, she asked herself, what the hell have you gotten yourself into?

To keep from thinking about that, she made a list of ways to kill someone in the Grand Teton National Park and have it look like an accident. Food poisoning. No, they ate out. A hunting accident. No hunting in the park. Car goes over a cliff. But as far as she could tell there was only one road in the park that climbed out of the flatlands, the road up Signal Mountain. And that was busy by day and closed at sunset. Car runs into something. But what? There were no obstacles, and the visibility was at least ten miles in any direction. Possible in the dark, but risky. A boating accident on Jackson Lake? Again, too risky, too much chance of being seen by the Forest Service, Park Service, Fish and Wildlife, or passing tourist. Grand Teton National Park, it seemed, was the safest place on earth.

Except for that high country, the back country that everyone was so quick to warn her about. Which brings us back to the camping trip. She had to find out more about that.

And then what? Suppose she came up with motive, means, and opportunity. Call in the authorities? "Well, you see, officer, I have reason to believe this man is going to kill his wife." Uh-huh. If they arrested everyone that someone thought might commit a crime, the whole world would be in jail. Bringing an end to crime — and civilization — as we know it. No, she'd have to convince Gwen. And she wasn't about to bet her life's savings on her chances of succeeding at that.

Well, well, the perfect no-win situation. Unfortunately, she wasn't in the mood to appreciate the geometric purity of it. So now what? She crumpled the paper napkin and stuffed it in her pocket. Press on, McTavish.

"We meet again," said Bryan, swinging up onto the stool next to her.

Stoner turned with what she hoped was a welcoming smile. "Hello, Bryan."

"Drinking alone?" He shook his head. "Not good for you. Not good at all."

"I'm not alone," Stoner said. "I have my friend Harvey with me."

"Where?"

"You're sitting on him."

Bryan laughed and signalled the bartender.

No, I don't mind if you join me, but it was considerate of you to ask.

"Where's Gwen?"

Bryan lit a cigarette. "My wife?"

Yes, that Gwen.

"She'll be along soon. Came home from Jackson and fell asleep. Whatever you two did in town, it must have been exciting."

Stoner smiled to herself.

"What's the secret?"

She started. "Secret?"

"You look like the cat that swallowed the canary."

"Oh," She waved one hand in the air. "A private joke."

"Now, now," Bryan said. "No secrets between drinking buddies."

"It's too complicated," Stoner said.

Tony brought his drink. "Care for another?" Bryan asked.

"I'm fine, thanks."

"So, what did you do?"

"Not much. Shopping. Lunch."

Bryan smiled. "And girl talk."

"Yeah," Stoner said. "Girl talk. How was your business meeting?"

"Fine."

Very informative. Now, how was she going to find out what she needed to know? She glanced up, saw Bryan watching her, and buried her attention in her drink. There was a long silence.

"Stoner?" Bryan said at last.

"Yes?"

"I have a problem."

She stared at him. Now he was studying his drink. Maybe someday she'd write a book on the visual fascination of alcohol.

"How well do you know Mrs. Burton?" he asked.

"I only met her once." Something told her to be careful, very careful.

"But you know she doesn't approve of me."

"I've gotten that impression."

"Do you know why?"

"Well...she seems to feel you and Gwen should have waited a while."

Bryan sighed. "I'm an impatient man," he said sadly. "When I see what I want, I take it. It's a fault I'm trying to change."

Well, you've made a terrific start. She stirred her drink.

"I know we should have waited," Bryan said. "But it's been my lifelong dream to come here..." his gesture took in the room, the Lodge, the Park, and probably the entire state of Wyoming. "... with the woman I love."

"Still and all," Stoner said, "a couple of months..."

"Gwen's a teacher. She goes back to work in September. By Christmas vacation the Park will be closed. That would make it June before..."

Stoner shrugged. "June's a nice month for weddings. Tradition and all."

"I was afraid I'd lose her by June."

Tell me about the Chicago job, Buddy-boy. She waited. He was silent. "Well," she said irrelevantly, "it'll pass."

He leaned back and looked her in the eye. "I think what really turned Mrs. Burton against me was the will."

Stoner looked away to hide her excitement. "The will?"

"Gwen changed her will. She left everything to me. I begged her not to, but she insisted."

"Why?"

"I don't know."

To prove she loved you, turkey. All you had to do was look pitiful, the way you are now, and she'd have done anything you wanted. And you know it.

Bryan flashed her an ingratiating smile. "I don't want her money. I don't need her money. Hell, I don't even know how much money she has."

Oh, cram it, Oxnard. You're her banker. You know how much money she has down to the penny. "How did you two meet?" she asked.

"We were planning to exchange some of her low-interest stocks for high-yield investments. They asked her to come in and talk it over. Women don't usually bother. They figure they don't know anything about finances. But she did." He ordered another drink. "The officer in charge of her account was out sick that day, so they asked me to fill in."

Stoner couldn't resist. "Then you do know how much money she has."

Bryan smiled sheepishly. "To tell you the truth, Stoner, just between you and me, the minute I saw her I was so taken with her I couldn't tell you what we talked about."

Gee-golly-gosh. "I don't see," she said, "what the problem is."

"Mrs. Burton. She won't let go of this stupid idea that I can't be trusted. Even you can see how much it's upset my wife."

Yep. Even dull, slow, retarded me can see that. "What do you want me to do?"

"When you get back to Boston, put in a good word for me with Mrs. Burton?"

In a pig's eye. "I'll do my best," she said.

Bryan lit another cigarette. "She drinks, you know."

"Gwen?"

"Mrs. Burton. Altogether too much for a woman her age."

"Well," Stoner said, "the elderly have run amok these days. AARP, Gray Panthers. One doesn't know what to expect next."

Bryan studied her. "You don't like me, do you Stoner?"

She felt herself blush guiltily. "I hardly know you, Bryan. How can I not like you?"

"You're rather cool to me."

"I'm sorry. I was a slow-to-warm-up child." Sometimes I never warm up. Sometimes I get colder and colder until everything around me turns to ice. All life slows to a halt. Flies stick to the windowsills. Steam freezes in midair. Push the right buttons, and I'll put the world into permanent paralysis. "Do you mind if I ask you a professional question?"

"Fire away," he said heartily.

"I have a little money saved up," she said. "Not a great deal, a few thousand. I'd like to invest it. What would you suggest?"

He thought for a moment. "Recreation."

"What?"

"Recreation. That's where the big money is now."

"I don't understand."

"Look," he said, "in our grandparents' day, what did people do to relax? Took drives in the country. Watched sunsets. Played cards." He flicked an ash on the floor, dismissing sunsets. "Things have changed. Now people want to see and be seen. They want to move, to make noise, to impact with the environment."

Jesus Christ.

"Put your money in recreational land development." He dropped his voice. "I'm working on a deal right now. A bunch of us are going to buy a parcel of land in New Hampshire, White Mountains, right along the Kancamagus Highway. First we put in a ski lodge and trails. Then expand for summer sports — trail bike paths, white water canoeing, golf courses, that sort of thing. Hunting in the fall. Eventually we'll build a domed stadium for sports and rock concerts. That's where the big bucks are, in rock concerts."

"Rock concerts." She had often thought rock concerts would be perfect sites for testing atomic weapons. Along with the World Series and the Super Bowl. A few carefully placed bombs and Poof! — there goes the patriarchy, present and future. "Isn't that government land?" she asked.

Bryan shrugged. "We'll take it to Congress. A few thousand dollars in the right hands and the votes are ours. Interested? Twenty-five thousand buys you in."

Stoner clenched her teeth. "I don't think I can come up with that much."

"Too bad." He looked at her sharply. "You don't approve."

"Not entirely."

Bryan laughed. "And you're a travel agent."

"I don't know what that has to do with it."

"You send a planeload of people to an island in the Caribbean. What do

59

you call that, conservation? You're exploiting the environment just as much as I am."

No, Stoner thought, I am not going to have a crisis of conscience right here. "Well," she began.

"You're as bad as my wife. Wake up, lady. It's a dog-eat-dog world, and it's the smart ones who'll survive. When push comes to shove, your feminine sensibilities aren't worth a plugged nickel."

Stoner downed her drink in one swallow.

"This country's full of idiots who could be making a killing. What do they do? Let their money sit in some conservative little bank and die a slow death. Take my wife..."

Okay.

"Has her money tied up in municipals. She could take it out, put it in our project, and make enough to spend the rest of her days sitting back and counting her profits. But she's afraid to touch it."

"Well, when she's dead, you can do anything you want with it."

He stared at her. "That was a lousy thing to say."

Oh, my God, she'd said it out loud! Panic pounced on her. "Just a joke," she said quickly.

"Not a very funny one."

"I have a strange sense of humor." The sensation was very like the moment your skates slip out from under you on the ice.

"You call *that* a sense of humor."

"A quirk," she said, backpedalling frantically. "Prenatal oxygen deficiency. Some days I don't dare leave the house."

He glared at her.

"I know, it's awful," she said. "Look, I'm sorry."

"Understand one thing," Bryan said. "Nothing would ever compensate me for losing my wife. Nothing."

"I believe you. I said I was sorry. I shouldn't drink."

"No, you shouldn't."

Gwen *would* pick that exact moment to appear. And wearing light blue. Stoner wanted to die.

"Well," Gwen said, "this looks like a fun group."

"I just had one drink too many and disgraced myself," Stoner said.

"Don't worry about it," Bryan said smoothly. "It happens to the best of us."

"Nevertheless, I'd better get dinner."

Bryan squeezed her arm. It looked like a friendly gesture. Except that he did it just hard enough to hurt. "Why not wait a few minutes and eat with us?"

"No. Food, now. My life depends on it."

She ran out of the bar.

In the lobby she stumbled into Smokey. "Ah," he said brightly. "Just the woman I wanted to see. Have dinner with me?"

Stoner hesitated. What she really wanted to do was run to her cabin, pack her things, and hitchhike to the nearest mode of transportation going east. On the other hand, dinner was probably what she needed most.

60

"Might as well," she said.

"Well," said Smokey after they had ordered. "You're in a mood."

Stoner ran her hand through her hair. "I'm sorry. I just had a run-in with Bryan Oxnard."

"And what's on his so-called mind?"

"Money."

The waitress brought two pathetic salads. Stoner picked at hers. "Why do they have such good food here, and such crummy lettuce?"

"Too far from the fresh markets." He looked at her curiously. "What did he say to you?"

"He invited me to invest in a vacation resort in the White Mountains."

"Well," said Smokey.

"How can they do that, Smokey?'

The ranger shook his head. "The right money in the right places .."

"But they're only a group of land developers."

"Go in with the lumber interests, I suppose. They've managed to worm their way into the forests out here."

"Creeps," Stoner muttered.

"Powerful creeps."

Their dinner arrived. Smokey cut into a steak that, with some timely CPR, might recover. "What's your involvement in all this, McTavish?"

"What?" She dropped a french fry.

"Seems to me you have more than a passing interest in those Oxnards."

"Uh, that sort of thing just makes me angry, that's all."

"Sure." He chewed thoughtfully.

"How was your day?" she asked.

"Not talking?" He smiled at her. "Okay, I'll keep my big beak out of your business."

"Oh, Smokey, I didn't mean. "

"It's all right, darlin'. I've always been nosy."

Stoner attacked her roast beef. "Listen," she said, "if you were going camping around here, where would you go?"

"Well..." He scratched his head. "The campgrounds around Amphitheater Lake and Lake Solitude are closed. Overused. Surprise Lake is worth the trip."

"Is it isolated?"

He frowned at her. "Not planning to go alone, are you?"

"You can camp about anywhere in the back country. Most folks go up one of the canyons."

That sounded promising. "How many of those are there?"

"That you could get to by horse..." He counted on his finger. "Eleven."

"Eleven!" Stoner groaned. "I'd never be able to go up them all."

"Thought you weren't going to camp."

"I might just ... look them over."

"That's a fair amount of riding," Smokey said.

"Oh, I don't ride."

His eyebrows shot up. "You planning to join the Marines, McTavish? You'll be walking for the next six years. Stick to the established trails.

Those canyons are killers. One misstep and we'd be waiting for you with the spring run-off."

"Huh?"

Smokey sipped his coffee. "I've known folks to go up those canyons, slip off, get caught in a small avalanche or mudslide, we don't find them until the spring when their bodies wash down."

"I thought everyone was supposed to register."

"That tells us where you were headed. It doesn't tell us where you went down. Even when we know, we can't always get you out."

Stoner shuddered. "Have you ever had to do that, Smokey? Bring someone out?"

He was silent for a while. "Often enough."

"I'm sorry."

"My job," he said brusquely.

"But," she pressed on, "which would you say are the *most* dangerous?"

"They're *all* dangerous," he barked. "Stay away from them, McTavish. I don't want to pack you out in a plastic bag on the back of a mule."

Stoner was touched. "I'll be careful," she said softly.

"Careful isn't good enough. Keep out of them."

"I wish I could promise," Stoner said. "I may not have any choice."

He shot her a puzzled look. "What's that mean?"

"It's my job, Smokey. Like you, sometimes I have to do unpleasant things."

Smokey was silent, the conversation putting him in a dark mood. She wanted to tell him the truth, but to go around implying that people were incipient murderers... She glanced up to see Gwen and Bryan enter the dining room. Gwen made a bee-line for their table.

"Hi," she said. "Feeling better?"

Stoner looked up at her. "Much. Did Bryan tell you what that was about?"

"He's not talking. How about you?"

"Not me. I'm too embarrassed."

Gwen laughed and put her hand on Stoner's shoulder. "You're impossible, you two."

"Yeah," Stoner murmured.

"Talk some sense into her," Smokey said. "Maybe she'll listen to you."

"Are you in trouble again?" Gwen asked her.

Her hand was still on Stoner's shoulder. Stoner felt as if someone was pouring warm water over her.

"She wants to hike up those damn canyons," Smokey groused.

"What do you want to do that for?"

Stoner shrugged. "It was just an idea. I don't know what everyone's getting so excited about. You and Bryan are going, aren't you?"

"But he's an experienced camper. And he knows the territory. He used to hunt here with his father?"

Smokey glared at her. "Poaching?"

"I don't think so," Gwen said, and smiled. "He's from Rock Springs, you know."

"Well," Smokey muttered, "tell him to watch his step."

Bryan sauntered up to them. "Are you coming, Gwen? Or should I order for you?"

"I'm coming."

"Wife says you're going camping," Smokey said. "Where?"

"That's a secret."

"Know what you're doing?"

Bryan grinned. "I know what I'm doing, Flanagan."

Gwen was rubbing her thumb nervously along Stoner's collar bone. If she tilted her head just a little, accidentally, her cheek would touch Gwen's hand. Stop it, she told herself. This is a serious male power struggle.

"Overconfidence," Smokey said. "Quickest way to get yourself killed."

"Honestly," Gwen said lightly. "You two are like little boys playing King of the Mountain." The pressure in her hand betrayed her tension. "Bryan, are we ever going to eat?"

"Sure," Bryan said. "See you later, Stoner."

Last chance. Pretending to look up at Bryan, she let her face rest for an instance on Gwen's hand, and felt herself go red. Gwen squeezed her shoulder. "You look exhausted," Gwen said gently. "Get some rest. Good night, Mr. Flanagan."

Smokey grunted.

"Make her go to bed," Gwen said. "She's had a long day."

"I don't trust that wise-acre," Smokey said when Gwen had left. "I'll give you odds he's never been to Rock Springs."

"What makes you say that?"

"Look how he's dressed. Suede jacket, for the love of God. Movie star cowboy. Makes my hackles rise." He assaulted his steak. "Nice little wife, though."

"Yes," Stoner said.

"Not his type at all."

"No."

"Now, if I were younger..." He shook his head. "Naw, not my type, either. Too soft."

"Who is your type, Smokey?"

To her surprise, he was silent for a long time. At last he looked up. "Stell Perkins," he said quietly.

"Stell..."

"You gonna sit here and jaw all night, McTavish?" His voice was gruff. "Or are you gonna get some sleep?" He stared down at his plate. "Look like somethin' the cat dragged in and wouldn't eat."

Stoner got up. "I'll see you at breakfast, Smokey." She hestiated, feeling she should say more, unable to think of anything to say.

"You want to see 'em make a movie," he said, "Come down by the Snake tomorrow. Park at Blacktail Ponds and walk north along the river."

"I'd like that," Stoner said. Impulsively, she bent down and kissed him on the cheek.

She ran all the way to Little Bear. There was no way she was going to sleep tonight. No way.

CHAPTER 5

But she did sleep. Overslept, in fact. It was well past nine by the time she had dressed and made her bed. Too late for breakfast, no point in hurrying. She rinsed out her new clothes and hung them over the porch railing, hoping the sun would take away some of their stiffness. Timberline Lodge was quiet, the guests gone off on projects of their own. She stood for a moment, smelling the pines and dust and last lingering smoke from the breakfast fires. Another glorious day.

As she came down the path she ran into Stell carrying linens to a recently-vacated cabin. "Morning, stranger.," Stell said. "We missed you."

Stoner held the cabin door for her. "Do you always keep track of your guests?

"Sometimes. I was about to take a coffee break. Join me?"

"If it isn't too much trouble." She followed Stell into the lodge.

"Go out to the campfire circle," Stell ordered. "I'll see what I can scrounge."

She was beginning to be able to look at the mountains almost calmly. In the dust-filled air of midmorning they were flatter, more distant, less intimidating. Stoner watched as a wisp of cloud toyed with Teewinot's thumblike peak.

"Corn muffins," Stell said, handing her a plate. "The best I could do, I'm afraid. Our chief cook runs the kitchen like an Army camp."

The older woman sat down and stretched her legs luxuriantly in the sunlight. "I must be getting on in years," she said. "It feels so good to sit."

"Where's Chipper?" Stoner asked, trying not to wolf her muffin.

"Over at the Ranger camp with Ted. They have a pipe that needs fixing."

"Oh, gosh, I was supposed to meet Smokey for breakfast."

"So he said." Stell stretched her arms over her head. "But I sent him into town for supplies, to take his mind off his movie people."

Stoner took a swallow of coffee, remembering their conversation last night. "Have you known him a long time?"

"Close to forty years," Stell said. "Met him when I came here as a brand new bride." She laughed. "He was some hot-shot in those days."

"Forty years. I didn't think he was that old."

"He won't see sixty again. None of us will."

Stoner calculated quickly. "You're old enough to be my mother," she said incredulously.

"Yep. So don't sass me."

"No, Ma'am," Stoner said. They laughed.

"John thought he was quite the ladies' man in his youth."

She called him "John". For some reason, it gave Stoner a warm feeling. Stell sipped at her coffee and leaned forward, hands around the cup, elbows on her knees. "We've come a long way, John and Ted and me. Through some rough times, and a lot of good ones. But we've held it together. That's what counts in the long run, holding it together."

Stoner looked out at the mountains. "Has he ever married?"

"A Ranger's life isn't much to offer a woman. Hard work, a little fun, and a whole lot of inconvenience. He gave it some thought for a while, but when you come right down to it, John Flanagan's married to those mountains. Some of the younger fellows marry, and get out of the service or take office jobs. But those old gals up there have him right where he lives." She sighed. "Hell, they have us all."

"What will happen to him," Stoner asked, "when he has to retire?"

"He won't," Stell said. "Some January day, when the time comes, he'll just walk up into the high country. With a quart of Irish whiskey."

Stoner put her plate down. "That's sad," she said.

"Sad?" Stell shook her head. "He's found the place he was meant to be. He's done the work he was put here for. And he's been loved." She smiled to herself. "So dearly loved."

Stoner felt tears well up in her eyes. She looked at the ground.

"Listen to us," Stell said, and slapped her knee. "Sitting here jawing like a couple of old ladies with nothing better to do than philosophize. What are your plans for today?"

"I thought I'd get a little work done. Go visit the motels in Jackson, drop by Teton Village."

Stell grimaced. "You won't like it."

"I don't suppose I will. And Smokey invited me to the movie set."

"The old blow-hard," Stell said. "Can't wait to show off." She got up. "Well, let me know if there's anything you need."

"Actually, I did want to take a look at some of the..." she hesitated to say it, "... canyons while I'm here. If you could suggest a good guide book?"

"There's a copy of Ptezoldt at the front desk. And some topograhpic maps. I can't give them to you, but you could borrow them for the day."

"Aren't you going to tell me not to do it?"

Stell looked at her. "You have eyes, don't you? Look at the maps. They'll tell you plainer than I could. Done with that coffee?"

Stoner handed her the plate and mug. "Thanks, Stell."

"Oh, don't keep thanking me. It makes me tired." She cocked her head to one side and looked Stoner over. "Old enough to be your mother. God Almightly." Taking the stairs two at a time, she strode into the lodge.

***

After two hours with Petzoldt, Stoner was incapable of rational thought. The gentleman was thorough. She had to grant him that. A real stickler for detail. Compulsive, even. Perhaps worthy of hospitalization. And his command of the language! Glacial moraine. Talus slope. Alluvial deposit. Poetry, sheer poetry. Unfortunately, she hadn't the slightest idea what they meant. Damn it, Herman or whatever your name is, I don't *care* about alluvial deposits. All I want is one lethal canyon. Is that too much to

66

ask, one perfect spot for murder?

He didn't give a damn. He was probably sitting on his little behind in his little pup tent on top of The Wall, whatever the hell that was, collecting royalties and scratching his memoirs into the granite for some other damnfool idiot to read some day. Five minutes alone with Mr. Petzoldt, that's all she wanted.

She sighed and turned back to her notes. Okay, let's see what we have so far. Between the maps and Heinrich P., she had narrowed it down to five. Avalanche, cutting west from Taggart Lake between Cloudveil Dome and Mt. Wister. Leigh and Moran, passing by Mt. Moran. Hanging Canyon — cute name, has possibilities — up to Lake of the Crags, around the north side of Mt. St. John. And Bannock, a slit between Grand Teton and Teewinot. Five. Given her inexperience, a climbing rate of one mile per hour (according to Fritz Petzoldt, who was probably part mountain goat), and the altitude (don't forget the altitude, God forbid), she should just be able to cover them all by her 57th birthday.

Frustration made her clench her fists. Damn! This trip was giving her emotions a real workout. All right, let's look at this calmly. You have a week. Play it cool. Ask questions. Pay attention. Dig into Bryan's background. Get Max Kesselbaum on the case. He used to be an FBI agent, before he gave it up for the joys of organic gardening. Maybe he still has Bureau contacts. Meanwhile, work on your cover story. If you're supposed to be here on a working vacation, you'd better be able to drop the names of a few of Jackson Hole's better motels.

She threw a few essentials into her knapsack, folded the maps, and locked the cabin door behind her.

***

By midafternoon, she had driven endless miles, passed out business cards like rice at a wedding, and collected several tons of brochures. She was also working on a crashing depression. The motel mentality, it seemed, possessed the remarkable ability to reproduce itself at every level. Sun-baked gift stores south of town sold plastic souvenirs, polished rocks, and cactus lamps to KOA campers. In the expensive resorts to the west, oil paintings, Indian jewelry, and hand-woven rugs were the attraction. But it was all the same.

Bryan had put the right name to it: exploitation. Ski trails crawled down once-wooded slopes like the slimey leavings of garden slugs. Golf course sprinklers tossed gallons of precious water into the thirsty air, growing grass where no grass was meant to be, so that silly men in ridiculous caps and plaid shorts could abuse little white balls with overgrown toothbrushes. And in winter, the voice of the snowmobile would be heard throughout the land. They were impacting with the environment, all right. With a vengeance.

Being a travel agent, Stoner was treated by the motel owners as one of their own. They welcomed her into private offices, plied her with coffee or liquor (which she declined — drinking at 6,000 feet could be hazardous to her health, as last night so poignantly demonstrated), and spun tales of expansion and profit. By the time she had heard the tenth scheme to infiltrate the few private holdings left in the Park, her polite smile had turned to plaster. When the manager of the Slumber Inn, a motel as original as its name, began to confide his plans for turning Timberline Lodge into a condominium city, she knew she was about to crack. Pleading a headache, she scurried out and drove as fast as she could back to the Park.

Puffy afternoon clouds were building up as she passed through the entrance station and headed north on Rockefeller Highway. She had to put as much distance as she could between herself and souvenir shops, disco bars, and the A and W Root Beer Drive-In. And her mind had registered, faintly, a number of taxidermists. She wanted to outrun that knowledge.

The Tetons were ephemeral in the dusty air. She reached the Blacktail Ponds turnoff, parked the car, and stood for a moment looking down on the still waters. Shrubby willows ringed the ponds. Water plants glowed lime-green as a passing cloud turned the sky's reflection to gray. A beaver shoved a bit of sapling silently through the water.

A car pulled up and parked. Illinois plates. Before the motor had stopped, two young boys got out and ran to the edge of the hill where she stood. Instantly they spotted the beaver, snatched up handfuls of stones, and began throwing them wildly toward the swimming animal. Furious, Stoner grabed the nearest upraised arm and twisted it. "What the hell do you think you're doing?" she yelled.

The child shrieked. That, of course, brought the mother. "Take your hands off him," the woman shouted. "Do you want me to call the police?"

"My dear woman," Stoner said evenly. The boy thrashed in her hand like a hooked trout. "This angel of yours was pelting a beaver with stones."

The mother snatched her child and held him close. He gave Stoner an angry, triumphant look and buried his head in his mother's stomach, whimpering. The older child watched with a pleased expression. "Well, he didn't mean any harm. He's *only* a baby."

"So was Genghis Khan, once."

By now the father had appeared on the scene. "Come on, kids. Leave the lady alone." He herded his family back to the car. "Goddamn Park's full of nuts," he said loudly.

As they pulled away, the boy looked back at her, grinned, and stuck out his tongue. Stoner gave him the finger. She turned back to the pond. The beaver was gone. The bit of sapling floated lonely in the water.

"*Damn* it!" She shouted into the hot stillness. Striding to her car, she gathered up the brochures and flung them angrily into the nearest trash barrel.

A footpath meandered north along the ponds, scarcely wide enough for walking. Stoner followed it, kicking up dust as she went. She found Smokey down by the water. Feet planted stubbornly in the ground, hands on his hips, he looked like the Palace Guard. He spotted her and broke into a grin. "Hey, McTavish."

"I'm not very good company." She dropped, cross-legged onto a patch of bare earth and pouted.

"What's up?"

"I've spent half the day playing travel agent, and just got into a brawl with a six-year old. I think I lost."

He looked down at her, an amused smile crossing his face. "I think you might be in the wrong line of work."

Stoner shrugged petulantly. "You and me both." She ground her heel into the dirt. "Don't you ever want to smash the little monsters?"

"Don't have to," he said. "The uniform terrifies them."

"Someday this whole valley will be one big amusement park. I wonder where they'll put the roller coaster."

He squatted beside her. "You're starting to think like Fish and Wildlife," he said. He paused. "Look, Stoner, there are people around here who don't want that to happen. They're getting organized, and they're passing laws to protect what's left. I've seen folks who wouldn't sit down to the same dinner table serving on committees together."

Stoner rubbed her hands over her face. "I'm afraid I'm not a very tolerant person, Smokey."

"Well," he ruffled her hair, "there's a lot to be mad about."

She drew lines in the dust with a bit of twig. "I'm frightened, that's the problem. They're going to destroy it all, and there's nothing I can do."

"It's not a one-woman crusade, you know." He looked up. "Where are you going with that axe?" he shouted at a man on the set.

"Tree's in the way," the man called back.

"That's your problem. Shoot around it." The man shuffled away. Smokey chuckled. "Want to hear something crazy, McTavish? The same government that's trying to sell off parts of the scenery, pays *me* to keep them out. Now, that kind of thinking's going nowhere fast."

Stoner glanced up at him. "I talked to someone who wants to build condominiums on Timberline land."

He guffawed. "There's a fool for you. Ted an Stell sold their development rights to the Park Service ten years ago. When they retire, it becomes government property."

"Then what?"

"Depends. Phil, the oldest boy, is a chemist. He won't want to run it. Ted, Jr. might. The Park Service can find someone else, or close it down to the public. You might come out here some day and find me bunking in your cabin."

"You mean Timberline Lodge might not even be here?" It gave her an odd feeling.

"Darlin', some day even *you* won't be here."

She stared at him. "Well, that's a comforting thought."

Smokey lit a cigarette, breaking the match and slipping it into his pocket. "Just trying to cheer you up."

"Some sense of humor," she said. "You should meet Marylou." She contemplated the shallow twists and turns of the Snake River. "How many of the owners have sold to the government?"

"Most. The rest will fall in line. Winters are long out here. They can be damn lonely if no one's talking to you." He tilted his head toward the mountains. "Look at them. They've seen dinosaurs, oceans, glaciers, Indians, tappers, tuskers, and now tourists. And you know what? They're growing half an inch a year."

Stoner stared at him. "You're kidding."

"I'm serious."

"My God, that's wierd."

"I'll tell you another one," Smokey said. "There are birds out here that walk under water."

"You don't expect me to believe that."

"Keep your eyes open, especially near waterfalls. You'll see."

She laughed. "Sure, Smokey. And I'll do it at midnight, and carry a burlap sack."

He shrugged amiably. "Suit yourself. But the point is, Stoner, there's a lot going on in this world we don't understand. And until we know what Mother Nature's got planned for us, don't go jumping to conclusions."

Stoner pulled her knees up and wrapped her arms around them. "What do you think?"

"I think," he said, "that old gal's having the laugh of her cosmic life. I think some day she's going to turn us all into crabgrass."

Stoner smiled. "You're quite a philosopher."

He grunted.

A slim blonde man, dressed in white shirt and riding pants, approached. His face was red and cracked from too much unaccustomed sun. "Howdy, Art," Smokey said. "This is my pal, Stoner McTavish."

He gave her an odd look, reached down, and shook her hand. "Pleased to meet you, Miss McTavish."

"Ms.," Stoner said.

"Chris wants to know when we'll have a full moon. We need some night shots."

Smokey pulled a dog-eared almanac from his back pocket and consulted it. "Tuesday."

"Will it be light enough?"

"If it doesn't rain."

Art glanced up at the sky. "Rain?"

"Fall's coming on fast," Smokey said. "Could snow by mid-September. I can't make any promises."

"Christ. We're already behind schedule."

"Well, don't blame the weather for your problems. Personally, I'd take the flat of my hand to your actors' backsides. It might solve some of your 'internal difficulties'. I know it'd be good for your ulcer."

"Shit," Art said, and stalked gloomily away.

"What was that all about?" Stoner asked.

"Leading lady hates the leading man, and vice versa. It's cost them two weeks already."

"That seems very childish."

"It should. They're fourteen and sixteen."

Stoner groaned. "One of *those* movies. I'll bet they have a dog." He jerked his thumb toward the set. "That's himself."

A large English sheepdog lay on its stomach, peering through shaggy hair.

"Dumbest dog I ever met," Smokey said. "Won't even eat unless someone shows him how. The other day a ground squirrel walked up to him, looked him straight in the eye, and walked off. Dog didn't as much as blink. That was one disappointed squirrel."

"He looks like a nice dog, though, poor thing."

Smokey took off his glasses and polished them on his shirt. "Yeah. All that beast means to anyone is money, and that's all it'll ever mean. It's not right to do that to a dog."

"Let's kidnap him."

"And have the Park overrun with Pinkerton agents? That pile of hair's insured for more than you and I'll earn in our lives. Better leave him alone. He won't miss what he never had."

Stoner felt the gloom begin to settle in again. "Smokey, why do we keep having these depressing conversations?"

"Celtic blood," Smokey said.

"Gwen's Welsh."

"Mother of God, they're the worst. At least the Irish drink it away. And write poetry."

"What about the Scots?"

"They go out and cut off a few heads." He glanced at her. "Just to pass the time, mind you."

The crew was packing up. "Losing the light," Smokey commented.

"Losing the light?" She squinted against the glare.

"Dust builds up, washes out the contrasts. Four o'clock's about their limit." He reached down and pulled her to her feet. "Give me a lift and I'll show you something."

He took her on a tour of the dude ranches inside the Park. Here, at least, the emphasis was on maintaining a way of life, not changing it. The involvement with horses left her mouth a little dry — the day, it seemed, revolved around the care, feeding, saddling, and riding of them, the night devoted to talking and singing about them (not that they weren't handsome creatures — from a distance) — but the life was relaxed and interesting. Her argument, she thought as Smokey directed her east from Moran Junction toward Jackson Lake Lodge — was not so much with the human race as a whole, as with that part of it which was selfish, irresponsible, loud, uncaring, unthinking, and rude. That part, in short, which Impacted with the Environment.

Jackson Lake Lodge, huge and sprawling, was no bigger than a matchbox beside the vastness of the lake. "Now," Smokey said as the setting sun thrust skyrockets of gold skyward behind Mt. Moran's snub-nosed peak, "tell me the land-grabbers will outlast this."

A soft evening breeze rippled the water, transforming the brief reflected sunset into living embers. The light drained rapidly from the sky. Moran and its companions, Woodring and Bivouac Peak, leapt out in silhouette. Black-centered clouds floated eastward, their edges burning. For an instant the earth was in flames. Then the light was gone, leaving behind a flat gray sky. Inside the lodge the lamps were lit. A planet sparkled over Rockchuck Peak.

Stoner felt her heart lift. "Thank you," she said.

***

She toyed with the cherry in her Manhattan. "Smokey," she ventured, "if you wanted to find out something about someone, how would you go about it? Other than asking."

He glanced at her quizzically. "Who are we talking about?"

"Oh ... just ... in general."

Tony delivered a bowl of peanuts. "My private stock," Smokey said. He cracked one and passed the dish to her. Stoner declined.

"I think..." Smokey adjusted his glasses. "... we're referring to that Oxnard fellow."

"No, I..."

"Come on, McTavish." He ate a peanut. "What are you up to?"

She could feel herself blush. "He .. there's something about him."

"He's a real burr under your saddle."

"Sort of."

Smokey took a handful of peanuts, cracked them, and put the shells in one neat pile and the nuts in another. "Well, I might be able to help you out," he said at last. "But I have to know what's going on."

Stoner hesitated.

"Think he's trying to pull a fast one?"

She nodded.

"And the wife?"

She shook her head.

"Listen, McTavish, I might look like a garrulous old gossip to you..."

"Oh, Smokey, it isn't that." She wanted to tell him. He might be able to help. Every inch of her trusted him. And it wasn't as though she had signed a contract not to bring anyone else into it. But, most of all, she wouldn't be stumbling through this alone.

Stoner glanced over at him. He was still cracking peanuts, but something about him was different. A tiny sagging of the skin on his face, perhaps. He looked — old. Old, and hurt. That did it.

"Gwen's grandmother thinks there's something funny about Bryan," She said. "She asked me to find out what I could." No point in telling *all* the family secrets before she had to.

"What's she going to do with the information?" Smokey asked. "Make trouble?"

That was something Stoner had never considered, that Mrs. Burton would use what she discovered against a perfectly innocent Bryan — everyone had a little something nasty in their past. She felt a twinge of guilt over the fifty dollars she had stolen from her mother. Anything could be blown out of proportion. What if they were all being manipulated by Mrs. Burton for her own purposes?

She shook her head. No, if Gwen's grandmother harbored hidden motives, they wouldn't have slipped past Aunt Hermione — who often said one look at a person's palm told her much more than she ever wanted to know about anybody. There were times, Aunt Hermione said, when she wished everyone could be required to wear gloves. And there were people who should definitely wear them at *all* times.

"No," Stoner said. "She's only worried. If he checks out all right, I'm sure she'll be relieved."

"I wouldn't," Smokey said.

"You wouldn't?"

"If I had a daughter, I'd rather her be married to a crook than a creep. A crook can be sent away. Creeps just stay that way."

Stoner smiled.

"How do you want it to come out, McTavish?"

She hesitated. "I don't want Gwen to be hurt," she said at last. "So I guess I want to clear him. The trouble is, I'd never be sure." She ran her hand through her hair. "No matter what the facts are, instinct tells me..."

"That he's headed our way," Smokey said.

"*Good* evening," Bryan made himself at home. "How did you find Jackson today?"

"It was hard to miss."

"Well, we missed *you* at breakfast." He snapped his fingers to get Tony's attention, and ordered a drink. "My wife was sure you'd been carried off by wild beasts."

"If he calls her "my wife" one more time...

"You certainly bring out her maternal instincts."

Smokey mutilated a peanut.

"I had work to do," Stoner said. "In Jackson."

"Yes. We found out." Bryan checked his appearance in the mirror behind the bar, and adjusted his tie. "Ran into Stell, fortunately."

"It doesn't hurt," Smokey said, "to keep track of someone who's out here alone, especially the first time."

"Suppose not." He scratched at an invisible stain on his jacket.

"Is Gwen joining you?" Stoner asked.

"In a minute. Don't tell me you're a worrier, too."

"Sometimes, yes."

Bryan laughed. "Women." He leaned around Stoner to address Smokey. "Tell me, Flanagan, do you understand them?"

"I try," Smokey grunted.

"Take these two, Bryan went on. "They spent half the day in town yesterday, and I can't get either of them to tell me what they did. What would you do in a case like that?"

Smokey fixed him with a cold stare. "I'd take the hint and mind my own business."

Bryan laughed again. It was a nasty sound. He flung an arm around Stoner's shoulders. She tried to crawl into her glass. "Come on, Stoner.

What went on in Jackson?"

She cringed under the feel of his arm. "Nothing interesting," she said.

He squeezed her shoulder, a little roughly. She couldn't tell if it was intentional. "Humor me."

Smokey put down his drink and stood up. "All right, boyo. Take your paws off her."

Steel flashed for a second in Bryan's eyes. Then he smiled and spread his hands in a gesture of innocence. "I'm only trying to get to know my wife's friend."

"You don't have to use the braille system."

Bryan looked at Stoner. "Did I offend you? I'm terribly sorry."

"Never mind," Stoner muttered.

"Ah," Bryan said, looking past her, "an open table. Gwen will be down in a minute. Have a drink with us?"

"I *am* having a drink," Stoner said stiffly.

Bryan shrugged. "Suit yourself." He slipped from the stool and sauntered to a table in a dark corner of the bar.

"Hope I didn't embarrass you," Smokey said.

"I'm glad you were here." She shuddered. "My God, he gives me the willies. He's obsessed with that Jackson trip."

"He's jealous," Smokey said.

Stoner looked at him. "Jealous! He's married to her, for Heaven's sake. I'm just a friend."

"That kind of guy doesn't want his wife to have friends. Unless he picks them himself." He finished his drink. "How'd she get mixed up with him?"

"I wonder that myself," Stoner said.

Smokey took a small notebook and the stub of a pencil from his breast pocket. "Bryan Oxnard." He wrote it down. "Where'd she say he was from?"

"Rock Springs."

"Anything else?"

"No, I'm sorry."

"Well," he stood up and pocketed the notebook. "I'll see what I can do."

"Smokey," Stoner said. "I don't want to involve you in this."

"Believe me, darlin', it's a pleasure." He gave her a wink. "But you watch your step, McTavish. There's nothing more dangerous than a jealous husband."

"On your own tonight?" Stell asked as Stoner passed the cash register at the entrance to the Highlands Room.

"I need some time alone. I've had enough conversation to last me a lifetime."

"Know what you mean. Some of those motel people can talk you into an early grave. By the way, did Mrs. Oxnard find you?"

"Who? Oh, Gwen. I haven't seen her. Is she looking for me?"

"Earlier today," Stell said.

"Bryan found me. Oxnard. That's a hell of a name. It sounds like a disease."

Stell smiled. "Something dairy cattle might get. We have fresh trout tonight."

"With heads?"

"I'm afraid so."

"Some other time, thanks,"

She looked over her menu and decided on pork chops, gave her order and settled back to think.

Today was Thursday. Six days, if her hunch about the camping trip was right. Gwen was safe for six days. And she had six days to ... what? She had absolutely no idea what to do next. Start hiking? Was that the best way to go about it? It would take her away from the Lodge, use up a great deal of time, and leave her in the end with possibilities but no certainties. There had to be a better way to find out Bryan's plans. But the only person who knew those plans was Bryan himself. If she could only get him to slip up, reveal himself...

Edith Kesselbaum! She made her living uncovering things people didn't want to say, things they didn't even know. After dinner, she'd put in a call to Dr. Kesselbaum.

That settled, Stoner sat back to enjoy her meal and do a little casual people-watching. There, in the far corner, was a good example of that peculiar species, the American Nuclear Family. Mother, father, male child of about nine, female of four. Son pouting and restless. Mother harried, angry, and probably suffering from elevated blood pressure. The interesting interaction was taking place between father and daughter. Daughter fumbles with fork. Father cuts meat into smaller pieces for her. Daughter bats eyes and puckers lips seductively. Father beams. Son, watching, gives daughter a good pinch. Daughter shrieks. Father speaks sharply to son. Daughter runs to crawl into Daddy's lap. Father cuddles and kisses. Mother sighs. Father feeds daughter by hand from his own plate. Son knocks over glass of milk and is sent from the room. Mother contemplates suicide.

It had to be innate. They couldn't learn it that young. By the time the kid was fifteen, her brother would be in jail for selling drugs, the mother would be in bed with chronic low-back pain, and Daddy would be pacing the floor waiting for her to come in from a date and threatening to punch out any boy who looked her way. Stoner glanced up at Stell, who was watching her watching them. She raised her eyebrows questioningly. Stell tilted her head, indicating the father. Right. He was the one who could stop it, and it was clear he was enjoying himself much too much. She wondered if Freud had ever considered that possibility.

At the table nearest her sat two elderly women in tweed suits and sturdy walking shoes. They were consulting a much-used copy of Peterson's *Field Guide to Western Birds*, checking off items on a printed sheet of paper. Life lists. They saw her watching. One of the women leaned toward her.

"Siskins," she trilled.

"Siskins?"

"Pine siskins." The woman pointed to her book. "We saw a whole flock today, near Granite Canyon."

"I'm... very glad," Stoner said.

"And a magpie. Colors like the rainbow."

"Someone told me," Stoner said, "there are birds out here that walk under water."

"Ouzel," said the woman firmly.

"Easel?"

"Do you play bridge, dear?" asked the other.

"Yes, a little."

"If you can find a partner, let's have a game. We're in Coyote."

"I'm sorry," Stoner said. "I can't tonight."

"Well, if you change your mind," said the first, "don't hesitate to drop in. We don't go out at night. Very few owls, you know."

"I hadn't realized."

They returned to their life lists.

Across the room a large round table hosted three boisterous couples. The men were loud and balding, with beer bellies over-hanging stiff new tooled leather belts. The women must have spent the day in the beauty shop. Their hair was elaborately sculpted and stiff, and they fingered it nervously. Costume jewelry hung like Spanish moss from their wrists, necks, and earlobes. They probably bowled together each Wednesday.

One of the women reached for the salt, straining beyond reason an already-strained shirt front. Two pearl snaps exploded, revealing her more-than-adequate breasts. She wasn't wearing a bra. Her husband whipped out his Polaroid Swinger and snapped her picture. An outburst of squeals, whoops, and bawdy comments filled the room.

Stell sneaked a peek at Stoner, trying to keep her face expressionless. A twitch at the corner of her mouth gave her away. Stoner grinned. Stell covered her face with her hands.

"With a crowd like that around," Stoner said as she stopped to sign her tab, "who needs television?"

"I love them," Stell said. "They come here every August. They've driven away at least sixteen of our stuffiest customers over the years. Want to come riding with me tomorrow?"

Stoner paled. "Not me."

"You don't like horses?"

"They don't like me. I've been on three horses in my life. The first threw me, the second ran away with me, and the third lay down and rolled over."

"Well, you're making progress. If you change your mind, let me know. I might be able to help."

Stoner looked at the floor. "Thanks, but I don't think..."

Stell laughed. "You face is a study." ·

The bird ladies approached. Close up, they looked even more alike, though one was a little older. "Remember," the younger said, "any time you want a bridge game, just let me know."

"I'll remember," Stoner said.

"I'm impressed," Stell commented when the sisters had left.

"What?"

"The Thibault sisters don't play bridge with just anyone. Was Petzoldt any help?"

"Some," Stoner said. "I don't think we get along."

"I'd give you the guided tour myself, but I can't get away for that long. Now, if you'd come back after September 15th..."

Stoner looked at her warily. "On horseback?"

"Hell, yes. You wouldn't catch me tramping up those gullies."

"Stell, doesn't anyone in Wyoming walk?"

"Not if they can help it."

A mob of hikers headed their way. "See you later," Stoner said, and moved off.

It was still too early to call Marylou for Dr. Kesselbaum's Wellfleet number. Knowing her, she had probably worked late and was having a genteel Continental supper in some dark little basement restaurant only Marylou would ever be able to find again. So now what? She could go out and look at the moon, but the moon hadn't risen yet. She didn't really want to be alone — after today the re-entry into solitude had to be more gradual. There was a fire in the lobby fireplace. The other guests were either eating or drinking, providing a comfortable background noise. Perfect. Picking up a copy of *Bonney's Guide to Jackson Hole*, she sat down to read.

She was hardly through the Hoback Entrance section when something jiggled her chair. "Hi," Gwen said, balancing herself on the arm and bending down to see the book. "What are you reading?"

Stoner held it up.

"Oh, God, *Bonney's Guide*. We spent the first three days here taking those auto tours. Remember, Bryan?"

He stretched out in the chair opposite, propped his boots (new, Stoner noticed) on the coffee table and folded his hands behind his head. "I'll never forget it."

"I made him stop at every point that's mentioned in the book. We never got the car out of first."

Bryan smiled. "Let that be a lesson to you, Stoner. Never marry a history teacher."

"I don't know," Stoner said. "It sounds like fun."

"Marrying a history teacher?" Gwen asked.

Well, now that you mention it... "The auto tour," she said quickly.

Gwen leaned back, slipping her arm across the back of Stoner's chair. If you touch me, Stoner thought, feeling the blood rise to her face, I won't be responsible for my actions.

"The amazing thing about Jackson Hole..." Gwen said.

If I reach up and scratched my shoulder...

"...is that nothing of major historical significance has ever happened here."

... my hand will be exactly on a level with her belt...

"They've had their share of outlaws and cattle rustlers, of course."

... and I can grab her around the waist and pull her down here on top of me...

"Even a casual murder or two."

... but who'd ever believe that was an accident?

"But nothing out of the ordinary. Nothing that didn't happen a hundred times over in little towns out here."

On the other hand, if she were to slip...

"Don't you find that amazing? I mean, this scenery demands drama on a grand scale."

... her arm would be around me, and I could bury my face...

"Even the movies they make here are minor ones. Who remembers 'Spencer's Mountain'?"

... in her breast. At which point I would dissolve into a tiny little puddle...

"Of course, there was 'Shane'."

... and never be heard from again.

"Shaaane," Bryan called in a little-boy voice. "Come back, Shaaane."

"Did you ever see 'Shane', Stoner?"

"Where?"

"She isn't listening," Bryan said.

"Oh, I'm sorry," Gwen said. "Am I boring you?"

Jesus, Mary, and Joseph, and all the Saints in Heaven. Stoner slid down in her chair.

Bryan was watching her, all too intently. She could see his mind working. "Of course you're not boring me," Stoner stammered. "I was thinking about ... historical significance."

"Odd, isn't it?" Gwen said.

"Yes. Yes, very odd." Dear God, get me out of this. I'll never sin again, I promise. Not by thought, word, or deed. She peeked up at Gwen. Well, maybe just a little. A little thought, that's all, a harmless little thought.

"How long are you staying?" Bryan asked abruptly.

"I ... I'm not sure. Into next week, I imagine."

He lit a cigarette and tossed the match toward the fireplace. It landed on the rug. He glanced down, saw it was out, and ignored it. "Seen Yellowstone yet?"

Stoner shook her head.

"Why don't you and Gwen go tomorrow?"

Her heart jumped.

"What about you, Bryan?" Gwen asked.

"I'm supposed to play golf with George Freylinghausen tomorrow. At the Racquet Club."

"I didn't know that."

"He asked me yesterday, while you were in Jackson."

Gwen was silent.

"It's business, hon," he said. He held out his hands. "It could be important to our future."

"George Who?" Stone asked.

"Freylinghausen." Bryan smiled at her. "Just the kind of name you'd run into at a resort, isn't it?"

Gwen's silence was tight.

"If you'd rather not," Stoner said to her, "it's okay."

"It isn't that," Gwen said, and touched her shoulder. Just thoughts, God. No words, no deeds. Pleasant little thoughts to sleep with — on.

"I don't know, Bryan," Gwen said. "I mean, it's our honeymoon."

Bryan assumed a contrite expression. "It's only one day, hon. I wasn't thinking when I made the date. Anyway, you went off yesterday."

"For a few hours. This is a whole day."

A whole day? A whole day? "If you'd rather not..." she said again, lying through her teeth, "it's okay."

"I *want* to go,"Gwen said. "It's just ... well, people don't do this sort of thing on their honeymoon, do they?"

All the time. All over the country. At this very moment there are thousands of newlyweds on separate vacations.

Bryan smiled. "I thought we weren't going to worry about what other people did."

"You're right," Gwen said. She sounded glad. She actually sounded glad.

"Great." Bryan got to his feet. "I'll make reservations for you on the bus tour. Then we'd better get going." He went over to the desk.

"Get going?" Stoner asked.

"We're driving over to Teton Village. Bryan wants to go dancing."

Stoner groaned. "How can you? *I'm* exhausted."

"I'm a manic-depressive," Gwen said, laughing. "Catch me on the way down."

"You're sure it's all right?"

"Of course I'm sure. I was a little taken aback by the business thing, that's all." She tilted Stoner's head up and looked at her. "I want ... very much ... to go to Yellowstone with you."

"Good," Stoner said, knowing her face was red enough to read a newspaper by in total darkness. A whole day. Alone. With Gwen. On a ... "I can't go," she said.

"What?"

"I can't go."

Gwen looked puzzled. "Why not?"

"I..." she studied her hands. "I get carsick."

"I have dramamine."

"What if it doesn't work?"

"Then you'll throw up," Gwen said.

"It's *embarrassing!*"

"Oh, Stoner. I think you're the most self-conscious person I've ever met." She ruffled Stoner's hair affectionately. "Be in the dining room at 7:00. The bus leaves at 7:30."

Bryan held the door for her, and waggled his fingers in Stoner's direction as they left.

Irresponsible, Stoner chided herself. You're out here on a Very Important Assignment, and you want to waste a whole day running off to

Yellowstone with that woman.

Yeah, she answered. Isn't it fantastic?

***

"Yellowstone!" Marylou shrieked in horror. "Isn't that where stuff comes out of the ground?"

"Yes, Marylou. Did you get my letter?"

"What letter?"

"I mailed it Wednesday."

"This is Thursday," Marylou said. "Do you think the Postal Service has discovered efficiency?" Her voice dropped. "Can we talk freely?"

"Yes."

"Mrs. Burton is having Harry Smythe check into Bryan's background. Incidentally, do you think there's some hanky-panky going on between those two?"

"I don't know, Marylou. I hope so. What about your father?"

"Max is above reproach. Really, Stoner."

Stoner sighed. "Can he get the FBI files?"

"He's off on a New Age retreat at Rodale Farms until the end of the month."

"Can I call him?"

"They're in seclusion. Anyway, I doubt very much that they have telephone service in Emmaus, Pennsylvania. Sorry, love. We really can't reach him."

"What's he doing there?"

"Oriental medicine or something. All I know is, it requires a massive amount of meditation. He's going to have the cleanest aura in Boston."

Damn. She tapped her pencil against the desktop. A dead end. "Look, I need to talk to your mother. Can you give me her number on the Cape?"

"Right-o. Got pencil and paper? Listen carefully. I can only repeat this once. One, eight-hundred..."

"Marylou, for Christ's sake, that's a toll-free number."

"Oops, sorry," Marylou said. "I got Time/Life Books by mistake."

"This phone call is going on your bill."

"Here we go. Ready?"

Stoner copied the number.

"By the way," said Marylou, "she's here now. Shall I put her on?"

"There are times," Stoner said, "when I wish you didn't have a sense of humor."

"I'm sorry," Marylou said seriously. "I'm a little frightened, Stoner. My dearest friend in the entire world is off chasing a blackguard around the frontier."

"Blackguard?" Stoner giggled. "Where did you pick up a word like that?"

"I've taken your advice. I'm trying reading as a hobby."

"*What* are you reading?"

"I'm not sure." She paused. "I love you, Stoner. Come home soon."

"I love you, too, Marylou."

"I'll never send you away again."

Stoner smiled. "Just put your mother on."

She heard rustling in the background, and pictured Edith Kesselbaum — tall, wiry, her black hair permanently askew, probably wearing some brightly colored, amorphous, filmy thing, chiffon or silk, no polyesters. "Polyester," Edith was fond of saying, "is the uniform of the opportunistic."

"Hello, Stoner," said a throaty voice. "How's tricks?"

"Hello, Dr. Kesselbaum."

Edith Kesselbaum sighed. "Ten years, Stoner. For ten years I've been asking you to call me Edith."

"It doesn't feel right."

"We must make a note to discuss your mother fixation."

"You've been saying that for ten years, too."

"We have to *concentrate* on it, Stoner. Concentration is the key to everything."

"Fine. How's Wellfleet?"

"Horrible, as usual. The library is abominable. But you know Max. He insists his organic doo-hickies grow best near the ocean, so what's to be done? What's on your mind, Stoner?"

She hesitated, wondering how to begin. "Has Marylou told you what I'm doing here?"

"We were just discussing it. I must say, Stoner, it's a very Christian thing you're doing."

"Dr. Kesselbaum, I don't know quite how to take that. Do you mean Christian as in Good, or as in meddling?"

"A little joke, dear." Her laugh was wicked, almost debauched. "How can I help?"

"There are things I have to find out, that I can only find out from Bryan. I'm not sure how to go about that."

"You mean you went out there without a plan of attack? Stoner, a plan of attack is of prime importance. *Never* set off without a plan of attack."

"But what should I do now?"

Dr. Kesselbaum thought for a moment. "What's your impression of this man?"

"Arrogant," Stoner said immediately. "Sure of himself. And materialistic. He looks at a sunset and sees parking lots."

"What about the wife?"

"I can't use her."

"Why not?"

"I just ... can't."

"Yes, of course," Edith said. "Marylou did mention something about sexual attraction. You wouldn't want to compromise her."

I give up.

There was a thoughtful silence on the other end of the line. "What I would do," Dr. Kesselbaum said at last, "is flatter his ego. Make him think he's won you over. He may try to impress you. Perhaps he'll tip his hand."

"Dr. Kesselbaum," Stoner said, "I haven't the slightest idea how to do that."

"Oh, my, of course, you wouldn't. You have so little experience with men. Do you recall any advice your mother might have given you?"

Stoner struggled to remember. "Don't talk about yourself, and don't correct their grammar. Don't let them think you know more than they do. Pretend to be helpless. And don't lift anything by yourself."

"That's rather rudimentary, Stoner." She made a choking sound. "Are you sure there's nothing more?"

"Dr. Kesselbaum?"

"Yes?"

"It's okay to laugh."

"I wouldn't dream of..." Edith began, then broke down. "Oh, Stoner, you're the world's last aging innocent."

"I know," Stoner said miserably.

"God help me, I don't even know where to begin. It would take months. Maybe years. You lack the proper instincts."

"I guess I'm on my own, huh?"

"I'm sorry, dear. I'm afraid you are."

"Well, thanks anyway."

"Just be careful, Stoner. And for God's sake..." She choked again. "... don't lift anything yourself."

"Good night, Dr. Kesselbaum." She hung up and sat on the edge of the bed, hands dangling between her knees.

Another day, another fifty cents.

CHAPTER 6

Stoner sat by the window, her coffee untouched, and studied the mountains. Fiercely delicate in the brilliant glare of early morning, the Cathedral spires punctured the August sky. A breeze touched the aspens and set their leaves to spinning as if war had broken out between neighboring flocks of sparrows.

Rather like whatever was happening inside her stomach. Sipping her coffee, Stoner identified the symptoms of impending flight. It was a mistake, this trip. It was one thing to pass a couple of hours in a hotel bar — quite another to be trapped all day in a small, moving object, with only each other for company and no chance of walking home if the going got rough. What if they argued? What if Gwen didn't like her? What if she didn't like Gwen? It was a possibility. She was realistic enough to know that her attraction to Gwen, so far, was largely physical (yes, Marylou ... yes, Edith Kesselbaum, I admit it). After all, the woman had gone and married Bryan Oxnard. Now who, in their right mind, would willingly take on a department store mannequin with a monstrous ego and a name like Oxnard? I mean, how can you have an extended conversation with someone like that? And now Stoner had gone and committed herself to spending eight hours out of her life with an empty-headed ball of fluff.

"Is that all you're having?" Gwen asked, indicating Stoner's coffee cup.

Her stomach tied itself into fifteen square knots and clove hitch. She nodded stupidly.

"If you're going to be sick, you might as well have something to be sick with." Gwen slid into her chair and ordered ham and eggs for herself, and toast and milk for Stoner. She looked out the window. "Another perfect day. Boring, isn't it?" She pushed a pack of dramamine across the table. "What are you brooding about?"

She couldn't remember. "How can you be so cheerful at this hour of the morning?"

"I can't help myself." The waitress brought her coffee. She took a swallow. "I think I'm becoming addicted to this stuff."

Stoner nodded.

"I never thanked you," Gwen said, "for letting me talk about Grandmother the other day. Sometimes I carry things around inside myself so long gangrene sets in. It helped. It really did."

"That's okay," Stoner mumbled.

Gwen cocked her head on one side and looked at her. "I really don't know how you're going to enjoy Yellowstone," she said, "if you insist on prattling on like this."

"I'm sorry. I..."

"I'm only teasing, "Gwen said, and touched her wrist. The touch traveled up her arm, through her body, and out the soles of her feet. When she

83

got up, she knew, there would be charred spots on the floor. "What's wrong, Stoner?"

"I'm afraid we won't like each other," Stoner blurted out in the most unsophisticated moment of her entire life. *Go ahead, laugh at me.*

"I really don't think there's much danger of that," Gwen said softly. "I know I like you." The corner of her mouth twisted in a wry smile. "But then, nobody's giving me medals for good judgment lately."

Stoner's heart melted. "Oh, Gwen, are you very angry about that?"

Gwen looked down. "No, not angry. Hurt, I guess. It's ... hard."

Swell. I can't wait until she finds out what I *think.*

"It's also a beautiful day," Gwen said. "Are we going to waste it being timid?"

"No," Stoner said firmly.

"Tell you what. I'll hold your hand if you'll hold mine."

Stoner choked on her coffee. Breakfast arrived like the U.S. Cavalry to the rescue. She nibbled on a piece of toast. "What did you do yesterday?"

"We took one of those white-water raft trips down the Snake."

"How was it?"

Gwen shuddered. "Now I know why they call it the Mad River Tour. You have to be crazy to do it. There you are, jammed into this huge rubber *thing* with twenty other suicidal idiots. With life jackets. Contrary to popular belief, those are *not* comforting. The water churns up around you — I swear it *grabs* at you. The banks get higher and close in. There's no visible means of escape. All the while you're being tossed around like a cork. And the worst part is, every other person on that death trip was *enjoying* it."

Stoner laughed.

"So there I was, thinking, 'Listen, guys, maybe you believe in an afterlife, but I'm not so sure, and I'd kind of like to hang around a little longer if it's not too much trouble,' when they landed the thing on this tiny little sand bar. Well, you look at the erosion problems they have out here, and you know that bit of land has about five minutes of existence left in it. And they get out all this food I and expect you to eat."

"I think I'd pass it up," Stoner said.

"With your stomach, definitely. Take your dramamine."

Stoner toyed with the bottle. "It'll make me sleepy."

"So what? As you can tell, I have a hard time making conversation, anyway."

"You know what? You're remarkable."

Gwen actually blushed. Blushed! "Are you going to take that stuff, or do I have to suffer the consequences?"

"All right, all right." Stoner sighed. "Here goes nothing."

***

By the fifth bear jam, the effects of the dramamine were beginning to wear off. The tour bus jolted to a halt, snapping her awake. She rubbed her face.

"Good morning," Gwen said.

Stoner looked up. "Oh, my God was I sleeping on your shoulder?"

"You were."

"I'm so sorry."

"Well, you started out aginst the window, but you looked so uncomfortable I moved you over. Besides, your teeth were rattling."

She covered her face with her hands. "I'm humiliated. Let me die."

Gwen patted her shoulder. "Pay attention, Stoner. We're having a Wildlife Event."

In the car ahead, tourists were waving cookies out the window, tempting the bears. An adult and two cubs ambled across the road. Rearing up on their hind legs, they leaned against the car, noses twitching. The bus driver flicked on the PA system and warned against feeding the animals.

"Somehow," Stoner said, "I'm not tempted." The bears reminded her of overstuffed chairs, all fat and fur. "Ungainly, aren't they?"

"I feel sorry for them," Gwen said. "They learn to get food from people. Then one day some tourists in a campground get nervous, and the rangers move them out into the wilderness. It must be frightening for them."

"There's a message in that," Stoner said. Her mind felt like moss. "But it eludes me."

"Beware of rangers bearing tranquillizer guns?"

"Never accept handouts from humans. They'll turn on you in the end."

"Oh, brother," Gwen said.

"I'm sorry."

"Will you stop with the apologizing?" Gwen said. "Good grief."

"Sorry."

Gwen hit her on the knee.

The bus lurched on through the woods. In a shaded, grassy clearing stood an immense, shaggy, horned animal. "What's *that?*" Stoner asked, alarmed.

Gwen leaned across her to look. "Bison."

"It got loose."

"Everything's loose out here," Gwen said. "We're the ones in the cage, hadn't you noticed?"

"Where are the geysers?"

"We're about to West Thumb. We'll stop in about an hour. How do you feel?"

"All right."

A large lake appeared on their right, flanked by mountains. "Yellowstone Lake," Gwen said. "That's the Absaroka Range." The bus pulled off into a parking area dotted with small buildings. Wisps of cloud drifted across the ground. "Odd," Stoner said. "You'd think the mist would have burned off by now."

"That isn't mist. It's steam."

"Steam?" Stoner said apprehensively. "From underground?"

Gwen laughed. "No, from the laundry. Really, Stoner."

"You mean there's hot water under here?"

"That's right."

Stoner ran her hand through her hair. "Do you think we should have come?"

"Wait a while. It gets worse."

"Worse?"

"Beyond belief."

Stoner looked at her. "Have you been up here before?"

"Last week."

"And you came back?"

"Apparently."

"Why?"

"Because I wanted to, silly."

"Why?"

"I'm fond of the company, for the love of Heaven." Gwen said loudly.

"Oh." Stoner jammed her hands in her pockets and slouched down in her seat.

"Don't make me make a scene" Gwen whispered. "It's one thing to be ejected from the Wort Hotel. Being thrown out here is something else again."

"Why are they stopping?"

"Pictures and natural functions. Want to get out?"

Stoner looked down at the ground. The bus had parked beside a steam vent. "Is it safe?"

"Probably."

"I think" Stoner said, "I'll wait until the odds improve."

Gwen looked at her. "Why are you so afraid? You've seen pictures of Yellowstone, haven't you?"

"Pictures can be faked," Stoner grumbled.

"Okay, but we get out at the next stop. Regardless."

They were moving again, around the shore of the lake, cutting north at Fishing Bridge. The stately disarray of lodgepole pine, Engelmann spruce, and alpine fir yielded to the rolling grasslands of Hayden Valley. Wildflowers shone like yellow jewels in the wide meadows, and in the distance bison grazed in placid unconcern. The sun, the gentle hills, the hum of the bus tires made her sleepy again. Then, suddenly, they were stopping.

"Prepare yourself," Gwen said. "This is going to be grim."

They got out and started off on a path labelled, innocently enough, "Mud Volcano Trail." Without warning the breeze shifted, tossing waves of foul-smelling air into their faces. Stoner felt herself go pale.

"Hang on," Gwen said. "It gets worse."

On either side, pools of gray, hot mud boiled sluggishly. The odor of rotten eggs grew thicker. Then they were face-to-face with Black Dragon's Cauldron, a seething, bubbling mass of putrid mud that oozed like vomit from the mouth of a cave-like opening in the rock ledge. Stoner stared at it. "Oh, my God," she said. "That's the most disgusting thing I've ever seen."

They moved to the edge of Sour Lake and looked out over still, greenish water. The edge of the lake was rimmed with a yellowish, crystalline substance. Dead trees, like fingers without flesh, clawed at the sky. Stoner knelt to get a closer look at the water.

"Don't touch it," Gwen said, pulling her back.

"What is it?"

"Sulphuric acid. The dark spots on those trees are burns."

She felt panic growing inside her. "I don't think we should be looking at this."

"I know what you mean."

Someone near them snapped a picture. "Don't do that!" Stoner shouted.

"Stoner, calm down."

"It's all wrong," she said quickly. "Something's going on here, and we're not supposed to see it."

"Stoner?"

"Someone made a mistake. This is supposed to be a secret. We're going to be punished for looking. I mean it, Gwen. Whatever's happening, it's not for human eyes."

"Do you know how many millions of people have looked at this? Half the human race should be in big trouble."

"Well, isn't it?"

Gwen looked hard at her. "You're serious, aren't you?"

"Yes, I'm serious. Some things are private."

"Come on, then. We'll wait in the bus."

"You don't have to leave on my account."

Gwen laughed. "Are you kidding? You want me to stand here and mess up my karma?"

They walked back quickly along the trail. "The rest isn't so bad," Gwen said.

"I hope not." Stoner watched the ground go by under her feet. "I'm sorry," she said at last. "Sometimes I think I catch a glimpse of something..." She trailed off.

"Maybe you do. Anyway, who am I to tempt fate?"

Stoner let that one pass.

"Why did you run away from home?" Gwen asked.

Stoner shrugged. "My mother and I didn't get along."

"How come?"

"She doesn't like what I am. Not that we ever talked about it. Mostly we argued about how I dressed, how I talked, and who my friends were."

"What about your father?"

"He didn't want to get involved."

Gwen sat on a bench in the parking lot, scraped up a handful of pebbles, and tossed them one by one back to the ground. "How old were you?"

"Eighteen. It was time to get out, anyway. I'm just sorry it had to be like that."

"But you still see them."

She could feel the familiar tension in her face and hands.

"I try to avoid it, but if I don't see them, they keep calling on the phone until I do." she sighed. "I guess I shouldn't complain. We have it down to twice a year now."

"I only go to the dentist twice a year," Gwen said. "But that doesn't make it fun."

"I wish I could tell them to get lost. Or not let it upset me."

Gwen leaned back and stretched her legs in front of her. "Families are funny things. They can hurt us in ways no one else can. I try to understand it, but I can't."

"Neither can I."

"What are the dinners like?"

"It starts over the appetizer with how much they miss me, how they don't understand how I can treat them like this, how they're getting old and I'm their only child, and why can't I move back to Rhode Island? My mother does the talking. My father drinks scotch and watches. After a while my mother starts to cry, and orders a whisky sour for her nerves." She paused. "I hate whisky sours."

Gwen traced slow circles with her fingertip on Stoner's back.

"By the time we get to the salad it's Aunt Hermione's fault. She's a crazy woman. She has me under some kind of spell. Then Marylou. *She's* taking advantage of me, and some day I'll be sorry I didn't listen to them, and they hope they'll be around to pick me up when I fall on my face." She laughed humorlessly. "With the main course we have personal appearance — my hair's too short, I dress like a hippie, if I could just try to be a little more feminine... If I'm lucky, we don't get around to marriage before dessert."

"Do you just sit and take it?" Gwen asked.

Stoner glanced at her, and away. "Usually. Once in a while I try to argue, and my father tells me not to upset my mother. That's his only contribution to the conversation."

Gwen rested her hand on the back of Stoner's neck. Shit, I'm going to cry. She blinked rapidly.

"What the hell, they pay for the meal."

"You pay more," Gwen said.

"I guess I should stop seeing them..." How do you explain to another person what you can't explain to yourself? "But I don't seem to be able to."

"Why?"

"I'm not sure."

What the heck? Tell the truth. "When I think about the fight there'd be if I stood up against them..." She spread her hands. "I hate unpleasantness. It hurts. The echoes of things that are said ... I hear them for weeks afterward. I feel chewed up, charred. And dirty. As if there were maggots crawling on me." She smiled apologetically. "I'm not very good at confrontation."

"Neither am I," Gwen said. She laughed. "Maybe we should write a book. *Winning Through Flight.*"

"*Creative Cowardice.*"

"*Zen and the Art of Strategic Withdrawal.* Let's get on it when we get home. It might meet my department's demands for publication."

"Well," Stoner said, "I can handle the autographing parties, but you'll have to do the talk shows."

"I don't know," Gwen said. "I'm shy."

"I hadn't noticed, though I had heard rumors to that effect."

"Rumors?"

"Mrs. Burton mentioned it."

"Poor Grandmother," Gwen said. "She suffered through the agonies of my adolescence. Seclusiveness, fits of unmotivated despondency. At least I didn't write poetry."

"How does one survive adolescence without poetry?"

"I'll let you know," Gwen said, "as soon as I'm sure I did. I may be a late bloomer."

The crowd was filtering back to the bus. Stoner sighed. "On to the next horror. This trip is going to warp me in ways I never dreamed of."

"You'll dream of them," Gwen said as she got up. "Keep your phone by the bed and call me if you have a nightmare."

Stoner followed her up the steps into the bus. Mrs. Burton had left out one tiny essential item in her description of her granddaughter. Gwen was undeniably — and unbelievably — nice. "Sorry," Stoner murmured as she tripped over someone's feet.

Gwen was standing in the aisle waiting for her. "You take the window seat for a while," Stoner said.

"Don't you want to see?"

"I can see enough from here. And, to tell you the truth, I'm tired of being ignored by the wildlife. It makes me feel, as they say, invalidated."

"God," Gwen said, slipping into the seat. "Invalidated by a moose."

It wasn't long before they were stopping again, this time at the Grand Canyon of the Yellowstone. Far below the rim, the tawny, sluggish river flowed between walls of sulphur-yellow volcanic rock. Upstream, the water poured in an ochre ribbon over the falls. A lizard darted out onto a sun-baked rock and tested the air with its tongue. A hawk soared overhead, wings outstretched and still. "Do you think it's looking for us?" Stoner asked.

"Maybe the lizard is lunch," Gwen said. "Want to walk?"

They started along the North Rim Trail. By a trash barrel a ground squirrel rummaged through discarded paper bags and napkins. Gwen stopped, reaching into her shoulder bag, and knelt down. She held out a peanut. The squirrel eyed her cautiously for a second, then darted forward, snatched the nut, and scampered up the nearest tree.

"I thought you didn't approve of feeding the animals," Stoner teased.

Gwen looked up, brushing the hair from her eyes with the back of her hand. "I don't think this little fellow will make the tourists nervous, do you?"

Staring at her, Stoner felt a warm glow in the pit of her stomach. "I wish I had a picture of that," she said.

Gwen reached for her hand and pulled herself up. "Well, you left your camera in Boston, dummy."

"Don't rub it in."

They walked on for a while. "How did you meet Bryan?" Stoner asked.

"The bank was reinvesting some of my money. He asked me to come in and talk it over. That was strange. Usually they just do it and send me a notice."

That ain't the way I heard it.

"I told him to go ahead, I didn't need to discuss it. But he insisted. Funny how things work out, isn't it? Do you believe in luck?"

"More or less," Stoner mumbled. She pretended to admire the scenery.

"You go along from day to day," Gwen said, "everything the same. You think you know how your life is going to be. And when you least expect it, someone comes along and turns it all upside down."

Tell me about it, Stoner thought grumpily.

"Did that ever happen to you?"

As a matter of fact, quite recently. "Once or twice," Stoner said.

Gwen leaned over the railing and looked down into the canyon. "How did it all come out?"

"I'm not sure," Stoner said evasively. "I'm waiting until the final out before I add up the score."

"What troubles me," Gwen said, "is I'm not sure I know the difference between a hit and an error."

Amen.

"Stoner, do you think my grandmother could be right about Bryan?"

She felt herself go pale, and knelt down pretending to tighten her shoelaces. "I don't know, Gwen. I've barely met him. Do you?" Yes, she wanted to scream, yes your grandmother's right. So get out now, while there's still time.

"To be perfectly honest," Gwen said, "sometimes I have a little doubt — not a big one, just … " She shrugged. "Maybe I jumped into something... But there was the Chicago job... "

There was no Chicago job. Stoner looked up. "What are you afraid of?"

Maybe it was the scenery that made Gwen look so small. Maybe it was something else.

"That he'll get tired of me."

She wanted to grab her and hold her. She reached for the railing instead. "It works both ways, you know. You might get tired of him."

"Impossible."

"Nothing is impossible."

Gwen shook her head. "That is."

Stoner felt herself dangerously close to tears again. For God's sake, Gwen, the guy is a creep, probably a murderer, and most definitely a slimey, sleazy...

"What's the matter?" Gwen asked. "You look fierce."

"Don't they ever feed us on this trip?" Stoner said irritably.

"Next stop. Can you hang on?"

"Sure," Stoner said. "Hanging on is what I do best."

***

90

"I've done something terrible," Gwen said. "I know it."

Stoner roused herself out of a blue funk. She was slouched down in her seat, knees digging into the back of the seat ahead, hands rammed in her pockets. "What?"

"I've offended you."

She shook her head. "You put yourself down. I hate it when people I ... care about do that."

"That's what Bryan says, too. I'm sorry."

Glorious. Simply glorious. That's lemonade in July, Indian summer, and snow for Christmas all rolled into one. Remember, McTavish, mainstream is mainstream, and alternative is alternative, and never the twain shall meet.

She wanted to touch her, but was afraid. "It's my fault," she said. "Sometimes I dig myself into a hole and pull it in after me."

"I thought I was the only one who did that."

Stoner forced herself to smile. "The whole country's laced with underground tunnels." She ran her hand through her hair. "You know, Gwen, Bryan's job at the bank may not be the greatest in the world. But the fringe benefits are fantastic."

Gwen looked away shyly. "Thank you."

Make conversation. Make conversation. "Mrs. Burton says you have a brother in Australia."

"Don. He left shortly before our parents were killed. You should meet him. You could exchange run-away stories."

"Why did he run away?"

"Our father ran the house like a Marine drill instructor," Gwen said. "We had a million rules. I mean, it was hard to get through the day without doing something wrong. And if you made a mistake, he'd come out swinging."

"He hit you?"

"Well, not me so much. He didn't have to. I saw what could happen, you know?"

Stoner cringed. Her chest felt tight.

"It was hard on Don. The older he got, the more he resented it. He'd rebel — in little ways at first. But you knew some day the whole thing was going to blow up. Sometimes we'd go out in Dad's car while he was at work. We were always careful. We knew he'd kill us if he found out, but I guess it was kind of a thrill for us to get away with it." She sighed. "Anyway, one day we got into an accident. An old man pulled out in front of us. It didn't do much damage, just a little scrape he probably wouldn't have noticed. But someone saw us, and told him."

"What happened?"

"It was late at night. He dragged us out of bed and started beating Don with his belt. I was petrified. He kept hitting him and hitting him. I tried not to cry. He always hit you more if you cried. But I was so scared I couldn't help it. So he started in on me."

Stoner hunched her shoulders. Her lungs felt as if they were full of lead.

"I thought he was going to kill me," Gwen said. "I really thought I was going to die. And then I did, sort of. I mean, something in me went dead. At least I could stop crying then."

She was silent for a moment. Stoner tried to breathe evenly, softly, as though even the air was fragile.

"Don was gone the next morning," Gwen said at last. "He took his college savings and bought a steamship ticket for Australia. He's lived there ever since."

"He left you here?"

"He tried to get me to go. But I was sure Dad would catch us. I knew I couldn't go through that again. Anyway, they were killed three months later, and I went to live with Grandmother. He's married now. I'd like to see him."

Stoner could feel herself shaking. "I could kill your father."

Gwen laughed. "You're too late."Then she turned serious. "I haven't cried since that night. Sometimes I'm afraid there's still a little part of me that's dead. Sometimes I do things, or say things, and they feel kind of ... far away." She hesitated. "Sometimes ... I feel that way with Bryan."

Oh, God.

Gwen glanced at her. "It's probably because it happened so fast. It's probaby newlyweds' nerves or something. Don't you think?"

"I suppose," Stoner muttered.

"Do you ever feel that way?"

"Sometimes." Not lately. Lately, everything in me is alive. Too alive.

"Do you have a lover?" Gwen asked.

"Not at the moment. Well, not for a couple of years, actually. Marylou thinks I should. I don't know."

"Why not?"

Stoner shrugged. "It's all great at the beginning, but if it goes bad... I take things too hard. I wish I could be easier, you know? Everything's such a big deal for me. Aunt Hermione says it's the Venus in Taurus."

"It's a nice quality. For your lover, I mean. They must feel safe."

"Sometimes too safe," Stoner said bitterly.

Gwen put her arm around her. "I'm sorry."

Don't do that. Unless you want to flood this bus with three years' worth of accumulated tears. A drop of warm dampness slid down her face.

Gwen tightened her grip. "It's all right if you want to..."

"I don't. Can we change the subject?"

"Now?"

"Immediately."

"I don't think I can."

"You would if you cared about me," Stoner said, in the lightest tone she could muster.

Gwen was silent for a moment. "I've only known you for a few days," she said at last, "and I find I care about you very much."

We are rapidly approaching a crisis of international proportions. "Gwen, I..." she began, and went blank.

"Maybe I shouldn't have said that."

"Why not?"

92

"Well, I rushed into marriage. You probably think I'm shallow."

Never. They can rip out my fingernails. They can put a gun to my head. But I'll never think you're shallow.

"I'm really not," Gwen said earnestly. "I don't make friends easily. Not real friends. But sometimes you meet someone, and right away you're ... sympathetic. Do you know what I mean?"

"Absolutely."

"It's been a long time. Maybe that part of me was dead, too."

She looked down, her hair falling forward to hide her face. "I don't ever want to hurt you, Stoner."

"I don't want to hurt you, either." But I'm going to. Unless Bryan turns out to be a sheep in wolf's clothing, I know I'm going to.

The bus pulled into a parking lot and wheezed to a halt. "Lunch," Gwen announced, and got up. "Don't feed the bears."

Stoner stumbled down the aisle after her.

***

At Mammoth Hot Springs, calcium-laden water oozed from the hillside and slowly hardened into travertine. Red, orange, and yellow algae and bacteria painted the mounds of salt-like rock. Chunky gray formations, rough as the legs of elephants, stood like monuments to death.

"Fascinating," Gwen said.

"Explanation, Mr. Spock?"

"None, Captain."

Stoner consulted the self-guiding trail booklet. "This is full of interesting facts. But it doesn't explain anything."

Gwen looked at her quizzically. "Stoner?"

"What?"

"Are you trying to *understand* Yellowstone?"

"I thought I might."

"If you can understand *this*, you can understand anything."

"It's a question of survival," Stoner said. "Mine."

***

By the time they got to the Geyser Basins, she was sinking fast. They made a quick trip through the maze of Paint Pots, and went back to the parking lot. She dropped onto a bench near a clump of stunted firs. "I don't know how much more of this I can take," she said.

"We're in the Valley of Fatigue. Don't worry. They sort of rush through the geysers. There's a separate tour we can take another day, if you ever want to see this place again."

"I want to see it. But right now my senses are battered."

"Hey," Gwen said cheerily, "the best is yet to come."

"What's that?"

"Old Faithful!"

Stoner shook her head. "Gwen, I have been belched at by Black

Dragon's Cauldron. I have been invalidated by bison. I have seen nature at its most obscene, and been terrified out of my wits. Through all of this I have remained relatively good-natured, despite a constant background din of hyperactive children. Do not, I beg of you, ask me to believe in Old Faithful."

"You'll be sorry," Gwen sang, and swung up into the bus.

Groaning, Stoner pulled herself up the steps. "And you didn't tell me we were going to climb Grand Teton four steps at at time."

Gwen sat down and patted her lap. "Put your legs up here. I'll rub them."

"You will *not*," Stoner squawked, turning a lovely shade of shocking pink.

***

The boardwalks around Old Faithful were jammed with tourists. Nothing was heard but the clicking of Instamatics. In the middle of the packed circle of humanity lay a pile of tan clay and pebbles. "I knew it was a trick," Stoner muttered. "They do all that publicity to get us here, and any minute some jerk in a clown outfit is going to jump out of that hole and laugh his head off."

Gwen hit her.

The crowd drew a collective breath.

"Here it comes," Gwen whispered.

The geyser gave a tiny burp, like a bubble of swamp gas.

"That was it?"

"Wait."

A two-foot long plume of steam rose from the vent.

Stoner applauded.

Gwen giggled.

A fat, balding man dressed only in shorts and binoculars gave them a dirty look.

Gwen clapped her hand over her mouth and shook.

Old Faithful erupted. A jet of boiling water shot into the pale blue sky. A puff of breeze sent downwind onlookers diving for cover. The geyser steamed and belched and hissed like a boiler gone berserk, then dwindled to a mass of seething mud. Stoner dropped to her knees and peered beneath the wooden walkway.

"What in the world are you doing?" Gwen asked.

"Looking for a valve."

Gwen's knees gave way under her. She sat on the ground, hugging herself, and laughed. Stoner crawled over beside her, tears streaming down her face. Her jaws ached. Tourists walked past them, staring, like Sunday strollers at the Zoo. "Control ... yourself," Stoner gasped, and started to hiccup. Gwen tried to look solemn, glanced sideways at Stoner, and fell over on top of her.

"We'd ... better ... go," Gwen choked between fits. "Oh, God, I'm dying." She struggled to her feet.

"Can't," Stoner said.

Gwen grasped her wrists and hauled her up. "Know what?" she said. "You're nuts."

* * *

Shadows were long and cold as they passed West Thumb and started south toward Teton. Gwen yawned. Stoner made a pillow of her jacket, folded the arm rest, and pulled Gwen's head down onto her lap. It was an act of consummate courage. "Stretch out," she said in her most casual "I-do-this-every-day-of-the-week-and-twice-on-Sundays" voice.

"I'm sorry," Gwen murmured. "Too much sun. Too many emotions."

Friend, what I could tell you right now about too many emotions.

The bus bounced along the road. Bless you, Oh God of Frostheaves. Stoner slipped her arm around Gwen. To hold her steady, of course. Stop that noise, she ordered her heart, you'll wake her. The other parts of her body could continue to do what they were, at the moment, doing most efficiently. As long as they were quiet about it. Actually, there was very little she could to to stop them, short of a general anaesthetic.

Carefully, she looked down. Gwen's eyelashes lay softly on her cheek, her breathing was deep as a baby's. A lock of hair had fallen over her face. Stoner held her breath and very, very gently stroked it aside with her fingertip. It felt like silk. Oh, Jesus, I knew her hair would feel like silk, I knew it, I knew it.

This was more than mere sexual attraction. This was total, heart, soul, and body love. Huge, enveloping, floating-to-the-ceiling love.

She dared to rest her hand, oh so lightly, on Gwen's head. Gwen stirred in her sleep, and twined her fingers around Stoner's. "Oh, my God, Gwen," she whispered. "I love you."

CHAPTER 7

Thank God for Smokey and their dinner date. Because of it, she had no choice but to delcine Gwen's invitation for drinks with Bryan. She would never have been able to resist on her own, and it would have been a perfectly horrible way to end the day. As it was, she didn't get back to Timberline Lodge until after ten. Stopping in the lobby, she picked up a Special Delivery letter from Marylou.

The three-quarter moon hung frozen in the still night. Smoke from the lodge chimney rose in ghostly column to the treetops, flattened, and settled back to earth, touching the air with a woody odor. Somewhere over in the Gros Ventres, a coyote yipped. Exhausted, Stoner trudged to her cabin. The gravel crackled under her feet. She fumbled with her key and pushed opened the door.

Something made the hair rise on the back of her neck. She stood for a moment in the doorway, listening. Silence. But there was, or had been, someone in her room. Carefully, she reached for the wall switch.

The room was empty. Everything was as she had left it. Or was it? Had she fastened both clasps on her suitcase, or only one? They were both fastened now. The desk drawer was not quite flush with the frame. Had she left it like that? And had there been that space between two of her shirts, as if one had been removed and replaced carelessly? Given the state she had been in since she got here, it was possible.

She checked through her possessions. All was in order. Nothing missing. Perhaps one of the chambermaids had been in. but it wasn't her day for clean sheets. Puzzled, she sat down on her bed, and remembered Marylou's letter.

It must be important. Special Delivery. Marylou didn't believe in the U.S. Mail. Well, she believed in it as an institution. But as an institution capable of transmitting communication from one place to another, forget it. For her to send a Special Delivery was rather like an atheist praying to St. Jude. She tore open the letter.

> Dear Stoner,
>   Come home. All is forgiven.
>   Love, Marylou
>
>   Seriously, pal, a thousand lifetimes have
> passed since you left. Christmas is just around
> the corner. I can't believe you would leave
> me, your dearest and oldest (and rapidly grow-
> ing older)friend, alone and bereft on Christmas.
> Loved talking to you on the phone, but it made
> me LONELY.
>   Have you seen any Indians? Do they have

96

electricity out there? Was that really a car I
rented for you, or a surrey (with fringe on top,
I hope)? Movies? Television? Without television,
how to do you know what's normal?

Business. Mrs. Burton put friend Symthe on
the trail of our golden boy. A quick check of
the bank's personnel file reveals nothing out of
the ordinary. Suspicious, eh? S. also contacted
some of the people who had given B. letters of
reference. They all had high praise for him, only wished he hadn't had to leave so abruptly (!).
The story is, he had to tend to a dying
father. (Up violins)

Now, get a good grip on your bra straps.
Here comes the shocker. Bryan's father apparently died twice. At least he left two different
jobs for the same death. I calls that funny, I
does — though of course you New Testament
types claim your boy can do it.

Upon receiving the news, Mrs. B. wept un-
consolably, conjuring up visions of darling
Gwyneth's death and-or dismemberment. But I
assured her there was nothing to fear with
Stoner McTavish on the case. You would not, I
told her, let Gwen out of your sight for a single
second. And I'm willing to bet those are your
sentiments exactly.

I must go sentence this letter to obscurity by
neglect, compliments of the Postal Service.
Write often. Come home soon. Try to have a
little fun along the way. And Stoner, love,
PLEASE BE CAREFUL!

Love you, Marylou.
P.S. Have discovered an adorable little
restaurant just off the Public Gardens. Perfect for
a seduction, and close enough to your place to
minimize awkward pauses. (There is no turnoff like a ride in a Boston taxi, believe me.)
You must take G. there upon your return.

Well, well. So there was a crack in Bryan's story. Two dying fathers. Not
much to go on, though. It could have been a mistake — another relative,
father recovers and relapses, the possibilities for error are boundless. Still
and all...

She jerked upright. What if Bryan had been in her room? Well, there
was nothing for him to — the cocktail napkin! No, she had burned that. It
had burned, hadn't it? She scurried to the fireplace and poked around.
Yes, there it was, only a charred corner left, and a bit of writing. She

peered at it. "Birth re..." Could be worse. It could have been the list of ways to commit murder in the Grand Teton National Park. What else? Gwen's picture. She dove for her suitcase.

The picture was there, safe and sound. Or was it? Had she left it turned to the side of the suitcase, or facing the center? But even if he *had* seen it, what did that prove? He already knew she was asked to look them up. It would only be natural that she would carry a picture, for ease of identification, wasn't it? Wasn't it? Not entirely.

Stoner, old friend, I do believe you have delusions of grandeur. Would Bryan Oxnard, Grandee of Ego, go to all the trouble of sending his blushing bride off to Yellowstone, simply to search your room? Of course not. Still and all, there was something uncomfortable about all of this.

Well, tomorrow she could ask Stell if anyone had been in Little Bear on official business. Meanwhile, she had promised Smokey she'd call when she got in. He was expecting news from his friend in Cheyenne, who was, she suspected, making a covert after-hours visit to the Record Bureau. Not that she was anticipating much excitement from that quarter. But perhaps they could get Bryan on charges of falsifying his age. She pulled Smokey's number from her pocket, and dialed.

"Employees' Residence."

"Could I speak with John Flanagan, please?"

"Yeah, hang on," the man said, and put her on the Wyoming equivalent of "hold".

The telephone was dropped with a loud clunk. Footsteps clomped across wooden floorboards. A screen door squeaked. *"Flanagan."* Pause. "I dunno. Some gal." Squeak. Bang. Clomp, clomp, clomp. "In a minute." Clunk. Sounds of television in the background, Idaho rancher justifying the mass clubbing of jackrabbits. "Figger they cost me $10,000 in crops last year. Folks back east don't understand what we're up against out here." Oh, I understand what you're up against. You're up against what happens when you poison the coyotes, exterminate the timber wolves, and shoot down every hawk between Chicago and Los Angeles.

Squeak, bang, clomp, clomp, clomp. "McTavish?"

"Hi, Smokey. Do you have anything?"

"Hang on." There seemed to be an inordinate amount of "hanging on" in the Tetons. Due, no doubt, to the mountaineering influence. "Hey, Claude," she heard Smokey say, "run get me a Coke, will you?" Clomp, clomp, clomp, squeak, bang. "Okay, we can talk, but make it fast."

"Smokey, is his name really Claude?"

"Naw, it's what we call the rookies. Here's the poop. My friend says there's no record of a Bryan Oxnard in Rock Springs or the state office in Cheyenne."

"Could he have gotten the wrong year?"

"He checked every year from 1940 to 1960."

"So fast?"

"You ever hear of computers, McTavish?"

"Oh." She spread out her roadmap. "Well, what about the Sweetwater county seat?"

"Rock Springs *is* the County Seat."

Stoner frowned. "But it's so *small*."

She could hear Smokey's chuckle. "The city of Boston has twice the population of the entire state of Wyoming. Think it over."

She thought it over. "That would explain why there's so much scenery, wouldn't it?"

"Any news on your end?"

"Some. I'm not sure what it means. Bryan left two jobs because of deaths in the family."

"It's possible."

"It was his father both times."

"Ah-haaa," Smokey said.

"Yes," Stoner said,

Smokey cleared his throat. "Look, McTavish, I know I said I wouldn't butt in. But it seems to me you're going to a lot of trouble about this buck. And there are times a government uniform can get you in places you wouldn't ordinarily get in, if you grasp my meaning."

"I get your meaning."

"Don't you think it's time to level with me, McTavish?"

Stoner hesitated. Yes, it was time. "Can you meet me at the Lodge for breakfast?"

"Has to be early. I've got to be on the set by 8:30. We might be getting some rough weather over the weekend."

"Rough weather? It's as clear as glass out there."

"Too clear. Say 7:00?"

"Fine. Smokey?"

Squeak, slam, clomp, clomp, clomp. "Here's your soda, Mr. Flanagan."

"Thanks, Claude." Clomp, clomp, clomp. The volume on the television went up. "Jesus," Smokey muttered. "They're taking them young these days. Something on your mind?"

"I just wanted to thank you for your help."

"Save it until I do something helpful." He hung up.

Well-well-well, as Marylou would say. Our first big break. Maybe not so big, but at least she had caught Bryan Oxnard in his first lie. She changed into pajamas and slipped into bed. It had been quite a day. Turning off the light, she folded her hands behind her head and gazed into the moonlight. Oh, what the hell? She pulled the pillow from the spare bed, wrapped her arms around it, and fell asleep pretending it was Gwen.

                                 ***

A heavy mist was falling the next morning, forming silver droplets that slid like tears down the dining room windows. Amorphous gray clouds screened the mountain peaks. The clatter of dishes was muffled. Even the children were subdued. The usual hikers were gearing up to challenge the altitude, but with considerably less than their usual enthusiasm.

"So that's the story," Stoner said. She stabbed a chunk of waffle. "I don't know, Smokey. Out loud, it sounds ridiculous."

Smokey rubbed his chin thoughtfully. "Let's see if I got it straight. You think Oxnard is planning to kill his wife."

"Maybe."

"And use the money he inherits from her...to do what?"

"Invest in land development in New Hampshire. My hunch is, he had his eye on something, but didn't have the cash. So he went through the accounts...working in the bank, it wouldn't be hard...until he found one that suited his needs. The right amount of money...not enough to arouse suspicion...the capital available, a young single woman who would be vulnerable. He arranged to meet Gwen, swept her off her feet, and saw to it...probably by claiming it was the last thing he wanted...that she wrote a new will making him the sole heir. He talked her into coming out here on their honeymoon, knowing it would be easy to stage a fatal accident in the back country." She shoved her hair to the side. "Sounds pretty far-fetched, doesn't it?"

"Yep. When's the camping trip?"

"Thursday."

He calculated. "This is Saturday. That gives us today, Sunday, Monday, Tuesday, and Wednesday."

"Unless he isn't going to do it here." She frowned. "He'll do it here. It's the chance of a lifetime."

Smokey sipped his coffee thoughtfully. "Five days to come up with enough evidence to put him in the slammer."

"Or convince Gwen." She felt sick. "Oh, God."

"What's the matter?"

"Do you know what this will do to her?"

Smokey glanced at her sharply. "Now see here, McTavish. There's a lot more than her feelings at stake if you're right."

"I know. We have to think cooly and clearly."

She looked up to see Gwen and Bryan enter the dining room and take a table in the far corner. A flock of butterflies came to life in her stomach. Very cool.

"Smokey," she said, "things like this don't happen in real life, do they?"

"Things like what?"

"Murder."

He laughed. "Don't ask me. I spend most of my time watching half-made movies."

"I'm serious. It's just ... crazy."

Smokey took off his glasses and polished them. "Well, now, from what I read, one out of every ten people in this country is insane. That gives us about twenty million or so to choose from. Of course, a fair number of them have been elected to public office."

"And most of the rest aren't going around plotting murder. Do you think Bryan's insane?"

"Nope."

"Do you think he's really going to do it?"

He eyed her for a moment. "You know, McTavish, you'd make life a lot simpler for yourself — and for me — if you'd decide once and for all

100

whether or not you think this character's guilty."

Stoner toyed with her waffle. "I don't suppose it makes much difference, does it?"

"Not a bit of it. If he's guilty, we'd better be on top of the situation. If not, nothing lost but time. Now." He pulled out his notebook and stub of pencil. "Let's see how the land lays. One, Bryan Oxnard claims to be from Wyoming, which he isn't. Two, there's something peculiar about his history."

"As far as we know."

He gave an exasperated sigh. "As far as we know. That lawyer fellow following up his leads?"

"I guess so."

"All right." He squinted and chewed on the end of his pencil. "Your breakfast's getting cold."

"I'm not hungry."

"You're never hungry. You'll be starved by noon. And I can't think with you *waiting* like that."

"Sorry." She tried to eat her sausage. "I wish I knew what to do next."

"Got it!" Smokey signalled for another cup of coffee.

"What?"

He leaned forward excitedly. "We're not getting anywhere with the man, so let's go after the crime!"

"Huh?"

"Get a list of all the unsolved cases of marriage-and-murder-for-money, and try to fit our boy with the suspects."

"What if he never did it before?" Stoner asked despondently.

Smokey shrugged. "Do you have a better idea?"

"How about those canyons? If we find out he's taking her up one of them, doesn't that tell us something?"

"Do you know how many people pack up those canyons in a year, McTavish? I don't think they all have killing in mind."

"But if you did," she persisted, "which one would you use?"

"Leigh, Moran, Avalanche, Bannock, or Hanging."

Stoner sighed. "I already *know* that. Which *one*?"

"*Any* one. And don't you go running off to look them over. Two hours from now you won't be able to see your hand in front of your face."

She chewed on a bit of waffle. "How do we get that information you talked about?"

"You leave that to me. Let's just say government employees often make useful friends."

"Smokey, you're not going to do anything illegal, are you?"

He put on an air of innocence. "Me? Never. But the less you know about it, the better."

Stoner tilted her head and looked at him. "You know, Smokey, I'm really grateful..."

"Hush," he cut her off. "I was having a dull summer. Besides," he glanced in Bryan's direction, "I wouldn't mind sticking it to that greaser myself."

Stoner laughed. "*Now* who's calm and collected?"

"I don't have to be. I only do the footwork." He snapped his notebook shut. "I'll make a few phone calls."

"Wait a minute, it's the weekend."

"All the better, less traffic around the files."

"What files?"

"FBI."

"Smokey!"

He grabbed for his check. "I didn't say that." Tossing a handful of change on the table, he hurried from the room.

Stoner sat back to finish her coffee. Across the room she could see Gwen and Bryan, laughing and chatting over their breakfast. Dilemma. Do I go over and talk to them, or do I develop functional blindness and make a bee-line for the door? She really didn't want to talk to Bryan this morning — not that she had ever cared much for the idea, but after yesterday she'd prefer to think of him as an abstraction. The thought of him, a real live human being, able to be with Gwen 24 hours a day, to talk to her, to touch her whenever he wanted — it was too much to bear. On the other hand, she couldn't ignore Gwen. Didn't want to ignore Gwen. Couldn't stand to ignore Gwen.

She finished her coffee and approached their table. "Good morning."

Gwen looked up into her eyes and smiled. "Hi," she said in that velvet voice.

Every ounce of blood in Stoner's body rushed into her earlobes.

"How was the Chuck Wagon?" Gwen asked.

"Amazing. I've never seen so much food. Smokey had to send me home in a wheelbarrow."

"Did you sleep all right?"

Stoner nodded.

"No nightmares?"

"Not a one." Her dreams, in fact, had been about Gwen. They had also been X-rated.

"Having trouble sleeping?" Bryan asked.

Stoner started. Oops, forgot him.

"She was a little unsettled by Yellowstone," Gwen explained.

He raised one eyebrow. "Really? I thought you people were made of stronger stuff."

Stoner went cold.

"Bryan, what do you mean by 'you people'?" Gwen asked sharply.

He dabbed at the corner of his mouth with his napkin, prissily. "Liberated types. You know, open their own doors, carry their own groceries, fix their own cars..."

"'You people' is a pejorative term," Gwen went on icily.

Bryan smiled in a disarming way. "No offense intended."

"And just for the record," Gwen persevered, "your wife considers herself one of those 'liberated types'."

"Hon." He spread his hands helplessly. "I really didn't mean anything by it. You know I didn't marry you to be my Barbie Doll." He glanced at Stoner and winked. "She's having a bad day. Think it's the full moon?"

"I am not having a bad day," Gwen said through clenched teeth. "At least I wasn't until now."

"The moon isn't full," Stoner said, and prayed Gwen would never look at *her* the way she was looking at Bryan.

"I surrender," Bryan said. "Two against one..." He pretended to mop his forehead. "Oh, boy. You girls really stick toge..."

"Women!" Gwen snapped. She threw down her napkin and left the room.

Stoner wished the floor would swallow her.

Bryan looked at her sheepishly. "Put my foot in it, didn't I?"

"I guess so."

He shrugged. "Well, I know how to bring her around."

"Really?" Stoner asked, knowing exactly what he had in mind.

"We've been running around too much. Time for a nice quiet afternoon..." He gave her a superior smile. "... in bed."

"I wouldn't know," Stoner said, ramming her hands into her pockets. "'We people' don't solve our problems that way."

As she turned on her heel, she could hear his mocking laughter.

Gwen caught up with her at the lobby desk. "Stoner, I'm so sorry," she said, putting her hand on Stoner's arm. "I hope I didn't embarrass you."

"You didn't embarrass me."

"I don't know what got into us. We've never squabbled before."

"Well, that's probably a miracle," Stoner said. "What are you going to do?"

"Raise his consciousness."

Stoner looked at her. It was going to be an interesting day for the Oxnards. Come on, Gwen, she wanted to say, walk with me in the rain. Let him raise his own ... consciousness. "Be careful, will you?" she said, surprising herself.

"What do you mean?"

"I'm not sure."

Gwen sighed. "Here he comes. I'd better disappear. Step one is to make *him* have to find *me*. See you later." She started to leave, then turned back. "By the way, Stoner, I didn't sleep at all last night."

"Wait. What do you..." But she was gone.

Bryan signed his tab and sauntered over to her. "Where'd she go?"

"What? Uh, I don't know."

He rubbed his hands together, grinning. "Hide and seek on a rainy day. I love it." The bastard was positively euphoric. "See you around, buddy." Whistling, he climbed the stairs toward the guest rooms.

Stoner clenched her fists and glared after him.

"Don't do it!" a woman's voice called.

She whirled around to see Stell grinning at her from behind the cash register.

"Don't do what?"

"Kill him. Do you know what a mess it would make on that rug?"

Stoner went over to her. "Sorry, Stell. He just makes me so ... angry."

Stell flipped her hand in a gesture of dismissal. "Aw, he's a horse's behind. Where've you been keeping yourself?"

"Yellowstone."

"The Thibault sisters are getting up a bridge game this afternoon. Want to join us?"

Stoner hesitated. "Well, I thought I might do a little hiking..."

"In this?"

She glanced out the dining room window. Even the base of the mountains was hidden now. The canyons must be completely socked in. No point in trying to see anything today. She'd learn more from the trail guide and topographic maps. "Sure," she said, "I'd love to play bridge."

"Come over to Coyote around two. We'll be partners. The sisters always stick together." She dropped her voice. "Personally, I think they cheat."

"They do?"

"A little system of signals, but harmless. They don't play for money."

"I guess I shouldn't be shocked," Stoner said. "My aunt cheats at gin."

"Maybe it comes with age."

"No, she always did. Listen, do you sell trail maps here?"

Stell shook her head. "Try the mountaineering school at Jenny Lake. It's an easy walk from here." She pulled out a telegram from beneath the counter. "This just came for you."

"For me? I didn't enter the Publishers' Clearing House sweepstakes."

Stell held it out. "Well, aren't you going to take it?"

"Nobody sends good news by telegraph."

"I can open it for you."

"I'll do it." She took the envelope.

"Shucks," Stell said.

Furtively, Stoner peeked at the message. "Trail dried up June 1975. Curiouser and curiouser. Love, Marylou."

Stoner rubbed her face.

"Bad news?"

"Not particularly. Business. Sort of."

"Speaking of business, one of the girls thinks she wants to go into the travel field. What would you advise?"

Stoner looked down at the telegram, toward the stairs to the second floor, through the mist to the nearly-invisible mountains. "Tell her," she said, "there's only one qualification. You have to be certifiably insane."

Letting the screen door slam behind her, she made a dash for her cabin.

**

Jenny Lake is known as the jewel of the Tetons, but under the rain the jewel is more pearl than sapphire. A shell-like depression at the base of Teewinot and Mt. St. John, its icy waters are freshened by glacial runoff and melting snow from Cascade Creek. Rich, dark earth, left behind by the glacier that gouged the lake and Cascade Canyon to the west, nurtures a dense forest of pine and fir.

Stoner touched a boulder that lay at the side of the trail. Its jagged surface tore at her hand. Immediately beyond the forest towered the mountain walls. Without the distraction of sun and sky, the granite stood out stark and rough, with knife-like edges and points. She walked to the north edge of the lake and looked back at the Cathedrals. They, too, had changed. In the sullen morning air they were ragged, hard, menacing. Single firs stood like guards against implacable rock. Torn and shredded clouds fingered their way between razor-sharp peaks. Tree trunks glistened in the dark overhang of woods. Jenny Lake was hard, and gray as pewter.

Stoner felt herself draw back as if threatened. This was not nice, not nice at all. She was glad she hadn't gone up into those mountains today. They looked as though they would eat you alive. Hurrying to Jenny Lake junction, she picked up her maps and nearly ran back to Timberline Lodge.

She built a roaring fire in the fireplace and changed out of her dripping clothes. Stretching out on the rug in front of the fire, she spread the maps and settled down to the task of finding a perfect spot for murder.

It had to be steep, but not impassable by pack train. All of the trails followed streams, but how high above the water were the paths? If they were level with the streambeds, there would be little or no drop-off. She needed a drop steep enough to kill a person, or guarantee the body would never be recovered.

Avalanche Canyon, despite its ominous name, followed Taggart Creek in a fairly gentle rise westward toward Mt. Wister. The creek branched, one arm stretching west to Shoshoko Falls and Lake Taminah. This, according to Petzoldt, was not a difficult climb. But who knew what he considered "difficult", crusty old masochist that he was? Still and all, she was inclined to reject it.

The South Fork, however, ascended sharply. There was no vegetation marked on the map. It must be above the timberline, or scraped bare for other reasons. She recalled the cruel rock she had touched. It would rip the flesh from your body as surely as a school of starving pirhanas. With a felt-tip pen, she marked the South Fork of Taggart Creek as a possibility.

Bannock was next. For more than a mile the trail overlapped Cascade Canyon Trail, according to the guidebooks a popular and much used attraction. Then it crossed Cascade Creek and cut southwest along a feeder stream, between Owen and Teewinot. The contour lines were tightly bunched here, the timber sparse. Another possibility.

Hanging Canyon and Moran, like Avalanche, seemed less likely — at least on paper — but Leigh had some rugged spots. It all depended on the placement of the trail. Stoner rolled over on her back and gazed up at the rough boards of the ceiling. Even if she eliminated Hanging, Moran, and Avalanche, there was too much territory to cover. And even if she could pick her favorite spot, who was to say it would be Bryan's? Smokey had better come up with something to stop this camping trip before it got started, because if he didn't...

Stoner shot upright. Suppose they couldn't find evidence to implicate Bryan. She would have to convince Gwen without it. And if she couldn't do that ... she would have to follow them and stop him in the act.

Her face went cold. Stop him? He was much bigger, much stronger... Don't think about that. Think about getting him before ... Maybe he'd give himself away.

She got to her feet and went to wash her face in cold water. Her brain felt like rubble. She glanced at her watch. It was nearly one, time for lunch. Stuffing a trail bar in her jacket pocket, she left the cabin.

The rain had given way temporarily to mist as she wandered along Cottonwood Creek and sat down against an aspen. Across the Park Road,

Timbered Island rose in a dark, solid mass out of the flatlands, its tight forest out of place against the sagebrush. Smokey said an elk herd had taken up residence on the glacial moraine. She pictured them in her mind, shy buff ghosts moving silently through the dripping trees.

She tore the wrapper from her trail bar and bit into it. It tasted exactly like cardboard, or other health food, probably a highly efficient source of protein, etc. etc. Well, it would have to do.

Cottonwood Creek gurgled and sang over oyster-shell rocks. Stoner rested her head on her knees, closed her eyes, and listened to the water sounds around her. From time to time a car splashed by on the Park road, but for the most part the valley seemed deserted. Raindrops fell from leaf to leaf with a leathery slap. The mist was soft on her hands and face. At a rustling noise, she looked up. Across the creek, a marten stared at her from the safety of a tree. Its alert black rodent eyes watched her curiously. "Sorry, fellow," she said aloud. "I don't have anything for you."

The marten continued to stare. Looking at the wise little animal face, Stoner found herself thinking of Scruffy, her soft mongrel dog. She could still remember his silky coat and deep brown eyes, the way he cocked his head when she talked to him. When he was pleased, which was much of the time, he would curl his body into a furry horseshoe, look at her over one shoulder, and grin. On their walks together he liked to hide in the underbrush and leap out at her unexpectedly as she passed. He slept at the foot of her bed. She talked to him for hours. He licked her face when she cried. When she refused to return home after running away, her parents had him destroyed.

Stoner picked up a rock and hurled it into the creek. Damn them! She ran her hand through her damp hair. The acrid fragrance of wet sage tickled her nose. She wondered what Gwen and Bryan were doing. She wondered if Gwen had raised his consciousness, and didn't believe for one minute that it was possible. Though he might pretend, the slug.

Time to go. The marten had moved to a higher branch, but still watched her. Stoner laughed. "All right, you little beggar, I'll bring you something tomorrow."

She knocked on the door of the Thibaults' cabin. "Ah," said the Elder, "Right on time. I like promptness. Come in. You're wet. Go sit by the fire." She gave Stoner a shove. "Galatea! That girl's here."

"She's not a girl, Hortense," came a voice from the bedroom. "She's a woman."

Hortense smacked her lips impatiently. "Sit down." She pushed Stoner into a chair by the fire.

"Thank you." She glanced around the cabin. It was much larger than Little Bear, with separate living room, bedroom, and kitchen. "Your place is lovely."

"Stayed here every year for the last seven," Hortense proclaimed, buttoning a tweed jacket over her firm bosom. Under the jacket she wore a soft white shirt. Sturdy walking shoes graced her large feet. Stoner thought she recognized him from the L.L. Bean catalogue.

"Do you do much of your own cooking?" Stoner asked.

Hortense shrugged. "My sister takes a crack at it now and then. And we have Stell and Ted over on Saturday nights, when the dining room's closed." She peered at her gold lapel watch. "Galatea! What *are* you doing?"

The younger Thibault popped her head into the room. "If you must know, I'm folding your damn underwear."

She disappeared, leaving Hortense to sputter incoherently. "How'd you get so wet?" she demanded.

"Outside. I had my lunch by the creek."

"Arthritis before you're fifty," Hortense said bluntly. "What's your name?"

Galatea appeared in the door. She was thinner than Hortense, dressed in slacks, a light overblouse, and sandals. Her glasses hung on a beaded string around her neck. "For Heaven's sake, Hortense, don't be rude."

"Rude. I suppose you want me to call her 'Hey you' all afternoon."

"I'm sorry," Stoner said quickly. "I should have introduced myself."

Galatea dismissed her apology. "My sister hasn't given you a chance." She held out her hand. "I'm Galatea Thibault."

"Stoner McTavish." She shook hands.

"And *this* mangy old bison..." Galatea gestured toward Hortense. "... is my older sister, Hortense."

"How do you do?"

Hortense pumped her hand once, brusquely. "Queer name."

"It's for Lucy B. Stone."

"Humph," said Hortense.

"Stell will be a few minutes late," said Galatea. "Some early check-outs."

"Hot-house flowers," Hortense declared. "Few drops of rain, they pick up and leave. Of course," she glanced sharply at Stoner, "there are those who lack the sense to come in out of it."

"Ignore my sister," said Galatea. "She's a bully."

"Oh," Stoner said.

Galatea turned to Hortense. "We're embarrassing her."

"Oh, no," Stoner said quickly. "Please don't think that ... Ms. Thibault."

"*Miss*," said Hortense. "And proud of it."

"Oh, don't start that," said Galatea. She patted Stoner's hand. "Call us Hortense and Galatea."

Stoner looked down at her hands. "I'll try."

"Now what's the matter with you?" Hortense demanded.

"Well ... I have a hard time calling ... older people ... by their first names."

Hortense gazed triumphantly at her sister. "You see? I told you she had manners. First time I saw her I said to myself, 'That girl has manners.'"

"She's not a *girl*," Galatea snapped. "Woman. She's a woman."

Hortense stared at Stoner. "How old are you?"

"Thirty-one."

"See?" said Galatea.

Hortense snorted. "What did *you* know at thirty-one?" She gave Stoner a conspiratorial wink.

"As much as you know now, you old crock. Tea." Galatea turned on her heel and stalked to the kitchen.

"Don't mind my sister," Hortense said. "She's a free thinker. It makes her touchy. Where are you from?"

"Boston."

"Not one of those rat-ridden Cambridge apartments, I hope."

"Hortense, for the love of Heaven!" Galatea shouted from the kitchen.

"Eavesdropping is rude," Hortense shouted back.

Stoner laughed. "I live with my aunt, on Beacon Hill. Are you from New England?"

"Hortense stared at her as if she'd gone mad. "Of course. We have a little house in Newton."

"You think it's little," Galatea said, putting down a silver tea service, "because *you* don't have to clean it."

Stoner jumped up. "Let me help."

"Don't bother. I only have to get the cakes." Galatea scurried back to the kitchen.

"*You* don't have to clean it, either," Hortense called after her.

"Of course I do, every Tuesday."

Hortense poured the tea and handed Stoner a cup. "Want any of that stuff?" She indicated the cream and sugar.

"No, thanks."

"She cleans on Tuesday because the cleaning girl comes on Wednesday. Isn't that ridiculous?"

"I think a lot of people do that," Stoner said.

"Hear that?" Hortense shouted. "She thinks you're ridiculous."

"That's not what I said."

Hortense chuckled and nudged her. "Let her think it. Stubborn old fool, wins every argument we have." She sipped her tea. "Who's your aunt?"

"Hermione Moore."

Hortense knit her brows. "Moore. Moore." She glanced up as her sister entered with a tray of cookies. "Do we know any Hermione Moore from Boston?"

Galatea settled catlike into a chair, one leg curled beneath her. "New England Horticultural Society."

"The worms didn't hort this year." ·

"This one's her niece," Hortense said. "What are you grinning about?

"Uh..." She stammered. "Nothing."

"Hermione and I worked on the dried flower arrangements," Galatea said, "for the Harvest Festival a few years back."

"Didn't talk much, as I recall," Hortense said.

"She's a little shy."

"Humph," Hortense grunted. "Must run in the family."

Blessedly, there was a knock on the door. "Sorry I'm late," Stell said. She nodded to Stoner. "I didn't mean to throw you to the lions."

"Don't be ridiculous, Stell," said Hortense. "We're harmless old ladies."

"You're a couple of coyotes," Stell said. She pulled off her sweater and tossed it on the sofa. "That's why I put you in this cabin."

"In that case," said Galatea, "Stoner must be a little bear."

Stell looked at her fondly. "Are you, Stoner?"

"Uh..." She ran her hand through her hair.

"For God's sake, Galatea," Hortense said. "You've embarrassed her again. Let's play cards."

***

Hortense snapped her fingers. "Blue Runner!" she exclaimed.

"Two spades," said Galatea.

"Now, wait a minute," Stell broke in. "No talking across the table."

Hortense ignored her. "Your're *that* McTavish?"

Stoner nodded. "My grandfather."

"Three diamonds," Stell said.

Hortense consulted her cards. "Four spades."

"Sister," Galatea said patiently, "we only need three for game."

"That's no trump."

"We have one on."

"Oh," said Hortense, momentarily abashed. "Well, you can make it."

Stoner passed.

Galatea and Stell passed, and Hortense put her cards down. "I have trouble with mine," she said to Stoner. "A friend in the city has a perfect crop every time. But mine — they're abundant, but there's something missing in the flavor."

Stell looked from one to the other. "Will someone please tell me what's going on?" She tossed a card on the table.

"Spades are trump," Hortense said.

"I *know* that. What are you *talking* about?"

"Beans, of course," said Hortense. "Pay attention, Stell."

"Beans?"

"Beans."

"The McTavish Blue Runner Stringless Hybrid Snap Bean," Stoner said. "My grandfather invented it. Or created it. Or developed it. Or whatever."

"I'm delighted," Stell said.

"Well, I can't understand what I'm doing wrong," Hortense said. "I follow the instructions to the letter."

"You bully them," Galatea said. "No plant in its right mind would grow the way you carry on."

"Maybe your soil's too rich," Stoner suggested.

"I took it to the county extension agent. He said that soil would never support life as we know it."

"That can't be it, then." She thought. "Light?"

"They only get two hours of sunlight, and that's filtered through the willow."

"Ah," Stoner said. "I'll bet they're too far from the garage."

109

"I'm afraid to ask," Stell said, "but why?"

"They need carbon monoxide. That's why they're ideal for city gardens."

"I always knew easterners were crazy," Stell said, taking a trick and leading.

Stoner laughed. "They're just mutants," she said.

"Don't bother trying to grow them here," said Hortense. "Your air's too clean."

Stell glanced up over her glasses. "I can get along very well without mutants, thank you."

"Some of your guests come pretty close," Hortense said.

"Now, Hortense," Galatea warned.

Stell sighed. "The ups and downs of the tourist business. Isn't that right, Stoner?"

"Yes."

"Stoner's a travel agent," Stell explained.

Galatea tossed her remaining cards on the table. "The rest are mine. Want to play another?"

Stell looked at the score pad. "We have a rubber each. Might as well." It was pouring rain again. "Fine with me," Stoner said.

"That bunch from Illinois ever pay you?" Hortense asked, sorting her cards.

"No. We thought of working through a collection agency, but that seemed coarse. One heart."

"By me," said Hortense.

Stoner counted her points. Oh, God. Twenty-one, and her partner had opened. They were talking about a slam. She had dreaded this moment all her life. "Two no trump," she said timidly.

"Well," said Galatea, "we might as well sit this one out."

Stell went to Blackwood. Stoner named her aces and breathed a sigh of relief when Stell decided to play it in hearts.

"So you're here on business," Galatea said.

"Partly business, partly pleasure."

"Still thinking of hiking those canyons?" Stell asked.

"Probably."

"I thought maybe the maps would change your mind."

"I'm afraid not."

"We had a group here a few years ago," Stell said as she played. "Mid-September, it was. They went up Leigh Canyon to Cirque Lake, got caught in an early blizzard, and all froze to death."

"Oh, Stell," Stoner said. "How awful for you."

"Sometimes I wish the Park Service would close the canyons."

"Hah!" said Hortense. "Can't you hear the hue and cry *that* would raise?"

Stell laughed. "I suppose."

"Never," said Hortense, "interfere with a person's right to be a horse's ass." She gave Stoner a pointed look.

"Nothing I can do about her," Stell said. "I'm not her mother."

110

Hey. That was a swell idea.

"What are you looking for up there, anyway?" Hortense asked. "Trying to catch yourself some muscle-bound jockey?"

Galatea giggled. "Jock, Hortense. The word is 'jock'."

"You never had much use for men," Hortense said. "All of a sudden you're an authority."

"Well, I had my share of beaux." Galatea laughed. "Remember Harold?"

"Handsome Harold, the Harvard Fairy," Hortense said.

"Not the Harvard Fairy, one of the Harvard Fairies." She turned to Stoner. "Our love affair ended the day I walked into his room and found him trying on undergarments."

Stoner was puzzled. "What's so terrible about that?"

"They were my undergarments."

Stell hooted. "You're trying to make me lose this hand."

"Well," said Hortense, "I hope your Ted doesn't do that."

"Your husband?" Stoner asked, shocked.

"My son. No, Hortense, he's perfectly straight." She laughed. "I suppose 'straight' isn't exactly the right word under the circumstances."

"Your son's gay?"

Stell smiled at her. "Don't look so horrified. One out of ten, you know."

They seemed to be very fond of statistics in Wyoming. Stoner cleared her throat. "Is it ... all right with you?"

Stell scowled at the dummy hand, then chose a card. "Oh, I went through the usual hoopla at first. I had visions of him running off to San Francisco to become an interior decorator, and hooking up with a suntanned Adonis who'd sit around in undershirts and call him 'Teddy'." She took the trick and led from her hand.

"But it's all right now?"

"Better change the subject," Hortense said. "You're exciting the girl."

"Shut up," said Galatea, and kicked her sister under the table.

"Well, I moped around for a while. Then one day I said to myself, 'Stell, old gal, you can continue making life miserable for everyone, or you can admit you love that boy and get on with it."

"What about your husband?"

"Whenever Ted's upset, he works it off making repairs. He reshingled every cabin that spring." She sighed. "Wish I had his way of going about things." She played her last card. "Seven hearts it is."

"Well played," Galatea said.

"No thanks to you, Galatea. We've been friends too long for you to think you can distract me with yesterday's news."

Galatea shrugged. "Nothing ventured, nothing gained."

Dear Santa. All I want for Christmas is Stell Perkins for my mother. Your friend, Stoner. P.S. Million-dollar bribe is under the chocolate chip cookies.

There was a knock at the door. "Come in," Galatea said.

The headwaitress stuck her head in. "Mrs. Perkins, may I speak to you for a minute?"

Stell motioned her in.

"I'd rather you come out, if you don't mind."

Stell passed the cards to Hortense. "Your deal."

"Now," said Hortense to Stoner, "tell me why a girl your age lives with her aunt."

"Really, Hortense," Galatea exclaimed.

"How am I going to find out if I don't ask? *She's* not volunteering the information."

"She may have personal reasons."

"Well, I shouldn't think they'd be *im*personal."

"I've lived with my aunt since I was 18," Stoner said. "We both like it. The only reason I'd get a place of my own would be to prove something, and that doesn't make much sense. Besides, in her own way I think she needs me."

"She's probably saying the same thing about you."

"Probably. I guess we need each other."

"Good," said Hortense, dealing the cards. "Too many young people these days afraid of ties. Think it's a mark of maturity not to need anyone. Mark of selfishness, if you ask me."

"Hortense has opinions," Galatea said sweetly.

"Now you take Stell Perkins," Hortense went on, sneaking a peek at Stell's cards. "That woman has a heart big enough for the whole world to find room in. Not that she's a push-over, mind you. Get her back up and you'll wish her mother'd miscarried."

Stoner counted her points. Not enough to open, thank God. "What gets her back up?"

"Meanness. If Jesus Christ himself said a mean word, she'd cut him cold."

"Damn," Stell said, coming back in.

Stoner looked at her. "Something wrong?"

"One of our chambermaids quit. No explanation, didn't even ask for her paycheck."

Hortense muttered something under her breath about "kids" and "irresponsibility."

"Oh, shut up," said Galatea. "Who was it, Stell?"

"Amy."

"I know her. Built like a *Playboy* centerfold."

"My goodness," Stoner said, startled.

"Galatea likes to think she's 'hip'," Hortense said. "But she only sees those magazines when she goes on antipornography marches."

Stoner looked at Galatea. "You really do that?"

"Last May she was arrested for spraying shaving cream on *Hustler*."

Galatea touched her hair modestly. "Maybe she got tired of working," she said to Stell.

"Amy wouldn't walk off like that. She's a Mormon. Hortense, did you look at these cards?"

"Of course not," Hortense huffed.

"There's another problem," Stell said, arranging her hand. "She didn't turn in her keys. If we don't find them, we'll have to change all the locks."

112

She sighed. "I hate to even ask it, Stoner, but is there anything missing from your cabin?"

Stoner stiffened. "I don't think so. But I did have the feeling someone had been in there yesterday."

"Well," said Stell. "Doesn't that about curdle the cream?"

"Do you think she might have stolen something?" Stoner asked.

"I don't know what to think. Instinct tells me no, but I've been wrong before."

"If you're short-handed," Stoner said eagerly, "I could fill in until you find someone."

"Thank you, Stoner. I couldn't let you do that."

"I don't mind."

"We can always get extra help from Colter Bay. I just pray we don't have a mess on our hands."

And I hope I didn't bring it on you.

"Well," Stell said, "nothing we can do at the moment. Whose bid?"

***

Bryan Oxnard was the last person in the world she wanted to see, but she had no choice. It was absolutely vital that she find out what she could from him about the camping trip — and she was curious to see what his reaction would be to the break-in at her cabin. She declined a dinner invitation from the Thibaults, depriving herself of the chance to meet the restless, elusive Ted Perkins — whose existence she was beginning to seriously doubt — and trotted through the rain to the Stampede Room.

The bar was jammed. Lodge guests, campers, and various Park employees jostled and elbowed and drowned out the sound from the juke box. She saw a table being vacated and pounced on it, ignoring the salvo of dirty looks from the standing drinkers.

She had just ordered a Manhattan when Bryan entered. Stoner caught his eye and waved. He got a drink from the bar and sauntered toward her. Remember, flatter his ego. She punched at an ice cube in her drink. Jesus, she'd have to be Helen Hayes to pull this off.

"Well," he said, sitting down. "This is a surprise. Where's your little green man tonight?"

"Beg your pardon?"

"The Eagle Scout. You're usually tight as two peas in a pod."

Careful. Can't afford to scare off the fish before he takes the bait. She forced a smile. "It's Smokey's day off. I suppose he's doing ... whatever he does on his day off."

"Drinking, no doubt."

"Like us." Keep that old smile going, Stoner. "Did you resolve this morning's crisis?"

He seemed bewildered for a second. "Oh, that. It was nothing. Did you enjoy Yellowstone?"

"I had mixed feelings."

"There's been some talk about a limited season for bear hunting up there. I'd sure like to get in on that."

A little something for your trophy room? Along with your wife?

"Though I suppose you don't approve of that, either."

Stoner shrugged. "I really don't know much about it."

He leaned back in his chair and looked at her. "So. Tell me about Yellowstone."

"I thought you'd seen it."

"I have. But I'd like your point of view."

On what? The commercial possibilities? "It's rather large,' she said.

The corner of his mouth twitched. "Once again the veil of silence."

"What?"

"You two certainly are secretive about your outings. It's a good thing I don't have a suspicious nature."

"For Heaven's sake, Bryan," she said in exasperation, "we rode in the bus, we looked at the scenery, and we talked."

"About what?"

"Geology and life."

He raised his eyebrows. "Ah," he said. "Life."

"Life."

"Whose life?"

"Mostly mine, as a matter of fact."

"And has your life been exciting?"

"Not very."

He took a swallow of his drink. "Eight hours is a long time for not very exciting."

"Not when you're carsick for most of it."

"Yes," he said, "Gwen did mention that." He gave her a look that was supposed to be sympathetic. "That must be awkward."

"Very awkward." She was, she realized, not only confused, but a little afraid of him. "Bryan," she said, forcing herself to look him squarely in the eye, "are you getting at something?"

A smile crawled across his face. "Is there something to get at?"

"Is there?"

"I find it curious," he said, "that my bride of little more than a week spends two days of our honeymoon with a stranger from back home."

"It was your idea, remember?"

"So it was." He took out a cigarette and let it dangle, unlit, from the corner of his mouth. "What's your interest in her, Stoner?"

Prurient. "I don't know what you mean."

"I mean, why are you so interested in her?"

She gripped the edge of her chair and hoped he didn't notice. "Mrs. Burton asked me to look her up," she said inadequately. With all the

114

workshops they offered at the Cambridge Women's Center, why couldn't they come up with one on Effective Lying? Women would flock to it like robins to a wet lawn.

"For what purpose?"

"To say hello."

He lit the cigarette with excruciating slowness and gazed at her, narrow-eyed, through a cloud of smoke. "I think, my friend, it's time to put our cards on the table."

This is not the time to run, she told herself, glancing at the door. "What?"

"You're working for Eleanor Burton, aren't you?"

Her insides turned to ice. "I work for a travel agency."

"But you're picking up a little extra on the side."

"To do what?"

"Break us up."

Relief hit her like Colombia Gold. "Right, she said, laughing giddily. "She offered me a king's ransom to unmask you as the fiend she knows you are."

"How much?"

That's a professional secret. But make me an offer. If it tops hers I'll swing over to your side."

He glared at her.

"Honest to God, Bryan. You've seen too many old movies."

He broke into a grin. "How was I? Convincing?"

Huh? She took a tighter grip on her chair. "Not very."

"Come on. I had you going for a minute."

"Well, maybe."

He rested his arms on the table. "Listen, it's fine with me if she wants to pal around with you. As long as she has a good time. That's what we're here for, to have a good time."

What the hell's going on? "I'm glad of that."

"Any friend of hers is a friend of mine."

Oh, I doubt that, Bryan. I sincerely doubt that. "That's nice."

"No reason why we can't all be buddies."

"No reason at all." Except that I wouldn't trust you to take out the garbage.

"After all, my wife's obviously very fond of you."

"Yes, well, I'm fond of her, too."

"We both are. Fond."

"It's fortunate," Stoner said, "since you're married to her."

He laughed. A little too loudly. A little too hard. Stoner examined her drink.

"How's your vacation going?" he asked.

"Fine." An opening. Seize it. An opportunity wasted is an offense against Fate, H. Moore. "Someone broke into my cabin yesterday."

"Did they take anything?" Not a twitch, not a blink, not a flicker.

"No."

"Did you report it?"

"Yes."

115

"Not much else you can do, then, is there?"

"I guess not." She ran her finger around the rim of her glass. A habit she had picked up from Gwen.

"Is there any reason," Bryan said with what she was sure was studied casualness, "why anyone would want to break into your room?"

"Not unless they have a travel folder fetish." She looked up at him in what she hoped was a helpless, feminine way. "I'm frightened." Thank God Marylou wasn't here to see this. She'd throw up. "What should I do?"

He muttered something sympathetic and unintelligible.

"I feel so vulnerable out there in the cabin." Forget Marylou. I might throw up myself.

"Maybe you should move into the lodge."

"I asked. They're filled."

"Well." He patted her arm reassuringly. "If you're ever afraid, you just call me. I'll come check the place out."

Wow! Big-time macho stuff. "I appreciate that," she said demurely. "It certainly is a relief to know you're there."

"Any time. Day or night."

She took a drink. "All set for your camping trip?"

"All set."

"I envy you," she sighed. "I'm so tired of motels and ski lifts and crowds. I wouldn't mind getting off on my own for a while."

"Maybe you should. There's plenty of wilderness out here."

"But I don't have much time, and I don't know the area. With my luck, I'd hike all day and wind up in the middle of a Boy Scout Camporee." She glanced at him hopefully. She hoped. "Do you know any place I'd be sure to be alone?"

He thought for a moment. "Hanging Canyon. No, that's too tricky to do on your own."

Now we're getting somewhere.

"Do you ride?"

"I'm afraid not."

"Too bad. There are a couple of trails that are *real* wilderness. But you couldn't walk them if you're in a hurry."

"Where are you and Gwen going? I'm only curious," she added quickly.

"Curiosity killed the cat."

"I wouldn't tell."

"How do I know you wouldn't let it slip," he said with an edge, "during one of your intimate *tete-a-tetes?*"

Stoner gazed at him calmly. "I didn't know you resented my friendship with Gwen."

"Not as long as it stays on the level of friendship."

So much for let's-all-be-buddies. Now we come to the truth of it. "What do you mean by that, Bryan?"

He tilted his head to one side and gazed at her quietly. "You know very well what I mean."

"No. I. Don't."

116

"It'll come to you." He got up and reached for her glass. "Care for another? I'm buying."

Stoner glared at him. Bryan shrugged. "Suit yourself."

Arrogant, self-righteous son-of-a-bitch. Furious, she shoved back her chair.

"Are you leaving?" asked a velvet voice.

Stoner turned and gulped. "Hello, Gwen."

Gwen slid into the chair next to hers. "Where've you been all day?"

"Playing bridge. How about you?"

"Making peace."

She swallowed. "All day? It took all day?"

"It does when you're doing it between chapters of a detective story."

"Oh. You like detective stories?"

"No, Bryan does."

Pack it in, Gwen. Run away with me. I'll live anywhere, even Yellowstone. He probably Does It with a book in his hands.

Gwen looked around. "Have you seen him?"

"At the bar."

There was a pause. Stoner fiddled with the pearl snap on her cuff, and noticed she had unconsciously put on the brown shirt, the one that brought out the emerald highlights in her eyes. Oh, God, I dressed for her.

"Stoner?"

"Huh?"

"Yesterday was lovely, wasn't it?"

Lovely? Wonderful. Superb. It was everything I've ever wanted in a day. It was a Nobel Prize-winning day. It was the best day of my life, and all past lives as well. "Yes, it was."

"You may think this is silly, but I wish we'd picked up a souvenir. It wouldn't matter what, just a bit of plastic to prove it really happened." She laughed. "I'm kind of sentimental that way."

You can have my heart. It isn't plastic, but it could be a living memorial. "So am I."

"I have a book shelf full of things back home. Tacky, worthless trinkets, mostly. But when I remember something especially nice, I can pick them up and say, 'That was real. Here's the proof.'"

Find a spot for me. Somewhere between the Lookout Mountain ash tray and the Luray Caverns pencil sharpener.

"I guess I'll have to leave them behind when I get home," Gwen said a little sadly. "There's no place for them in Bryan's apartment."

There's no place for you, either. But we could live in Mammoth Cave.

"Anyway..." Gwen brushed her hair back from her forehead. "He'd think it was stupid."

Want to hear stupid? Let me tell you about the conversation I've been having with your adoring husband.

"Did Stoner tell you about the intruder?" Bryan asked, intruding. He kissed her. Stoner looked away.

"What intruder?"

"I think someone broke into my cabin," Stoner said.

"How awful. Why would anyone want to break into *your* cabin?"

117

"You don't have to be insulting. How do you know I'm not a famous international dope smuggler? Wanted on ten continents. Interpol has a file on me so thick they had to build a separate room for it."

Gwen smiled a little uncertainly. "Are you all right?"

"Fine." Swell. Terrific. Never better. Sitting around watching you and Big B play kissy-face is one of my favorite all-time entertainments.

"Get you a drink, hon?" Bryan asked, mauling Gwen's shoulder.

"Please."

He elbowed his way back to the bar. Mr. Bryl-Creme. The boy most likely to suceed. Our father, who art in heaven, deliver us from hysteria and other associated forms of psychosis.

Gwen put her hand over Stoner's. "Stoner, what's wrong?"

Stoner looked at her. Christ, she was wearing that pale blue and tan plaid shirt again. I love you, I love you.

"Am I unbuttoned or something?" Gwen asked.

"No! Gwen, do you have any idea how..." Beautiful you are?" "Never mind."

"What is it?"

"Nothing. It's nothing."

Gwen smiled and squeezed her hand. "You're a mess."

"I think Bryan resents the time we spend together," Stoner blurted out.

"What makes you say that?"

"Just a ... a tension I feel in him."

"Don't be silly, Stoner. He's never said an unkind word about you."

Of course not. He stores them up to say *to* me. No point in repeating himself, wouldn't be cost-effective.

"I'm sure you're imagining things," Gwen said.

You took your hand away when you saw him coming. I didn't imagine that.

"Here you go, hon," Bryan said, putting Gwen's drink in front of her and straddling a chair. "Cheers."

Barf.

Gwen glanced at her. Stoner looked down.

"Listen," Bryan said. "What do you say we all take the breakfast cruise to Elk Island tomorrow?"

"What?"

"It sounds like fun," Gwen said.

"Rain," Stoner mumbled.

"It's already clearing. Want to, Stoner?"

She looked at Bryan. "I'm sure you two want to go alone."

He smiled. "We have a lifetime to be together," he said, his eyes adding, "and don't you forget it."

Gwen touched her wrist. "Please?"

She felt like a rabbit in a trap. "All right, sure. But we'd better take separate cars. I have to stop by Signal Mountain Lodge."

"Maybe we should all go," Bryan said. "I'd like to see how you operate."

I'll bet you would. I'd like you to meet my acquaintance, Bryan Oxnard. Double entendre is his first language.

"Sorry," she said. "There are some things I'd rather do alone."

"Too bad."

Now I get it. He's not going to let me out of his sight. I have a little shadow who goes in and out with me, and what can be the use of him is more than I can see.

He turned to talk to someone at the next table. Gwen leaned close to her. "You see?" she said. "He really does like you."

She pushed back her chair and stood up. "I have to get dinner."

"Where?"

"Jackson Lake Lodge."

"Well, I guess we'll see you in the morning."

Gwen's expression was puzzled, and a little hurt. Stoner reached out to touch her, thought better of it, and shoved her hands in her pockets roughly. "Right. In the morning."

She was partway across the room when she heard Gwen call. "Stoner? Colter Bay Marina."

"Colter Bay Marina," she said, and hurried out.

She wanted to cry.

CHAPTER 8

Night had settled in by the time she started back to Timberline. The clouds had lifted and were breaking up, scattered across the sky like pieces of a jigsaw puzzle. Behind the Gros Ventres, the ripening moon began to climb. The wall of Douglas firs on the Jenny Lake Road opened to her headlights, and slipped silently shut when she had passed. For a while the road led due west toward the base of the Cathedrals. Owen, Grand, and Teewinot gazed down indifferently. Their silver tips and stark white glaciers hung in the darkness like the crests of waves poised to break. A few fires gleamed cozily in the campground.

The cabin was brittle with cold. Stoner lit a fire and paced the floor restlessly, unable to shake her feeling of isolation. The silence was oppressive. Her nerves were raw. She needed human contact. Maybe if she wrote to Marylou...

> Dear Marylou,
> Lack of evidence to the contrary, I agree with Mrs. Burton. Bryan Oxnard is a bastard. I don't know what kind of a spell he cast over Gwen, but he has to be stopped. Any doubts I had about this assignment are gone. You can tell Mrs. B. she doesn't have to pay me. This one is *gratis*, with my pleasure...

Well, really, how childish can you get? About one step above slipping a note under his door: "Dear Bryan, I hate you, Love Stoner." She crumpled up the paper and tossed it in the fireplace, picked up a novel, and walked down to the lodge.

She settled deep in an armchair, propped her feet on the flagstone hearth, and opened her book. The lobby was deserted. Even the crowd in the bar had left. The juke box played a soft ballad. She could barely make out the low murmur of Tony's voice as he chatted with a lone customer. Over on the reservation desk, the nightlight cast a dim golden glow. A log collapsed, releasing a shower of sparks. The room smelled of years of accumulated woodsmoke. She read a few pages, burrowed deeper into the chair, and nodded off.

She was awakened by a touch. Stell was tucking a blanket around her. "I didn't mean to disturb you," Stell said. "It's turned cold."

Stoner rubbed her face. Stell poked at the fire, her large, strong hands moving logs as if they were twigs. When she had finished she sat on the hearth and gave Stoner's ankle a squeeze. "Are we wearing you down, Stoner?"

Stoner tried to stifle a yawn. "I don't know how you do it, Stell. Do you ever rest?"

"I have all winter to rest, after the Cocktail Hour."

"Cocktail Hour?"

"It begins on Columbus Day, and ends at jail or unconsciousness, whichever comes first." She got up. "Coffee?"

"I feel like you're always feeding me."

"Wouldn't do it if I didn't want." She started toward the kitchen. "Bring the blanket. The fire's low. Where's your jacket?"

"I forgot." She wrapped the blanket around her shoulders and trundled into the kitchen behind Stell.

"Wonderful," Stell said. "Catch pneumonia. Ruin your vacation. Hortense had a few choice words on that subject over dinner. She's taken quite a fancy to you."

"She has?"

"So has Galatea, but Hortense is harder to please. Picky."

Stoner huddled next to the dying fire. "I'll have to drop in and see them when they get home."

"That'd mean a lot to them," Stell said. "Hortense in particular. She doesn't see many young people. She used to get out a lot, but she can't any more. Bad heart. Throw a log on the fire, will you?"

"How bad is it?" Stoner asked, hoping Stell wouldn't notice that she had added an extra log for longevity.

"I've seen her go downhill in seven years. Not that she'd want it known." She put the coffee on to heat. "Every September when they leave I think I might not see her again. When I put the padlock on Coyote, my hearts breaks a little. Not that I'd want it known."

Chipper got up from her rug and jumped onto the hearth. With a mighty moan she flung herself down, propped her head on Stoner's leg, and gazed adoringly at her. Stoner fondled the old dog's ears.

"You certainly have won her over," Stell said. "Strangers usually frighten her."

Stoner smiled down at Chipper. "We understand each other. They frighten me, too." She watched Stell pour coffee. "Have you heard anything from Amy?"

"I called her father, but she wasn't home yet. He'll have her call when she gets in." She handed a mug of coffee to Stoner and eased herself into the rocking chair. "This is my favorite time of day," she said. "Nothing to do but rock and daydream. That's how I'm going to spend my old age. Rocking and daydreaming."

The fire crackled lazily.

"You know the only thing I regret, Stoner?" Stell said. "I never had a daughter." She rocked, resting her head against the back of the chair. "I used to dream about it. How we'd work the kitchen together, talk things over in the evenings. Just like this. Ted and I are close as a man and woman can be. But there are things, things I wouldn't try to talk with him about. Not that he wouldn't understand, or try to. But he'd understand them differently, the way men do." She sighed. "My sons are good sons, good men. But I sure wish one had been a daughter."

Ahem. I have a suggestion...

"Funny," Stell said. "I always imagined she'd be a lot like you."

Stoner looked down at her hands.

"Your mother's a lucky woman, Little Bear."

Her face tightened. "I don't see much of my mother," she said tensely. "I left home when I was eighteen."

121

"Why?"

"She didn't like me."

"Why didn't she like you?"

"Because I'm a lesbian."

"I'll be damned," Stell said. "Imagine not liking your own kid." She rocked for a moment. "Ted Junior says gay life is hard." She laughed. "Actually, he says it sucks. He's about as good a poet as he is an interior decorator. Has it been hard for you?"

"No, I've been lucky. A little paranoid around the edges, but that comes with the territory. I guess, when most of the world wants to keep you out, it's all the sweeter when someone lets you in."

"Ever want to be different?"

"Now and then. But at those times I'd want to be different no matter what I was."

"Wish you were a man," Stell said. "I'd fix you up with my son."

"Then I couldn't be your daughter."

Stell chuckled. "That's the truth. Always some fly in the ointment." She looked down at Stoner. "Do you mind me talking to you like this?"

"Not in a million years. Most people won't, you know. I guess they're afraid they'll get it if they talk about it."

"I *hope* it's not catching," Stell said. "I'm too old to start over."

"I don't think you'd have much trouble, Stell."

"And what would I do with Ted? Turn him out to pasture with the horses?"

Stoner grinned and shrugged. "Well, if he likes horses..."

Stell reached over and slapped her on the foot. "Don't talk dirty to your mother."

Oh, my God, I'm going to die of happiness.

The phone rang, shattering the peace.

"Damn," Stell said. She pushed herself up from her chair and went out to the desk.

Stoner glanced at the fire. It was popping along cheerily. But it could burn down fast, the wood was dry. Then it would be time to go. Feeling only slightly guilty, she tossed on two more logs.

She was dozing off when Stell slammed into the room, marched to the ovens, took out her sourdough starter, and began churning up a batch of bread. Clouds of flour burst in tiny explosions.

"Uh ..." Stoner said at last, tentatively.

Stell grunted and flung another cup of flour into her bowl. She beat the dough into submission. "Amy's father."

Stoner waited through another round of banging and kneading.

"He leaves tomorrow. Before breakfast." She slapped the dough against the table. "I'd toss him out tonight if it wouldn't cause a ruckus."

"Amy's father?"

"Bryan Oxnard."

Stoner froze. "Stell?"

Stell shoved a wisp of hair out of her eyes. "I knew he was a mangey tomcat first time I saw him."

"Stell, what's going on?"

122

"He tried to get cute with her."

"With Amy?"

"Well, he sure didn't try it with me. I'd have neutered him for life."

"Please, Stell. Tell me what happened."

"Yesterday. She went up to change the sheets. Put his hairy hands on her."

"Why didn't she come to you?"

Stell attacked the bread again. "Thought I'd blame it on her. Probably thought it was her fault. You know how girls are. So she hid out in the woods all afternoon and hitched into Jackson first thing this morning."

"What about the keys?"

"Lost them."

"In the woods?"

"In the scuffle."

The pieces fell into place. Stoner took a deep breath. "Stell, there's something I have to tell you."

"Yeah? What?"

"I think he did it to get the keys. To get into my cabin."

Stell stared at her. "*Your* cabin?"

Stoner nodded.

"Well?"

"I don't ... I don't know how to say this..."

Stell rammed her hands on her hips. "Start talkin', kid, or start walkin'."

"You see..." She was shaking. "I'm not really out here on vacation... Stell, I really didn't mean to involve you in this."

Stell took a menacing step toward her. "Stoner..."

"Gwen's grandmother thinks Bryan's going to kill her. Gwen. I came out here to stop him."

"Son of a bitch," Stell said in an awed tone.

"I think he suspects me," she went on, clutching the blanket tight around her. "I think he wanted those keys to get into my cabin. To look for ... evidence. Honest to God, Stell, I didn't know he'd try anything like this. It never occurred..."

"Pipe down," Stell said. "I'm thinking." She came over and sat down.

"I know it sounds incredible. I know people don't do this sort of thing..."

"Yeah, yeah. That's what they said when Hedda Gabler killed herself." She rested her elbows on her knees and folded her hands.

"Stell, please don't throw them out," Stoner said urgently. "If he goes, I'll have to follow him. I might lose him. He doesn't know anything for sure. I don't know anything for sure. Smokey's trying..."

"Smokey! Is that old buzzard in on this, too?"

Stoner nodded.

"Jesus. Intrigue right under my nose and I don't even know it. I'm losing my grip." She looked at Stoner. "How you figure he's going to do it?"

"You mean you believe me?"

"Of course I believe you. Nobody could make up something *this* far-fetched."

"They're going on a camping trip," Stoner said. "I think he's going to make it look like an accident."

"And that's why you're so all-fired interested in those canyons."

"If I could just figure out which one..."

Stell laughed. "That's no problem. He'll have to register the trip."

"He will?"

"If he wants it to look like an accident."

"What if he puts down the wrong one?"

"Well, that'd be mighty suspicious, wouldn't it?" She rubbed her arms. "What do you plan to do about it?"

"Expose him beforehand if I can. If not, I guess I'll have to follow them."

"And do what?"

"Stop him."

"How?"

"I don't know."

Stell picked up a stick of wood and tapped it rhythmically against her foot. "Well." She thought for a moment. "I don't suppose it's entered that thick head of yours that this is dangerous."

"It's ... occurred to me."

"You must be pretty fond of that gal."

"Well..." Stoner said awkwardly, "she grows on you."

Stell folded her arms and leaned against the side of the fireplace. "Son-of-a-bitch," she said again. "Tell me one thing."

"All right."

"I want the truth."

"The truth."

"Are you *really* a travel agent?"

Stoner grinned. "I'm really a travel agent."

Chipper whined in her sleep. Stoner stroked her. "Will you let them stay?"

Stell thought it over. "If it's you he's after, I don't suppose he'll be robbing other guests. I guess I can sit on it for a few days."

"Thank you," Stoner said. "You won't be sorry."

"I'm *already* sorry."

Stoner hung her head. "So am I."

"Now, you listen to me, Stoner. If you find yourself in trouble, you come straight to me. Do you understand?"

"Yes, Ma'am."

"I want to know *where* you are every minute, and *why*. If I find out you've been sneaking around doing some damnfool thing, you're going to know trouble like you never knew trouble."

"I'm going to Elk Island in the morning. With Gwen and Bryan. And then to Signal Mountain Lodge. I'll be back here for lunch."

"You bet you will," Stell said. "Wait'll you see their prices."

"Hey, Stell," Stoner said shyly. "You're a real friend."

Stell glared at her. "Only until you cross me." She stood up and began turning out the lights. "Go to bed. Take that blanket with you. Come on, Chipper."

"Well, sleep well."

"I'm not going to sleep at all, thanks to you," Stell said gruffly.

"Stell?"

"Now what?"

"I really am sorry."

"OUT!" Stell shouted, pointing to the door.

The moon was high, the flatlands coated with silver. Stoner sighed. She didn't want to leave here, ever.

**

Saturday's rain had given the world a crisp polish. Stoner was at the Colter Bay marina early. The still waters of Jackson Lake offered a mirror image of the mountains and flawless sky. Where the lake was still in shadow, mist curled upward from the surface like dwarf phantoms. Over on Elk Island, smoke from breakfast fires rose in thin columns. She scraped her foot in the grainy, pebbled earth, and took a deep breath. You'd have to be subhuman to commit murder out here.

Looking up, she saw Bryan coming down the path. Alone. Stoner returned his wave without enthusiasm, and went to meet him.

"Gwen isn't coming," he said. "We'll have to go without her."

She felt a prickle of apprehension. "What's wrong?"

"Sinus headache. It happens every time the weather changes."

"We can make it another day..."

Bryan gave her an odd smile. "We have reservations. It's seven o'clock in the morning. I don't think they'd be able to fill our places, do you?"

She didn't know what to do.

"Gwen told me to go ahead," Bryan said. "She didn't want to spoil things for all of us."

Gwen doesn't appreciate the intricacies of this situation.

"Well..." she said.

He crossed his arms and studied her with an amused expression. His eyes were mocking. "Not afraid of me, are you?"

Stoner bristled. "Of course not." Not that you'll ever find out, pipsqueak.

"I won't bite."

But you might spill the beans. If I play it right. Like last night? Definitely not like last night. Today, we keep the old demon emotions in their place.

"Unless," Bryan said, "you have scruples against dating men."

"I have scruples," Stoner snapped, "against dating married men." Also idiots, creeps, lechers, and toads. You qualify on all counts.

"But this isn't a date, is it?"

Let's call it a fact-finding mission. She looked around at the crowd gathering for the trip. Nothing life-endangering could happen in this mob. She shrugged. "Why not?"

Bryan laughed. "You flatter me."

About ten minutes from shore, she realized she should have brought

125

dramamine. The low, rhythmic thrum of the launch's motor set up ripples and shock waves in her stomach reminiscent of "The Poseidon Adventure". Stoner clutched the railing and prayed for a miracle.

Bryan, mercifully, was indisposed to talk. It was, in fact, a silent trip. Grainy-eyed parents, unenchanted by their children's cute antics this early on a Sunday morning, kept enthusiasm to a minimum. The launch crew went about their work quietly, efficiently, with a detachment Stoner envied. They probably had rich fantasy lives.

She wasn't going to make it. Think of something else. Travel games. Make a list. Great Issues and Questions of our Time. Is the gypsy moth infestation the result of Reagan's economic policies, or are they both symptoms of a deeper problem?

Not long ago, if you played your stereo too loud, your mother told you to turn it down, and the neighbors called the cops. What happened?

"A" deposits $1000 in bank "B" and receives 6% interest. Bank "B" lends $1000 to "C" at 16% interest, and charges "A" 12¢ for handling the deposit. What is the annual income of bank "B"'s president?

Can the laws against telephone harassment be extended to include salesmen who call you at home?

What did Freud want?

Is there a conspiracy between the midwest steel industries and the producers of limestone to create acid rain?

Who owns the sun? Who owns Congress? Who owns *them*?

"You might at least talk to me," Bryan said.

"Bryan," Stoner said sweetly, "you have two choices: silence or vomit."

"You're sick?"

"Quite."

"You should have told me. I'll get you a Coke." He disappeared into the cabin.

With all the chugging and pounding, you'd think they'd at least be making progress. Elk Island seemed no bigger than before. Maybe even smaller. Her mouth tasted like tin. Come on, Bryan.

"Here you go," he said.

"Thank you." Don't think, drink. She waited for repercussions.

"Better?"

"Maybe."

"We'll be there soon."

Never. This is how I'm going to end my life, adrift on a sea of nausea and scenery.

The launch nudged the dock. The crew deserted. "Come on," Bryan said, and offered her a hand up. Considering the circumstances, she accepted it. Don't think this is a truce, Bryan. It's a temporary suspension of hostilities.

She settled for a breakfast of fried potatoes — no coffee, and certainly no undecapitated trout — and another soda, and carried her plate to the edge of the crowd. Bryan sat beside her.

All right, students, our homework assignment for today. Devise a conversation you can have with someone you hate, who is going to try to kill

126

someone you love. You must be polite at all times. You must also find out the following:

1. Where is he going to do it?
2. When is he going to do it?
3. How is he going to do it?

Compose a haiku containing your answers. No cheating, and no looking at each other's papers. Grades will be assigned randomly.

She cleared her throat. "This is lovely country. You must hate the east, coming from here."

Bryan cannibalized a trout. "I prefer the east. There's more going on."

"Still, there must be things you like about it. Enough to want to spend your honeymoon here."

"It's okay for a vacation."

Or a murder.

"I used to hunt here with my father," he said.

"Oh. Is that where you're going camping? Where you used to hunt?"

"No." He put his plate aside and stretched his legs. "You certainly are interested in that camping trip."

She brushed her hair to the side nervously. "Well, I envy you. I wish I could do something like that."

"Maybe I'll take you. Just the two of us, alone in the wilderness. What do you think of that?"

She laughed. "I think Gwen might have something to say on the subject."

He picked up a pebble and tossed it into the lake. "My wife trusts me."

We are each permitted twenty-three moments of idiocy in a lifetime. Unfortunately, Gwen has chosen to consolidate all of hers into one momentous mistake. "To do what?"

"That was very good," Bryan said. "Nothing I like better than a good fencing match."

It is said that wolves smile at their prey as they move in for the kill. Bryan grinned. "I like a woman who can hold her own."

Oh, go hold *your* own. "Come on, Bryan, it wasn't even vaguely clever."

"But I'll bet you can be clever. Very clever."

She sighed wearily. "What are you doing, Bryan?"

"I'm not doing anything. I think you're an attractive woman. Is that a crime?"

"Go easy on the bull-shit, will you? People are eating." I can't believe I'm sitting here saying these things.

"You shouldn't be so self-effacing. Any man would find you attractive."

Yippee. "I'm not interested."

"Or any woman." He looked hard at her. "I'll bet you've had lots of women, haven't you?"

She glared at him. "If I have, you'll be the last to know."

Bryan chuckled. "Not the type to kiss and tell, huh?"

"Bryan," she said, "I don't think this conversation is going anywhere. But I am." She stood up and marched her dishes to the serving table, then headed for the shore. Bryan followed.

"Come on," he said. "Tell me. Man to man."

She whirled on him. "What the hell is the matter with you?"

"I'm only trying to get to know you," he said innocently.

"*Why?*"

"So I can understand what my wife finds so fascinating about you."

Fascinating? Gwen thinks I'm fascinating? Damn it, she was blushing.

Bryan smiled. "That pleases you, doesn't it?"

"Go to hell," she muttered.

"You like her, don't you? You like her very much. You wouldn't mind getting her in your sleeping bag, would you?" He took a step toward her. "Want to know what it's like to screw Gwen, Stoner? Want to know? I can tell you. I've done it plenty of times."

"Stop it."

Get me out of here. Dear God, get me out of here. She clapped her hands over her ears.

"You think about that, don't you, Stoner? At night, before you go to sleep, you lie in bed and think about what she'd be like."

"You're disgusting."

He laughed in her face. His breath smelled of fish. "*I'm* disgusting? Pervert."

She looked wildly for a way out. He was backing her toward the crowd. She started to her left. He stepped in front of her and grabbed her hands.

"Let go of me, Bryan."

"I know she flirts with you," he said in a low voice. "I've seen her touching you. I've seen those knowing smiles she sends your way. I've seen how she looks at you. But it doesn't mean a thing, Stoner, my love. She's like that with everyone."

She twisted in his grip. "If you don't let go of me, Bryan, I'll scream. I'll scream the snow down from the mountains."

"I don't think you will," he said smoothly. "I don't think you want to spoil things for all these nice people."

He really *is* insane. She opened her mouth. Before she could draw breath, he clamped his lips over hers and shoved her against the rough trunk of a tree. She tried to push him away, and felt his tongue, forcing her teeth apart, probing the back of her mouth. She gagged, and brought her knee up sharply toward his groin.

Bryan jumped aside, laughing. "No you don't, little girl. You don't pull that one on me."

"Bastard," she hissed. "I'll tell Gwen."

"And I'll tell her you came on to me. Who do you think she'll believe, her devoted husband or a love-sick queer?" He grinned at her, teeth bared, his eyes shooting hatred like bullets into hers. "Her grandmother tried every trick in the book to keep her away from me, and where did it get her? I won then, and I'll win now." His eyes narrowed. "But I'll tell you something, Stoner, my love. I'll tell you what turns her on. You think about *that* while you're lying in bed playing with yourself. You can think about what *I'm* doing to her. You can think about what *I* can get, any time I want it. You can think about what you'll *never* have."

"Leave me alone!" she screamed, and burst into tears. Panic sent her running. She didn't care where, she didn't care who saw. Anything, anything to get away from him.

A bearded young man at the edge of the crowd stood up. "Hey, lady, you all right?"

"She's my wife," she heard Bryan say. "A little quarrel. You know how it is. She'll come around."

She sat on the shore and cried until her stomach ached. Bastard! She pounded the gravel with her fist. Bastard, bastard, bastard!

***

There is one certain fact about the human race: anyone in distress will be left absolutely alone. The other tourists avoided her on the ride home as if she were Typhoid Mary. Some gave her openly hostile looks. She didn't care. Only one thing mattered to her now. She had to keep Bryan away from Gwen.

She caught up to him as he was getting into his car, and grabbed his sleeve. "I have one thing to say to you, Bryan."

He looked at her.

"If you do anything to hurt her, in any way, you'll pay for it. If it takes the rest of my life, I'll track you down and make you pay."

"Why would I do anything to her?" he asked. "I love her."

She turned on her heel and stalked away. As she left the parking lot, he pulled up beside her. "A word of warning, my impulsive friend. Stay away from my wife. Stay away from my camping trip. And stay away from Bannock Canyon."

He gunned the motor and peeled out, spraying her windshield with gravel.

She stared after him open-mouthed. Bannock Canyon! He had dropped it as casually as a gum wrapper.

Things are looking up, she thought as she turned toward Timberline Lodge. I might have done it the hard way, but I did it.

She saw him again, his car stopped along the side of the road, hood raised in the universal distress signal. Flat tire, Oxnard? Eat it raw. She leaned on the horn and sped past him to the Jenny Lake turnoff.

***

She dashed for the lobby. Thank God, Stell was there. "Have you seen Gwen?" she demanded.

"A while ago, What's up?"

"Where is she?"

"Out for a walk."

"Where?"

"I don't know. Stoner..."

"Well, where do you *think* she went?"

"Stoner, what's the matter?"

"Please, I have to know."

Stell turned to the map behind her on the wall and put on her glasses. "Well, from the way she was looking at this thing, I'd guess ... Inspiration

Point."

"Great. See you later." She dove toward the door.

"Whoa!" Stell shouted, and grabbed her arm. "What's going on here?"

"No time."

"If it's Gwen you're after, you'll meet her coming or going. Now, settle down and tell me what this is all about."

Stoner ran her hand through her hair. "She didn't go on the trip. Bryan and I had a rather ... unpleasant encounter, and I'm afraid for her. How did she look?"

"Pale."

"Like sinus?"

"Something like that."

"Gotta go."

"*Stoner.*"

She turned back. "Yeah?"

"Take a jacket. It looks like rain."

She raced to her cabin and stumbled through the door. The cabin girl had been there. Her wastebasket was emptied, her towels straightened. Her bed was freshly made. The fireplace had been cleaned. So, even if by some remote possibility her note to Marylou had escaped burning, it was safely in the dumpster. And every minute of Bryan's time from last night until now was accounted for. Grabbing her jacket, she headed for the trail to Inspiration Point.

***

She crossed Lupine Meadows, swung northwest around Jenny Lake, and started to climb. The trail rose sharply through tall forests of spruce, fir, and lodgepole pine. Cascade Creek danced beside the path. Indian paintbrush glowed like rubies in patches of sunlight. Through breaks in the trees she could see the silver peaks of Owen and St. John. At Hidden Falls, she stopped for breath. At this altitude, you could rupture a lung taking the dog for a walk.

At least the exertion had taken the edge off her panic. All right, Bryan was dangerous, crazy dangerous. But no more dangerous than he had been before. No more dangerous to Gwen, anyway. His attack on herself had been — jealousy, anger, a warning. It didn't mean that he was going to dash home and dismember his wife. Still, she didn't want to let Gwen out of her sight. But that would only arouse his suspicion — and his anger — more. So what? So, he might take it out on Gwen. Maybe she should stay away from them. And spend the next four days crawling with anxiety?

Can four days of anxiety cause ulcers? Brain damage? Okay, let's look at this calmly. If he tries anything in their room, someone will hear. If he tries anything outside their room, someone will see. Therefore, he won't try anything. Except in Bannock Canyon.

Hell, he might do anything, anytime. He isn't going to care about people hearing, or seeing. He didn't care this morning. But who knows how that looked from the outside? Like a matrimonial squabble, no doubt.

Jesus, will I ever get the taste of him out of my mouth? She cupped her

130

hands and drank from the foaming, icy deluge that poured down the jagged cliffs. Mother Earth, I hope you have healing powers, beause this daughter of yours sure do need healing.

She splashed the chilling water on her face. All right, all right, what's the least common denominator here? More than anything else, Bryan wants Gwen's money. Therefore, he will not do anything to jeopardize his chances of getting it. Therefore, he will not do anything to cast suspicion on himself. Therefore, he will not do anything to make her back off from that camping trip.

I hope.

Meanwhile, what can I do? One — she tossed a pebble into Cascade Creek — find a way to put Gwen on her guard. Two — she tossed another pebble — keep my eye on them as much as possible. Three — another pebble — keep pursuing his past, try to come up with solid evidence against him. But most of all — she scooped up a handful of stones and hurled them against a rock — STOP HIM!

The sky was fading to gray. Thin clouds crept in around the mountain peaks from the west. Push on. Find Gwen. By the time she reached Inspiration Point, her knees were shaking. But the view was magnificent. Jenny Lake lay below, small, silver, and reflective as a pocket mirror. The Gros Ventres were visible to the south, and to the east the Mt. Leidy Highlands and the whole, long, river-threaded basin of Jackson Hole.

She felt a drop of cold rain on her shoulder, then another, and looked north into the most terrifying bank of clouds she had ever seen. Like oily smoke, they boiled down through the canyons and crevices above her. Rips of lightning stabbed the ground. Cannonades of thunder cracked through the valleys. Jesus!

Storm in hot pursuit, she scrabbled and scrambled down the path. As she rounded a curve, she saw a familiar figure and skidded to a halt. "Gwen," she shouted over the thunder, "where have you been?"

Gwen glanced at her and looked at the ground. "Walking."

"What?"

"Walking."

"Where?"

Gwen gestured toward the forest. "Around."

"Walking *around*? In the *woods*? There are *bears* in there, Gwen. Moose. Elk. Timber wolves, probably."

"What?"

Gwen's hair whipped across her face.

"We have to get out of this," Stoner yelled.

The wind grabbed a clump of trees and shook them like rattles.

Gwen's face was white. "I'll be all right."

The clouds opened.

"Are you nuts? This one's a monster!"

She grabbed Gwen's hand and dragged her to the base of the cliffs that banked Hidden Falls. There was a shallow *cul-de-sac* topped by an overhang of rock. Lightning crackled through the treetops as she plunged inside, pulling Gwen with her.

Stoner gasped for breath. "You weren't going to stay out in that, were you?"

131

Outside a tree crashed to the ground somewhere in the forest. Gwen shrugged. She was trembling. Stoner peeled off her jacket and threw it over Gwen's shoulders. The wind shrieked. Branches creaked and shattered. Rain swept in furious torrents through the woods and gushed in waves from the overhanging rock. "It has it in for us," Stoner said. "I knew we shouldn't have looked at Yellowstone." She reached up and pushed carefully on the granite roof. The rock was firm.

She slid down into a sitting position, her back against the wall of stone. Gwen didn't move. "Sit down. It could be a long wait."

Mechanically, Gwen obeyed. Stoner looked at her. Something was terribly wrong.

"I missed you this morning."

"Yes."

"Bryan said you had a headache."

"Did he?" Gwen looked away.

"Is it better?"

Gwen didn't answer. Definitely, terribly wrong.

She steeled herself. "Gwen, there's something I have to tell you. This morning, Bryan..."

"Bryan?"

"Bryan and I ... we had a little trouble." She wasn't listening. "*Gwen.*"

"This morning?"

"Gwen."

"You went to Elk Island this morning."

"That's right."

"I couldn't go. He didn't want me to go."

Wait a minute. Are we on the same plane here? "Gwen, what's wrong?"

The wind blew harder. It cut through pine branches like an axe-blade. Ear-splitting retorts ricocheted from canyon wall to canyon wall as the storm roared down the mountains like a runaway freight.

Gwen looked blankly at the ground. She was still shaking. Stoner bit her lip. When in doubt, act. She slipped her arm around Gwen's shoulders. Gwen dropped her head to her knees, but didn't pull away. "We ... had a fight," Gwen said after a long time. "That's why I stayed home."

Shit. Stoner pushed her hair back from her forehead.

"He called me stupid and childish and ... the look on his face." Gwen shuddered. "I haven't seen that since... He said I had to stay...I couldn't stay..." Her voice trailed off.

Stoner held her tighter. "Tell me."

"I never expected... He's never been angry before... I thought it would be all right to tell him."

"Tell him what?"

"I wasn't trying to ruin it. I only asked. He woke me up. I was asleep and I woke up and he was standing there, in the doorway. Staring at me. I knew. I knew someone had told him."

The wind hurled curtains of rain across the mouth of their shelter. Stoner pulled Gwen's head down against her shoulder. "Please, Gwen, try to sort it out."

Gwen pressed against her, her fingernails biting into Stoner's arm.

132

"Don't let me cry."

"Talk to me."

"He woke me up."

Stoner felt the hair rise on the back of her neck. She wanted to scream, to run, to stop it. She forced it down. "It's all right," she said, stroking Gwen's shoulder. "Just talk to me."

"He wanted to kill me. It was in his eyes."

"Who, Gwen? Your father?"

Silence.

"Bryan?"

Gwen pulled back and looked at her, shaking her head as if to clear it. "Bryan wouldn't want to kill me ... would he?" she asked in a very small voice.

Yes. Damn it, yes!

"Would he?"

This wasn't the time. "I don't know," Stoner said.

"He wouldn't. He loves me. He said he loves me." She looked at Stoner pleadingly. "Would he?"

Stoner forced herself not to look away. She cleared her throat. "What did you fight about?"

Gwen shook her head. "I can't remember. I said ... he was shouting ... everything got all mixed up."

"Try."

The storm was moving on to the east now. The wind dropped. Thunder rumbled distantly. Heavy drops still fell from the trees, but in the air only a fine mist remained, tangy with wet pine and earth.

"It was the camping trip," Gwen said at last. Stoner froze. "I asked him if he wanted to cancel the camping trip."

"Why?"

"I thought he was worried about the money. He's been ... distant. I said we could do it another time. It was only a suggestion. I didn't mean anything by it."

"I guess it's important to him," Stoner said lamely. I can't tell her now. I can't make it worse. She gritted her teeth.

"He wanted to make love afterward," Gwen said timidly. "I was .. afraid. He was ... seemed rough. Like a stranger. I couldn't help it, I kept thinking how ... alone I am out here."

"No," Stoner said firmly. "You're not alone out here."

"While we were making love...I hated him. But I couldn't stop him. I was afraid to stop him. Stoner, I'm so ashamed."

"Don't be." Where I come from, we call it rape.

"I don't know what to do."

"Gwen, I want you to promise me something. If you feel afraid, for any reason, no matter how silly you think it is, please come to my cabin. Or to Stell."

"Stell?"

"She'll understand."

Gwen gave her a puzzled look. "What do you...?"

Stoner touched Gwen's face. "Just promise."

"I promise."

A pencil-thin finger of sunlight broke through the clouds.

"Stoner, what going on?"

"You mustn't go through this again."

"Am I losing my mind?"

"No. Just be careful, okay?"

"Of Bryan?" Gwen said incredulously.

Stoner rubbed her face. "Yes."

Gwen stared at her.

"When you sense things ... well, I believe in instinct."

The sun beat down on the wet forest floor in pools of blazing green and gold. Gwen brushed the damp hair from her eyes and got slowly to her feet. "I have to go. I have to apologize to him."

"A few more minutes won't matter."

"He'll be worried. I have to get it over with."

"Gwen!" She scrambled out into the sunlight after her.

"I mean..." Gwen turned and ran.

"Let me come with you," Stoner called.

Gwen didn't look back. The forest swallowed her.

Stoner trotted down the trail to the edge of Jenny Lake, slipping on the rain-slick ground. She twisted her ankle and pulled up short. Damn it! Gwen was nowhere around. She limped past the lake and across the meadow, and slammed noisily through the lodge door. The lobby was deserted.

Now what? Kick open the door to their room and burst in, guns blazing? If only she could. Beaten, she went to her cabin.

It was a mess. The contents of her luggage lay strewn about the floor. Her clothes had been torn from their hangers and dumped in the middle of the rug. Gwen's picture lay on the hearth, ripped in two. The bed looked like a rat's nest. And lying in the center of her pillow, arranged as neatly as the Crown jewels, were Amy's keys.

Stoner gazed at the mess, and began to laugh. If this was his idea of a threat... If his mind operated on *this* level... Perhaps, at last she had the advantage.

***

"Don't count on it," said Edith Kesselbaum.

Stoner gripped the phone. "What do you mean?"

"*I've* never been able to outthink a psychotic. And, believe me, I'm no slouch."

"Is that what he is, psychotic?"

Edith sighed. "Stoner, dearest, I realize you lack professional training. And being, as it were, counter-culture, you are inclined to be tolerant of a wide latitude of behavior. But surely you must recognize that mindless acts of vandalism are not the acts of a sane, mature human being."

"Well," Stoner said, "I thought it was odd."

"Yes, Stoner, quite odd."

"Dr. Kesselbaum, do you think I'm stupid?"

"You're a romantic, Stoner. Which means...'" she went on, anticipating Stoner's next question, "... that you will always attribute to your fellow man or fellow woman far more intelligence, self-restraint, insight, and purity of motive than he or she possesses." She sighed again. "Oh, dear, nonsexist language can be so awkward and time-consuming. Still, the American Psychiatric Association is quite adamant on the subject."

"What can I do?"

"Nothing, I'm afraid. They pay little attention to one of their own. They would totally ignore the opinions of a lay person."

"Huh?"

"Besides, I distinctly recall that you were positively orgasmic with joy when the ruling went through."

"About Bryan, Dr. Kesselbaum," Stoner said patiently.

"My advice to you would be ... to come home immediately. The man obviously has the instincts of a wounded animal. But perhaps I malign our animal friends."

Stoner smiled. "I think so."

"Yes, I frequently wonder if the advantages of the opposable thumb outweigh our evolutionary losses. Has it ever occurred to you, Stoner, that the human experiment may have been a failure?"

"Every day," Stoner said.

Dr. Kesselbaum indulged in a philosophical silence.

"What about Gwen?" Stoner asked.

"What's your assessment of her mental state?"

"Well, keeping in mind that I'm a romantic..."

"I always have that in mind, Stoner."

"I think she's cracking up."

"*Must* you wallow in slang? What do you mean by 'cracking up'?"

Stoner meditated on it. "I think," she said at last, "she's confused. His behavior is changing in ways she doesn't understand."

"Because she lacks half the data, you see. She doesn't perceive what you perceive, being blinded, as it were, by passion. She is not, one might say, playing with a full deck."

"She may be short on spades," Stoner said sadly, "but she sure has the joker."

"Ah, yes, the joker. In the ancient decks, the Fool. The card of innocence, ignorance, but possessing the instinctual wisdom of the newborn."

"Dr. Kesselbaum, are you going Jungian?"

Edith Kesselbaum gasped. "Oh, my God, I hope not. I would be expelled from the Psychoanalytic Society in rags and tatters."

"Well, I can't just *leave* her here."

"In his clutches? Certainly not."

"What should I do? Kidnap her?"

"No, too many risks involved."

"I guess so," Stoner said. "She's had self-defense training."

"Well, there's a plus for your side."

"Not if she doesn't think to use it."

"Or uses it on you. I shudder to think..."

135

"I have to do something, Dr. Kesselbaum."

"Under the circumstances, I would say...'" She thought for a moment. "Punt."

"Punt?"

"Fourth down. Long yardage. Punt."

Stoner kneaded her forehead in desperation. "Can't you be more specific?"

"Play it by ear."

Stoner groaned.

"It isn't hopeless, dear. There's a good chance, in his mental state, he'll make a mistake."

"What kind of mistake?"

"Stoner, you have the single-mindedness of an elephant."

"I *need help*."

"Well, take this Hammock Canyon business..."

"Bannock Canyon."

"That's what I said, dear. Are you paying attention?"

"Yes, Dr. Kesselbaum."

"In my professional opinion..."

Ah, that was a good sign.

"In my professional opinion, he targeted the murder spot for you. He had delusions of grandeur, obviously. I think he'll go right ahead with his plans as originally conceived."

"And what should I do?"

"Let him think he has you on the run. You may catch him with this FBI file business, of course. But just in case you don't..."

Stoner held her breath. "Yes?"

"Familiarize yourself with the scene of the crime. You may be able to get the jump on him. Is there anyone there you can call on for help?"

"I think so." She thought of Smokey.

"Good. Now there's one very important thing to remember."

"What's that?"

"Get him before he gets you."

"Thank you very much, Dr. K. You've been very helpful." I think.

"One thing, Stoner..."

"Yes?"

"Are there any McDonald's out there?"

"Not that I've found. But I did see an A&W Root Beer."

"Oh, thank God," Dr. Kesselbaum breathed. "Good-bye, Stoner."

Good-bye? That had a ominous ring. Stoner stared at the phone for a moment before hanging up.

CHAPTER 9

As she was drifting off to sleep, a thought struck her. Gwen was probably, at this moment, in bed with a homicidal maniac. A surge of adrenalin went through her. Now, wait a minute. Remember, he wants money, not blood. He's not going to risk that with an assault rap. It has to look like an accident. Nothing will happen to her before that trip. But something had already happened to her, this morning. She tried to forget how Gwen had looked on the trail. It was impossible. The demons of insomnia, well-armed, somersaulted into her room and set up shop.

She tried to read, but couldn't concentrate. She wrote a letter to Marylou. It didn't work. She built up the fire and stared at it until it died to coals. She paced the floor. She took a warm bath and a dramamine. She counted sheep. She counted the minutes. She counted her heartbeats. Coyotes barked and fell silent. Something scurried past the bathroom window, something small, something with claws. A pine cone fell on the roof and rolled off to the ground. There was a faint, irregular sound of dripping as moisture gathered on the leaves of plants, coalesced, and dropped. Silhouettes and shadows appeared, vague pockets of dark on dark. Slowly they arranged themselves into the shapes of trees. The night grew pale. A breeze sprang up, close to the ground. To the east, a gray smear spread behind the hills.

Cue the birds. A tentative, questioning "cheep". Then another, and another. A flutter of wings. Up jays. A call. A squawk. Hey, man, that's *my* tree. Squawk. Who do you think you're shovin', man? Squawk. Squawk. Keep your damn claws to yourself. Okay, everybody, let's hear it for MORNING.

Stoner got up from the porch, tested her knees and ankles. I dunno, lady. Wheel bearings rusted, shocks gone, transmission shot. Tell ya' what, give me ten bucks and I'll haul it away for you. She put her hands on her lower back, stretched, and moaned. Quick, Mom, the Doan's Pills. Walk it off. Better still, put it out of its misery. This won't hurt, my dear. You'll fall into a deep sleep, and wake in a far, far better place.

A cuticle of yellow appeared on the horizon. Down at the lodge, a screen door slammed. A wisp of white smoke rose from the chimney and evaporated into the morning air. Ah, they've chosen a new Pope.

She caught sight of Smokey, plodding up the path to the kitchen door. He stopped, unaware of her, tipped his hat to the sunrise, and went inside. Dishes clattered. The machinery of life was starting up.

Stoner washed, dressed, and hurried down the trail. She slipped in through the kitchen door. Smokey leaned against the sink, a mug of coffee in his hand, chatting with the cooks. Odd, seeing all these strangers in Stell's kitchen. But Chipper, in her usual place by the fire, raised her head and panted a welcome.

"McTavish!" Smokey boomed. He got her a cup of coffee. One of the cooks was cutting up potatoes and onions for home fries. His cleaver beat a tattoo on the slicing board. The air was rich with the odor of smoke and frying bacon. Sweet rolls were rising on the open hearth.

Stoner gave a deep sigh.

"Rough weekend?" Smokey asked.

"Rough enough. What's the word on our project?"

"You're not going to like it."

Her heart fell. "No files."

"Oh, we've got files, McTavish. We've got files up the wazoo."

"How many?" she asked, and held her breath.

"One thousand, seven hundred and thirty-two."

Stoner sagged against the wall.

"I hope you didn't have plans for today," Smokey said.

"Not now."

Stell breezed in through the dining room door. "*Good* morning, Stoner. John."

Smokey grunted.

"Here," Stoner said, digging the keys from her pocket.

"Where did you get them? Or will I be sorry I asked?"

"Bryan left them in my cabin."

Stell looked at her. "What was he doing there?"

"A little amateur intimidation."

"Bastard," Stell said.

Stoner laughed. "I'll have to leave the swearing to you. I'm fresh out of euphemisms. Were they at dinner last night?"

"Yep."

"How are things?"

"Quiet. Subdued. Oxnard was his usual smiling self."

Stoner looked down at the floor.

"Worried?" Stell asked.

"Very."

"What do we do now?"

"Stoner's going to go through some FBI files," Smokey said. "She told you about this, huh?"

"She told me," Stell said. "Some of it. I hate to think what she *didn't* tell me."

"Know what you mean," Smokey said. "Sure wish I didn't have to work today."

"The sagebrush is depending on you," Stoner said. "Stell, did you find out anything?"

"Sure did. He's booked through our stables."

Stoner leaned forward eagerly. "And?"

"Thursday. Bannock."

"Mother of God," Smokey said.

* * *

"One thousand, seven hundred, and thirty-two," Stoner said later in the

138

dining room. "I can't believe it."

"You will when you see them."

She jabbed at her blueberry pancakes. "Index cards?" she asked hopefully.

Smokey shook his head. "Print-outs."

"Summaries?"

"Every detail. The Bureau is thorough."

"All unsolved?"

"All unsolved."

She stirred a spoonful of sugar into her coffee angrily. "What have they been doing with their time?"

"Persecuting social activists." He destroyed a sausage patty. "I'm sorry, McTavish. I'd hoped to be more helpful."

"It isn't your fault." She rubbed the back of her neck. "I thought the men in this country had all the money."

"They soon will," Smokey said.

Bryan and Gwen came in and went to a table in the corner. Stoner caught his eye and winked, as if they shared a secret. Bryan returned her wink.

"What's that about?" Smokey grumbled.

"A little sanity test. We both failed." She poured more syrup on her pancakes. "I don't know, Smokey. Do you think this is a waste of time?"

He shrugged. "You got any better ideas?"

"No."

"Neither do I." He got up. "Well, I got to go. Don't envy you."

"Maybe they'll be interesting," Stoner said.

"I looked through a bunch. That computer's no Agatha Christie." He handed her his key. "Good luck."

Luck. She dumped two more teaspoons of sugar into her coffee. It'll take a lot more than luck. Three pairs of eyes might help, or a quickie Evelyn Wood Speedy Reading course.

She glanced over at Gwen, but Gwen was facing away from her. Bryan looked up and grinned. This has to work, because if we get down to Thursday...

"Good day, Stoner."

She started. "Miss Hortense," she said, rising.

"Oh, sit down. This isn't boarding school."

"Will you join me?"

"No, thank you," said Hortense. "We're off to the Gros Ventres."

"I see."

"Bald eagles. How's your cold?"

"Cold?" Stoner said. "I don't think I have a cold."

"Of course you do. Dripping wet the other day. Can't avoid a cold."

"I..." Stoner said, flustered, "I guess I'm getting over it."

"Stay buttoned up." She plucked at Stoner's sleeve. "Cotton. No good in this weather."

"I have a sweater."

"Where?"

"In my cabin," Stoner said.

"Wonderful," Hortense said. "The cabin won't catch cold."

Galatea hove into view. "*Now* what are you picking on her about?"

Hortense pursed her lips. "None of your business." She poked Stoner with her elbow. "Pneumonia is just around the corner. Take my advice."

"Yes, Ma'am. I will."

"Manners," said Hortense as Galatea steered her away. "Not much sense, but the girl's got manners."

"How many times do I have to tell you," said Galatea, "she's a *woman*."

Stoner went to pour more syrup on her pancakes, but the pitcher was empty. The pancakes were disintegrating into a soggy mass. Sugar binge. A sure sign of derangement.

I wish I didn't have to leave her alone with him. I wish there were some way to keep an eye on them. Anxiety formed a little knot in her stomach. Now I know how mothers of teen-aged daughters feel.

Hey, they made it through the night, right? And through the morning festivities, whenever they are. How was it this morning, B? Still her best time of day? Or do you like it better when you get to play rough? Does that give you a little thrill, Bryan, that scared, frozen look in her eyes? Kind of like the way a trapped animal looks, in that split second when it knows it's going to die? Really gets it up for you, doesn't it?

She threw down her napkin and strode from the room. If it was going to be *this* kind of day, it was just as well she had to spend it with computer printouts. Basket weaving, in fact, might be more appropriate.

"Is the cooking that bad," Stell asked from her perch behind the cash register. "Or is it the service?"

"The clientele."

Stell sighed. "That's the problem with democracy. We have to let in the trash." She reached over the counter and touched Stoner's shoulder. "Take it easy, Little Bear. You're doing the best you can."

Stoner clenched her fists. "Stell, I feel so damned helpless."

"I know. But just keep plugging. Try to have a little faith."

"In what?"

Stell thought. "A Just and Merciful God?"

Stoner rolled her eyes Heavenward.

"Dumb luck?"

"I need all of that I can get."

"Well," Stell said, "you can only do what you can do."

"That's real comforting, Stell."

"What do you expect? It's Monday. Look, Stoner, get those files and bring them over to my office. I can give you a hand between disasters."

Stoner hesitated. She was tempted. "Oh, I don't want to involve you in this any more than I have to."

"Stoner, I'm *involved*. It's *my* Lodge, they're *my* guests, you're *my* friend... and he looks like a towel-swiper to me."

"Dr. Kesselbaum says he's crazy. That should make me feel differently about him, I guess. But it doesn't."

"Me, neither," Stell said. "Whoever Dr. Kesselbaum is."

Stoner leaned on the counter. "Listen," she said in a low voice. "let's forget all this horsing around and just throw him off the top of Grand Teton."

"I don't think that's a good idea," Stell said.

"Why not?"

"Because his wife is headed our way."

Stoner's arm slid out from under her. Her head banged on the counter top.

"Hi," Gwen said.

Stoner cleared her throat. "Hello," she squeaked.

"Are you coming down with something?"

"Hey, gals," Stell said. "Mind moving into the lobby? We have a regiment of rock-crawlers approaching."

They retreated to an out-of-the-way corner.

"When they make the movie of Stell's life," Gwen said, "I want to play her."

"You feeling okay?"

"A little shaky," Gwen said. "But life goes on."

"Yeah."

"I really scared myself."

No, damn it, *Bryan* scared you. And he scares me, and Stell, and Smokey, and Dr. Kesselbaum. Your loving husband, Gwen, is the Terror of the Tetons. She glowered at the floor.

"Anyway," Gwen said. "I wanted to return your jacket, and to thank you."

"Thank me?"

"For being a friend."

Stoner shrugged. "Just remember what you promised me." She took her jacket.

"I remember."

Suddenly, unexpectedly, Gwen reached out and embraced her. "Stoner, you're terrific."

Gwen's stomach was firm against her stomach. Her thighs were firm against her thighs. Her breasts were soft against her breasts. The jacket hit the floor with a thud. Her blood pressure knocked the top off the Richter scale. She put her arms around Gwen and felt her knees start to give way.

Gwen pulled back and looked at her. "Are you all right?"

"Fine," Stoner said, bracing herself against the wall. "I'm fine." Every cell in my body has just turned into a suction cup. Other than that...

"What are you doing today?"

Oh, I thought I'd sit around and count my nerve endings. "I don't know. How about you?" What poise. What composure. What'll I do if I faint?

"We're going over to Teton Village."

"Well, stay away from dark alleys." Stoner gulped air. Oh, Jesus, heavy breathing.

"Are you sure you're all right?"

"Yeah. Yeah, I'm fine. A little dizzy. Altitude."

"Want me to walk you to your cabin?"

"No!" My cabin is not a safe place for you right now. Dark alleys, deep woods, strange men's cars, and my cabin. "I'll be fine. Really." She gestured limply toward the dining room. "Bryan must be wondering. . ."

"Well, okay. If you're sure."

"I'm sure. I'm sure." Oh, dear God, get her out of here.

"Want to meet for a drink tonight?" Gwen asked.

Tonight? Tonight? No, I think I'll be dead by tonight. "Fine."

"Around seven?"

Seven what? Oh, yeah, seven o'clock. "Fine."

"Well, I'll see you then."

"Yeah. Then. Yeah."

Gwen picked up her jacket and held it out to her. "You dropped this."

Move the arm. Open fingers. Grasp jacket firmly... Not her hand! The jacket!

"Stoner?"

Whatwhatwhatwhatwhat? "Yeah?"

"Enjoy your day."

"Oh, I will. I certainly will. You too."

Gwen moved away from her reluctantly. "Stell, she said, "is she all right?"

"I think it's that time of month," Stell said. "Don't worry. I'll mop up."

Gwen went slowly back into the dining room.

Stell collapsed over the cash register.

Stoner glared at her. "Say one word," she said, "one word and I'll leave without paying my bill."

"Oh, my God, Stoner. Your face is worth the price of admission." She wiped a tear from the corner of her eye. "So is hers."

"Stell, I'm warning you..."

"So," Stell said. "That's how the land lays."

Stoner bolted.

                              ***

"Are you going to help?" Stoner asked feistily, "or are you going to sit there and smirk?" She was sprawled on the floor of Stell's office, back against an easy chair. Computer printouts carpeted the floor.

"I'm not smirking," Stell said. "I'm thinking."

"Well, tell me what you think of those." She indicated a pile of possibilities she had set aside.

Stell put her glases on and picked up the papers. She glanced through them. "What are they?"

"Missing widowers. They all inherited money and disappeared. Wives died of suspicious causes."

"This one's oriental." She put it on the reject pile. "This one lost an arm in Vietnam. This one would be seventy years old now. I don't think they're what you're looking for."

Stoner rolled over on her back. "This is hopeless. I can't even concentrate any more. What time is it?"

"A little after three. How many more?"

She counted them. "A hundred and eighty one."

"Let me finish up. You've done more than enough for one day."

"I just need a break."

"In more ways than one, I think," Stell said.

Stoner closed her eyes. "They're so unimaginative. The only one I've found that was even vaguely creative is poisonous mushrooms."

"It's hard, isn't it, Stoner? Being in love with her?"

"It'll do in a pinch."

"Is she nice to you?"

"Yes."

"She'd better be."

Stoner pushed herself up on one elbow. "How should I handle it, Stell?"

"I can't answer that for you."

"But you worked it out. You and Ted and Smokey."

Stell smiled. "It took us twenty years, Stoner. We did some things right, and some things wrong. Everyone got hurt a little. And we had some laughs along the way. I guess what got us through was that we never stopped loving each other."

Stoner gave a bitter laugh. "We have a slightly different situation here. The only one who wishes the best for everyone is Gwen, and that's only because she doesn't know what's going on."

"If you ask me," Stell said, picking up a stack of printouts and putting on her glasses, "she'd do well to wash the sleep out of her eyes and take a look around."

"She's under his spell," Stoner said.

"Hunh."

Rolling over on her stomach, Stoner found herself face-to-face with the bottom shelf of Stell's bookcase. She scanned the titles. The usual complement of mysteries — Crime Club edition — indigenous to all vacation spots whose business revolved around sunshine. A worn paperback copy of *The Virginian*. Michener's *Centennial* (back east it would be *Hawaii*, or Roberts' *Boon Island*). A couple of pre-World War II romances, probably considered very daring in their time but safe now for children's reading. Jack London, of course. "Where's the Zane Grey?"

"Up one."

The next shelf contained the lead-and-cactus thrillers. Also about three years' worth of outdated Readers' Digests. "I wouldn't expect you to have these," Stoner said.

Stell glanced up. "They belong to Phil. He was saving them in case he wanted to become a dentist."

"I want to do the right thing, Stell. But I don't know what that is."

"You could be wrong about him, you know."

"It's occurred to me." She brushed the hair out of her eyes. "But he's certainly going out of his way to make my life miserable."

"Jealousy?"

"Maybe." The branch of a pine stroked the windowpane. "Then why the lies about where he was born? Why the gaps in his history? That can't have anything to do with me."

Stell took off her glasses and looked at her. "You're a loving person, Stoner. When the time comes, you'll know what to do."

Stoner sighed and reached for the flies. "Well, right now I have to get through the next three days. The next two and a half days. After that ... If I bungle it, there won't *be* any after that."

"I don't know anyone I'd trust more," Stell said.

"Do you mean that?"

"With all my heart."

She stared down at the page. "You know, sometimes I have trouble believing this is real. I half expect we'll get to the end, the lights will come up, and the audience will leave the theater."

"Want to know a secret?" Stell said. "I still expect that to happen at the end of my life."

"Really?"

"Really. What worries me is the reviews."

There is a moment in each day when Nature holds her breath. The wind dies. The sun pauses in the sky. Dust settles. Birds fold their wings, and deer lie down in shadows. A moment of silence in memory, perhaps, of that instant long forgotten when a single bolt of lightning punctured a sea of gases, and two molecules were joined to begin the long, slow climb toward life.

Then an acorn drops. A fish breaks the surface of a pond. A moose snorts in the willows. The wind touches a leaf. And the day begins its inexorable descent into evening.

Stoner looked up. "Stell, do you believe in God."

The older woman laughed. "That old crank?"

"But you believe in something."

"I believe that everything that happens was meant to happen." She hopped down from the desk. "And that includes dinner."

***

By six-thirty, she had finished, sorted, packed the files in their cardboard boxes, ruined her eyes, developed a tension headache, and learned absolutely nothing. She dragged herself into the bar, huddled over a Manhattan, and passed the time wondering how they could make marischino cherries without Red Dye #2. And why they couldn't make red M&M's out of the same thing. M&M's just weren't the same any more. They might as well go the way of Collier's Magazine.

Smokey slid onto the stool next to her. "Well?"

"Nothing."

"I figured as much. You're eyeing that drink like it was the Golden Gate Bridge."

Stoner sighed heavily. "The files are in Stell's office. What should I do with them?"

"I'll take 'em. They'll heat the bunkhouse through November." He ordered a gin on the rocks.

"Gin?" Stoner stared at him.

"Time for serious drinking," he said. "And serious thinking." He tossed off the drink, ordered another, and swirled it around in his glass. "Fingerprints," he said at last.

"Fingerprints."

"Send them to Washington and see if he has a record."

"Terrific," Stoner said glumly. "What do I do, go up and ask him for them?"

Smokey shook his head slowly. "I don't know about you, McTavish. Are you sure you're cut out for this line of work?"

"I know I'm not."

"You have a drink with him, and lift his glass."

"And how do I do that?"

He waved away her question. "Brazen it out."

Brazen? *Brazen?* I've never brazened in my life. "I'll try," she said.

He patted her hand. "Good ... woman."

Gwen and Bryan entered the bar and took an empty table. Stoner slipped from the stool, drink in hand. "Wish me luck."

"Luck of the Irish."

"I'm not Irish."

She generated a smile and approached their table. "Good evening."

Bryan stood and offered her a chair.

"Did you get some rest today?" Gwen asked.

"Uh-huh."

"Let me freshen your drink," Bryan said. Before she could answer, he had snatched her glass and headed for the bar.

"How was Teton Village?"

"Hot and scenic." Gwen unbuttoned her cuffs and turned back her sleeves. It was absolutely, positively the most sensual act Stoner had ever seen. "May I tell you a secret, Stoner?" Gwen leaned dangerously close. "I hate Teton Village."

Stoner grinned.

"All that wall-to-wall carpeting," Gwen went on. "It's indecent."

"Maybe it comes in handy in the winter." Her mind caressed an image of night, snow, a deep, soft rug — and firelight flickering on a certain naked body. Pay *attention*, for Heaven's sake.

"... to Cheyenne tomorrow. Why don't we spend the day together?"

"In Cheyenne?"

"*Bryan's* going to Cheyenne. We could do some hiking, and go into Jackson for dinner. Have you seen the show at the Pink Garter?"

"Why's he going to Cheyenne?"

"I don't know," Gwen said. "Something about his father's estate."

Now what's he up to?

"Doesn't he want you to go with him?"

"He said he doesn't want to worry about me sitting around hot and bored."

Stoner was tempted. But with Bryan out of the way, it would be a perfect chance to check out Bannock Canyon.

"We could walk up to Emma Matilda Lake and spy on the moose."

Damn. There was nothing in the world she'd rather do. "I wish I could," she said. "I've been much too lazy. I really should work."

Gwen looked disappointed. "I understand."

No, you don't. You don't understand that I'd give anything to be with you...anything but your life. "My evening's free, though," she said. I can give myself that, at least.

"Great." Gwen's face lit up. "We can find the fanciest restaurant in town and disgrace ourselves."

Recklessly, Stoner touched her hand. "Let's. We'll create a scandal they'll hear about all the way to Park Square Station."

"And be the talk of the MBTA."

"To say nothing of the Cambridge Women's Center."

"Here we are," said Bryan, putting down their drinks. He flicked a glance at Stoner's hand touching Gwen's.

Choke on it, Bryan. She didn't move.

Gwen did. "Stoner has to work tomorrow," she said, taking her glass in both hands.

"That's too bad."

"But we can spend the evening together."

"Good." He turned to Stoner. "I won't be back until morning. I'm glad I can leave her in good hands."

Liars go to hell when they die, Bryan. Think it over. "This is certainly a strange honeymoon, you're on." She couldn't resist baiting him.

Bryan smiled his oily smile. "Is it? I really don't have much basis for comparision. Do you?"

"Only what I see in the sit.coms."

"Well," he said, "take good care of my girl."

Condescending ass. "I think," Stoner said cooly, "Gwen is capable of taking care of herself."

"But you wouldn't mind, would you?"

Gwen looked from one to the other. "What's going on?"

"Nothing," Stoner said quickly. "Bryan and I had our differences yesterday. We only need to cool down."

"Maybe I should leave you alone," Gwen said.

"Good idea," said Bryan. "What do you say, Stoner? Want to have it out here and now?"

"I think we've covered the essentials," Stoner muttered.

Gwen slammed her glass against the table top. "Look," she said angrily. "Cut it out, or tell me what this is about."

Stoner looked down at her hands. "Sorry."

"To tell you the truth, hon," Bryan said, "I'm jealous."

Stoner stared at him in disbelief.

"I've always envied women," he went on. "They have such an ... easy... time together."

Oh, barf.

"Being affectionate and all that." He looked like a starving spaniel.

"It's how you're brought up," Gwen told him soothingly. "You'll learn in time."

It's a good thing these glasses are cheap. I might have to wreck this place with my bare hands.

Bryan glanced at his watch. "We'd better get going. We're meeting some people for dinner at Triangle X." He motioned to the waiter and ordered another Manhattan. "Put it on my tab."

"Stoner?" Gwen said.

She looked up.

"Where should we meet tomorrow?"

"Your place, or hers?" Bryan said, and laughed.

"I might be late," Stoner said tightly. "I'll call you."

The waiter brought her drink. As they left the bar, Bryan ostentatiously patted his wife's bottom.

Stoner jumped up, stiff with rage. Listen, you horse's ass, I'm going to get you. I'll make you pay for every smug look, every snotty remark, every second of anxiety you've caused her or me. So you'd better keep a sharp eye out. Because I'm waiting. I'll wipe that superior look off your face if it takes the rest of my life.

Oh, for God's sake, you sound like a ten-year old. She sat back down and took a swallow of her drink. Relax. You can't afford to let him get to you. From now on, you're going to need every ounce of cool-headedness you can muster. Don't lose your head, and the final at-bat will be yours.

She looked down at the table. The glasses were gone, cleared by the waiter when he brought her drink. On a busing cart in the corner stood a small mountain of dishes, Bryan's glass buried among them. No way to find it now. Stoner dropped her head in her hands. This was *really* the last straw.

***

She ate alone and quickly, picked up a bus schedule, and went to her cabin to think. The early bus to Cheyenne left at 7:30. The Highlands Room opened at 7:00. That meant he would have breakfast in Jackson, not at Timberline. He would be gone until Wednesday. Not enough time for the Fingerprint Angle. She had just run out of options.

Okay, plans. Keep the anger up and the depression down. We're going with Bannock Canyon. And if it turns out to be a wrong guess, let's make it a *thorough* wrong guess. Map. Go over Bannock with a fine-toothed comb. Find every likely spot, and check it out. Try to think like Bryan Oxnard.

What if he doesn't do it right away? Prepare to live on nuts, berries, and trail bars. Dress warmly. Have Smokey get you a gun. You have to catch him in the act.

Warn Gwen. How? Be convincing. Make a logic-tight case. There *is* no logic-tight case. People don't do this sort of thing, remember? But she can be warned. Surely her instinct for self-preservation will make her cautious. If she has any.

Find that spot. The closer the lines are bunched together on a topographic map, the steeper the fall. That narrows it down. To about a dozen. What about the surrounding terrain? Places to hide. Smooth drops with nothing to break the fall. Added attractions, like sharp rocks. The maps are no help here, no substitutes for personal observation.

Stoner brushed back her hair and sighed. Time to make friends with a horse.   ***

It is one of the Great Mysteries of Human Nature: if you are convinced you can't possibly sleep, you will. Stoner changed into her pajamas and got in bed, ordering a wake-up call for seven. Before she turned out the light, she looked around the little cabin, with its varnished walls and rustic furniture and cheerful stone fireplace. Someday, when this was over, she would come back here. Maybe with Gwen. She was asleep almost as soon as her head hit the pillow.

The insistent ringing of the telephone awakened her. In darkness, she groped for the bedside lamp and glanced at her watch. Midnight. Apprehensively, she picked up the receiver. "Hello?"

"Stoner, dear," said Aunt Hermione brightly.

"Aunt Hermione, is everything all right?"

"Of course it is."

"Marylou, is she okay?"

Aunt Hermione laughed. "Such a worrier, Stoner. Marylou is fine. We had dinner together tonight — at a perfectly awful restaurant, incidentally. She thought it was going to be French, when it was actually French-Canadian. No comparision, believe me. Marylou was fit to be tied, of course."

"Aunt Hermione..."

"Edith has returned to Wellfleet. Max is back from his retreat, levitating among the zucchini I suppose. Edith was in a foul mood over it, but a marriage is a marriage regardless of the libraries. Though I've often wondered if marsh hay is really the mulch of choice, as so many claim. Thalassa has come out in favor of seaweed, you know."

"Aunt Hermione," Stoner interrupted, "did you really call me at two in the morning to discuss mulch?"

"I can just hear the caterwauling when the news hits the Horticultural Society. What did you say, dear?"

"It's two o'clock in the morning..."

"Is it really? Why are you calling at this hour? Is something wrong?"

"Aunt Hermione," Stoner wailed. "*You* called *me.*"

"So I did. I wonder why." There was a pause. Stoner could picture her aunt, gray hair a frizz around her face, powder blue bathrobe trailing the ground, holding the phone in one hand and trying to light a cigarette with the other. She heard the hiss of a flaming match, then a long exhale.

"I've had a dream," Aunt Hermione announced. "It has that prophetic feel to it. And you know how seldom I have prophetic dreams. Not like you. You have them all the time. Are you *positive* you're not psychic, Stoner?"

"I'm positive."

"And there was that odd incident of the cat and the Blue Runners. Somehow you *knew* he was going to eat them."

"I knew he was going to eat them because he'd been at them for months. Years. I'd chased him off a hundred..."

"But that very day. That very *day* you told me. 'Aunt Hermione,' you said. 'The cat is going to eat the Blue Runners.' What do you call that if not psychic?"

I give up. "Why did you call me, Aunt Hermione?"

"Because of the *dream*, of course."

"What about the dream?"

"Well, it wasn't very clear. But I definitely had the feeling you were in danger. It was a warning. Stoner, you must stay away from rocks."

Hysteria was imminent. "Aunt Hermione, there's nothing *but* rocks out here."

"Oh, dear, how unfortunate." She was silent for a moment. 'I don't suppose...,"

"If I were to avoid rocks," Stoner said, "I couldn't leave my room. I'd starve."

"They don't have room service?"

"No, they don't."

Aunt Hermione clucked her disapproval. "Well, there's nothing to be done, then. I don't suppose you could stay away from ... *unnecessary* rocks?"

Stoner smiled. "I'll certainly do that. Good night, Aunt Hermione."

"Oh, another thing, dear. I need a favor. How friendly are you with those Native Americans?"

"What Native Americans?"

"The ones you met out there."

"I haven't met any that I know of."

Aunt Hermione mused. "Odd. There were Native Americans in my dream. I'm sure of it."

"Perhaps I'll meet some."

"Well, if you do, I wanted you to ask them for something."

"Jewelry?" Stoner said. "There's very nice Native American jewelry in the stores here."

"No, not jewelry. Though I've always admired those squash blossom necklaces. But they're much too expensive."

"I can shop around." Why are we discussing the price of jewelry in the middle of the night?

"Never mind. What I was thinking of was recipes for herbal medicines. The sort of thing one finds around here these days is suspect, what with every Tom, Dick, and Harry inventing their own, as it were. But if one went right to the source..."

"I'll do my best. Any particular tribe?"

"Yes, the dream was very specific. Something about a tree."

"A tree?"

"A tropical tree."

"Wait a minute." She reached for her copy of *Bonney's Guide* and turned to the index. "Indians. Arapahoe..."

"Banyan!" said Aunt Hermione. "It was a Banyan tree."

At the same moment she saw the name: Bannock! Bannock Canyon ... Banyan. "Aunt Hermione..."

"Never mind, dear. I just remembered. They weren't very friendly." She hung up.

CHAPTER 10

D-Day dawned bright and clear. Not a cloud in the sky. There should be rain and thunder, stinking mists and terrible winds. Wizened crones croaking blood-chilling warnings in Satanic tongues, proferring the steaming entrails of slaughtered goats. Blind prophets in blood-smeared rags railing against the gods. Salamanders falling from the Heavens like living hailstones. Floods. Famines. Devastation.

Stoner stirred her coffee and nibbled moodily on a piece of toast. Horses. Nasty beasts. Nothing that big was intended to be sat upon by mortals. Look at the menacing way they switch their tails. Once they were as small as dogs, it's said. But that was before the Bomb. Ask Godzilla.

Dear God, I've tried to lead a good life. I've only broken the minor commandments — not honoring my father and mother, forgetting the Sabbath, taking your name in vain, coveting my neighbor's wife. But not his ox. Or his ass. I swear to you, God, I never for a minute coveted Bryan's ass. So why are you making me get up on a horse? You never made Job get up on a horse. You were too smart, weren't you? One mention of a horse and you can kiss *that* believer good-bye.

"Well," said Stell, sitting down with a cup of coffee. "I hear our quarry has gone to earth. Or at least to Cheyenne." She wrinkled her nose. "Is *that* your breakfast?"

Stoner nodded. Thought I'd make it easier to sort the remains. This is "Be Kind to Cornoners" week. "Have you seen Gwen?"

"She went back to bed. Said she was going to sleep all day ..."

Alone.

"... and do the town with you tonight."

"That's right."

"Better watch your step," Stell said. "Jackson can be rough after sundown."

"Really?"

"Some nights there's loud talking on the corners until midnight."

Stoner laughed. It occurred to her that she should tell Stell what she was planning to do. Maybe even ask her to come along. But there are things a woman has to do alone — be born, die, go into labor, and get on a horse for the first time.

"What are your plans for the day?" Stell asked.

"I don't know. Write some reports, take a walk." Make out my will.

"A little vacation from Bryan Oxnard?"

"I've done everything I can," Stoner said. "The ball's in his court. We were going to try to lift his fingerprints from a glass, but I lost it."

"For the love of Heaven, why didn't you tell me? There are a hundred ways I can get his fingerprints. Everything he touches passes through my hands. I can get you his fingerprints, his signature, even his blood type if he cut himself shaving."

"My God," Stoner exclaimed. "We never thought of that."

Stell sighed. "You and Flanagan. Don't do it the easy way if there's a hard way to do it."

"Could you get me those things? Smokey said to leave them in his cabin."

"I'll drop them off there for you. Ted and I are going into town this morning. Phil and his wife and kids are here for the week. Now that I know my chickens are safe, I guess it'll be all right to leave. You going to stay out of trouble?"

"I'm going to try."

Stell got up. "Well, that'll have to do. Where's Smokey sending that stuff?"

"Cheyenne, I think."

She shook her head. "Won't work. Quickest way's to send it by Greyhound, and they don't have another run until tonight. Well, it's worth a try. What's Bryan doing in Cheyenne, anyway?"

"Beats me. He said it was something about his father's estate. But of course we can't find any record that he's from around here."

"Maybe he changed his name," Stell said.

"To *Oxnard*?"

"You've got a point there. See you tomorrow."

***

Sorry, Spike, the Governor's call came too late. The execution's on.

She stuffed her jacket into her knapsack with a couple of trail bars, filled the canteen she had bought at Jenny Lake, and slipped the map into her back pocket. Slinging the knapsack over one shoulder, she closed the cabin door. There was a finality in the "click," a feeling of pushing off from the top of an amusement park slide. And no getting off until you reach the bottom.

***

Jake, the wrangler, was trying to coax a saddle onto a vicious-looking creature at least 20 feet tall. The man was short and stocky, with dark hair and weathered brown skin, and dressed in patched jeans and faded western shirt. His boots were scuffed and caked with manure. On his belt buckle was engraved something about saddle bronc riding and the 1965 Calgary Stampede. An unlit cigarette dangled from the corner of his thin-lipped mouth. If he wasn't the Last of the Old West, he was doing a darned good imitation.

Stoner cleared her throat. "I — uh — need a horse for the day."

Jake looked her up and down. He grunted non-committally. "Rode before?"

"Yes, preferably," Stoner said in alarm.

"Not the pony. You."

"Oh! Yes, yes, of course."

He gave her a dubious look, shuffled into the stable, and returned — in-

152

stantly, it seemed — with a great black brontosaurus of a beast, saddled and ready. "Here ya' are," Jake said. "This here's Blacky. He's real gentle."

"He?" she croaked. "A stallion?"

"Gelded." Jake pointed to the appropriate missing part.

"Oh."

He stood holding Blacky's bridle. Protocol would seem to dictate that she mount. "He's — quite large, isn't he?" she squeaked.

"Large? What kinda horse do you usually ride, lady?"

"Tennessee Walker," Stoner said, the only thing that came into her mind.

Jake patted the horse's neck. "Hell, Walker'd think this here pony was his colt. You gonna get on?"

Here goes. My first career faint. She swung up into the saddle. Wide, isn't he? Just slip your feet in the metal stirrups and make yourself comfortable, Mrs. Jones. Doctor will be in in a minute to have a look at that rash.

Is that the earth down there?

Look, fellows, I don't want to put a damper on your day or anything, but something tells me this mountain is alive.

Jake walked around the horse, adjusting the stirrups and talking. "These might be a bit longer'n what you're used to. You don't post a quarter horse."

You don't what? Which quarter? Hey, officer, you got it all wrong. Do I look like somebody who'd send a horse through the U.S. Mail?

"Ever rode Western before?"

Stoner shook her head.

"Ain't much different. Jist more to hold onto. There."

He gave the horse a slap on the rump. Don't *do* that! Blacky merely shuffled his feet and jangled his bridle.

"Don't hafta worry about Blacky," Jake said. "He's a good pony. Neck reins."

"What?"

"Neck reins."

Stoner looked around. "Where?"

Jake stared at her. "You sure you've rode before?"

"Of course. Back east we call them something else."

"Neck reins ain't what they wear. It's what they does."

"Oh."

"Say you wanta go right," Jake explained. "Steada pulling on the right rein, you let the left rein rest on his neck."

"How clever," Stoner said. "Whatever for?"

"Keeps you other hand free for your gun or rope or whatever."

"Fascinating."

Jake spat in the dust. "Yeah." He grabbed Blacky by the bridle and started off.

"Hey!" The earth lurched.

"Quarter horse is a workin' horse," Jake said, leading them around the corral. "He ain't gonna get it in for you like some of them eastern critters.

153

Do what you tell him, long as it makes sense."

This isn't so bad, after all. Jake slipped his hand from the bridle and walked away. He hooked one boot over the bottom rail of the fence and watched her.

We're on our own, Old Paint. She let the horse take her.

"Okay?" Jake yelled.

"Okay."

"Bring him over here."

He handed her a clipboard. "Sign."

"What is it?"

"Waiver of responsibility." He glanced at her from under thick brown eyebrows. "Routine."

Recalling a movie she had once seen, Stoner crooked her right leg around the saddle horn and took the paper. Hey, this was all right.

Jake copied her name into his register. "Destination?"

She hesitated. "Leigh Canyon."

"Nice country up there," he said, scribbling.

"Can I get back by nightfall?"

"Depends how far you go. Keep a good, steady pace, but don't tire your pony. When the sun hits Moran, turn around."

She thought for a moment, then gave in to temptation. "Maybe I should try Bannock instead. Is it shorter?"

Jake growled. "Stay outa that one. It's a killer. Path's bad."

THEN WHY ARE YOU LETTING BRYAN TAKE HER THERE? It's a conspiracy. You're all in it together. The Park Service, the Forest Service, Fish and Wildlife, Oskar Petzoldt, the Sheriff's Office, the Wilderness Society, and the Congress of the United States. Accessories, all accessories. WHY DOESN'T SOMEBODY DO SOMETHING?

"Sit still, lady. You're upsettin' the pony."

"Oh, sorry," she said. "I didn't mean to annoy him."

"You ain't annoyin' him. You're scarin' him half to death."

That makes two of us. She patted Blacky's neck.

"I'm goin' down to Laramie this afternoon. Funeral of an old pal. Nephew's takin' over for a couple days. Don't let him cheat you. Rate's ten bucks a day."

"All right."

"Now, this here pony ain't pretty, but he's trail-wise. If he don't wanta run, don't make him run. If he don't wanta stop, don't stop. If he takes off, hang on. We got bears around here."

Stoner nodded.

"You cartin' food and water in that thing?" He pointed to her knapsack.

"Yes."

"Topo map?"

She pulled it out and showed him.

"Okay, you're set. Pick up the trail here on the west side of Jenny. It'll take you past Cascade Canyon and on up to Leigh Lake. You'll see Indian Paintbrush Canyon first, then Leigh. Cascade's nice if you decide not to go as far as Leigh. Keep left in Cascade. About a mile in you'll see a trail that cuts southwest. That's Bannock. Pass it up." He gave the pony's nose a pat. "You keep out of trouble," he said to Blacky. "Anything happens to her, Stell'll have my tail."

154

"What?"

"Inexperienced rider goin' out alone. No rule against it, but the feelin' runs pretty high."

"Then why..."

He spat again. "You'd just run over to Jenny Lake stables. No tellin' what they'd give you. Besides," he said, turning away, "ain't nobody gonna call me no damn chauvinist pig." He went in the barn and slammed the tack room door.

Well, guess I'm not the only one on a working vacation. Galatea Thibault's been making the rounds. Clinging to the saddle horn, she started off down the trail.

Across Lupine Meadows, the way was flat and the going easy. She decided to risk trotting, and touched her feet to Blacky's sides. Immediately he picked up speed. Bumpy, but not impossible. Let's try third. His gait shifted, smoothed out into a lope. Not bad. Not bad at all. She lifted one hand from the saddle horn. Hey, Slim, the Oxnard gang just robbed the east-bound stage. Shot the driver and took off with that pretty little widow from over to Dodge. Saddle up and let's ride!

At the entrance to Cascade Canyon they started to climb. Blacky slowed to a puffing, grunting walk. Stoner leaned forward. Looks like they came this way, Slim. Fresh tracks. He's tricky, all right, but he can't outsmart Marshall McTavish. Keep the beer cold, Kitty. This time tomorrow that mangey polecat won't be good for nothin' but buzzard bait.

They passed Hidden Falls, and the little cave where she and Gwen had waited out the storm. It made her sad. Gwen should be here now, the two of them riding up into the mountains for a picnic. Someday, when this is over...

The little horse picked his way up the trail, around boulders and downed trees, pushing steadily upward. His hooves thudded on the packed earth. Cascade Creek sang. The sky was high and pale. They entered a stand of pine and spruce. Sunlight flashed through breaks in the trees. The forest was cool. She gave Blacky his head and dug the jacket from her knapsack, tossing it around her shoulders.

At the entrance to Bannock Canyon, the trail became ragged and climbed sharply through an alpine meadow. Blacky trudged dutifully forward, stopping now and then to nibble at tufts of bear grass. Owen and Teewinot loomed overhead. Their sharp crags sliced the sapphire heavens. Streams criss-crossed the meadow and poured glacial runoff into Cascade Creek. Another forest, thin and sparce. The sun crested Teewinot, stabbing the canyon with searing light and burning, dust-choked heat. Stoner shrugged out of her jacket and tied it to the saddle, hanging her knapsack from the horn. The trail was so steep now she had to lie along Blacky's neck to keep from pitching backward.

They emerged from the woods onto a sun-drenched section of trail. Stoner whistled softly and reined in her horse. On her left a wall of granite rose steeply, covered with rocks and pebbles. A scattering of dead trees clung to the slope. The mountain dropped away as sharply to her right, a delta of granite and limestone dotted with jagged boulders. The aftermath of an avalanche. It had spilled from the summit of Teewinot, scouring the mountainside to plunge at last over a precipice into a creek bed hundreds of feet below.

Stoner felt a tightening in her chest and stomach. She had found the place.

Stark, hostile, evil. Teewinot cast its shadow across the trail. Angular boulders, rocks like Stone Age knives. The stream was barely audible.

Blacky shifted uneasily on the narrow path. Saddle leather whimpered. Other than that, there was silence.

Too much silence.

She took a rock from the mountain wall and tossed it lightly down the slope. On impact it began to roll, picking up speed and dislodging bits of talus, triggering a miniature slide. The rocks tumbled over the edge and vanished, silently. The gravel on the slope came to rest with a low hiss.

Stoner felt tears spring to her eyes. There was no defense against this place. It demanded human sacrifice. One misstep on the narrow trail, and horse and rider would be gone in an instant. He was bringing her here. Here, to this place of stone and cold and death.

Blacky snorted and pricked up his ears. She heard it, too. Or felt it. Someone else was here.

Cautiously, she turned in the saddle. A flash of red, back in the woods. Too large for a bird.

Cover. Back to the woods? The trail was too narrow here for turning. Cross the slide, exposed and vulnerable? Get down, hug the mountainside, and lead the pony back to safety.

She kicked her right foot free of the stirrup and shifted her weight to dismount.

A sharp "pop". Blacky reared. She grabbed for the saddle horn but missed. The little horse reared again. His eyes were white with terror as she hit the ground sliding. She was on the slope.

Rocks bit like daggers into her shoulders and back, tearing her shirt, ripping her skin. Jesus! She gritted her teeth against the pain and dug her feet into the gravel. It slipped like ball bearings, carrying her closer to the edge. She grabbed at a passing boulder, and felt the skin strip from her hand. Choking back a sob, she kicked harder. Find a foothold. The avalanche was moving with her. Dust clogged her nose and mouth. Rocks clattered off the walls of the canyon below. On her back she was as helpless as a beetle. With a last desperate effort, she flung her weight uphill and rolled onto her stomach. Something crashed into her side, stopping her breath. Rocks and gravel poured over her legs. She had stopped moving. Just beyond the boulder that had caught her, sliding debris vanished over the edge of the cliff.

For a moment she lay still, listening to the silence, afraid even to breathe. Her body was on fire. Slowly, carefully, she lifted her head.

Something was moving, up on the trail. Something — red. She tried to make it out. Dust blinded her. She blinked rapidly to clear her eyes. It had disappeared.

"Hey!" she yelled. "Is anyone there?"

Her voice echoed back at her.

"Help me. Please."

Silence.

A gray-white boulder, studded with quartz, hung at the edge of the trail just above her. Through the dust and blazing sunlight it seemed to move.

Not seemed to. It *was* moving!

The boulder rocked slowly back and forth, then tipped forward, hung for an instant, and began to fall toward her. Another flash of red, on the trail behind it.

"Bryan!" She screamed.

Her voice was drowned in the crashing of rock.

The boulder lumbered toward her, picking up speed. Smaller rocks tumbled and danced before it.

I don't want to die.

It was almost on her now, blotting out the sun. Stones poured over her in waves.

I don't want to die.

There was a roaring in her ears, like the roar of a freight train.

She turned her face to the ground and waited.

The rock rumbled closer. The ground shook. Her heart pounded. Oh, God. Oh, God. Oh, God. The boulder against which she lay gave a sickening lurch. There was a sharp crack, and echoes like a string of Chinese firecrackers.

Silence.

Thought returned slowly. She was alive. Her boulder had held. She waited, knowing the numbness would pass, and pain and fear return. Please, Gwen, she prayed silently, if I don't get out of here, remember to trust your doubts.

He was still up there. She had to make him think the rock had hit her, make him think she was dead. Sooner or later, he would leave.

And then what? Move, and you might go over the cliff.

And if by some miracle you make it to the trail, how will you get back to Timberline? What if you can't walk? Blacky's gone, maybe dead. Or maybe he's run back to the corral. If he comes home riderless, someone will look for me.

In Leigh Canyon.

All right, one thing at a time. It was dark under the pile of stones. There was safety in darkness. Take shallow, even breaths. The movement of the smallest pebble could set it all in motion.

Carefully, she turned her attention to each part of her body. Nothing felt broken, but she couldn't be sure. Her legs and hips were bruised, but the stiff new denim jeans had been some protection. Her shirt was in shreds, her arms and hands and back scraped and bleeding. There was a burning sensation where the granite had torn at her. Push it back. Push it back while you still can. Dust filled her eyes. Her mouth was dry. Her chest ached with each breath.

Think of something else. Think of Gwen... No! Thinking of Gwen heightens physical awareness.

She created a clearing in her mind. A clearing in a cool, deep wood. Stone wall ringing the clearing. A stream trickles through the rocks and drips into a shallow pool. Examine the wall in intricate detail. Learn every nuance of hue and texture. Slowly, slowly. Moss. Smell the moss. Feel the dampness. Listen to the water, hear every tiny splash. There are ferns growing around the pool. Study them. Stroke their fronds. They are like feathers, rows of tiny feathers, each carrying a single spore.

Now the coolness is tangible. A bird unexpectedly drops down and drinks from the pool. Let go now. Let the scene carry itself. Consciousness drifts upward toward reality. Bring it back. Gently, easily, hold it softly as a bubble. Hands touching her now. Soothing, comforting, protecting. All inside now. Safe. Drifting.

She came alert hours later, sensing a change in the air. The shadow of Mt. Owen arrowed down the canyon. Listen for sounds of life. Use your body as a sensor. Mind blank, wait for impressions.

Nothing.

Carefully, she pushed at the rocks until her head was clear.

Night was coming on fast. Objects would lose their clarity soon, distances grow deceptive. The rock slide stretched above her, fragile and menacing. Behind... She knew what lay that way. She eased herself to her knees, and gasped aloud at the unexpected stabs of pain. Her head pounded. Don't faint.

Every movement must be perfectly planned. No more mistakes. No more reckless acts.

And now, ladies and gentlemen, in the center ring, Stoner McTavish will attempt the impossible. A death-defying act of self-preservation. No safety net. No second chance. And no rehearsal.

I can't.

You're quite the comedian, aren't you, Stoner? As if you have a choice.

I can stay here.

Okay. Do that. And on Thursday — if you're still alive on Thursday — you can watch Gwen die. You can congratulate Bryan when he wins.

It was just a thought.

She braced herself against the boulder and looked toward the trail. A few hundred yards to her left the slope levelled out and met the forest. If she could cross it diagonally...

Pressing close to the ground, she inched forward, away from safety. The rocks beneath her legs gave way. She was slipping toward the precipice.

Go limp. Dead weight.

She stopped moving. Carefully, she tested the ground. There was nothing under her left foot.

Dig your fingers into the ground, under the rocks. She searched gently through the rough stones. And touched solid earth. Packed hard. She scratched into it with her fingernails. Her heart rattled like a terrified bird's.

Don't think about that. Don't think of anything but the next few inches, and the next, and the next...

Dig. Anchor. Slide. Reach. Dig. Anchor. Slide. Reach. The light faded. The canyon filled with night. Dig. Anchor. Slide. Reach...

Her hand touched grass. Dead, brittle, but grass! She slid forward another few feet, and collapsed on the trail with a sob of exhaustion.

With darkness the cold came down hard. She began to shiver. Her body screamed as she stumbled to her feet and started down the trail. Something caught her eye at the side of the path. Her knapsack. The canteen had fallen out. No chance of finding it in this darkness. But the trail bars were inside. At least that was something.

How far had she come this morning? Five miles? Ten? The map was still in her pocket, but it was too dark to see it. As if it mattered.

The full moon had risen by the time she stumbled into Cascade Canyon. Cold light filtered through the trees and lay in phosphorescent pools on the trail. Her knees trembled. Her breath came in frosty sobs. She paused to rest and the chill caught up with her, creeping into her bones, stiffening her muscles. The knapsack dangled from her belt; her hands were too raw to carry it. She slipped it on as a buffer against the cold. The rough canvas chafed her torn back like a file. Fighting back tears, she shrugged it off.

Keep going. Keep going.

Robot-like she plodded ahead, the only sound the steady "thunk, thunk, thunk" of her footsteps. The toe of her boot caught on an exposed tree-root and sent her pitching forward. She threw herself against a rock, tearing the scabs from her hands. Warm blood trickled between her fingers.

Something darted at her from the shadows. Automatically, she dropped to the ground and huddled, terrified, against the earth.

The owl glided peacefully over the meadow.

She dragged herself to her feet and trudged on.

From Inspiration Point, Jackson Hole lay like a silver lake beneath the moon. She looked for lights, but there were none. Even the lodges were dark. Nothing was alive out there. And nobody was searching for her.

A wave of self-pity swept over her, and close behind it bubbled hysteria. Mustn't give in to that, or to the overwhelming desire to lie down on the ground and sleep. Or freeze. It must be close to forty degrees, maybe colder. And it would be even colder than that before morning.

Keep on truckin'.

The knapsack banged her leg, reminding her of the last trail bar. She dug it out. Her hands were trembling, so badly she could only fumble at the wrapper. Biting a corner of the cellophane, she tried to tear it open with her teeth. She was too weak. She choked back tears of frustration and dropped it back into her knapsack. No littering in the Park. Punishable by fine or expulsion from the premises. Maybe she could get Bryan on a charge of unauthorized disposal of household waste.

The thought of him gave her an unexpected surge of energy. Bryan Oxnard. Bryan Oxnard. Her feet kept time to it. She repeated it over and over like a mantra.

The moon had begun to slide behind the mountains when she limped up the steps to her cabin. The key. What if she had lost the key! She pulled it out, unlocked the door, and stumbled inside.

Snapping on the bedside lamp, Stoner sat on the edge of her bed and let her hands dangle between her knees. She ought to wash and change. She ought to do something about her wounds. She looked down at her hands. Blood, dirt, bits of torn flesh. They looked like hamburger. She didn't care. She was done in. Poor hands, I can't help you.

There was a soft knock at the door. She glanced around wildly. She couldn't let anyone see her like this.

"Stoner?"

Gwen. Not her. For God's sake, not her.

"Stoner, I can see your light. I know you're in there."

Go away. Please, go away.

"Please let me in, Stoner."

Have to get rid of her.

"I've been looking for you all evening. I was worried sick. I couldn't sleep. Let me in."

Hide in the bathroom. She started to get up. Her legs gave way beneath her. She needed help. "The door's not locked," she said hoarsely.

Gwen looked at her and gasped. "My God, Stoner." She knelt beside the bed and took one of Stoner's hands in hers.

"Horse threw me."

"I have to get you to a doctor."

"No!"

"You're all torn up."

"I'll be all right. Nothing's broken." She glanced up. "Please, I can't argue. I'm so tired." She forced herself to say it. "Please help me, Gwen."

Gwen brushed Stoner's hair to the side and touched her face tentatively. "Stay here," she said.

Stoner laughed humorlessly.

Gwen filled the ice bucket with warm, soapy water and brought it to her. "Soak your hands in there," she said. She went to build the fire.

Okay, one quick plunge. "Christ, that stings."

"It can't be helped. Want to come over here?"

She shook her head. The cabin filled with warmth, turning her muscles to jelly and melting away the protective numbness. It was going to be a bad night.

"You look like the losing side in a gang war," Gwen said as she wiped the dirt from Stoner's face with a fresh towel. "How are your hands doing?"

She held them up.

"Better. But I don't like that gravel."

"I'm not too crazy about it myself," Stoner said.

Gwen sat beside her and took her hand, touching the wounds with her towel. Stoner winced.

"I think," Gwen said, "the less either of us thinks about what's going

160

on here, the better off we'll be.''

Easy for you to say.

Gwen worked on her for a while. "Well, I guess you'll live. Anything else?''

"I ... cut my back a little.''

"Turn around. The light's bad.''

Stoner turned.

"Oh, Stoner.'' Her face was white. "It's ... awful.'' Gwen propped her elbows on her knees and folded her hands behind her head. "I think I'm going to be sick.''

"You can't,'' Stoner said desperately. "You have to help me.'' She was dangerously close to tears.

"We really should go...''

"Gwen, I'll die if I have to leave here. Please.''

Gwen sighed, and stood up. "Take off your shirt.''

"Now?''

"Now.''

"Here?''

"Here.'' Gwen smiled. "Stoner, I've seen women without shirts before. Close your eyes if you're embarrassed.''

She unbuttoned the shirt and started to pull it off. Her whole back caught fire.

"Okay,'' Gwen said. "I'll take it from here.'' She got fresh water and carefully soaked the strips of blood-encrusted cloth embedded in Stoner's skin.

Slowly, she peeled away the material. It hurt. Jesus, it hurt. Stoner squeezed her eyes shut and bit her lip.

"Tell me what happened,'' Gwen said.

Stoner shook her head.

"It'll take your mind off of this.''

"Told you. Horse threw me.''

"Well, it must have dragged you all the way from Montana. I thought you were afraid of horses.''

"I am.''

"Were you alone?''

"Yes!'' she screamed as a jolt of pain went through her.

"I'm sorry, Stoner. Is it very bad?''

"If I were a masochist,'' Stoner said, "I'd be in Heaven.''

Gwen sat back. "Oh, shit.''

"What's wrong?''

"You're all full of ... dirt and gravel. I'll have to clean it out.''

Stoner closed her eyes.

"How could falling off a horse do all this?''

I had help, friend. Wait until you see what your loving husband has planned for *you*.

"Do you have an antiseptic?''

"First aid kit in the suitcase,'' she mumbled.

Gwen rustled around. "Good God, is this thing left over from World War II?''

Stoner tried to turn and look. It was a mistake. "Aunt Hermione's," she said.

"Your so-called first aid kit consists of three band-aids, a bottle of iodine, and a pack of halazone tablets."

She started to shake inside. "I knew this was my lucky day."

"It's going to hurt," Gwen said.

"It already hurts."

"Well, it's going to get worse." Gwen hesitated. "Let me call Stell.She probably has something..."

"No." She hit the bed with her hand. "I don't want her here. I don't even want you here. Oh, God."

"You'd better lie down," Gwen said, helping her. "I'm sorry, Stoner. I didn't mean to nag. I'll try to make this fast."

It was like an army of fire ants crossing her back, stinging her over and over. Stoner ground her face into the pillow.

"I wish you'd scream," Gwen said.

She shook her head vehemently. If I start screaming now, I'll never stop. I'll just go on screaming, and screaming, and screaming for the rest of my life.

Gwen threw a ball of tissue on the floor angrily. It was soaked with iodine and blood and gravel. "I hate this," she said.

"Just get it over with." Another white-hot knife cut through her. She grabbed for the bedframe. Her hands smarted. It isn't fair. It isn't fair. She pressed herself into the bed, trying not to move, involuntarily pulling away. Make it stop. Please, God. I can't take any more.

Tell me what you want from me, God. I'll do anything. Anything. Anything to stop this.

Something was snapping inside her. Little popping sounds like the breaking of twigs. Ripping. Nerves exploding, swelling and bursting like bacon on a hot fire. "Jesus Christ!" she screamed.

Gwen put her hand on Stoner's head. "Only one more." She finished, gathered up the tissues silently, and dropped them into the wastebasket. She took the ice bucket into the bathroom, emptied it, and slammed it as hard as she could against the floor. "God damn it!" It shattered in a burst of plastic shards. "Excuse me," she said.

Stoner swung her legs around and sat up. "Think nothing of it."

Gwen took Stoner's pajamas from the peg and held them out to her. "Do you need any help?"

She shook her head.

"Then I'd better clean up in here. The way things are going, you'll step on it and get tetanus." Her voice was tight.

Stoner stood up shakily. "Gwen, are you mad at me?"

"No, idiot. But I'd rather not have hysterics right now, if it's all the same to you." She slammed the door and wrenched on the water.

Mechanically, Stoner changed her clothes, wincing as the soft cotton touched her back. Buttons. They danced in front of her eyes. The buttonholes ran from her. It was her hands. Shaking. Concentrate.

"Here," Gwen said. "Let me."

"I can..." She was shaking harder. Her teeth were chattering.

Gwen rested her hand along Stoner's cheek. "You're used to going it alone, aren't you, Stoner?"

The words went through her like an arrow.

Everything fell apart.

"I can't do it," she said, and burst into tears.

Gwen wrapped her arms around her carefully, cradling Stoner's head against her shoulder.

She cried for all of it: for Aunt Hermione's squash blossom necklace, for Scruffy, who couldn't understand why she had to leave; for the cat she hadn't even liked very much; for Stell and Smokey; for Marylou, who had to make a joke of life; for Gwen, and what was to come...

And then she cried for herself, because she was tired and in pain and afraid ... not just now but a little afraid, all the time, somewhere deep inside. Because she couldn't keep going and had to. Because she went to bed alone, and got up alone, and made her own appointments with dentists and doctors. Because her mother didn't like her and her father didn't care. For lovers who had left. For promises she couldn't keep. For friendships that had died. For the shy, awkward child she had been and still was. Because living was too hard. Because she couldn't do it anymore.

"Stoner," Gwen said, and held her tight and stroked her hair, and made soft, comforting sounds.

She burrowed deep into Gwen's shoulder. Just for a little while. Please, just hold me for a little while.

Gwen rested her head against the back of Stoner's neck.

"I'm sorry," Stoner mumbled.

"Don't be an ass."

"I ruined our evening."

"I don't care how much you hurt," Gwen said softly. "If you say anything like that again, I'll hit you."

She had cried herself out. She sat up and fumbled for a tissue. Gwen handed her one. She glanced up.

Gwen was looking at her with an odd, inward expression. Her face was wet.

"You, too?" Stoner asked.

"Me, too."

"Why?"

"Because of you." She pulled back the covers. "Get in bed now."

Painfully, Stoner crawled between the sheets and lay back.

"Do you have extra pajamas?" Gwen asked.

Stoner indicated her suitcase. "Are you staying?"

"Yes."

"You don't have to."

"Yes, I have to." She went into the bathroom and changed her clothes, built up the fire, and turned out the lamp. Firelight flickered in the room. "Stoner," she said, sitting beside her and stroking her hand, "when we get home... If you ever need me, any time you need me... You know."

"Thank you." Sleep was coming on fast. "Gwen, I have to tell you about..." Bryan.

"Tomorrow," Gwen said. She tucked the covers lightly around her, then bent down and kissed the top of Stoner's head. "We'll talk tomorrow."

"But I have to..." She began to drift off.

Gwen got into bed. "Goodnight, Stoner."

CHAPTER 11

There was someone in her room. Someone moving around, quietly, stealthily. What do I do now? Pretend to be asleep and hope they'll sneak out again? Jump up and surprise them in the act? Slowly, she opened her eyes.

Gwen had one foot up on the chair, tying her shoe. Her back was toward her.

"What are you doing here?" Stoner asked, and sat up. Her whole body was one solid ache. "Ow," she said. She remembered.

Gwen turned toward her, laughing. "Jerk."

She was buttoning her blouse. Stoner caught a glimpse of her right breast. Round, firm, the color and texture of cream. It was the most beautiful breast Stoner had ever seen.

It's a good thing I'm half dead and have scruples.

A touch of pink brushed Gwen's cheeks.

"Gwen, are you blushing?"

"Of course I'm blushing."

"Why?"

"You'd blush, too, if I'd said to you what you just said to me."

Stoner buried her face in her hands. "I didn't say it out loud. I didn't."

"You certainly did."

"Oh, my God, I'm humiliated. I can never speak to you again. I'll have to move out of Boston..."

Gwen laughed. "Well, you're not going anywhere today." She came over to the bed. "As long as you're sitting up, let me see your back."

She braced Stoner with one arm and raised her pajama top. "Not bad," she said, "considering the working conditions."

"Gwen, I'm so sorry I said..."

"Oh, be quiet," Gwen said, and traced Stoner's shoulders with her fingertips. "It was the nicest thing anyone ever said to me."

She felt her body contract into a deep, warm, visceral, and very pleasant knot. "Don't make fun of me, Gwen."

"I am not making fun of you," Gwen said seriously. "It's very nice to be liked by someone I like. Especially someone who appreciates women."

Just hang me from a radio tower and use me for a beacon. "Would it be okay with you," Stoner said in a tiny voice, "if we forget this happened and start the day over?"

"After breakfast." She ran her hands through her hair and tossed a couple of logs on the dying fire. "I won't be a minute."

"Wait. There's something I have to tell you."

"You can tell me," Gwen said firmly, "after I have coffee." She closed the door quietly behind her and trotted down the path.

How do you tell the woman you love that the man she loves is planning to kill her?

If she believes you, you break her heart.

If she doesn't believe you, you can never be friends again.

Either way, you lose. She loses.

But you have to do it.

Stoner sighed. Well, you certainly can't do it lying in bed in your pajamas, with dirty hair. Carefully, she pushed back the covers and stood up.

Showering and dressing held all the joys of a Medieval torture chamber. Her legs were bruised. Her joints burned with every movement. The shower was like needles against her skin. The palms of her hands were dry and stiff, and when she moved them tiny cracks tore open and bled.

She dressed as well as she could, and stumbled back to her bed. If she could only lie here and heal... But that was impossible. She had to think. She had to plan. She had to act.

Act? Take action? And how do you do that when your body is covered with invisible monsters that bite and claw and beat you with red-hot hammers? How do you plan when your thoughts can't reach beyond the surface of your skin?

Footsteps pounded on the cabin steps. The door banged open. Stoner looked up.

"Here's your breakfast," Gwen said brusquely. She put the tray down on the bed.

"Aren't you having any?"

"No." Her lips were thin, her face pale. She avoided Stoner's eyes.

"Is something wrong?"

"Bryan's back. He got a ride from Cheyenne early this morning."

Oh, God, now what had he done to her? "Gwen." She reached toward her. "What's happened?"

"Don't touch me?" Gwen barked.

She felt herself go dead. "Have I done something?"

"You've done plenty." Gwen's eyes flashed fire. "He told me all of it."

"All of ... "

"You're working for my grandmother. She sent you here to break us up." She laughed unpleasantly. "All this time you've pretended to be my friend, and it's all been a lie."

"No, Gwen. You don't understand."

Gwen's eyes bored into hers. "I know about Elk Island. He showed me your letter to Marylou." Tears spilled down her face.

It was all a set-up. The invitation. The fight with Gwen. He watched me leave the cabin... "Listen to me!"

"No! I was stupid enough to trust you once. But I'm not stupid enough to be hurt again. Damn you, Sto..." Her voice broke. She turned and ran.

Helpless, Stoner watched her go. There was an aching hollowness in her chest. Mechanically, she reached for the coffee and took a sip. It was cold.

Stoner hung her head. She had never felt so alone in her life.

***

Well, what are you going to do? Sit here and listen to your hair dry?

I don't know.

You have one card left. Play it.

It's the two of clubs, and spades are trump.

She got up slowly and left the cabin, heading for the lodge. Stell met her in the lobby. "Come into my office."

"I can't. I have to find Gwen."

"She's in the dining room and they've just ordered. You have plenty of time." She crossed her arms and barred the way. "Stoner," she said firmly. "You are coming with me."

Stell closed the office door and pointed to the footstool. "Sit there. I have something for those scratches."

Stoner looked at her. "Who told you?"

"Nobody had to tell me. You're walking like something out of 'Revenge of the Mummy.' Pull up your shirt."

Why not? It's all I do any more.

"Actually," Stell said, spreading a cool soft cream on her back," Gwen told me. What's the big idea, kid?"

"When did you see her?"

"Just now."

"How did she look?"

"Like Medea on a bad day. Are you going to answer my question?"

Stoner twisted around and looked up at her. "What did she say?"

"She said you'd fallen off a horse, that you'd gotten badly cut up, and she couldn't do anything for you. I asked you what was the big idea."

She does care. At least enough to tell Stell.

"I asked you, Stoner."

"That's about the size of it, Stell. I fell off a horse."

"Where?"

"Bannock Canyon."

"Why didn't you come to me?"

"I couldn't. It was late."

"Late!"

"The horse ran away," Stoner said apologetically. "I had to walk home. It was after midnight..."

"I don't care what time it was. You should have called me."

"I'm sorry. I just couldn't."

"I could wring your neck, Stoner. Where did you get the horse?"

She hesitated. "From ... your stables."

"Jake?"

Stoner nodded.

"I'll kill him!" Stell bellowed. "I'll murder him with my bare hands."

"I'd have gotten it somewhere else. He knew that."

"I suppose you would," Stell grumped. "Hands."

Stoner held them out. "You might as well know all of it," she said. "Bryan did this. He tricked me into going up there. He scared the horse. And then he tried to kill me."

Stell glanced at her "How'd you get away?"

"Dumb luck."

"Well," Stell said, wrapping a bandage around her hand, "what do you do now?"

"Tell her the truth."

"Where do you think that'll get you?" She gestured at Stoner's other hand.

167

Stoner held it out. "I don't know. It's all I can do. Have you heard anything about the fingerprints?"

"John called this morning. They told him it'd take a week. Does Oxnard know what you're after?"

"No. He thinks I want to break them up."

"Riles easily, doesn't he?" She put away the first aid kit and took Stoner's wrists in her hands. "Look at me, Little Bear."

Stoner looked up.

"I want you to promise me that you'll be very, very careful."

"I'll be careful." Stell, I think you're wonderful.

"Very careful."

"Very careful." She stood up.

"All right. Now, get out of here..." She swatted her on the rear end "...before I do something we'll both be sorry for."

"Stell, can I take you home to meet my friends?"

"No. If they're all like you, I'd be out of my mind in a week."

***

She paused at the entrance to the dining room and took a deep breath. Well, here goes nothing.

She marched up to Gwen and Bryan's table.

"I want to talk to you, Gwen."

Gwen glanced at Stoner's hands and looked away.

"Have a little accident?" Bryan asked, grinning.

She ignored him. "Gwen?"

"Go away," Gwen said softly.

"Not until you listen to what I have to say."

Bryan half rose. "My wife asked you to leave."

"Your wife," Stoner said, turning on him, "can speak for herself."

Gwen was silent.

"Five minutes," Stoner said. "Just five minutes. Outside."

"Don't let her bully you," Bryan said to Gwen. "She wouldn't dare cause any more trouble."

Stoner looked him in the eye. "I don't have a lot to lose," she said coldly, "do I?"

"Leave us alone," Gwen said.

"I'm not talking to 'us'. I'm talking to you." She waited a moment. "Are you coming? Or should I make a scene?"

"I'm not coming."

Stoner picked up a bread-and-butter plate and hurled it to the floor. It smashed.

"For God's sake," Gwen whispered. "People are looking."

"Come outside with me," Stoner said in a low voice, "or I'll wreck this place piece by piece." She picked up a glass.

"That's enough," Bryan snapped.

"Stuff it, Bryan," Stoner shouted.

"All right, all right." Gwen put her napkin down and got up.

168

"Honey..." Bryan said

Stoner turned on him. "Go play with yourself, *Honey*." She followed Gwen out to the campfire circle.

"What do you want now?" Gwen said furiously.

"Sit down."

"I'd rather stand, if it's all the same to you."

"It's not the same to me," Stoner barked. "Sit *down*."

Gwen sat on the top row of seats and glared at the mountains.

Forgive me, Gwen. Forgive me for this. She ran her hand through her hair. "I'm sorry I had to do that."

Gwen stared straight ahead.

"There's something more I have to tell you."

"More lies?"

"Gwen, I haven't lied to you."

Gwen looked at her sharply. "You haven't done anything but lie since the minute I met you."

"I never lied about how I feel about you."

Gwen looked down at the ground.

How the hell do I start? "Gwen, I don't know how to say this..."

"Well," Gwen said, "don't ask me for help."

That stung. Stoner bit her lip. "Thank you for telling Stell..."

"I'd have done the same for anyone."

Stoner swallowed and dropped onto the bench beside her. "You really know how to hurt, don't you?"

"We're evenly matched."

"Gwen, I never wanted to hurt you." She started to reach toward her, but checked herself.

"Then you shouldn't have taken ... 'the assignment'." Her voice was bitter.

Don't take it away. Please, Gwen, don't take it all away.

Gwen turned and glared at her. "Why did you sneak around behind my back? Why did you lie to me?"

"There wasn't any other way."

"Try honesty."

"Your grandmother tried that. It didn't work."

"My grandmother thinks I'm a child."

"Do you mean," Stoner said, "if I had told you what I think, you would have listened?"

"I don't know."

Stoner stared at her. "You have ... doubts?"

"I didn't say that. I said I don't know." She got up. "This isn't getting us anywhere. I'm leaving."

Stoner jumped up and grabbed her, pushing her back to her seat and holding her there. "Listen to me. This isn't about how I *feel* about Bryan. I'm talking about murder."

"What?"

"You husband is planning to kill you."

"This is absurd." She twisted in Stoner's hands.

"On the camping trip. There's a place in Bannock Canyon. Just beyond

169

a spruce forest. The trail narrows, at the edge of an old avalanche. He's going to push you over and claim it was an accident."

"You don't know what you're talking about." She tried to pull away. Stoner tightened her grip. "I know what I'm talking about. He tried to do it to me."

"No!"

"Remember how he acted when you wanted to cancel the trip? He's going to kill you, Gwen."

"Let go of me!" Her face began to crack.

"Bryan's crazy, Gwen. He's two different people. I've *seen* it."

Gwen shook her head vehemently from side to side. Her tears exploded like sparklers in the sunlight. "Stop It, Stoner. Please stop it."

"He wants your money. That's why he married you."

"God damn you!"

"I don't want anything to happen to you."

"Bryan loves me."

Frustrated and angry, Stoner shook her. "He tried to kill me. I saw him. He was wearing that red..."

Gwen froze in her hands. Her eyes went dull.

Oh, God, what have I done? Stoner clenched her teeth. "You wanted the truth," she said softly. "There it is." Let me hold you, Gwen. Let me hold you until this all goes away.

Gwen slapped her.

Stunned, Stoner put her hand to her face.

They stared at each other.

Gwen scrambled to her feet. "I hate you, Stoner."

"Don't go on that camping trip."

Gwen spun around. Angry tears poured down her face. "Get out of my life."

"At least take a gun. Gwen, I love you."

"Will you go to hell?" Gwen screamed, and ran into the lodge.

Stoner rubbed her face where Gwen had hit her. Well, at least she knew what to do now.

Stell was at the reservation desk. "How did it go?"

"It didn't."

"Are you feverish?"

"No, why?"

"Your face is red."

"She hit me," Stoner said.

Stell threw her pencil down. "I know you love her, Stoner, but that woman is causing a lot of trouble for a lot of people."

"She's confused."

"Fucked up," Stell snapped. "Up, down, and sideways."

Out of the corner of her eye she saw Gwen and Bryan leaving the dining room. "Stell," she said urgently, "make it look as if I'm checking out."

"Now what?"

"I don't have time to explain."

Gwen spotted her and ran for the stairs. Bryan hung back.

"It's the last thing I'll ask," Stoner pleaded.

Stell got out her account book, put on her glasses, and pretended to read. "Where are you going?" she asked under her breath.

"The Ranger Station."

"When will you be back?"

"Tomorrow. Look, this has to be convincing. See if you can keep him here until I return the key."

Bryan was lingering in the lobby. He pretended to leaf through a magazine.

"Here's the damage," Stell said loudly.

"Fine. I'll bring a check when I drop off the key."

"Sorry you have to cut your vacation short."

"I'm needed at home."

Bryan sauntered over to her. "Leaving?" he asked.

"Yes."

"Get what you came for?"

"Not exactly." She moved toward the door.

Bryan leaned on the door jamb, blocking her way. "I heard about your accident. That was rotten luck, Stoner."

It certainly was. For you. "Bad planning on my part," she said.

"Where did it happen?"

Oh, God, what do I do now? "Cascade Canyon ... I think."

"You think?"

"I'm ... not sure." Inspiration struck. "Look." She led him to the maps tacked on the wall of the lobby. "I started out here," she said, tracing the route with her finger. "And turned ... oh. I shouldn't have turned. It was Bannock Canyon, then."

"A little confused?" he asked condescendingly.

He doesn't believe it. "It must have been Bannock. That would explain why I didn't see any hikers, Well, I *thought* I saw someone, but when I called for help they disappeared. Actually, they couldn't have disappeared because they weren't there at all." This wasn't working. "I guess I was ... hysterical."

Bryan smiled. "You're not a very good liar, Stoner."

She froze. "What?"

"You intended to go up Bannock Canyon all along. Didn't you?"

"No, I really didn't care where..."

"You went up there to see where Gwen and I are going camping."

"No, I..." If he guesses I know, it's all over. He'll wait until it's safe before he does it. Maybe on the trip home. Maybe in Boston. I can't follow them around for the rest of my life.

Bryan laughed. "There's nothing more ridiculous than a love-sick Bull-dyke."

"What the hell do you mean by that?"

"You wanted to see what it would be like so you could think about it, didn't you? You wanted to imagine her up there with me, but instead of me it would be you."

She couldn't believe her ears. He really thought she had done all of this because she wanted Gwen for herself. As if they were two German Shepherds fighting over a bitch in heat. He had no idea she suspected...

Don't smile. Keep the eyes demurely cast down. Floorward. Now, shuffle the feet a little. That's right. Project extreme discomfort. Humiliation. "I have to leave," she murmured. "My plane..."

Bryan put his arms on either side of her head, trapping her. "What's the matter, Stoner? Embarrassed? You should be."

"If you don't mind..." She pretended to duck under his arm. His hand shot out and grabbed her by the arm.

"When did it happen? When you met her? In Jackson? At Yellowstone? When did your little 'assignment' turn into a romantic interlude? Or was it before you ever took the job? Was it when you saw her picture?"

She didn't have to fake the blush that flowed into her face. Or the nervous tremble around her lips.

He grinned. "So that was it. Love at first sight. Well, don't feel too bad. You aren't the first woman in history to make a fool of herself."

"I have to leave," she said evenly.

"You know, Stoner, I'll miss you." He gave her arm a little shake. "I've enjoyed toying with you. In your own stupid way, you're a lot more fun than my wife."

She looked up at him, ready to kill. "Let me go, Bryan."

He tossed her aside as if she were an annoying gnat. "Have a nice trip. And next time, stick to your own kind, queer."

Stoner turned on her heel and stalked off. We'll finish this tomorrow, Bryan. In Bannock Canyon.

***

She ran to her cabin, stuffed her clothes into her suitcase, and tore back to the parking lot. Tossing the suitcase into the trunk of her car, she looked up. Bryan stood outlined in a second-story window, openly watching. She stared back for a second, and went into the lobby.

"Sorry," Stell said. "I tried hold him."

"It's okay. He saw."

"Will you please tell me what's up?"

"I'll spend tonight at Smokey's. First thing tomorrow we'll round up some help and catch him in the act."

Stell frowned. "You still think he'll go through with it? After all this?"

"He'll go through with it." She laughed, and felt giddy, euphoric, and maybe a little reckless. "He's put two and two together, and come up with seventeen."

"I don't know, Stoner. Why don't you let Smokey take it from here?"

"I wouldn't miss this for the world." She was as light as a feather as she ran back to her car.

***

The sky was high, clear, and endless as she drove toward Blacktail Ponds. Rolling down the windows, she let the hot wind roar through the car. She smelled the dust and the sage. She sang.

The speedometer registered 70. With an effort, she slowed to 55, then watched it creep up again. I'm going to get him. I'm going to get him.

172

This is dangerous, said the small voice of reason. You must be careful. Everything is at stake.

Tomorrow. She could picture the scene. Bryan, riding along as arrogant and unconcerned as a prince. Biding his time. Oh, he could afford to bide his time now. There was nothing in his way, nothing to stop him. Whistling, he approaches the slide. Now. The moment is now. It excites him sexually, a tingling in his loins. He makes his move.

And then, in one magnificent chorus of green, from behind every rock and tree — the entire Forest Service.

His face. Bewilderment. Disbelief. Fear giving way to humiliation. He pales. His smile of triumph fades. His features melt into a scowl of defeat.

Oh, it was going to be a wonderful day.

The Moose entrance station sprang up ahead. Stoner slammed on the brakes, screeched to a crawl. Concentrating, she crept through the exit and turned left onto Rockefeller Highway. She pushed the pedal to the floor.

At times it is hard to tell the difference between joy and fear.

I'm going to get him. I'm going to get him.

She was grinding her teeth.

Blacktail Ponds overlook shot by on her left. She jerked to a stop, backed up, and spun the wheel. The car came to rest in a shower of dust and gravel.

She locked the door and glanced down into the backwater of the Snake. The pond was still and hard as a mirror. In it the Tetons hung inverted and probed the river bottom. Something grabbed her stomach and twisted it hard. Her knees gave way. Stoner dropped to the guard rail and gasped for breath. She was very, very frightened.

Tomorrow yawned like an open door. Terror lurked behind it. She looked at the future. The future looked back. She wanted to run. She couldn't move. The minutes slipped away, each one pushing her closer to tomorrow.

If I stay where I am, and breathe very carefully, maybe I can stop time. Maybe this moment, this precise moment will last forever.

It slid by her, a wisp of breeze, and became the past.

And then she thought of the one thing she had been trying not to think of all along. Gwen.

Some words, once spoken, cling to you with razor-sharp teeth. And no matter how hard you try to shove them away, no matter how fast you run, you can't outrun the pain. "I'd have done the same for anyone."

Stoner began to cry.

There was no one there to comfort her this time.

Instead there was a Winnebago full of tourists.

She got to her feet and stumbled down the path to the movie set.

"McTavish!" Smokey grinned and waved.

Sanity returned. "Do you have anything to drink?" she asked.

"Only what's in the canteen." He handed it to her.

It turned out to be Irish whisky. It burned her throat in a satisfying way.

Smokey took her chin in his hand and turned her face toward him. "You

173

look like an abortion," he said.

"I need help."

"What happened to you?"

"I had a run-in with Bryan." She couldn't go through it all again. "Look, I'm in a hurry. Can I stay in your cabin tonight?"

"We'll find an empty bunk. What kind of trouble are you in, McTavish?"

"He's going to try it tomorrow. In Bannock Canyon. I know the exact spot. Can you get some friends to help us surround it?"

Smokey puffed out his chest. "I can come up with enough Rangers to surround the whole damn canyon."

"With guns?"

"With telescopic sights." He grinned. "Ah, McTavish, you've given a whole new meaning to the Forest Service." He offered her the canteen.

Stoner shook her head. "What about your job? The movie?"

"We'll sell 'em the rights to the story."

"I have a lot to do. I'll explain the whole plan tonight."

Taking a pull at his canteen, he waved her off.

***

Jake's nephew and his pals lounged on the grass by the corral, bored and adolescent. Stoner introduced herself. "I took a horse out yesterday. The black one. I fell off and he disappeared. Did he come back?"

One of the hands roused himself with an aggrieved expression. "Blacky?"

Stoner nodded.

"Hey, Jim, Blacky's here, ain't he?"

Jim looked her up and down. "Yeah."

"May I see him?"

Greatly burdened by life, Jim got up and led her to the stable. "Figure you owe us about twenty bucks, seein' you didn't bring him in yourself."

"Of course." She paid him. The registration book lay open on the table.

"Bill!" Jim hollared into the stable. "Get the black." He turned to her. "You want him again today?"

"I just want to be sure he's okay." She needed a few minutes alone with that book. "Uh ... I lost my jacket. It was tied to the saddle. Could you see if it's around somewhere?"

Jim grunted and slouched into the tack room. Quickly, she turned the page to Thursday. It was blank, but something had been erased. Puzzled, she flipped back to Wednesday. There it was. "Oxnard. Two riding, two pack. Bannock Canyon. 11:30."

Stoner held her breath. He was planning to do it today. She checked her watch. 11:00. Get out of here, fast.

"You're outa luck," Jim drawled. "Came home clean."

There was one thing she had to know. Bill was leading out the horse. She ran her hands over its body, and found what she had been looking for. On Blacky's left flank, a lump about the size of a dime. She pushed the hair

174

back to reveal a red swelling. "What would cause this?"

Bill peered at the spot. "Horsefly, maybe. Ain't serious."

"How about an air rifle?" she asked. "I thought I heard something, right before he threw me. There were children playing around. Maybe one of them..."

"Maybe. Ain't supposed to have guns in the Park, but sometimes they do."

"Thanks." She slipped Jim five dollars. "Sorry to trouble you."

All right, now what? Bryan's change of plans eliminated guns and Smokey's friends. And she was only half an hour ahead of him. Give me a break. No gun, no help, no time. All she had left were her wits, determination, and a body that was ready for the trash heap.

Hide the car. Find a horse. She moaned aloud at the thought of riding again. Yesterday's adventure had done nothing to enhance her love of the sport. She turned into the drive to the Rangers' cabins. First one on the left, she recalled. The parking area was at the back, hidden from the road. Score one for our side. From the corral she heard a whinney. Smokey's horse. Score two. She ran into the cabin, dropped her suitcase, found pencil and paper, and scribbled a note.

"Flanagan. They're going today. I'm taking your horse. Make a Novena. McTavish."

Bridles and saddles hung neatly in their places in the barn. How the hell do you dress a horse? Which goes around what? Hearing footsteps behind her, Stoner turned guiltily. A woman approached, in the familiar green uniform. Score three.

"Hi," Stoner said cheerily. "I'm a friend of Smokey Flanagan. He said I could borrow his horse."

"Yeah?" The woman had long black hair and eyes like steel marbles. She chewed her gum and looked Stoner over. Slowly.

"I ... don't know which saddle is his. Could you ...?"

"Name?"

"Stoner. Stoner McTavish."

The woman looked at her, expressionless.

"I was named for Lucy B. Stone."

"Yeah?"

"It was my aunt's idea." Somehow this wasn't the way the conversation was supposed to go.

"Where from?"

"My aunt?"

"You."

"Oh. Timberline Lodge. We eat together. Smokey and I. Often."

"Otherwise."

"Otherwise?"

The woman gave a single chew. "Where from otherwise?"

"Boston."

Silence.

"That's in Massachusetts."

"So I heard." She seemed to arrive, reluctantly, at a decision. "Jessie Eisenberg." She shook Stoner's hand, gripping it hard. Stoner winced.

175

"Gonna ride with hands like that?"

Stoner brushed her hair aside nervously. "I thought I could. What with the neck reins and all."

Jessie pointed her chin toward Stoner's hands. "How'd you get that?"

"I had an accident."

"Can't lift much."

"No," Stoner said. "Not much at all."

Jessie hauled the saddle and bridle from the wall and strolled to the corral.

Here we go again, Stoner thought. She fought down panic and swung into the saddle, muscles screaming. The horse shifted uneasily. Stoner grabbed for the saddle horn.

"Been on a horse before?" the woman asked.

"On and off."

"Don't pull his head back so far."

"Thanks," Stoner said. "If you see Smokey, tell him I left a note in the cabin."

"Okay."

"Is there a shortcut to Bannock Canyon?"

Jessie eyed her. "Stay out of there. It's wicked."

Stoner sighed. "A killer. I know. I'm supposed to meet someone there. I'm late."

"Map?"

She dragged the battered topographic map from her pocket.

"Okay," Jessie said. "Out of here take Lupine Meadow. There's a trail around Moose Lake. At the north end of the lake cut northwest up the side of Teewinot. Steep and rough, but it'll do." She chewed her gum ruminatively. "He knows where you're going?"

"Yes."

Jessie checked her watch. "'Bout four o'clock I'll come looking."

Stoner looked down. "Thank you," she said, touched.

"Don't look very tough," the woman said.

Stoner blushed.

"Pony's name's Pinto. Thinks highly of you."

Apparently they had banned personal pronouns in Wyoming. "Pinto?"

"Flanagan."

"Thank you. I think highly of him, too.'

Jessie shrugged. "He's okay. For a man."

Stoner grabbed the saddle horn, dug her heels into the horse's side, and set off at a gallop. A few hundred yards down the trail, the significance of Jessie's last remark struck her. Well, well.

She tied the pony to a tree out of sight of the trail and stretched out behind a rock to wait. The sun was warm. A fly buzzed overhead. Below her the narrow path picked its way across the avalanche. Stoner shuddered.

Don't think about it.

Be ready.

A Canada jay called in the woods, voicing a private complaint. Somewhere on the side of Teewinot a rock dislodged itself and tumbled down the mountain. The sun climbed higher. A wisp of cloud formed and dissolved and formed again, rehearsing a variety of shapes. From far below she could make out the impatient gurgle of the creek. Pinto munched rhythmically on tufts of bear grass.

Suddenly he stopped, tested the air, and snorted. Stoner strained her ears, but no sound came to her. Pinto jangled his bridle and pawed the earth. His ears flicked. He quivered.

The grunting of horses, coming up the trail.

Stoner tensed.

A red-shirted rider emerged from the forest, followed by another in pale plaid. Two horses piled high with gear plodded behind. Bryan and Gwen. They approached the slide with excruciating slowness.

What if they ride on through?

It has to be here.

If he doesn't do it here...

They had reached the center of the avalanche, beyond the point where Stoner had fallen. There was no protective boulder on the slide there.

Bryan stopped.

Stoner began crawling toward her horse.

"Why are we stopping? Bryan?"

Keep stalling, Gwen. She got to her feet and sprinted, fumbled with the knots, shook the reins free.

There was a squeak of saddle leather. Someone dismounting.

"What are you doing?"

"It looks tricky. I'll lead my horse across and come back for you."

Steady plod of hooves. Clatter of loose gravel. Then Bryan's footsteps, coming back.

Damn, she couldn't see them. And if she moved out, he could see her. She inched forward, stroking Pinto's nose to keep him quiet.

Shout. Warn her.

No, he has to reveal himself. Unless Gwen knows his plans, it's useless.

Oh, Jesus; Gwen, don't do anything. Ask for explanations.

She held her breath.

"Okay," Bryan said. "You can get down now."

"I don't know, Bryan. It looks awfully..."

"Get down!"

"Don't pull at me, Bryan. I'll fall."

Wait.

Now!

Not yet.

"Bryan, cut it out. It's too dangerous. Let's go back."

"It's perfect."

"Stop it. Do you want me to fall?"

He laughed nastily. "I didn't bring you up here to look at the scenery."

That's it. MOVE!

She stepped out onto the trail, holding Pinto close. Beyond the pack horses she could see them. Bryan yanking at Gwen's arm. Gwen struggling to hold on, beginning to slip sideways in the saddle.

I can't reach her. Jesus Christ, I can't *reach* her!

Pinto tossed his head.

She jumped away from him. "Pinto! Go!" she shouted, and struck him with her fist.

The pony lunged forward toward the slide. Stoner raced after him.

Bryan looked up, startled, and threw himself against the mountain wall as Pinto thundered by in a whirlwind of dust.

She skidded to a halt beside Gwen's horse.

"Well," Bryan said. "Look what the cat dragged in. What's new, cowgirl?"

"Get out of here, Gwen." She kept her eyes on Bryan.

Gwen didn't move.

Damn it, this is no time to go into shock. "Don't be afraid. Put it in reverse and go."

Bryan grinned. "Nice day, isn't it?" One hand was behind him. With the other, he reached into his pocket, dug out a cigarette and lighter, and lit it. He studied the smoke. "No breeze. Do you think that means rain?"

"Gwen, move it."

"There's no hurry." He brought the hidden hand forward and held up the reins to Gwen's horse. "She isn't going anywhere."

She glanced up quickly. Gwen was staring at Bryan, her face tight. Stoner leaned toward the horse and nudged Gwen's foot with her shoulder, trying to waken her to action. "Please, Gwen, get down. Run. I'll keep him here."

Bryan laughed. "Well, cowgirl, what do we do now?"

Stoner glared at him. "Why?" she asked furiously.

"Why?"

"She'd have given you the money. All you had to do was give her one of your abandoned-puppy looks. Why this?"

His eyes met hers. "And ruin all my fun?"

Her stomach knotted with fear. Oh, God, he's really insane.

Bryan took a drag on his cigarette. "You know, I'd almost decided to put it off. It was too easy." He exhaled smoke through his nose and tilted his head toward Gwen. "Stupid cow."

Gwen didn't move.

"I thought of taking her back to Boston," he went on. "Playing with her a little. Just enough to scare her. Just enough to make it interesting."

His voice was low, hypnotic. She shook her head to clear it.

"Then you showed up. An obstacle. I like that. Even though I had to leave you a trail a mile wide."

Stall. Think. "If you wanted me around for excitement," she said, "why did you try to kill me?" Come on, Gwen, come on.

Bryan shrugged. "You got to be a bore. If there's anything worse than a fucking cow, it's a fucking bore." He straightened and flicked his cigarette aside. "Well, let's get on with it."

"Stay away from her!"

"Want to beg, Stoner? That might be amusing. Go on, kneel down and beg for her life."

"Bastard."

He grinned. "There's nothing wrong with begging. You wanted me to beg for her money. And I might have, cowgirl, if it was her money I wanted."

She couldn't bear the tension. She wanted to lash out at him. She wanted to turn and shove Gwen and her horse and the pack horses all the way to South Dakota. She clenched her fists.

"Now I've made you angry," he said. "Good. I like anger." His eyes glinted silver. He held out his hands. "Come on."

Stoner hesitated. Hold him off for ten seconds. Fifteen seconds. Will that give her enough time to...? But Gwen was frozen in the saddle. Or was she? Was there something different about the tension in the foot against her shoulder?

Bryan took a step forward.

Stoner centered her balance. All right. Okay. I'll take you with me.

He licked his lips and smiled, his raw male strength heightened by madness.

Another step. His arms hung at his sides. He could almost touch her now.

He dropped the reins.

She took a deep breath, watched his right foot leave the ground, swing forward . . .

"Bryan," Gwen said softly.

His eyes shifted toward the sound.

Stoner lunged.

Something caught her around the throat, slamming her backward into the horse's side, cutting off her breath. The horse lurched forward and reared.

Through the billowing dust she saw Bryan, arms thrown up to protect his face from slashing hooves. For a moment he teetered at the edge of the precipice.

He fell.

The echo of crashing boulders filled the air like a subway's roar. Above the thunder of cascading granite, she heard his scream.

Then there was silence, broken only by the clack of pebbles coming to rest.

Choking, she twisted around to look at Gwen. Her face was chalk, her eyes staring. Her hand locked around Stoner's collar.

She pried herself loose from Gwen's fingers and gently pushed the horse back to the safety of the forest. She whistled. Pinto trotted to her and began grazing at the side of the path. Bryan's horse followed.

Stoner held up her hand. "Come down now," she said.

Gwen hesitated, then slipped to the ground. Her legs buckled. Stoner caught her, barely noticing the hurt as Gwen clung to her. She hunched her shoulders to turn her body into a protective cocoon, and wrapped her arms around her.

"It's over," Stoner whispered, knowing that for Gwen it was only beginning.

CHAPTER 12

She sat on the kitchen steps and drew pictures in the dust with a stick. The Tetons seemed to be sleeping in the bright mid-morning air. The parking lot was nearly deserted; the trail to her cabin wound silently through the pines. Behind her, she could hear the last of the breakfast dishes being stacked for lunch. A breeze touched the heads of Indian Paint Brush in the meadow, and set them swaying.

I don't want to go.

Stell came out and sat beside her.

"Well, Stell said.

"Well."

"How did the inquest go?"

"Okay, I guess. She wouldn't talk much." She drew a circle on the ground.

"No change?"

Stoner shook her head. "They made her identify the body. I don't know why they had to do that."

"The law transcends compassion," Stell said.

"She has nightmares. When she sleeps."

"It takes time." Stell patted her arm. "I don't think you've slept much yourself."

"I don't suppose I have." She rubbed the back of her neck.

"What I don't understand," Stell said, "is why he moved the trip up to Wednesday."

"When he thought I was dead, he went back to Jackson and checked into the Motel 6 at the edge of town. He used a false name, but the night clerk recognized the description and the car. In the morning, he picked up the camping gear and came back here, the way they'd planned. Gwen told him I was still alive. He knew he had to turn her against me, so he showed her a letter I'd written to Marylou — he found it in my fireplace before he met me at Elk Island — and said I'd tried to make a play for him, to break them up. That seemed to work, but when I forced her to come outside and talk to me, she was pretty shaken when she got back. I guess he figured he had to act fast, before she started to put the pieces together.

"He convinced her they needed to get off by themselves right away, to take her mind off what had happened. Jake was in Laramie, and his nephew didn't know enough — or care enough — to be suspicious when he changed their reservations."

She broke the stick. "Gwen was hurt and confused by what she thought I'd done to her. And a little afraid of him, I think. He'd gotten pretty ugly about that trip once before. She wanted to believe him, and didn't know what else to do. So she went along."

Stell took a chunk of stale bread from her pocket and tossed it to a passing jay. "It's lucky you checked the reservation book. Or was it luck?"

"I was worried about Blacky. And I knew I'd have to follow them, so I wanted to see what time they'd be leaving." She shrugged. "Guess I'm a little impulsive."

Stell laughed. "Compulsive or thorough. At least she's talking about it to you."

"Only to tell me that much. Only because I pushed."

Not that there's been much time. The local police, State police, Forest Service, Park Service all had questions, and all wanted answers, and they positively refused to share questions or answers. They wouldn't even share pencils, as far as she could tell. Through it all Smokey stood to the side, hands on hips, ready and eager to break heads if necessary, in case things got nasty. Stell had dealt with reporters as if they were Jesus Christ himself talking mean. What few reporters there were. Accidents didn't hold the public's attention for long. But there had been phone calls to make, arrangements to ship Bryan's body to Boston since they couldn't come up with any living relatives.

The times they were alone, Gwen wrapped herself in a world of her own, closed in with her private thoughts like a mussel at low tide. Whatever she was going through, she was going through alone.

Stell took Stoner's hand in hers and laced their fingers together. "The police report came through, Stoner. He had a record."

Stoner looked at her. "What for?"

"Assault. Assault with a deadly weapon. Both women." She squeezed Stoner's hand. "You're not going to like this. Rape."

She hunched her shoulders. "Christ. Where?"

"Wisconsin, Arkansas, and New Mexico. He must have been desperate, to go to Arkansas."

"Was he... married to any of them?"

"The first two. He was engaged to the third."

"Jesus," Stoner said. "He made a career of it."

"Well," said Stell, "he'd have had to retire when he lost his looks. Come to think of it, he's not too pretty now."

"Stell!" She tried not to laugh, and failed.

The older woman looked at her. "It's good to hear you laugh again. I'll miss you, Little Bear."

Stoner sighed. "I'll miss you, too. I'd like to come back some time, if you'll have me."

"If I'll have you? What's that supposed to mean, if I'll have you?"

"I wasn't exactly an easy guest."

Stell punched her on the side of the leg. "You broke up what was otherwise a very dull season." She looked around at the forest. "Summer's about over. I can feel it in the air."

"In New England there will be cobwebs on the lawns now."

"New England," Stell said. "It's a world away."

Blinking back tears, Stoner traced Stell's knuckles with the tip of her finger. "Do you think I'll ever ... see you again?"

"Don't be an idiot," Stell said roughly. She slipped an arm around Stoner's shoulders. "You're part of the family."

"Stell, may I tell you something awful?"

"Why not? I'm used to bad news from you."

"I don't want her to marry again."

Stell took a deep breath. "I'm going to make a speech, Stoner. Maybe it'll mean something to you, and maybe it won't. But I want you to listen."

Stoner looked at her.

"I want you to have what you want, Little Bear. But life unfolds in its own way, and sometimes you think it's all going against you. But when times are hard, remember that a day is only one day, a year is only one year, and a lifetime is a very long time to live.

"There's something we've learned through the years, John and Ted and I. The sweet moments are sweeter, and the bitter moments less bitter if you have a loving friend. And no matter what the future holds for you and Gwen, I can't imagine a more loving friend than you."

Stoner rested her head on Stell's shoulder. She smelled of fresh bread. For the rest of my life, whenever I smell that I'll think of her. "Thank you," she said.

After a moment Stell dislodged her gently. "Now, I have messages for you. Smokey sends his love."

"I wish he could have been here."

Stell smiled, "He's hiding. Hates goodbyes. Tonight he'll sit in the kitchen and drink your health until we have to pour him into bed."

"I wanted to thank him for taking over these past days. I couldn't have done it without him."

"Well, you had your hands full with her. Jessie called."

"She found us, you know. She brought the horses back."

"She said to tell you, next time you're caught with five horses on your hands, try trying them together."

"Oh."

"And, Stoner, that doesn't mean tying the tail of one horse to the nose of the horse behind."

"I didn't do that," Stoner said.

"You're capable of it. The Thibaults will see you back in civilization." She stood up. "I guess that wraps it up."

"I guess it does." She stared at the ground miserably.

Stell ruffled her hair. "Come on. It's not the end of the world."

Stoner looked up at the mountains.

"They'll still be here," Stell said. "Next year."

"Yeah."

"Here she comes." Gwen was walking down the path, her sneakers sending up little puffs of dust. Stell went to meet her.

Stoner hung back. A few thin clouds flew like pennants from the peak of Grand Teton. The glaciers sparkled in the morning sun. Well, so long. She turned quickly and strode to the parking lot. "All set?"

Gwen nodded. Stoner took her suitcase and locked it in the car trunk. She wiped her hands on her jeans. "We might as well go."

Stell cleared her throat. "Take care of yourself, Gwen," she said, wrapping her arms around her.

"You, too, Stell. I'm sorry about..." She faded out and slid into the

182

passenger seat.

"Next time you come," Stell said to Stoner, "bring Marylou."

Stoner laughed. "I wouldn't do that to you." She scraped her feet in the gravel. "Well..."

"Well..."

"I wish you'd let me pay for my room and all."

"I told you," Stell said. "You're family."

Stoner threw her arms around Stell's neck. "I love you," she said.

"Be good, Little Bear," Stell said, holding her. "Now get out of here before I make a fool of myself."

Stoner ran for the car, turned the key in the ignition, and pulled out onto the highway. She didn't trust herself to look back.

Jackson Hole was two days behind them. Two days of silence, and sunscorched hills. Two nights of silence broken only by the rumble of trucks on the highway outside the motel rooms, and the rustle of Gwen's bedsheets as she tossed in her sleep. Two days and two nights of silence, and wondering what to do.

The flatlands gave way to wheat. Miles of hot, white sun, over miles of fields of tawny grain that stretched to every horizon. Only wild sunflowers and an occasional windmill relieved the enervating monotony.

One trouble with Nebraska was, you didn't know if it was worse with the windows open or shut. The air in the car was stifling, but when she opened the windows wide, the hot wind scoured her face.

Another was Interstate 80, which was long, fast, straight, and bypassed everything but Stuckey's. At times you could catch a glimpse of a small, gray town from the highway. Towns built by speed when the railroads headed west, destroyed by speed when the Interstates headed east. If things were different, they could get off the main road, go down into one of those little towns with names like Roscoe and Darr and McCool Junction, look at the grain elevators, watch the trains, have lunch in Mike's Bar and Grill or Ethel's Luncheonette, hang around the general store, and feel what life was like in the backwaters of time.

But things weren't different.

Then there were the bugs, genetically programmed to self-destruct in the exact center of the windshield on the driver's side. She pressed the washer button, and managed to spread a milky white smear over the entire field of vision.

Given silence, sun, bugs, and Nebraska, at what point does one cease to be legally responsible for one's behavior?

She glanced over at Gwen. Her face was expressionless, her eyes empty. Her skin had an odd opaqueness despite her tan. The veins on the back of her hands stook out like little blue glass tubes.

What the hell am I doing in this Godforsaken American heartland with this stranger?

Shock, she reminded herself. It'll pass in time. Be patient.

Did I ever know this woman with the mahogany eyes and fawn-colored hair and a voice like velvet? We giggled together in a bar in Wyoming. We touched in Yellowstone. I held her through a storm. She held me. What happened?

Bryan Oxnard happened.

He's dead, and he's still with us.

A thin layer of dust coated the inside of the car. Her lips felt cracked and gritty. The wind twisted and bruised the grain into patterns like ocean waves. Amber waves of grain, my Aunt Matilda. I can live a thousand years without another amber wave. Sell it to the Russians. Give it to the Eskimos. Shoot it into outer space. Bury radioactive waste in it. Who needs it?

They passed another in an endless series of disintegrating gas stations. Dessicated wood, windows empty or cracked, framed in rotting curtains. Coca-cola signs that dangled like suicides from rusting chains. Flecks of paint, molted from the walls, littered the paper-strewn ground. Dead pumps turned slowly and inexorably to rust, melting back into the earth.

"The alchemy of the twenty-first century," she said, "will be the science of turning rust back into iron ore."

The wind never stopped blowing.

"This must be a great place to be from. It's a hell of a place to be *in*."

A grasshopper splattered on the windshield.

"Women used to go insane out here in the early days. I can see why."

Gwen smiled politely.

"We're almost to Grand Island, whatever that is. Feel like some lunch?"

"If you do."

Damn it, agree with me. Disagree with me. Take some ridiculous position. Don't just *sit* there.

How about a little compassion, McTavish? She gritted her teeth and pressed harded on the accelerator.

Five miles of grain drifted by in silence.

"Say something!" Stoner yelled.

Gwen started. "I'm sorry."

She ran her hand through her hair. "No, I am."

"I'm not very good company," Gwen said. "Why don't you take a plane home from Omaha? You shouldn't have to be stuck with me."

"I'm *not* 'stuck with you'." Sure, Gwen, leave you. You'll wrap this car around the first tree you see. If there *are* any trees left in the country. Probably in Ohio. Cleveland. Do you want your last sight in the world to be Cleveland?

A pair of fornicating beetles carried out a desperate lovers' pact against the glass. "That settles it," Stoner said. "Now we *have* to stop."

Peering under the chalky mess, she spotted a diner ahead. A lone car in the parking lot suggested human life. To one side lounged a dilapidated but apparently functional gas station. "Gosh," Stoner said, pulling the car off the highway onto a rudimentary dirt road, "my prayers have been answered."

The gas tank filled, the windshield cleaned, she parked beside the restaurant. "I don't know. It's not the Copley Plaza."

Gwen pointed to a water-stained, fly-specked card scotch taped to a front window. "It passed the Board of Health."

"Yeah, but when?" She shrugged. "If it's good enough for Tom Joad, it's good enough for me."

Hamburgers and French fries. But not Wort Hotel hamburgers and French fries. This hamburger was thin and greasy. The roll was stale. And the potatoes had soaked in oil for three days. Flies clung in stomach-turning clumps to limp strips of flypaper. The waitress, whose name was probably Shirley — or Charlene — leafed through a movie magazine.

"I know this place," Stoner said. "It's the set for 'The Petrified Forest'."

Gwen stopped picking at her salad and looked up, meeting Stoner's eyes. The old butterflies started up in her stomach.

"Where are we?" Gwen asked.

"Relative Obscurity."

"What?"

"Famous people come from here. 'He came out of Relative Obscurity.' Or is that, 'He came out *in* Relative Obscurity.'?"

"Where did you come out?"

"The Ritz Carlton. It was the social event of the season."

"You're crazy," Gwen said.

"It's the altitude."

"Yeah." She looked away.

Okay, we do not make overt, audible references to Jackson Hole. Stoner contemplated her hamburger. "I think I may be related to this thing," she said. "Gwen, are we still friends?"

"I thought we were."

"Then I wish you'd talk to me."

Gwen stabbed a wedge of plastic, hard-boiled egg. "There's nothing to talk about," she said tightly. "You know everything."

"I don't know what's happening inside you."

"I can't."

"Gwen..."

"Don't, Stoner, please?" She put down her fork, lining it up neatly beside the plate. "I really can't eat any more," she said, and got up. "I'll wait for you in the car."

"Gwen, I ..."

"It's not you. Honestly." She left the restaurant.

Stoner took a bite of soggy potato. It tasted like tears. She dropped it on her plate.

"You done?" Shirley — or Charlene — asked in a bored voice.

"Yes, I think so."

Shirley piled the dishes with all the grace of a roller derby queen, and carried them, salad dressing oozing from between the plates, to the counter. "You want more coffee?"

"No, thanks."

Charlene dumped the dishes, unscraped, into a sink of greasy, sudless, and undoubtedly luke-warm water. "What's the matter with your friend?"

"My friend."

"Looks like the walking dead. Them eggs was boiled up fresh this morning. She too good to eat our cooking?"

Stoner drew herself up. "There's been a tragedy in the family."

The waitress shrugged. "Oughta eat."

185

"One hardly," said Stoner coldly, "engages in normal behavior at a time like this."

"Reckon one hardly does," said Charlene — or was it Shirley — with a smirk.

Stoner paid the bill. "By the way," she said casually as she took her change, "what do you have to do to be licensed by the Board of Health? Flush the toilets once a week?"

"You must be from the east."

Stoner leaned toward her confidentially. "I'll let you in on a secret, Shirley. I just murdered that woman's husband. Now I'm going to take her out to the nearest irrigation ditch and ravish her." She tossed two pennies on the table and let the screen door slam behind her.

"Let's get out of here," she said to Gwen, "Before she calls the cops."

"What did you do?"

"You really don't want to know." She tossed Gwen the keys. "You drive. I'll ride shotgun."

Grinnell, Iowa

I have to get away from her.

She sat on the edge of the bed and listened to Gwen running water in the bathroom. A truck roared by. Out here, the fifty-five mile speed limit had gone the way of the Wooley Mammoth. Another hundred and fifty miles behind them. Another silent meal.

Maybe I'll volunteer for the first solo space flight to Jupiter.

Toothbrush in hand, Gwen came out of the bathroom. "It's all yours," she said. She turned out her light and huddled in bed.

Stoner gazed at the formless mound of bedclothes that ostensibly contained a living human being. She sighed. "They say there's a hill outside of Iowa City. That should be exciting." She closed the bathroom door.

Fists clenched, Stoner lay on her back and watched the rhythmic flashing of the motel sign. Light, dark, light, dark. A beetle attacked the window. She wanted to scream, she wanted to strike out. Gwen's silence flowed around her. She was suspended in cold, hollow space. Light, dark. She wanted to smash the sign. We'll both be insane before this is over. Light, dark.

To hell with it. She got up and sat on Gwen's bed. She touched her shoulder. "Gwen, I can't keep going this way. I know I said things that hurt you. You said things that hurt me. I don't care about that now. Yes, I went out there to do a job, but that changed. It changed the minute I met you. Please don't close me out, Gwen, I ... love you."

Gwen began to cry. "Stoner, help me. Please."

She slipped into bed and pressed Gwen to her and held her hand.

Gwen sobbed, long and hard.

It tore the heart from her.

"I can't stop," Gwen said brokenly. "I can't stop remembering."

Stoner stroked her back. "Try to relax," she said. "You'll make yourself sick."

But it poured out of her in a flood, on and on.

Don't Gwen. Don't hurt any more.

It couldn't have been more than minutes, but it seemed like hours. Gradually, her sobbing gave way to trembling. And then she was quiet.

"It's all right now," Stoner said.

Gwen turned over on her back and looked at her. "I didn't want to do this," she said. "I didn't want to ask any more of you."

Gently, Stoner wiped the tears from Gwen's face. "Don't you understand anything about love?"

"I used to. A long time ago." She turned on her side and nestled against Stoner's shoulder. "Why did he hate me?"

"He didn't hate you."

"He didn't love me."

"No." She ran her hand down Gwen's back. Her muscles were long and firm. "Those emotions were beyond him."

"I don't know how that can be," Gwen said.

"Neither do I." Her hand came to rest in the small of Gwen's back. Careful.

"After all that happened, why did you stay? Why did you come after us?"

"Because I love you."

Gwen lay in her arms, soft and quiet. Her eyelashes brushed Stoner's neck.

"You should have talked about it, Gwen." Her heart was pounding. Her fingertips tingled. Her lips felt thick. Not *now*, for God's sake.

"I was ashamed of the things I had said to you. I was afraid you wouldn't forgive me."

Stoner smiled at her. "Gwen, you're impossible." Impossibly lovely. Impossibly ... desirable.

Get a grip on yourself. She rolled onto her back, out of temptation's way.

"Why didn't I see what he was," Gwen said, "all this time?"

"You're very trusting. It's an admirable quality, but it has its disadvantages."

Gwen was silent for a long time. Good, she's falling asleep. She felt her heart rate subside, and began to drift.

"Stoner," Gwen said in a very small voice.

"Yes?"

"Would you ... make love to me?"

Adrenalin shot through her. "What?"

"Would you make love to me? Please?"

"Me?" She squeaked. Her muscles turned to mush.

"If you don't want to ..."

"I want to," Stoner said. "With all my heart."   The problem is, I'm totally paralyzed.

"I wouldn't ask, but ... I feel so ... alone. I need you, Stoner."

Feeling suddenly very strong, and very protective, Stoner turned on her side and slipped her arm under Gwen's head. Carefully, gently she unbuttoned Gwen's nightshirt and slid her hand between her breasts. Gwen tensed. "Have you even been made love to by a woman before?"

"No."

187

"Frightened?"

"A little." Her face glistened in the pale pink neon light. Her eyes were dark.

"I'll stop any time you say. Don't be afraid to tell me."

Gwen looked up at her. "I'm just ... nervous."

Stoner caressed the hollows at the base of her neck. Gwen touched her face.

"If there's anything you want, or don't want, it's all right."

"I only want ... to know you're here."

Stoner smiled. "I'm here, Gwen."

Gradually she let her fingers drift across Gwen's breasts, and felt them rise to meet her. She lowered her head and massaged her nipple gently with her tongue. Gwen caught her breath and buried her hand in Stoner's hair. She moved her mouth to Gwen's other breast and nibbled softly with her lips.

Slowly she stroked Gwen's body. Over her shoulders, across her breasts, down her stomach and thighs, over and over, making circles until Gwen's skin danced in tiny tremors under her fingers. "I love you," she said hoarsely.

"Stoner," Gwen whispered.

She kissed her eyelids, the bridge of her nose, the corners of her mouth, and eased her hand between Gwen's legs. She was warm and damp and soft. Rhythmically, she moved her hand up and down, up and down.

Gwen tensed, clutched at her. "Not so fast," Stoner said. "Let yourself enjoy it."

"You're driving me crazy."

"That's part of the fun."

She went on smoothing her, fondling her, first in tiny ovals, then back and forth. Gwen's skin grew firm beneath her fingers. Perspiration broke out over her body. She felt herself grow damp, felt her own blood rise to the surface of her skin, then fall. Rise and fall, rise and fall in a warm tide. Gwen's breathing quickened, and her own warmth ebbed and flowed in rhythm with Gwen's breath.

Gwen's body convulsed. Again. And again. She grabbed Stoner's hand, held it tight against her. Then she went limp.

Stoner kissed her on the mouth.

For a while Gwen lay still, still pressing Stoner's hand. Her breathing was long and deep.

Gwen opened her eyes and looked at her. "Holy cow," she said.

Stoner grinned. "Holy cow?"

"Holy cow."

Then Gwen's hands were on her bare skin, touching her, giving to her. It was delicious. "You don't have to..." she said without conviction.

"Be quiet."

Gwen made love to her. Very slowly. Very deeply.

***

Boulders rumbled down the mountainside, inexorably coming nearer. She pressed her face into the gravel, unable to move, paralyzed with fear. Not again. Please, not again. The unseen clatter of breaking rocks grew louder. She tried to force herself to her knees, but the ground held her. Something touched her shoulder.

Her eyes flew open.

"Stoner," Gwen said, "wake up."

The chambermaid's cart rattled harmlessly past the window.

The pounding of her heart shook her. She breathed deeply until it subsided. "Sorry. Nightmare." Turning her head, she saw her own naked shoulder, and Gwen leaning over her, and remembered.

We made love.

"Are you okay?" Gwen asked.

"Fine, fine. What time is it?"

"Ten-thirty."

Stoner pushed at the covers. "We have to check out."

"Aren't we supposed to languish in a haze of romance and fulfillment?"

"We're *supposed* to be out of here." She moved to get up.

Gwen pulled her down. "Wait a minute. I want to look at your back."

"Once you've seen one..." She struggled to roll over.

"Oh, shut up," Gwen laughed, and pushed her head into the pillow. "You weren't self-conscious last night."

"That was last night," Stoner growled.

Gwen ran her finger lightly across her shoulders and down her spine. "You're going to have scars."

I'm going to have worse than that if you touch me between my shoulder blades. "Don't *do* that," she squeaked as Gwen touched her between the shoulder blades.

"Why not?"

"It turns me into a raving maniac."

"Good." Gwen kissed her. Right between the shoulder blades.

"I mean it, Gwen." She fought against her, half-heartedly. "If you don't stop, we'll never make Ohio by nightfall."

"What so special about Ohio?" Gwen kissed her again, and stroked her back. "You have relatives in Ohio or something?"

Oh, good Lord, everything's tingling. "Gwen..."

"What?" She slipped her warm, naked body over Stoner's and pinned her down.

"You're ... wanton."

"You bet I'm wantin'," Gwen said. Her lips brushed Stoner's earlobe. She nibbled it softly.

A surge of warmth flowed through her loins as Gwen touched her breast. She felt her hips began to rock — not quite against her will — beneath Gwen's thighs. "Cut it out."

"Say 'please'."

Not on your life. With all the strength she could muster, she rolled on her side to face Gwen, and wrapped her arms around her. Gwen's hand found her softness. Her hand found Gwen's. Together they touched and

189

stroked until her body exploded with delicious pin-pricks of pleasure.

After a few minutes she opened her eyes. "Gwen?"

"Quiet," Gwen said. "I'm languishing in a haze of fulfillment."

Propping herself on one elbow, Stoner gazed down at the woman beside her. Gwen's hair was damp, and clung in waves to her forehead. Her lips were full and red. Her lashes lay softly against her face. Stoner took her hand and kissed the palm. "You're not wanton..." And the bridge of her nose. "Or wantin'..." And the base of her throat. "You're relentless."

The laundry cart was in motion again. "We have to get dressed," Stoner said.

Gwen opened her eyes. "Who cares?"

"*You* try explaining this. In Iowa." She jumped from the bed, grabbed the spread, and headed for the shower.

"Some lover," Gwen grumbled good-naturedly.

"Get *up*."

"Oh, all right." Gwen started ripping the bed apart. "I'll pack while you bathe. If I can find your pajamas."

"For God's sake," Stoner said, sneaked one last appreciative look, and slipped into the bathroom.

As she was rinsing her hair, she heard a tap on the door. "Stoner," Gwen said, "does this mean we're more than friends?"

***

"Don't you want your bacon?" Gwen asked.

Stoner looked down at her untouched meal. "I'm not hungry."

"Really?" She helped herself to Stoner's toast. "Sex makes me ravenous."

"Not so loud," Stoner said quickly. "This place is packed."

"It'll give them something to talk about over the winter." Gwen nibbled on the bacon. "Anyway, they probably know."

"What?"

"Look around. We're the only people in here eating breakfast."

Stoner hid her face in her hands.

"At least drink your coffee."

She tried. "I can't."

"Look," Gwen said, consuming the last piece of toast and half of the cold scrambled eggs, "one of us has to be alert enough to drive. And it sure isn't going to be me."

Those hands. I've never seen anything like those hands. I'll bet she can do anything with them. Pick up bubbles. Open old olive jars. Cure lepers. Make the blind see. Calm frightened children. Lower fevers. I *know* she can bring frozen passion back to life.

All right, Marylou, I admit it. You were right. As usual. I needed to be in love. But not just in love. In love with this one, particular, out-of-all-the-millions-of-people-in-the-world, gentle, mahogany-eyed woman.

Gwen folded her napkin and looked up. "Stoner?"

190

"Why did you do that?"

"What?"

"Fold your napkin?"

"Why not?"

"It's a *paper* napkin."

Gwen threw it at her. "I have to ask you something."

"Anything."

"Was I ... okay?"

Were you okay? *Okay?* My knees may never support my weight again. I'll have to spend the rest of my life in a wheelchair. "You have a natural talent," she said.

"Oh, thank God. I was afraid I couldn't do anything but teach history."

Stoner laughed. "If you teach history the way you make love..."

Gwen shook her head. "I can't believe I did that. I've never been so ashamed in my life."

I knew it. I knew this was coming. Stoner looked down at the table. "Well," she said sadly, "it isn't everyone's cup of tea."

"I'm thirty years old, for Heaven's sake," Gwen said furiously. "To go and do a stupid, adolescent thing like that..."

Stoner felt a rush of anger. "If that's what you think, to hell with it." You're all alike. It's fine for a few hours of burning madness, a casual romp and tickle. But in the morning ...

"Stoner?"

"Go read the graffiti on the ladies' room wall. You'll feel right at home."

"Stoner, what are you talking about?"

"Adolescent sex," Stoner spat out. "Arrested development. What's *your* theory? We can't separate from our mothers? Inadequate fathering? Primary narcissism? Can't relate to men? Listen, Gwen, my experience with men haven't been half as bad as yours."

"What in the world is the matter with you?"

"We call it heterosexual privilege," Stoner grumbled. "I'm sorry you're ashamed. I'm sorry you think making love with me is stupid and adolescent."

Gwen grabbed her hand. "Stoner, stop this."

She snatched her hand away. "Don't patronize me."

"Listen to me, damn it. That's not what I'm talking about."

"Then what?" Stoner demanded, not giving an inch.

"I'm talking about asking you that question. Just like a man."

She glanced up. "What?"

"How was I, Babe? D'Ja come?" Gwen said, *macho voce.*

"Oh."

Gwen squeezed her hand. "I think it's time to talk about this, don't you?"

I am *not* going to cry. I am *not* going to break down in the middle of the Grinnell Greasy Spoon surrounded by Iowa farmers.

"Come on," Gwen said, pulling her up. "Let's get out of here." She handed Stoner some money. "Pay the bill with this. Yours, too. After all, I ate it.''

"Where are you going?''

"To the ladies' room. To read the walls.''

***

There was a hill behind the diner. It offered a view of corn to the north, corn to the south, corn to the east, corn to the west, and weeds underfoot. Stoner sat cross-legged on the pebbly ground and inspected a black-eyed susan. Today the scenery would fade to the familiar. The sky would lower and grow gray with smog. There would be cities with tall buildings, towns crowded up against one another like mussels on old pilings. The stench of automobile exhaust. Polluted streams, oil-slicked puddles. And everyone would be in a hurry.

She picked a leaf of crabgrass and slit it with her thumbnail.

"What are you thinking about?'' Gwen asked.

"Home.''

"Will you be glad?''

She shook her head. "I'll be glad to see Aunt Hermione and Marylou. But I'll miss the mountains.''

"So will I.'' Gwen tossed a pebble down the hill. "You'll be different there, won't you?''

"Not very.''

"I can't imagine you in other clothes, indoors. You belong around sagebrush.''

Stoner stretched out on her back. "I couldn't live there.''

"Why not?''

"Horses.''

Gwen laughed. The velvet had come back into her voice.

"You'll be different, too,'' Stoner said.

"I don't know what I'll be.'' She made a little pile of stones. "I read the walls.''

"Cute, huh?''

"I can't imagine what it's like, knowing that at any moment you'll be reminded that someone you never met hates you.''

"I try not to think about it,'' Stoner said. "I couldn't live my life if I did.''

"It's so very cruel.''

"There are all kinds of cruelty, Gwen. Living isn't easy for anyone.''

A flock of swallows whirled overhead, going south. So soon.

"Stoner, about last night...''

I don't want to hear this. "Last night was last night. It's okay.''

"I want to talk about it.''

"I'd rather not.'' Please, Gwen, don't spoil it.

"I have to.'' She rested her elbows on her knees and looked at the ground. "I don't know what it means for me. I'm ... confused. About myself. About the future. I was so sure of...'' She took a deep breath. "...Bryan. And I was so wrong. I don't ... trust what I know any more.''

Stoner swallowed. "I understand that."

"But I'm sure of one thing. I love you."

Something punched her in the stomach. It brought tears to her eyes.

"I've loved you since that night in your cabin. When you let me hold you." She looked over. "You made me feel ten feet tall."

Stoner closed her eyes.

"I wasn't using you last night, Stoner. I hope you don't think that."

"I don't think that," she said softly.

"Everything I did or said was ... from my heart. And I don't regret it. I'll never regret it. Ever."

"Neither will I."

"There's so much I don't know about you," Gwen said. She grinned. "I don't even know what you *really* eat for breakfast."

Stoner threw a pebble at her.

"It's something to look forward to."

"Yes," Stoner said.

"It's time to go."

"I guess it is." Stoner got to her feet reluctantly. She stared out toward the northwest, as if she could have one last glimpse of the Tetons. But there was only corn and sky.

Gwen came up behind her and wrapped her arms around her neck and kissed her neck gently. "They were beautiful," she said.

CHAPTER 13

"Mood swings," Gwen said. She tossed her suitcase on the bed. "All my life I've tried to avoid mood swings. I'm sorry, Stoner."

"Don't be sorry." She shoved the Gideon Bible into a drawer and slammed it shut. "And don't joke about it. It's perfectly understandable."

"The crazy thing is, I keep wanting to blame myself."

"If God had intended us to be rational, He would have made us rational."

"Do you believe in God?" Gwen asked, slipping out of her clothes and into her night shirt.

"No. If there *is* a God, I have no respect for Him."

"Well, how could you respect anyone who creates Ohio?"

"If you think this is bad, wait until you see the New York Thruway."

Gwen sat on the edge of the bed. "I hate feeling like this," she said sadly. "Especially after this morning."

Stoner went over and embraced her. "It'll happen. Just don't close up."

"I won't." She put her arms around Stoner's waist and buried her head in her chest.

"This is how it's going to be, Gwen," she said, cupping her head in one hand. "For a while. Bryan wasn't a very nice man." If anyone ever hurts this woman again...

Gwen took a deep breath. "Do you want to use the bathroom first?"

"You go ahead. I'll change."

I wonder what the sleeping arrangements are for tonight, she thought as she dried her face. I hope she doesn't want to make love.

Are you crazy? You don't want to make *love*?

Not now. Right now I only want to ... protect her.

When she came out of the bathroom, she noticed that Gwen had moved all the pillows into one bed. She slipped in beside her.

"Stoner," Gwen said softly. "Do you mind just ... holding me?"

Heaven is falling asleep with the woman you love in your arms. Even in Ohio.

***

Gwen pulled the car over to the curb in front of the Beacon Hill brownstone. Stoner got out and retrieved her suitcase from the back seat. She leaned in the window. "I'll see you in a couple of days."

Gwen nodded.

"Gwen, are you going to be all right?"

"Sure." She pushed her hand through her hair, a gesture she had picked up recently.

Stoner smiled and took her hand. "Memories?"

194

"I'm afraid so."

"I wish I could help."

"It's one of those things," Gwen said. "No one can do it for me."

"Well, if you need me, I'm as close as the telephone."

Gwen looked at her. "That seems awfully far away."

"Yeah, it does." Stoner stroked Gwen's face with the back of her hand. "I'll miss you."

"You aren't the only one."

A car behind them honked impatiently. "He must be from out of town," Stoner said irrelevantly. "In Boston you roll down the window and shout."

"Hey, lady, you gonna stand there all day?"

Gwen sighed. "I'd better go. I'll come down to the travel agency the day after tomorrow. If I can find it."

"Just look for a delicatessen with travel brochures. That's us." Impulsively, she leaned forward and kissed Gwen on the mouth. "Don't forget me."

Gwen put her hand on the back of Stoner's neck. "How could I? You rattle my cage."

"Come on, girls. Break it up." The driver gunned his motor.

"That's the trouble with New England," Stoner said. "No flair for romance." She tilted Gwen's face toward her. "Remember, any time you need me."

Gwen reached for the ignition. "Goodbye, Stoner."

She watched the car until it turned the corner, out of sight. A delivery truck growled menacingly. She ran for the sidewalk. She felt out of place, here in the middle of Boston in her western shirt and jeans. Traffic rattled by impersonally. Children shrieked on the Common. A pigeon landed in a flurry of wings and picked at the cracks in the sidewalk, complaining to itself. A picture formed in her mind, of Gwen that day in Yellowstone, feeding the ground squirrel, looking up. She felt an aching hollowness. Mountains, sagebrush flats, Stell, Smokey ... already they were like a dream. It was truly over. Sadly, she turned and walked up the steps to her home.

***

Aunt Hermione was with a client. She could tell by the way the house felt, as if it had never been lived in. Aunt Hermione claimed it was because she had to "gather the vibrations" for a reading. Stoner suspected the real reason was that her aunt infused the house with so much life, constantly moving about, touching things, making adjustments, that when she was sedentary it could think of nothing to do but stand with its hands in its pockets and stare stupidly out at the street. Whatever the reason, it was a signal to her to go out in the kitchen and make tea.

She put the kettle on and went to the window. The Blue Runners were in fine form, their tendrils laden with beans poking through the openings

195

in the wicker birdcages. The teakettle whistled and she realized she had been standing with her hands in her pockets, staring stupidly out at the garden. She patted the window sill. "I know how you feel, old friend."

"Talking to the walls, dear?" Aunt Hermione plunged into the room to an accompaniment of clattering beads and jangling bracelets. "Whew!" she gasped, peeling off her brightly flowered smock. "Through for the day. The waning moon is brutal. It must be in something." She smothered Stoner in a pillowy embrace. "Home at last. You look wonderful."

'So do you." She reached for the teapot.

Aunt Hermione pushed her toward a chair. "You stay right there." She clattered about the kitchen.

"I can make the tea," Stoner said.

"Not very well, dear."

She grinned to herself. All things considered, it was good to be home.

"Now," said her aunt, amid the tea paraphernalia. "I don't want you to tell me a thing. We're having company for dinner and there's no point in repeating yourself."

"Who?"

"Edith and Marlou Kesselbaum. I hope you didn't want a restful first night home. You know Marylou. She can't wait to hear every grisly detail."

Stoner stirred her tea. "It's all right."

"I have two pieces of perfectly awful news for you," Aunt Hermione said cheerfully. "First of all, we're getting a new cat."

Stoner smiled. "I guess I can live with it."

"And here's the truly terrible part. Have a cookie, dear." She passed the plate.

"The cat's pregnant?" Stoner asked, taking one.

"Oh, I certainly hope not. Grace assured me she was altered. Still, stranger things have happened. That Israeli child, for instance."

"What Israeli child?"

"You know the one. With the inn and the manger and those three silly old men? Well, it was a long time ago. I shouldn't expect you to remember."

"Jesus?" Stoner asked, trying to keep a straight face.

Aunt Hermione snapped her fingers. "That's the one. How clever of you. But, then, I've always said you were clever."

"Aunt Hermione, why are you nervous?"

The older woman looked at her. "Because I'm so grateful to see you safe and sound." She pulled a handkerchief from her pocket and dabbed at her eyes. "I did miss you, Stoner."

Stoner got up and hugged her. "I missed you, too," she said, her heart melting.

Aunt Hermione patted her cheek affectionately. "Don't squat like that, Stoner. You'll get stiff knees."

Stoner got her tea and stood leaning against the sink. "I can't sit any more. We've been in the car for five days."

"Five *silent* days," Aunt Hermione said accusingly. "Your last letter to me was postmarked Douglas, Wyoming. And Marylou's received nothing but postcards. I must say, dear niece, you write marvelously uninformative postcards. One need never worry about leaving them lying about."

"What's the other bad news, Aunt Hermione?"

"We're getting a cat."

Stoner closed her eyes and shook her head. "You told me that. What else?"

"Your parents are coming to Boston. They expect you to have dinner with them."

Puzzled, Stoner looked up. "Why? They don't even like me."

Aunt Hermione popped her glasses on and peered at her. "Well, some things have changed around here."

"You know those rumors we keep hearing about parents who love their children? I think they might be true. I met one."

"Really? Who?"

"Stell Perkins."

"Perkins, Perkins." Aunt Hermione frowned for a second. "Oh, the inn-keeper!"

"I guess you could call her that." She hesitated. "Do you mind if things are a little chaotic around here for a couple of days? I'd like to put my parents in their place. You might get some nasty phone calls."

"Of course I don't mind. You know I love excitment." She studied her. "Yes, there's definitely a change in you. A great deal must have happen-ed in Wyoming."

"And in Iowa."

"Iowa! Something happened in Iowa?"

"We made love," Stoner blurted out loudly.

"Well, there's no need to *announce* it, dear. I'm sure all of Beacon Hill could care less."

Stoner felt her face pass scarlet for magenta. "I didn't mean to say anything," she muttered. "It slipped out."

"I didn't hear a thing," Aunt Hermione said. "Aren't you curious to know how we disposed of the *corpus delicti*?"

"The what?"

"The Oxnard remains."

"Aunt Hermione," Stoner said, shocked.

"What do *you* call him, the dear departed?"

I give up. "What did you do with the ... with Bryan?"

Her aunt nibbled at a cookie. "We tucked him away in the cemetery, all nice and cozy. Grace D'Addario . . . you don't know her, Stoner, she's a witch ... sprinkled some herbs and did a lovely ritual dance."

Stoner choked on her tea. "She *what*?"

"Calm yourself, Stoner. Don't eat and exclaim simultaneously."

"Aunt Hermione, you could have been arrested."

"I know, dear. And we did get some very strange looks from a funeral procession that came by..."

Stoner groaned.

"But we couldn't afford to take any chances on the evil escaping from below ground. The moon was in Scorpio, you know, and Grace felt we were just in the nick of time." She poured herself another cup of tea. "Of course, much of what went on was Greek to me. Not my area of expertise, I merely did as I was told."

Stoner braced herself. "And what was that, Aunt Hermione?"

"A few simple dance steps and a bit of chanting."

"Oh, God."

"Sometimes I worry about you, Stoner. You're so conservative. More tea?"

"No, thank you."

"I was dying to open the coffin and take a peek, of course. But it would have been tactless, with Eleanor right here."

"You had Mrs. Burton with you? Dancing and chanting?"

"Of course. She's the nearest living relative, since you and Gwyneth were doing God-knows-what, cavorting about Iowa."

Stoner turned and beat her forehead against the wall.

"She has a lovely singing voice."

"Mrs. Burton," Stoner said weakly.

"You wouldn't know it to hear her speak, would you? I've urged her to join the Azalea Choir."

"The Azalea Choir."

"At the Horticultural Society."

Stoner collapsed into a chair. "Aunt Hermione, life with you is like life in the Twilight Zone."

"Why, thank you, dear. What a sweet thing to say." She sipped her tea placidly. "What time is it?"

"About..." she checked her watch. "...five fifteen."

"You'd better run and wash up. Our guests are due at six."

"What are we serving?"

"I picked up an adorable little roast at the butcher's."

Something dawned on her. "Aunt Hermione, do you realize you've invited Edith *and* Marylou Kesselbaum for dinner on the same night?"

Aunt Hermione clapped her hands to her cheeks. "Oh, dear Lord. What can we do?"

"You run down to the deli," Stoner said, getting up. "I'll hit McDonald's." She paused in the doorway. "I'm awfully glad to be back."

**

The telephone rang.

"Bother." She tossed the dish towel over the sink. She lifted the receiver. "Hello," she said coldly.

"Stoner? Is that you?"

Her stomach gave a little flip. "Gwen?"

"You sound so odd."

"I just broke my mother's heart," she said, carrying her coffee to the table. "I thought she was calling back."

"You did what?"

"That's the official position at the moment."

"But what did you do?"

"I refused to have dinner with them. I'm afraid we're in for a long siege."

"Oh, Stoner, I'm so sorry."

"Don't be. It was inevitable."

"Are you ever going to see them again?"

Stoner shrugged. "I don't know. It depends on how it goes. How are you doing?"

"Fair. I needed to hear your voice."

"It's good to hear yours," she said.

"Stoner? Are you blushing?"

"None of your business."

Gwen sighed. "I wish I could see you."

"I'll be right over."

"No, it's too late, and too far."

"I guess it is." She hesitated. "Gwen, I told Aunt Hermione about ... Iowa. She won't tell anyone. Do you mind?"

"Of course I don't mind," Gwen said softly.

"It just slipped out."

"I said I didn't mind."

"She wouldn't think anything strange about it."

"I DON'T MIND!" Gwen screamed. "No, Grandmother," she said, turning away from the phone, "nothing's wrong. We talk to each other this way all the time."

There was a mumble in the background.

"I know it isn't ladylike, but it doesn't *mean* anything."

Another mumble.

"Fine. You go on to bed. Goodnight, Grandmother." She turned back to the phone. "Good grief."

Stoner grinned. "Having some problems over there?"

"Honestly! I love her dearly, but she's been all over me like a fungus this evening."

"Well," Stoner said, "she was pretty frightened."

"I know. I told her we'd go up to Nova Scotia for a few days. Maybe that will settle her down."

Oh, shit. We certainly are back. "Sounds like a good idea."

Gwen laughed. "And you sound like you're lying through your teeth."

"I'm spoiled. The re-entry's hard." Hard! It was wrenching. She brushed away a tear that had somehow escaped.

"You're invited."

"I can't. I wouldn't be fair to leave Aunt Hermione with the fallout."

"If I come down to the agency tomorrow, can Marylou make reservations for us?"

"That's what we're in business for. And if she can't, I can."

"No," Gwen said. "I don't want you to."

"Why not?"

"It's hard enough to leave. I don't want to feel as if you're sending me."

I love you, I love you, I love you.

"Stoner?"

"What?"

"I thought you'd hung up."

"No, I'm still here."

"I have to keep reminding myself of that."

Stoner sighed. "So do I."

"Phone calls are frustrating, aren't they?"

"Yes."

"But better than nothing."

"Slightly."

"Very slightly. But I'll see you tomorrow. Around eleven?"

"Fine."

She paused. "Stoner?"

"What?"

"Your eyes drive me wild."

Stoner swallowed hard. "Is this turning into an obscene call?"

"It might. Goodnight, Stoner."

She turned out the lights and went upstairs. She unpacked, pulled back the covers, and propped the torn picture of Gwen against the lamp on her bedside table. Her bed felt very large. And very empty.

***

"For the love of St. Peter," Marylou wailed. "Will you *stop* fussbudgeting? You're driving me crazy."

"I'm *trying* to bring order out of this mess." She looked at Marylou. "Which, incidentally, *I* didn't create."

"Order," said Marylou, "is *not* putting the Grand Canyon folders in the Virgin Islands file."

Stoner dropped into her chair and buried her face in her hands. "Damn."

"Relax. You're only nervous because *she's* coming."

"Go away," Stoner mumbled.

Marylou patted her head. "All right, we'll clean up."

Stoner got to her feet.

"*I'll* clean up," Marylou corrected herself. "Read your mail."

Half-heartedly, Stoner opened a few envelopes. Propaganda. She tossed it on the desk. "Junk."

"We're in the junk business."

"This place certainly looks it. Aren't you going to empty the wastebaskets?"

"No," said Marylou. "I might have put something important in there."

"Two weeks," Stoner said, waving her arms. "I leave you alone for two weeks and you turn this place into a landfill.''

Marylou placed her hands on her hips. "Call United. Talk to Miss Mellowtones. It'll cool you off.''

"I have nothing to say to Miss Mellowtones.''

"Book a party of twenty-five on a flight to London.''

"*What* party of twenty-five? Marylou, if you're supposed to get twenty-five people to London, why aren't you doing it? Do you know how hard it is to get that many reservations? Did you talk to them about charters?''

Marylou chuckled. "That'll be the day, when we get a party of twenty-five. We're not Crimson Travel, pet.''

"What are you talking about?'' Stoner asked wildly.

"Just book the flight. You can cancel it later. It'll keep you out of trouble.''

Stoner screamed.

"Be quiet,'' said Marylou. "Do you want every cop in Boston coming through that door? You think this is a mess now. Believe me, once the mounted police get through with it...''

Stoner curled up in the fetal position.

"Good. Stay that way until I've finished.''

After a while Stoner ventured a peek. A corner of Marylou's desk was beginning to emerge. "Have you looked up hotels in Nova Scotia yet?''

"No, I have not looked up hotels in Nova Scotia yet. I haven't finished the fall housekeeping.''

"She'll be here any minute.''

Marylou ignored her.

The door opened.

Stoner felt the blood rush to her face.

"Yes?'' said Marylou, going up to Gwen. "May we help you? My partner is having a minor nervous breakdown, as you can see, but perhaps I...''

"For Heaven's sake, Marylou. That's *her*.''

"Who?''

"Gwen,'' she shrieked.

"Oh!'' She held out her hand. "I didn't recognize you. But of course I only got to look at your picture for about ten seconds before she snatched it.''

"I didn't snatch. I never snatch.''

"Uh,'' Gwen said, "maybe I should come back later.''

Stoner dropped her head on the desk and covered it with her arms.

"Nonsense,'' said Marylou. "If you want to be helpful, do something about...'' she gestured toward Stoner. "... *her*.''

"You're Marylou,'' Gwen said.

"I try.'' She looked Gwen up and down. "You weren't kidding, Stoner. She's delicious.''

"Marylou!''

Gwen laughed. "Thank you. I think.''

"I'll get you for this,'' Stoner said under her breath.

"Uh-oh,'' said Marylou. "Put my foot in it.'' She touched Stoner's hand. "I'm sorry. Friends?"

Stoner nodded mutely.

Gwen crossed to her desk and put her hand on Stoner's shoulder. "Stoner?"

"Damn it." She was close to tears. "I wanted everything to be perfect."

"Everything *is* perfect." Gwen glanced at Marylou. "Did Stoner tell you our plans?"

"I'll have something for you in a minute," Marylou said. "If you'll tell her to forgive me."

Stoner sighed. "Oh, Marylou. Of course I forgive you."

"Excitable, isn't she?" Gwen said to Marylou.

"Under certain circumstances."

Stoner shot her a warning look.

"Now." Marylou rubbed her hands together. "Let's get this show on the road." She went to her desk and pulled out some forms.

"Are you sure you can't come with us?" Gwen asked.

"I'm sure. And your grandmother must want time alone with you."

Marylou muttered something that sounded very much like, "Who wouldn't?"

"Excuse me?" Gwen said.

Marylou waved a brochure. "Too wooden. The hotel. Stuffy."

Stoner ground her teeth.

Gwen went behind her, put her arms around her, and rested her cheek on Stoner's head. "Denim," she whispered. "I knew you'd be wearing denim."

"Gwen..."

"Aha!" announced Marylou. She held up a folder. "How about this?"

Stoner glanced at it. "Marylou, that's a swinging singles' resort."

"My grandmother's seventy-two," Gwen said.

"Oh," said Marylou. "Well, you make me nervous. Go take a walk while I work this out."

"Come on," Gwen said, and started for the door.

"Stoner," said Marylou, "could I have a word with you before you go? A little problem with these vouchers..."

"I'll wait outside," Gwen said.

Stoner picked up the travel vouchers and studied them. "What's the trouble?"

"Very interesting," Marylou said.

"What's interesting?"

"All this touching and hugging. There's only one thing that makes people act like that."

"What?"

"Sex."

Stoner threw the vouchers in her face. "I hate you, Marylou." She bolted for the door.

"I want to hear all about it," Marylou called after her. "Every detail."

They sat down on a bench near the swan boats. The park was nearly deserted in the heat. An old woman in a faded wash dress fed the pigeons from a bag of bread crumbs, cooing softly. There was a dryness in the air.

"Season's turning," Stoner said.

Gwen nodded.

"Did you sleep last night?"

"A little. The nightmares are back."

"I'm sorry." Stoner took her hand.

"It's a matter of time, I guess." She looked at the ground. "Stoner, I don't know how to thank you for..."

"Don't."

The leaves of a willow pattered in an updraft.

"Gwen," Stoner said suddenly, "sometimes the Bryans of this world win, and sometimes they lose. What matters is to keep going."

"I suppose."

"Otherwise, they always win."

Gwen rubbed her face. "You know the worst thing he did, Stoner?" He took away my ability to believe in myself."

"That's what you gave me," Stoner said softly.

Gwen squeezed her hand.

There was a long silence.

Gwen giggled. "Marylou," she said. "She's outrageous."

Stoner grunted.

"You've been friends a long time, haven't you?"

"Twelve years."

"I think I'm jealous."

Stoner looked at her. "You are?"

"Some day I'll have known you for a long time, too. I'll like that."

"So will I." Stoner reached into her pocket and pulled out a narrow chain with a brightly colored, unpolished rock pendant. "I've had this since I was a kid," she said. "I found the stone on a perfect day." Awkwardly, she dropped it into Gwen's hand. "I'd like you to have it. For luck."

"It's beautiful," Gwen said. Her eyes were wet. "Thank you." She slipped it over her head, and held the rock in her hand. "Stoner, I wish I weren't so mixed up. I wish I knew ... how I love you."

"You love me," Stoner said. "That's what matters." She touched Gwen's hair. "Stell told me something. A lifetime is a very long time to live. The important thing is to hold it together."

They watched a swan boat unload its passengers.

"I'd better go," Gwen said. "Grandmother's waiting." She got up. "I'll stop by and get the reservations from Marylou."

"I think I'll stay here for a while."

"Stoner? It won't always be like this."

"I know."

Gwen turned and walked off. Draping her arm along the back of the bench, Stoner watched her go. Sunlight glowed on her fawn-colored hair. Her body was firm and strong and graceful. Stoner smiled. Gwen was wearing her pale blue plaid shirt and khaki pants and desert boots.

As would anyone with good taste.

THE END